DEATH
OF A
HERETIC

DEATH
OF A
HERETIC

PETER
TREMAYNE

HEADLINE

First published in Great Britain in 2022 by
HEADLINE PUBLISHING GROUP

1

Cataloguing in Publication Data is available from the British Library

ISBN 978 1 4722 6543 2

Typeset in Times New Roman PS by Palimpsest Book Production Limited,
Falkirk, Stirlingshire

Printed and bound in Great Britain by Clays Ltd, Elcograf S.p.A.

HEADLINE PUBLISHING GROUP
An Hachette UK Company
Carmelite House
50 Victoria Embankment
London EC4Y 0DZ

www.headline.co.uk
www.hachette.co.uk

For Caroline Lennon,
'The Voice of Fidelma';
reader of the English language audiobooks,
making Fidelma come alive on the airwaves;
in appreciation of a talented actress and friend.

Fuerunt vero et pseudoprophetae in populo sicut et in vobis erunt magistri mendaces qui introducent sectas perditionis et eum qui emit eos Dominum negant superducentes sibi celerem perditionem.

But there were false prophets also among the people, even as there shall be false teachers among you, who privily shall bring in damnable heresies, even denying the Lord that bought them, and bring upon themselves swift destruction.

2 Peter 2:1

PRINCIPAL CHARACTERS

Sister Fidelma of Cashel, a *dálaigh* or advocate of the law courts of 7th-century Ireland

Brother Eadulf of Seaxmund's Ham, in the land of the South Folk of the East Angles, her companion

Enda, commander of the Warriors of the Golden Collar, the élite bodyguard to the King of Muman

At Ara's Well

Aona, the innkeeper

Adag, his grandson

At the Abbey of Imleach Iubhair

Abbot Cuán, Abbot and Chief Bishop of Muman

Brother Mac Raith, the *rechtaire* or steward

Prioress Suanach, head of the sisterhood

The Venerable Breas, the *fer-leginn* or chief professor

The Venerable Lugán, the *leabhar coimedach* or librarian and master of all students

Brother Anlón, the physician

Brother Áedh, in charge of abbey firefighters

Brother Sígeal, the *echaire*, master of the stables

The builders
Sítae, *Ollamh-Ailtire*, the master builder
Cú Choille, a missing master carpenter
Patu, a senior carpenter
Mothlach, a stone mason
Tassach, a coppersmith

The students
Brother Garb, a senior student
Brother Étaid, his *anam chara* or soul friend
Sister Fastrude, a Burgundian student
Sister Ingund, a Burgundian student
Sister Haldetrude, a Burgundian student

The Frankish visitors
Deacon Landric, the steward to Bishop Brodulf of Luxovium in Burgundia
Brother Charibert, servant to Bishop Brodulf

The Chief Brehon's group
Fíthel, Chief Brehon of Muman
Urard, his secretary and scribe
Aidan, warrior of the King, accompanying the Chief Brehon
Luan, a fellow warrior

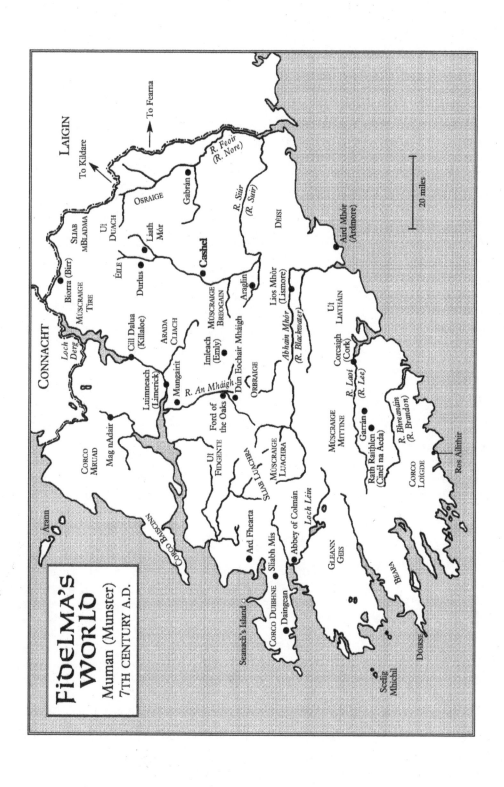

FIDELMA'S WORLD
Muman (Munster)
7TH CENTURY A.D.

LAIGIN

To Fearna

To Kildare

OSRAIGE

Gabrán

R. Feoir
(R. Nore)

SLIAB
MBLADMA

UÍ
DUACH

Liath
Mór

R. Siúir
(R. Suir)

DÉISI

Biorra (Birr)

MÚSCRAIGE
TIRE

Énle

Durlus

Cashel

Aird Mhór
(Ardmore)

CONNACHT

Loch
Derg

Cill Dalua
(Killaloe)

ARADA
CLIACH

MÚSCRAIGE
BREOGAIN

Araglin

Lios Mhór
(Lismore)

UÍ
LIATHÁIN

Mag nAdair

Luimneach
(Limerick)

Mungairit

Imleach
(Emly)

Dún Eochair Mháigh

Abhaín Mhór
(R. Blackwater)

Corcaigh
(Cork)

R. An Mháigh

ORBRRAIGE

CORCO
MRUAD

UÍ
FIDGENTE

Ford of
the Oaks

SLIAB LUACHRA

MÚSCRAIGE
LUACHRA

MÚSCRAIGE
MITTINE

R. Laoi
(R. Lee)

Garrán

R. Bhreanáin
(R. Brandon)

Arann

Loch Léin

Rath Raithlen
(Cinél na Áeda)

CORCO
LOÍGDE

CORCO BAISCINN

Ard Fhearta

Sliabh Mis

Abbey of Colmán

GLEANN
GEIS

BEARA

Ros Ailithir

Seanach's Island

CORCO DUIBHNE

Daingean

DÓIRSE

Scelig
Mhichíl

20 miles

AUThOR'S NOTE

This story takes place during the month called, in Old Irish, *Cét Samain* – 'the beginning of summer'. This approximates with the month we now call May. The year is AD 672.

Some readers may realise that we have already visited the Abbey of Imleach Iubhair – 'borderland of yew trees' (*The Monk Who Vanished*, 1999). Today, Emly, as it is now anglicised, is just a small village fourteen kilometres west of the county town of Tipperary (The Well of Ara). Founded in the fifth century by the pre-Patrician St Ailbe, Imleach Iubhair was once the premier teaching abbey of the kingdom of Muman (Munster) and the seat of its Chief Bishop, but there is little to show of that now. It remained a 'Cathedral City' until 1587. It was the principal ecclesiastical See of Munster until it was officially combined with the See of Cashel.

The early abbey buildings were replaced by a thirteenth-centry cathedral, which was destroyed during the conquest of 1607. By the end of that century it was reconsecrated as an Anglican cathedral, which, by 1827, had fallen into disrepair, when it was rebuilt. The modern Catholic church was built in 1882. The lake that fronted the old abbey has long vanished. There are still remains of five ancient holy well sites, including Tobair Peadar (Peter's Well). This became dangerous and was blocked up. It was from here an underground passage was reported to lead from the well head to the hill of Knockcarn, regarded as the abbey's ancient burial ground.

Imleach was a mixed house, a *conhospitae*, inhabited by male and female religious. It was governed by a *comarbae* (the 'heir' of Ailbe) but the title of abbot, originally from the Aramaic word *abbas* (father), was becoming a popular title for the head of such communities. For women, to the Aramaic word was added the Latin suffix -*issa* to make *abatissa* or abbess. I have used the title 'prioress' (*prioressa*), also borrowed into Old/Middle Irish, for the role of one in charge of the female religious in a *conhospitae,* or governor of their own religious house.

Some readers might be surprised that, even by Fidelma's time, Christianity was not a united religion but consisted of many divergent theological ideas, each with its supporters. Heated debates were numerous in various councils as to what concepts and teachings should be accepted and followed. The Edict of Milan in AD 313 had Rome recognise Western Christianity as a legitimate religion. Ten years later it was accepted as the official religion of the Roman Empire. Emperor Constantine (AD 285–337) realised that the Christian movement was fragmented with a diversity of interpretations. Leaders met in Nicaea in AD 325 to agree on fundamentals, and these became the basis of the Nicene Creed. But this did not unite all Christians.

Councils continued to argue. The Roman historian and former soldier Ammianus Marcellinus (c. AD 330–391/400) observed the often violent and dogmatic conflicts and commented: 'No wild beasts are so cruel as the Christians in their dealings with one another.'

The Council of Rome of AD 382, under Pope Damascus, accepted the choice of the twenty-seven texts chosen by Athanasius, Patriarch of Alexandria, which would constitute the New Testament. This led to arguments and the attempted destruction of many very early Christian writings not accepted by Rome.

The *Gospel of Philip*, mentioned in this story, is one of the Coptic texts, dated to the second/third centuries AD. It was discovered in a sealed jar, along with other early Christian writings, in Nag Hammadi, in Egypt, in 1945. The 1,200 Nag Hammadi texts are now in the Coptic Museum in Cairo, Egypt. They were buried in the fourth century to save them from destruction after the Council of Rome decision on what were acceptable to comprise the New Testament. The *Gospel of Philip* was named after the Apostle Philippos of Bethsaida (died AD 80 in Hieropolis), one of the original Twelve Apostles.

Numerous councils, in several parts of the Roman Empire as well as outside the empire, continued to evolve their own interpretations. By Fidelma's time six major Ecumenical Councils had been held in an attempt to standardise the religion. The third council held in Constantinople (AD 680) was still debating the human and divine aspects of the Jesus Christ. By this time there had been over thirty different interpretations of Western Christianity. Some ideas were accepted while others were abandoned or condemned as heresies.

Pelagius (active c. AD 380–418), was declared a heretic, but his teachings survived long among the Irish and other Celtic peoples of these Western lands. Ioannis, as Pope-Elect John IV, wrote a letter to the Irish bishops in AD 640, telling them to stop following Pelagius' teachings. Pelagius' works continued to be read and debated into modern times. For those readers fascinated by the writings and philosophies of Pelagius, I recommend *Pelagius: Life and Letters*, D. R. Rees, 1988.

The *Banshenchus* (*The History of Women*), which must surely take its place as the earliest European feminist history, survived in verse and prose form in the monastery of Daimh Inis – 'Island of Ox' (Devenish, Lough Erne, County Fermanagh). The abbey was founded by St Laisrén mac Nad Froich (died AD 564), popularly known as Mo Laisse. This text lists prominent women from the fifth and sixth centuries and entries continue to AD 1193. Among them is the daughter of King Failbe Flann, mentioned by her religious title.

In the following story, there are some references to previous Fidelma adventures, which it might be of help to mention. Fidelma's attendance at the Council of Streonshalh (Whitby) in AD 664, where she first met Eadulf, is related in *Absolution by Murder* (1994). This is when King Oswy of Northumbria decided his kingdom would follow Roman rites and not those of the insular churches and teachings from Ireland. Fidelma and Eadulf's attendance at the Council of Autun, in Burgundia, in AD 670, is related in *The Council of the Cursed* (2008). At this council it was decided that all religious houses in the Frankish kingdom and neighbouring Gaul should follow the Rule of Benedict rather than the various rules of the Western (Celtic) churches. Fidelma's adventure in AD 664/5 in visiting the Abbey of Bobbio (Bobbium), founded by Columbán and his Irish disciples in northern Italy, is related in *Behold a Pale Horse* (2011). The adventure in which Fidelma travels to Eadulf's home of Seaxmund's Ham, in the land of the South Folk, in the kingdom of the East Angles, is told in *The Haunted Abbot* (2002).

The incident in the Abbey of Darú (Darrow), to which Fidelma makes reference, is 'A Canticle for Wulfstan', first published in *Midwinter Tales 4*, Little, Brown, UK, October 1994, and in the USA in *Ellery Queen's Mystery Magazine*, May 1995. It was collected in the Fidelma short story volume *Hemlock at Vespers*, 1999.

Those toponymists among readers might be interested in knowing the modern equivalents of places mentioned in the kingdom of the Franks. Bituriga (Bourges); river Dea Matrona (the Marne); Evoriacum (Faremoutiers); Latiniacum (Lagny-sur-Marne); river Liger (Loire); Luxovium (Luxeuil-les-Bains); Martyr Nazarius (Saint-Nazaire) and Nevirnum (Nevers).

CHAPTER ONE

'There was a big fire at the abbey last night, lady.'

The news was broken in a cheerful tone by Adag, the seventeen-year-old grandson of the innkeeper, as he was placing a jug of ale on the table at which Fidelma and Eadulf were seated. Although the inn stood at the Well of Ara, some fifteen kilometres from the Abbey of Imleach Iubhair, 'borderland of the yews', local people still referred to it as '*the* abbey' because its influence dominated the area. The abbey was one of the oldest in the kingdom and it was acknowledged that its founder, the Blessed Ailbe, had been one of the first to bring the New Faith to Muman, the largest and most south-westerly of the Five Kingdoms of Éireann. It had become the premier teaching abbey of the kingdom, in which the abbots were also the chief bishops to the kings who dwelt at Cashel, where Fidelma's brother, Colgú, now ruled.

Fidelma glanced with interest at the youth.

'A big fire?' she asked. 'What happened? I heard that there is a lot of new building works going on there. Aren't they replacing many of the ancient wooden buildings by stone constructions?'

Adag shrugged. 'My grandfather will tell you all about it when he comes in. I gather you did not come here by the highway that passes the abbey gates, otherwise you would surely have seen something of the fire.'

'Eadulf and I rode from Dún Trí Liag, so we came across the mountains from the south-west.'

The youth went to the nearby fire to adjust one of the blazing logs that was threatening to fall.

'Why would you be visiting there?' the boy demanded over his shoulder. 'It is the fortress of Congal of the Dál gCais, who claims to be of royal lineage and does not let anyone forget it. He is not a nice person. He expects us to serve him and his kinsmen without charge and he treats my grandfather with utmost arrogance.'

Fidelma admonished him with mock disapproval. But she had known the boy since his birth and also knew that he spoke the truth. 'Don't voice your opinion too loudly and to too many people, Adag,' she warned. 'Congal is also a person who does not hesitate to use his power and the law to seek retribution if he feels slighted.'

In fact, the reason Fidelma and Eadulf, together with Enda, the commander of the élite Warriors of the Golden Collar, had visited Dún Trí Liag was because of a legal argument Congal had just had with one of his own clansmen. He had accused the man of stealing a bull from his herd. The man denied this but his innocence continued to be dismissed. The clansman decided to assert his rights under the ancient law and sat *troscud* before the gates of Congal's fortress, refusing food and drink, to force the noble to agree to place the matter to arbitration. Fidelma, as a *dálaigh*, was qualified to judge such cases, and so was sent to hear the arguments. It was a fact that, before the hearing, the bull had been found wandering in the nearby hills, having broken loose from its field. Congal reluctantly conceded his accusation was without merit and, with even more reluctance, agreed to compensate the clansman for his false accusation with a heifer from his herd.

If the truth were known, Fidelma felt more relaxed now that she and her companions were away from Congal's fortress. He was reputed to be a man of short temper, who held grudges. In

Fidelma's estimation, where Congal was concerned, 'trust' was not a word that came readily to mind.

The inn door opened with a sudden blast of cold air. Aona, the elderly innkeeper, entered followed by the young warrior, Enda, who pushed the door shut behind them. Enda had been helping Aona water and feed the horses in the inn's stable.

'What's this I hear about a fire at the abbey?' Fidelma asked the innkeeper as he came to check that his grandson had brought them all they required.

'Ah, so young Adag has told you? I was just telling Enda about it.'

Enda lowered himself on a bench by the table and reached for the jug of ale to pour himself a drink. There was no false etiquette between these comrades who had shared so many adventures together.

'I wasn't surprised at Aona's news,' he commented. 'There has been a lot of rebuilding at the abbey in recent times. Being built in the middle of a forest of yew trees, the oldest buildings are of wood. Recent abbots have encouraged the replacing of the wooden buildings by local stone. Fires do often happen when such work is happening.'

Fidelma turned to the innkeeper. 'What do you know of the origins of the fire? What caught alight?'

Aona shrugged. 'I only heard a few details from a passing traveller this morning,' he replied. 'Apparently it was not a big fire but confined to one of the old wooden buildings that they say was designated as the *tech n-óiged*.'

'The guest house?' Eadulf intervened in surprise. 'I thought the abbey no longer put guests in those original structures. Was anyone hurt?'

'The traveller said that some foreign cleric visiting the abbey was fatally injured,' the innkeeper replied. 'A few of the brethren, as well as some of those involved in the building work, were injured while trying to put out the conflagration.'

'A foreign cleric, you say?' Fidelma was interested.

'The traveller told me that he thought the man was a bishop from some kingdom over the seas.'

Fidelma pursed her lips in a troubled expression. 'A visitor to our kingdom and a bishop . . .? Do you know who this bishop was or whence he came?'

The innkeeper made a dismissive gesture with his right shoulder. 'The traveller did not know. He was only a passing merchant and not staying at the abbey. He had stopped there only briefly, at the gates, to get water for his horse. He simply heard that the bishop was an important visitor from overseas and had not been at the abbey for very long.'

'Sadly, fires are not uncommon in wooden constructions where food has to be prepared and cooked for so many people,' pointed out the innkeeper's grandson. He had the resigned acceptance of youth at the news of such a catastrophe.

'What you say is true,' Eadulf agreed. 'People are not often vigilant in the presence of fire.'

'It is of concern that a foreign bishop, a visitor to our kingdom, has become a fatal victim of a fire, and in the premier abbey of this kingdom,' Fidelma pointed out thoughtfully.

'Is it known how the fire started? Was there some accident?' Eadulf asked.

'The merchant told me no more than I have told you,' the innkeeper replied. 'There are a hundred and one ways a fire can start.'

'What concerns me is this bishop's rank and station,' Fidelma persisted. 'An explanation of how this misfortune came about might be needed because, under law, there could be a consideration of recompense if a fault is identified.'

Eadulf had been enough years in the kingdom to know what was passing through Fidelma's mind. The abbey was, in legal terms, responsible for any compensation due, and, as the abbot was also chief bishop of the kingdom, any fault might reflect on the kingship itself. Colgú might have to pay compensation to those in whose service this bishop had come to the abbey.

'It is nearly midday,' Eadulf said quickly to Fidelma. 'What if we have our midday meal here? Then there will be plenty of time to visit Abbot Cuán at Imleach to gather what details we can and you can ensure that nothing is amiss. I believe that is what is passing through your mind.'

Before Fidelma could respond, Enda was nodding in agreement.

'It is a good suggestion, lady. The horses need a little rest now that they have been foddered and watered. So let us have food first and then we can ride to the abbey.'

Fidelma modified her stern expression. 'And you, of course, want to put the care and rest for the horses first? Otherwise you would have delayed the journey to Imleach?'

For a moment Enda looked embarrassed and then realised the humour in her eyes.

The old innkeeper intervened and saved him finding a response. 'If it is a cold meal that you prefer I have some salted venison, hard-boiled goose eggs, and a salad with green leaves, watercress, salad burnet and wild garlic mixed with the shoots of recently flowered hawthorn. Alternatively, there is leek, softened, if it is a sharp taste that you are wanting. There is plenty of fruit and honey to follow, or warm barley cakes flavoured to your taste.'

'Nothing heavy for me,' Fidelma assured the innkeeper. 'We still have some riding to do, whether we go to the abbey or back to Cashel.'

'But we'll have another jug of ale,' Enda called as Aona made for the kitchen of the inn after his grandson.

There was a short silence when they were left alone.

'I would have preferred to rest this night in Cashel.' Fidelma addressed her companions quietly. 'I have a feeling that we might be delayed awhile by this matter before returning.'

'You are too anxious,' Eadulf rebuked her. 'The death of a foreign bishop does not necessarily mean there is a responsibility on the abbey or the kingdom.'

'All going well, we could still be in Cashel by this evening,' Enda agreed. 'Even at a relaxed pace it would not take us long to reach the abbey.'

In that he was right. The road that way was well kept by pilgrims as well as the merchant traffic going to and from the old abbey. It was classed under law as a *ramat,* a road leading to a noble's fortress. It was appropriate that Ailbe's abbey was called Imleach Iubhair, 'the borderland of yew', because the rounded, heavy-branched growths dominated the area, stretching down to the little lake beside which the abbey had been built. The yews were strong, the most durable of trees, with their curved needle-covered branches from which bows were cut both by hunters and warriors. Along the verges of the road that ran between them, were clusters of thorn bushes, forming hedgerows and crossing open spaces. There were whitethorn and hawthorn on which were emerging, among the shiny, dark green leaves, little clusters of flowers. As the month progressed these would swell into beautiful white speckled flowers with yellow centres. It was a sure sign that early summer was on the way.

In more open spaces, along the dry banks, were hoary cress. In childhood Fidelma had learnt that you could, at this time of year, grind the seeds for seasoning various foods. The presence of the cress indicated the nearness of water, and now and then the three riders saw the reflection of the lowering afternoon sun on fast-flowing streams, lighting small specks of damselfly hovering and darting along the surface. The area boasted a tiny lake and at least five deep wells of pure sweet water rising from the distant mountains and hills. Their presence was undoubtedly what attracted the Blessed Ailbe and his followers to form their community here.

In the sky a few predator birds searched for a late meal.

Dominant among them were the long, pointed wings of merlins, searching for stretches of moorlands where their hunting skills could be used at their best. Here and there were a few feral goats, with straight spreading horns, feeding on gorse and heather. In the warmer months they were found in high rocky places, but in winter they descended to lower levels. Fidelma reflected it was late in the year for them to be about, foraging so low.

The countryside was not entirely deserted by man. They saw a couple of religious, recognisable by their clothing, fishing a stream. As the waters were low and shallow, she suspected the men were from the abbey and not after salmon but the eel-like *náid*, or lampreys. They were a favourite dish of Abbot Cuán, although an acquired taste.

The abbey itself was situated on a slight rise to the north side of the highway. This was the main gate, and the abbey buildings ascended this rise, while immediately to the south was a long, low-lying hill called the Hill of the Cairn, which was used for a burial ground exclusively for the dead of the abbey and was known as the 'tombs of the blest'. The road ran on, passing a small lake towards the west.

Fidelma and her companions approached the familiar old, grey limestone entrance buildings, which had been the first to be erected at the front of the abbey, over a century before the subsequent abbots had determined that the entire complex would one day arise in stone as befitted the premier abbey of the kingdom. However, a lot was still to be achieved and Abbot Cuán, on his appointment less than a year before, had determined that it would be entirely rebuilt before he died. Half of the abbey was now reported to be constructed in stone, while the rest still remained in their original wooden form.

Fidelma and her companions turned up the slight rise in the track, which ran past the main gates. There seemed no sign of anything untoward but every now and then, as the wind blew, a faint but pungent smell of burnt wood permeated the air. There looked to be no gatekeeper to welcome them and the great oak doors remained closed.

It was Enda who edged his horse forward towards the bell rope and, reaching forward, tugged at it three times. The distant clang of the bell resonated from beyond the walls. Only a short time passed before there was movement at the top of the wall over the arched gates and a head appeared as if to examine who was without. It was gone before Enda could shout up their identity.

Enda was about to tug the bell again when one of the great wooden doors began to move. A man clad in religious robes slid forward through this aperture to face them. Young looking, of average height and with straw-coloured hair and pale features, he regarded them with light, almost colourless eyes. His brows were drawn together in a frown as he examined them and then his thin lips broke in a smile as he recognised them.

'Fidelma of Cashel!' he exclaimed. 'I thought I was not mistaken when I looked down just now.'

She returned his smile. 'It has been nearly a year, Brother Mac Raith.'

'And at that time we were in the land of the Uí Fidgente with our lives in danger,' the young man affirmed.

'Now you are the new *rechtaire,* the chief steward of this abbey?'

'And Cuán is now our abbot,' Brother Mac Raith added, before turning to Fidelma's companions. '*Salvete,*' he greeted warmly. '*Receperint, amicis meis epularer.* You are all most welcome.'

Eadulf and Enda returned the greeting in traditional fashion.

The steward stood to one side, gesturing them to come forward with one hand while shouting to unseen companions to open the doors widely to allow them to enter into a large courtyard with their horses. One of the brethren, a burly man who, by his clothing, was clearly the *echaire,* the master of the stables, led two stable lads forward to take the horses as the visitors dismounted.

'It is good to see you again, lady,' Brother Mac Raith was saying as he led them towards the main building of the abbey across the courtyard. 'I think the abbot will want to greet you immediately. Your arrival will do much to alleviate the anxiety that has been laid upon this abbey.'

There was no disguising the unease and fretfulness that the steward exuded in spite of the friendliness of his greetings.

'We have heard of the fire,' Fidelma said. 'I gather the accident has cost the life of a visiting bishop. We have ridden here from Ara's Well to see if there was any help we can render; otherwise we would have been on our way to Cashel.'

Brother Mac Raith's response was a worried grimace. 'Abbot Cuán will be doubly heartened by your arrival then. Perhaps it will be best if I take you and your companions immediately to him? For the moment, leave your bags and horses with Brother Sígeal, our master of the stables.'

The steward motioned them to follow him, quite neglecting the usual ritual greeting ceremony: the washing of feet and hands of travellers entering an abbey community. This did not go unnoticed by Fidelma, who gauged it as an indication of the man's concern so did not mention it. The steward hurried, in almost ungainly fashion, up a flight of stone steps to an upper level and along a dark corridor to what Fidelma dimly recalled from past visits as the abbot's quarters. The concern of the steward did not go unnoticed by Eadulf or by Enda either. They shot meaningful glances towards Fidelma as they came to a halt before an oak door. Here the steward paused and knocked and, on instruction from beyond, he slipped quickly inside. Only a moment passed before he flung open the door again and beckoned them forward.

The bent figure of Abbot Cuán was already coming out from behind his big desk with the aid of his stout walking stick. There was a smile of welcome mixed with relief on his features.

'Let no man say that God does not answer his prayers when he is in dire need,' he greeted her. 'You are most welcome, Fidelma of Cashel, and you, Eadulf, and Enda also. You have all been remembered fondly in my thoughts from our time among the Uí Fidgente. Your arrival is opportune.'

Abbot Cuán, who was short in stature, was inclined to look even smaller, being bent over his walking stick. Fidelma remembered that he had broken his leg in a fall from his horse years before. The break had not healed well and left him with a limp and a reliance on his stick. He was inclined to be fleshy and pale of skin and his hair was a nondescript brown, his eyes dark. His hair grew in tufts around the tonsure of the Blessed John. His features always reminded Fidelma of the mournful look of a dog that knew it had done wrong in the eyes of its master and was now looking for signs of forgiveness, although she knew that this was entirely misleading. The hint of his true character was in his gentle but firm commanding tone.

They had been through much together and so they shared a camaraderie that their social positions would not have entirely explained. They had shared dangers before the peace was finally made with Prince Donnenach of the Uí Fidgente and Fidelma's brother, Colgú of Cashel. Cuán had been *airsecnap* or Deputy Abbot of Imleach then, and Brother Mac Raith had been one of the scribes. A conspiracy that had led to the death of Abbot Ségdae, which involved the previous steward, Brother Tuamán, had brought them all together during the previous year.

'We were at Ara's Well, on our way to Cashel, when we heard that you had had a fire and a fatality,' Fidelma replied to his greeting. 'So we came here to be of service to you.'

Brother Mac Raith was arranging chairs for them to be seated while the abbot resumed his chair and put his stick aside.

'The fire was in one of the remaining wooden structures at the back of these abbey buildings,' Abbot Cuán explained without preamble. His voice was tired and dry as though he were repeating words that he had used several times before. 'It was the original guest house, which was due to be pulled down and rebuilt in stone. I know what you will ask, Fidelma. It was the choice of our distinguished visitor to stay there rather than in our new stone-built guest accommodation.'

Fidelma stared at him in surprise.

'Our guest said that a wooden house is warmer and more comfortable than the stone buildings,' the steward explained. 'He said he found the wooden building more equitable to his health and comfort.'

'Who was he?' she queried.

'He was a Frank: Bishop Brodulf of Luxovium,' replied the steward.

'He perished in the fire,' confirmed the abbot. 'I would like to say a few words about the fire itself before I explain about this bishop.'

Fidelma noted that the abbot did not seem unusually upset by the death of a bishop in his abbey. She waited for him to continue.

'Although we have had some rain in recent days, I must assume the wood of the guest house was dry, for there was no stopping the flames when they erupted. I have to say that we did all we could to extinguish them.'

'Do you know how the conflagration was ignited?' Eadulf asked, coming to the point impatiently.

Abbot Cuán sighed as if exhausted. 'We have not learnt yet. Brother Áedh, who leads a small group of the brethren, having learnt how to deal with fires, is investigating. The flames were seen only when it was too late to quell them. Usually, the waters around here are sufficient for Brother Áedh and his small band of followers to extinguish any conflagration before it becomes serious. Since our community has expanded in recent decades, the task is difficult. Now we have scholars from many kingdoms come here to study. We are looked upon as the principal religious centre of the kingdom. It is true that my predecessor was persuaded to obtain a few of those hand-held water pumps, which it is said that Ctesibius of Alexandria developed, but they are of little use against such large fires.'

'With respect, I think that we deviate from the important matter,' Fidelma interposed in a heavy tone.

Abbot Cuán bowed his head. 'I am sorry. I am probably trying to justify why we were unable to save our distinguished guest from this inferno. The flames spread quickly, as Brother Áedh will explain.'

'And this Bishop Brodulf was the only fatality?' Fidelma pressed.

'He was the only one in the guest house and the only fatality, although we have several among the brethren and the volunteers from among the builders who suffered burns in their attempts to douse the flames. We thought our guest might have escaped, and only after the flames subsided did we realise he had perished. We thought our guest house was safe from fire.'

'There is no such place as one safe from fire,' Eadulf pointed out. 'Buildings will contain wood and pitch and all other combustible materials. Those water pumps that you mention are no use. I have seen them in my travels and I know they can spray too little water to have any effect on extinguishing a fierce flame.'

'We were talking about the fatality,' Fidelma pointed out, the iciness of her tone showing her irritation at not getting to the facts she wanted. 'Who was this Bishop Brodulf?'

'As I said, he was a visitor to this abbey from Luxovium.'

'Luxovium?' Fidelma frowned, trying to place the name.

'It is in Burgundia, a kingdom of the Franks. Luxovium is one of the communities that was founded by our own Blessed Columbán.'

'We have been to Burgundia,' Eadulf reminded Fidelma. 'Two years ago, we accompanied Abbot Ségdae and other prelates to an abbey in Burgundia called Autun.'

'Ah, yes, it was a council where it was decided that the Rule of Benedict should be the normal rule in abbeys and religious communities,' Fidelma remembered thoughtfully. 'I attended there as an adviser to our representatives on the incompatibility of our laws and governances with these new Roman laws.'

'Since the Romans took over the New Faith as the state religion, they expect all Christians to accept Roman Law in return,' Abbot Cuán almost sneered. 'As if a thousand years of culture can be overturned by a decision of the majority from another culture.'

'Was it about the decision at Autun that brought this bishop here?' Eadulf frowned.

'In a way. He came here to see our theology and methods of instruction, knowing that we had refused many of the decisions of those supporting the Roman councils.'

'Luxovium, as you say, was where Columbán established one of his early communities,' Fidelma reflected. 'I heard about it when I was in Bobium, which Columbán also established. I was told that Luxovium was the old sanctuary of a Gaulish river goddess, Souconna, a sacred place of the Old Faith, where there were hot and cold springs. Columbán and his followers probably set up their community there because of that.'

'Is Luxovium still governed by missionaries from this land?' Eadulf asked. 'That would explain why a bishop from that abbey travelled here.'

'The Frankish kings have accepted Rome,' Abbot Cuán corrected dourly. 'Columbán and his followers were expelled from the area because they were celebrating the Paschal rites as we were taught to do in this kingdom.'

'You are right, lady,' Brother Mac Raith agreed. 'It was to Bobium that Columbán and his followers fled when they were exiled from Luxovium. The religious there were replaced only by those who swore adherence to the new Roman rites.'

'So why would this bishop be visiting here, especially since you have rejected the rules decided at Autun?'

'Bishop Brodulf certainly lost no opportunity to remonstrate with our scholars about our beliefs and interpretation,' the abbot agreed. 'I believe he came here with the explicit authority of the Frankish king, Clotaire, a descendant of the very king who exiled Columbán from Luxovium.'

'We met Clotaire at the council in Autun,' Fidelma remembered. 'He is not someone to insult lightly. So this bishop implied he had authority from Clotaire to visit here?'

'Whatever authority he had, Bishop Brodulf was not a welcome visitor to this abbey,' Brother Mac Raith remarked. They stared at him, surprised by the dislike in his voice.

'All should be welcome providing they do not abuse the laws of hospitality,' Fidelma pointed out sharply.

'Abuse? That is exactly what Bishop Brodulf did,' the steward returned, defensively.

It was the abbot who explained.

'Bishop Brodulf did so verbally, even insulting the *Cáin Ailbe,* by whose rules and precepts we run our community.'

'I cannot see what more we could do to maintain fraternity and equanimity between us,' the steward added. 'But when these foreigners call us pagans and unbelievers, it is hard to maintain a sense of brotherliness.'

'You used a plural: "these foreigners",' Fidelma pointed out.

'The bishop came with two companions,' the abbot explained. 'Both were from Burgundia.'

'Did they manage to escape the flames? Were they among those who are injured?'

Abbot Cuán shook his head. 'They had separate accommodation in the main guest quarters in the rebuilt part of the abbey.'

'So who was with the bishop in the wooden guest house, if not his companions?'

'He was alone,' Brother Mac Raith answered quickly. 'It was by his own wish and instruction. He informed me that his rank entitled him to his own accommodation and not one to be shared with those of lesser rank.'

Abbot Cuán shrugged, seeming to express sadness. 'Brother Mac Raith quotes his words exactly. I would say that this bishop possessed the fault of arrogance.'

'Those of lesser rank?' Fidelma mused thoughtfully. 'Who were these two companions from Burgundia who were travelling with him?'

'One is named Deacon Landric and the other Brother Charibert. He treated them like servants rather than companions.'

'So, this bishop was alone in the guest house when the flames enveloped it?'

'That is so,' Brother Mac Raith confirmed.

'If this bishop was sanctioned to come here by the Frankish king, Clotaire,' murmured Eadulf, 'then it is imperative to find explanations for his death.'

'We must ensure whether there is, or is not, a fault that would give rise to any claims by the Frankish king,' Fidelma decided. 'If there is a whisper of a fault, then Clotaire would lose no time in demanding compensation. The task of the abbey is to make sure that everything has been done that could have been done to save Bishop Brodulf from perishing in the flames. Otherwise, it might lead to a dispute involving the two kingdoms that could escalate into war.'

ChapteR two

Abbot Cuán decided that his steward, Brother Mac Raith, should conduct the visitors without delay to the site of the ruins of the guest house. Fidelma realised that the abbot avoided any unnecessary walking due to his injured leg. Brother Mac Raith now led them through passages into areas where some stone buildings were clearly very new. These were interspersed among some of the oldest of the stone structures, such as the chapel. The steward proudly pointed out one almost as large as the chapel, which was the *praintech*, the refectory. Opposite that was the *scriptorium*, the library. Nearby, they were told, was the entrance to the newly built guest apartments. Fidelma was impressed to see how the old abbey had been expanded.

They crossed a courtyard with a small fountain and proceeded through a stone arch. Here, the buildings changed dramatically. There were several wooden buildings on either side of a long broad stretch, almost like a road. The steward was especially proud to indicate that some of these were the students' quarters. These stood on the right and comprised two long wooden cabins, each of a single storey; one being for the male students and the other for the female students. Like other famous *conhospitae*, such as Mungairit and Lios Mór, the abbey of Imleach could also boast scholars from many kingdoms attending under the guidance of their professors and studying with various teachers.

Brother Mac Raith made a point of stating that a significant number of students were Angles and Saxons. Many had recently arrived following the decision made at Streonshalh to accept the Roman doctrines and reject the Irish rites.

The buildings on their left, opposite the students' quarters, needed no explanation from the steward. Here were a number of artisan buildings being worked by members of the abbey of both sexes. There were leather workers, shoemakers, carpenters and brewers making cider from barrels of apples. Even potters had their place among them, while at the end was a coffin maker. A smith was at work at his forge outside. Then there were weavers, embroiderers and others doing needlework. There were also constructions here that were obviously for food storage and other preparations.

Standing nearby was an apothecary, marked clearly by the sign outside. This was an image of an *echlasc*, or short horse whip, above the door. Why this had become a symbol for those practising the healing arts seemed to be because, under ancient law, it was required that a physician should be provided with a good horse to travel to wherever patients needed him. The symbolic removal of the *echlasc* meant the removal of the authority to practise the healing arts.

At this point, Fidelma and Eadulf came to a halt at the change of scenery. It was quite a surprise for them to survey an almost limitless building site with the sounds of work rising from it. There appeared great activity, with groups of workmen plying their various crafts. Sturdy oxen loaded with baskets filled with lime-stone blocks from some quarry or store stood waiting patiently in line for their burdens to be unloaded. It surprised Fidelma that there were still many wooden buildings and that, in spite of a few isolated stretches of a half-constructed palisade, the area was more or less open to the surrounding woods.

It seemed two tracks, one on the west and the other on the east, gave the builders access to the site. Brother Mac Raith explained that the builders had set up a main work camp a short distance away on the western side among the yew trees. The camp was for the artisans and general labourers to store or make special items for the work, and also contained their living quarters. Opposite, towards the east, there were fenced fields and paddocks constructed for the numerous oxen or asses used to transport heavy loads of stone and wood to and from the building site.

Brother Mac Raith noted with satisfaction the visitors' impressed expressions.

'Abbot Cuán is determined that when he surrenders the abbacy at the end of his life . . . God give him a long and fruitful one . . . he will leave the abbey fully built in stone and the new buildings will be observed with awe and pride by future generations as befits the premier abbey of the kingdom.'

'There appears to be a lot of work still going on in spite of the fire. Are the majority of the builders members of the brethren?' Eadulf asked.

'We have not yet attracted enough brethren with all the talents that are needed to rebuild such a community,' the steward replied, shaking his head. 'Talented workers in stone and wood are scarce, especially those needed to erect such imposing edifices. However, we have been able to contract the services of a great master builder named Sítae.'

If this name was meant to provoke a reaction from Fidelma or Eadulf, the steward was disappointed.

'I was thinking that there is a propensity on a building site to accidents,' Eadulf observed. 'A smouldering piece of wood, something inflammable . . .?'

Brother Mac Raith seemed immediately protective of the master builder's reputation.

'In the time that Sítae's men have worked here, there have been no fires,' he declared firmly before realising what he had said.

'Until now,' Fidelma replied dryly. 'As Eadulf observes, in such large-scale works it is inevitable that there will accidents. It is the law of averages.'

'This is true,' the steward admitted reluctantly. 'But there have been few even minor injuries among the builders. One does expect some injuries due to falling masonry and such like. We have been blest with few serious injuries and no deaths. Sítae's artisans are to be highly praised.'

'I could not help noticing the exquisite craftsmanship of the woodwork and the carving, especially in the abbot's chamber,' Fidelma granted. 'You have an exceptional carver of red yew. The carpentry is some of the best I have seen.'

'Ah, that is the work of the master carpenter, Cú Choille.'

Eadulf smiled at the name. 'Doesn't that mean "the hound of the wood"?' he queried. 'That is an appropriate name for a wood carver.'

'He is responsible for all the special red yew carvings you see around you, on the doors and other places. Cú Choille, like Sítae, was a pedant on safety measures when he was in charge of overseeing the team that worked in wood.'

'*When* he was in charge of the workers in wood?' Eadulf caught the inflection.

'Sítae informed me that Cú Choille had to leave yesterday to return to his home for some personal reason.'

Fidelma raised an eyebrow: 'You say that he left yesterday?'

'Yes, lady. Sítae will have a hard task to find another as excellent as he was.'

'I presume that his home is not near here?'

'I believe he came from a southern peninsula among the sandstone mountains of An Ceaoha. He was a rare craftsman, whose work will be a great feature of this abbey for many centuries to come.'

'I am sure it will be, judging by the care that I observe,' Fidelma agreed. 'It is so beautifully done. Why did he leave? Did you complete his contract?'

The steward stared at Fidelma for a moment and then a smile spread across his face as he realised her possible thought. 'I saw him first thing yesterday morning and he left after noon. The fire at the guest house occurred in the early hours of this morning. There were no accidents with wood being set alight during the time he was here. I can assure you of that.'

Fidelma shrugged. 'I was not implying anything. I just need to be clear about the sequences of events. So let us move on to the ruins of the guest house and you can explain as we go.'

Even if Fidelma, Eadulf and Enda had been insensitive to the acrid smell of freshly burnt wood, mixed with a curious pungent and unpleasant caustic combination of scorched and incinerated materials, the blackened oblong area to which the steward was leading them clearly showed them where the burnt house had stood. The blackened area indicated the dimensions of the building that had formerly stood on its own. There was also space at the back where the building was separated by a stretch of ground from the palisade wall.

There was, indeed, little left of the building. Only one or two charred heavy supports and beams stood upright. These remained in isolation, showing that the building had once had a first floor and the oddly shaped remains of a much-reduced wall were evident to one side. In another corner was the charred evidence of a stone construction, which Fidelma had no difficulty in recognising had once been a small oven.

Fidelma and her companions stood in silence as they examined the blackened pile. Fidelma mentally took in the dimensions of the remains, counting the number of *deis-ceim* measurements indicated by each wall. The place had been about the equivalent of eight metres by five. She knew that the law actually set out what dimensions were allowed for such buildings.

'I presume that the body has been removed?' she asked, glancing at the piles of incinerated material.

Brother Mac Raith grimaced in distaste. 'What remained has been taken to our physician, Brother Anlón. But it did not need a physician to confirm Bishop Brodulf was dead.'

'In a suspicious death—' Eadulf begun pedantically, but Fidelma interrupted him.

'The law treats all deaths by fire as worthy of being scrutinised by a physician so that the circumstances of the death are not made on presumptions alone.'

Brother Mac Raith shifted his weight uncomfortably. 'Well, Brother Anlón is highly proficient in medical knowledge. He will probably have examined the body by now.'

'We will have a word with him in a moment.' Fidelma cast her gaze back to the blackened pile that had been the house. 'Where was the body found?'

The steward pointed to an area that Fidelma, by the general shape of the building, assessed would be at the back.

'So Bishop Brodulf was found away from the main door?'

'It is only a guess, lady, but I would say that he would have been in the bed chamber when he became a victim of the fire. That would have been on the upper floor. That floor collapsed to the lower level as a result of the fire. The body was found on a burnt wooden frame, which was probably the remains of the bed.'

'So he was in bed when the fire erupted and was overcome by fumes?' Eadulf asked quickly.

Brother Mac Raith responded with an eloquent shrug. It seemed that he was not prepared, or not knowledgeable enough, to respond.

'You seem to be saying that he was overwhelmed by the fire while in his bed and died before he could get up?' Eadulf reiterated. 'Doesn't that seem strange?'

'I am not competent to answer,' the steward replied.

'This guest house had two floors, then?' Fidelma asked. 'But there was no one else here when the fire started?'

'As Abbot Cuán explained, the bishop insisted that this guest house was his alone,' affirmed the steward. 'It was his choice. He was using a bedroom on the second storey at the back, just above there . . . so when the floor collapsed . . .' He shrugged and pointed once again to where the body had been found.

Fidelma was thoughtful. 'And you said that even his companions could not be accommodated here because they were considered of lesser status?'

'You will have to speak with Deacon Landric, who accompanied him, as to why the bishop insisted on isolation,' Brother Mac Raith replied.

'Has it been ascertained where the fire began?' Fidelma then asked.

'Apart from removing the body of the bishop, Brother Áedh, who is our expert on such matters, has presented no report for the moment. I expect him to join us shortly. I would say, from the little I know, it is most likely that the fire would start in the kitchen area. An ember from the kitchen fire might have sparked, setting alight something that could easily catch fire, like dry wood or the tar that insulates the boards of the house. You can see the remains of the stone fireplace.'

He pointed to a corner where there was a blackened construction of stone and clay. Fidelma frowned as she examined the scorched remains.

'Is it not remarkable that, if the fire started there, on the lower floor and at the opposite end of the building to the bishop's bedroom, and with the bishop asleep in his bed, the flames spread so rapidly that they engulfed him before he could save himself?'

Once again the steward dismissed the question with a shrug. 'I am not competent to judge such matters, lady,' he added. 'Brother Áedh is the person to speak to. He is in charge of a group of the brethren that are trained to stand ready to fight any fires that occur. Áedh himself suggested organising this group as a precaution, in view of all the building work taking place.'

Fidelma tried to control the momentary smile as she realised the name Áedh actually meant 'fire'. 'I trust he was not one of the firefighters who were injured during the conflagration?'

'There was some scorching to his hands, but nothing serious. A couple of his men were likewise injured, and two of the builders who tried to help, but none seriously.'

'If you can point me to where we may find your physician, then after that we must find this Brother Áedh,' she said. 'Also, someone should be placed here to keep an eye on this area to make sure no one touches anything until we have examined it again. Enda can help in that.'

The young warrior immediately agreed; he had been feeling useless with no task to do.

Brother Mac Raith was surprised when Fidelma said that she and Eadulf already knew where to find the physician. They went to do so, allowing the steward freedom to go in search of Brother Áedh.

Fidelma and Eadulf remembered that building where they had noticed the *echlasc* symbol outside. Now, a tall young man stood at the door. Fidelma thought he had the look of a chief mourner at a funeral. He was extremely thin, with hands that had long tapering fingers, almost skeletal, showing clearly below the folded sleeves of his robes. He had a long face with pale skin and eyelids like hoods, that seemed constantly closed except to open briefly when interest was aroused, showing his dark eyes.

'Brother Anlón?' she queried.

'You are the *dálaigh* come to examine the remains of the foreign bishop?' Even his voice was mournful, except when he came to the end of a sentence, which was marked by a slight lifting in tone.

'I am Fidelma of Cashel,' she replied solemnly. She was surprised that the physician already knew of her arrival and intention.

'No need for surprise,' the young man smiled wanly. 'In this place, news is like a breath of wind being blown swiftly. I watched Brother Mac Raith showing you the remains of the old guest house where the foreign bishop met his death. Therefore, who else would you be?'

He stood aside and motioned them to enter. The smells and odours were familiar, as both Fidelma and Eadulf had spent many hours in the apothecary of her late mentor, Brother Conchobhair, at Cashel. The pungent smell of herbs, so strong it was almost suffocating, made her catch her breath. At the far end of the room something black and disfigured was stretched on a table and, as much as she had seen death, Fidelma found herself trying not to focus on it unless she had to.

'I suppose there is little one can say about a person who has perished in a fire,' Eadulf began as he followed her inside. He had studied the healing arts at the medical school of Tuaim Brecain, but never completed his studies. Even so, he still carried his *lés,* or medical bag, on his travels and his knowledge had often been of importance to Fidelma in her investigations. Eadulf glanced at the remnants of the corpse. 'There was not much left to examine. All one can do is hope that the fumes or even the heat eliminated the air so that it would cause the victim to be rendered insensible before the end. It is a grim way to die.'

A scowl of disapproval crossed the pale features of Brother Anlón. 'I am willing to stand aside and let your own physician make his examination,' he said sharply to Fidelma.

Fidelma glanced irritably at Eadulf, who now realised that the physician had taken his comment the wrong way.

'I was but expressing an assumption and, not being a qualified physician, I would make no deductions,' he said hastily.

24

'In this case it would not have mattered what assumptions you might make.'

They stared at the tall pale physician, puzzled by the comment. 'Why so?' Fidelma demanded.

'Because the bishop was dead before the fire started,' came the flat reply.

There was a moment's surprised silence before Fidelma asked: 'How have you reached this conclusion?'

Brother Anlón turned to a nearby work bench and picked up a long bent and discoloured objected. It was blackened by burning. The physician held it out towards them. In spite of its burnt and twisted shape, they could recognise it clearly as some sort of knife whose handle had been burnt off, although the blade was clear enough to identify its purpose.

'A dagger?' Eadulf asked unnecessarily.

The physician gave him an almost pitying glance. 'A dagger,' he confirmed with irony. 'The foreign bishop was stabbed through the heart with this dagger before the flames started.'

'Are you saying that—' Fidelma began.

'I am saying that Bishop Brodulf was stabbed to death before there was an attempt to have the body consumed by fire,' Brother Anlón replied flatly. 'The bishop was murdered.'

CHAPTER THREE

They had barely time to absorb the implication of the physician's statement before Brother Mac Raith entered.

'I have Brother Áedh outside,' he announced. 'He says that he has examined the site and has drawn some conclusions about the cause of the fire and how it was able to spread so quickly. The master builder, Sítae, is also outside and obviously wants to hear Brother Áedh's report.'

Fidelma was silent a moment before she turned to Brother Anlón.

'You will keep your medical report to yourself until I have had time to discuss the matter with the abbot.'

The physician indicated his assent with a gesture of his head.

There were two men waiting outside. One was clad in the robes of the brethren. He was a young man, sturdy of build with an athletic appearance. There seemed an excitable quality about his features, which suited his mass of ginger, curling hair and darting bright blue eyes; eyes that never seemed to stay focused on any one object.

The second man was older than the other. There was a tough quality to his features. He wore a sleeveless faded leather jerkin, which did not hide the muscular arms and barrel chest, his weather-beaten torso carrying scars one would associate with warriors and battle. He had a shock of black, unkempt hair, and dark eyes that seemed like black orbs without pupils. His features were given an added sinister quality by a nose that had been broken at some stage. His appearance spoke of a life spent out of doors, and there was something about his manner that made clear he was used to giving orders. He was the first to speak.

'I am Sítae. I am the *ollamh-ailtire*.'

Fidelma sensed a hostile quality in his tone.

'All the demolition and rebuilding is in my charge,' he went on quickly. 'I am here to make clear to you that the wooden guest house was not under my jurisdiction. My builders were not due to start work on demolishing that building until after the foreign bishop and his party had left the abbey.'

'You will have time to express your opinions shortly.' Fidelma matched his aggressive approach with indifference. 'As a *dálaigh*, I will make my first task to hear how the fire started and other details from Brother Áedh. I am informed that Brother Áedh is in charge of keeping the abbey buildings safe from fire.'

The younger man immediately shook his head.

'There is no such thing as a building that is safe from fire,' he corrected pedantically. 'I am sure the master builder here would agree. Stone can be a better deterrent to fire than wood, but all buildings are constructed with some elements of combustible material. Whether by stone or by wood, there are always additional flammable materials: wood, straw, wattle, daub. So neither material is truly safe from igniting to some extent or another.'

Eadulf smiled briefly, for he had pointed out the same thing shortly before to Abbot Cuán.

'At the moment,' Fidelma said patiently, 'I am interested in how this particular fire started and why it was so quick to spread its destruction.'

Sítae interrupted before Brother Áedh could reply.

'While I would agree with Brother Áedh that no building is safe from fire, I must repeat that I am here to assure you that there is no fault among my workers or on myself. This fire started in the night when my men and I were at rest in our camp outside the abbey. As soon as we heard the alarm, we rushed forward to offer our help to Brother Áedh and his men fighting the fire.'

Before Fidelma could repeat that he should wait until his opinion was asked, Brother Áedh was speaking.

'That is true,' he confirmed. 'We are grateful. Two of Sítae's men suffered burns alongside several of my own men in our attempts to quell the fire. Nevertheless, fires can frequently spring up on building sites after workmen have left for the night. As you can see, lady, all this back part of the abbey is largely a construction site. I think the origin of the fire must, with due respect, lie among the buildings materials.'

'I protest on that point,' Sítae snapped. 'It is easy to dismiss matters by blaming any failures on materials, if not on the men.'

Fidelma ignored him and continued to address Brother Áedh.

'Let us walk over to the ruins and you may show me what you, as someone knowledgeable as to how fires start and spread, have thus far observed.'

The master builder was clearly annoyed at being ignored but before he could start to protest, Fidelma took the opportunity to raise another question with him.

'To whom do you answer according to your contract with the abbey?'

The man drew himself up proudly. 'I answer directly to Abbot Cuán. As I said, I am an *ollamh-ailtire*. These workers are all contracted to me as I am master of all the crafts of stone work, and carpentry and attendant trades. Before this, I have worked on many churches, abbeys and fortresses in this capacity.'

'This abbey is a great undertaking,' observed Eadulf quietly.

'Many of the wooden buildings here need to be replaced in stone while those already built in stone need renovation. My workers and I are, in fact, recreating this abbey. I have eighteen master craftsmen under me and some thirty-three labourers to haul and place stones.'

'The restoration of this abbey . . . or the rebuilding of it . . . started a long time ago under Abbot Ségdae,' Fidelma pointed out. 'But you, Sítae, could not have been long in the work here?'

'Nearly a year,' replied the burly man in a patronising tone. 'I was previously in the territory of the Corco Duibhne, building a fortress. When Abbot Cuán took office here he realised that it needed a talented master builder to create a team to achieve what the abbey should be. It was to become a lasting memory to that blessed man, Ailbe, the founder of this abbey.'

'So you felt you were chosen?'

He failed to see her sarcasm.

'I am sure, when you see all the work that has been done, you will agree that my craftsmen are the best.'

Fidelma's face was grave. It was clear to Eadulf, who knew her temperament, that she had taken a dislike to the master builder.

'That may be so, but at the moment, Sítae, we have the remains of a fire to investigate and the death of the foreign bishop on our hands, as well as injuries among those who fought to extinguish it.'

'Indeed, indeed. And a body to be buried after the *aire*, the watching of the body,' Brother Mac Raith reminded them anxiously. 'The legal requirements must be met. Sítae is aware of that.'

Fidelma regarded him curiously. 'Why would the burial of the bishop's remains be of concern to the master builder?' she enquired.

It was Sítae who responded immediately. 'As Brother Áedh told you, in the fight to douse the flames, some of his men were injured. These are the same men who dig the graves in the abbey cemetery and know the rituals of measuring and carrying the body to the grave.'

Sítae was speaking before Fidelma could understand what the steward meant.

'I was telling Brother Áedh that, as his men had sustained some injuries, my men could fulfil the necessary work of preparing the grave for the remains of the bishop. In fact, one of my men, Patu, a carpenter by trade, has previously performed the task of measuring bodies and preparing graves.'

Brother Mac Raith added quickly, 'I see no objection to the generous offer by Sítae, provided he seeks the approval of the abbot. In view of the condition of the body I see no need for lengthy *aire*, once your legal approval is given. We could even perform the ceremony tomorrow at midnight.'

Fidelma was indifferent. 'I do not see that this is my concern. The ultimate decision would be the abbot's, so I suggest you discuss it with Abbot Cuán.'

They came to a halt once more before the blackened ruins where Enda was waiting for them. Fidelma turned to Brother Áedh. 'Now, as the expert on fires, you will tell me your views. Obviously, if you could cite evidence, as if you are giving testimony in a *dáil*, a legal court, it might eventually be used for that purpose.'

The young man straightened his shoulders. 'As the steward has probably informed you, it has been the policy of this abbey to start rebuilding its original wooden complex in more durable materials. We stand in an area where this has not been started. You will see around you that there are many buildings still in the original wooden constructions. This guest house was due to be pulled down long ago, except that the foreign bishop insisted on staying in it for the duration of his visit.'

'I think he was due to depart from the abbey within the next day or so,' the steward intervened.

Fidelma waited quietly, hoping Brother Áedh would continue with his account.

'I was roused by the steward in the early hours of this morning with the news that there was a fire. I went to the door and I could hear the noise of the alarums. I summoned my small band of firefighters, who, as I say, I had recruited and trained myself. I took charge, organising volunteers and lines of bucket men to the nearby stream and wells to supply water. By this time the entire building was alight. The fire had spread rapidly. I would also observe that our small hand pumps were useless.'

He paused and then added quickly: 'The previous abbot, Abbot Ségdae, had furnished the abbey with these hand pumps, which they say the Greeks devised years ago. But against a fire that has already developed, they were no more effective than a child spitting at it.'

'You saw no chance of saving the building?'

Brother Áedh shook his head. 'The building was even then beyond saving. Several of my men were injured and some badly burnt about the hands in the conflagration.'

'When you arrived, I presume that there was no way you could enter the building to fight back the flames?'

'None; the building was too well alight. All we could do was ensure that the flames did not spread to other nearby buildings and simply wait until all the combustible materials were exhausted.'

'You say that you and your firefighters had trained yourselves to tackle such fires?' Eadulf asked.

'I had suggested to the steward a year ago that a small group should be formed who would know how to fight fires. I had studied and learnt the techniques and so trained them myself. The steward endorsed the training of a small group from among our more muscular brethren. We have had no major problems before but accidents are inevitable on such a large building site.'

'The fire is nothing to do with my men,' the master builder repeated angrily. 'I think the *dálaigh* is waiting to hear some evidence of what actually happened and not general insinuations.

I will argue that the fire is neither the fault, nor even the accidental fault, of any of my building team. My honour price backs it.'

'I have heard you,' Fidelma replied impatiently. 'But I am still waiting for some attempt at explanation. So let us start to discover the cause of this fire. Now, Brother Áedh, can you offer an opinion? Looking at the building when it was on fire and looking at the remnants, do you get any idea as to where the fire started?'

Brother Áedh had no hesitation. He pointed to the far corner where the body of the bishop had been found, just as Brother Mac Raith had previously.

'Given that the cooking area was diagonally opposite to where the bishop was found, you would say that the fire did not start by accident in the cooking area?'

'You can see that the only stones used in the building were in that place. It was no accidental cooking fire. Anyway, I am sure that the steward has informed you that the foreign bishop did not cook for himself, nor did any of his attendants come to cook for him. As far as I recall, he attended all his meals in the *praintech*, the refectory, along with the majority of those who serve in this abbey.'

Fidelma glanced at Brother Mac Raith. It was important information that he had neglected to tell her.

'Do you confirm this? You were uncertain when you mentioned the cooking area.'

Brother Mac Raith was defensive. 'I could not be sure if Bishop Brodulf had any special meals made for him outside of the three meals that are served to all in the abbey. The bishop made a point of joining all the senior members of the abbey in the *praintech* for all meals.'

'Which are?' asked Fidelma. When the steward looked surprised at her question, she explained: 'Individual communities often have different arrangements for meals, especially a *conhospitae*, such as this.'

'We make no difference between the sisterhood and the brethren,' replied the steward. 'We all sit together. There is the *longud,* the first meal; then the *etar-shod,* the middle meal when the sun is at its zenith. Finally, we have the *praind*, the evening meal. Most of our religious attend that as being the last meal of the day, when thanks are given for the success of the day's labour.'

'And Bishop Brodulf always attended all of these meals?' Eadulf pressed.

'He liked to make his presence known, especially during the last meal.'

'So it is logical that no other meals would have been cooked for him here?'

'I suppose not. If he required anything, then his servant, Brother Charibert, would have made the arrangement,' the steward pointed out. 'You will recall, Brother Charibert did not stay in this guest house. He stayed in the new guest apartments just beyond the students' quarters.'

'That is some way for a servant to come to attend to the needs of his master,' Eadulf observed.

Fidelma had been about to make a comment, but then shrugged. She would see what Brother Charibert had to say later. She turned back to Brother Áedh.

'This confirms what you say. There being no meal cooked here, the fire did not come from this area. So you say it started at the far corner? You pointed to the area where the bishop had his bed on the upper floor? Could it have come from a candle or a lamp left alight when the bishop fell asleep?'

'I doubt that, lady.'

'You sound positive. Why so?'

'A fire starting from a candle, or even a lamp filled with oil or a flammable resin, or some such, might well have started the fire. However, the bishop would have to have been incapable of waking up. Even in difficult circumstances, the fire would have woken him at some point and he would have endeavoured to put it out, or escape from the room. As we found the body still on the remains of his bed, which had collapsed directly from the floor above, he had been unable or incapable of movement. When the flames burnt through the support of the floor of his bedchamber and it fell on to the floor beneath, the bishop was still lying prone on the remnants of his bed.'

Fidelma gave a warning glance at Eadulf. She did not want to reveal that they knew well the bishop had not been roused when the fire started because he was already dead. However, she wanted to know what Áedh could add to the story.

'Are you saying that there is no way that the fire could have started in the bishop's bedchamber by some accident with a candle or lamp?' she pressed.

'That is precisely what I am saying.'

'But the fire started from the bedroom?'

'I did not obviously make myself entirely clear,' Brother Áedh replied with a sniff. 'I said it started from that direction. To be explicit, I would say that it developed from the ground floor underneath the bedchamber. I will explain. In examining the condition of the wood one can usually gauge the intensity of the heat. Very well. While the fire burnt fiercely, the wood shows that the lower floor was exposed to flames more intensely than the upper one in which the bishop slept. This is not to say that the intensity of the fire in the bedchamber was negligible. It was enough to almost destroy the body and other surrounding items. Almost, that is; but not to the extent of the lower floor. So the lower floor was the source of the flames.'

Sítae, the master builder, who had been suppressing his desire to say something during this time, shifting his weight and muttering, now could not hold himself in.

'What Brother Áedh seems to be asking us to believe is that

there was some accident that started the fire on the lower floor at the back of the building. He wants to imply that I and my men are responsible. I protest!'

'At the moment, there is nothing to protest about,' Fidelma replied sharply before an argument developed. 'We are simply eliminating factors by looking at the evidence. The point here is that if the lower floor was the source of the flames, then how were those flames ignited to spread so quickly through the rest of the building?'

'Such evidence was almost destroyed.' Brother Áedh addressed her, but with a curiously triumphant glance at Sítae.

'*Almost*?' Fidelma asked quickly.

'I truly did not want to lay the blame on the master builder. However, come round to the back of these ruins and I will show you. True, it is not complete evidence, but . . .'

They followed him in curiosity. At the other side of the guest house Brother Áedh pointed along the blackened line of burnt wood and ash that had once been the back of the building.

'See those burnt support posts? That was where the back door to the guest house stood. Also you will see a little area that had been an extension, and from the stone there you will understand what it once was.'

'You can continue to explain,' Fidelma invited.

'Thus, if guests wished to discreetly go to the outside toilet, they did not have to go out of the front entrance but could use this more secluded route, leaving the place by a back door.'

'And so?' Fidelma murmured impatiently.

'We stand at the back door,' the man continued, unperturbed. 'Now, between the back of the guest house, which is still marked clearly by the extent of the ash, you see a space between it and the border fencing of the abbey, which is untouched. The tall boundary fence of wood remains. The builders will be changing this when they erect the new stone wall.'

The master builder gave an irritated exclamation. 'What did I say? This is leading to a claim against us. I am told that the border space was made years ago so that there was a clear *fortach* between any building and the outer wall of the abbey. And, yes, we will be trying to replace the wooden wall with a stone one. But because this building was still used as a guest house, we had not sought to do any major work near it. You can see for yourself where we have already stopped working to allow the people in these buildings to relocate.'

Eadulf frowned slightly, having worked out the measurement of the *fortach* to be five metres roughly. Some of this borderland space between buildings and fencing was grass and with many muddy patches in which herbs and plants were grown.

Fidelma stirred impatiently, shifting her weight from one foot to another.

'What are you trying to tell us, Brother Áedh?' she demanded. 'I have been patient in trying to follow you and am not sure where exactly you are leading. Are you truly claiming what the master builder is saying that you are?'

'A moment more of patience,' Brother Áedh insisted, his tone clearly trying to conceal his emotion. 'I have said that the fire started on this side. You see that from the back door. Now a lot of the ground has been churned up by my men moving round to try to quench the flames. But look closely at the ground between the back of the building and the border wall. Look down carefully. Some areas of the earth have not been touched. Do you see anything on the grass or the rough earth?'

Enda, whose sharp eyes and ability as a tracker were part of the training of becoming a Warrior of the Golden Collar, tilted his head to one side. He pointed.

'He is drawing our attention to the light dusting of yellow powder here and there on the ground.'

'Yellow powder,' confirmed Brother Áedh, not disguising his

triumphant tone. 'Can anyone identify what the yellow powder might be?'

It was Eadulf who bent down to pick up some of the powder between his fingers, rubbing it between them before sniffing it cautiously.

'Pale yellow and crystalline, the odour is like eggs that are rotten. I forget what you call it in your language.'

'*Scraib!*' Fidelma declared.

'That's right,' Eadulf confirmed. '*Scraib* . . . sulphur dust.'

Brother Áedh nodded like a master confirming the knowledge of his pupil. 'Most of you will know that sulphur dust ignites easily and can even cause an explosion when in confined areas.'

Eadulf was suddenly made enthusiastic by the knowledge.

'Brother Áedh is telling us that sulphur dust was brought here to the back of the guest house. That is dangerous. Toxic gases can form when it is set on fire. If it is solid and in a bulk, like in a brick, it will still burn moderately, but as dust it has an explosive force. It can be ignited just by friction, giving out sparks and flames and—'

Fidelma cleared her throat as she interrupted him.

'I think we can all deduce that the powder of *scraib* is certainly enough of an aid to turn a dry burning building into a conflagration.' She turned to Brother Áedh. 'And what are your deductions from this?'

'I have thought long and hard. This fire was no accident. It was deliberately set and fed. I was concerned that a building, even an old one, with dry wood, daub and wattle, could burn down so quickly and so thoroughly. Now I believe it was fed when it was set alight, and fed by someone who had brought a bucket of sulphur dust to use, spreading it as an incendiary.'

He pointed to an area of soft earth, which must have been behind the outside toilet.

'See that indentation? I would say that is where the bucket of sulphur stood. Someone placed the bucket there so that it was hidden. Sometime in the early hours, I believe that person returned here to the back door and, when they were ready, used it to help spread the flames.'

There were several moments of silence while each of them digested what the fire expert had said.

'It is a plausible theory,' Fidelma agreed eventually. 'At the moment, it is no more than a speculation, but it is a very good one.'

'I think there is only one matter to be considered,' Brother Áedh replied. 'The answer to one question and then you have the person responsible for setting the fire.'

'Only one question?' Eadulf asked with a frown.

'Who has access to sulphur dust?' Brother Áedh responded. 'It is not so common, yet would have to be available in large quantities; enough to fill a large bucket.'

'He accuses me and my men!' Sítae shouted.

'He has not said that,' Fidelma responded firmly.

'He does not have to say it,' the master builder said slowly. 'He knows that we use sulphur dust in our work. But we have never brought it into the building site here. We maintain a quantity in secure condition up at our encampment. We would never leave any amount within the abbey grounds.'

Brother Áedh shrugged. 'I shall say no more. Who else but builders would use it?'

'The knowledge of its use is not only confined to builders,' Eadulf pointed out. 'Its use has been known since ancient times as a flammable material. The Romans used it in their ceremonial fires.'

Sítae was scowling. 'You seem to know a lot about it.' He turned suspiciously to Eadulf. 'You tell us who else uses it?'

Eadulf paused for a moment at the suspicious face of the man and then smiled.

'It is known and used by apothecaries and physicians,' he replied. 'It is used to purify the air, to cleanse a room and, if taken as an inhalant, as a medicine. It neutralises phlegmatic illness and balances the body of ill humours.'

Brother Áedh grimaced sourly. 'In other words, a physician, or an apothecary, as well as a builder, might have knowledge and access to a supply and its use. Even so, we do not have too many such professionals in this abbey who could have access to a whole bucket of sulphur dust.'

His accusatory glance was aimed at the master builder.

'When do you use this sulphur dust, Sítae?' asked Fidelma. 'Where is this matter usually kept?'

'We use a small amount as an aid to splitting stone. It is stored in our camp in a special stone container, which has a heavy stone lid. It would be difficult for any stranger to remove any of it unnoticed, let alone a full bucket of the powder.'

'Who said it was a stranger who did so?' Brother Áedh sneered.

Fidelma, seeing the aggressive movement of the body between the two men, decided to end things.

'I have noted all your comments and I must thank you both for your assessment,' she said. 'There is much to consider. You will know that, as a *dálaigh,* I am bound to conduct this investigation in accordance with the laws. I have some matters to discuss with the abbot. Further investigation will have to be made before any resolution is reached. You may both be called upon again for official statements but, in the meantime, talk as little as you can about this matter.'

Fidelma turned sharply towards the main abbey buildings, leaving Brother Áedh and Sítae staring disconcertedly. Then they glowered at each other for a moment before turning and moving off in opposite directions. Brother Mac Raith had hesitated to make sure of their departure but was now hurrying after Fidelma.

'Should we say that this bishop was murdered before the fire?' Eadulf whispered to her.

'We will discuss the situation with Abbot Cuán first,' Fidelma replied firmly. 'We must follow the legal protocols before we start making speculations.'

'I am not sure I understand,' Eadulf protested.

'You have been with me a long time, Eadulf, and you have learnt much about our law. Colgú may be my brother and a king, but I am still under our legal system; I am only a lowly advocate. I may be personal *dálaigh*, a legal adviser, to my brother, but I am not Chief Brehon. When it comes to the death of a foreign prelate I cannot override the fact that this death took place in the abbey of the Chief Bishop of this kingdom but one in which the King also has authority in civil matters. However, even a king has to act in accordance with his Chief Brehon, while in ecclesiastical matters it is the Chief Bishop who advises him. I can do nothing unless I am given such authority and even with authority we are dealing with a crime against a foreigner of some status.'

Eadulf was silent. He realised that Fidelma was punctilious about following protocols.

She suddenly halted and turned to the steward.

'Talking of protocols, we shall probably have to spend this night as guests of the abbey. I realise it is in your purview as steward to grant visitors permission to do so. I should make an official request to you.'

Brother Mac Raith did not seem surprised, but was flattered at being asked nevertheless.

'You do not have to make such a request, lady. Your chamber is already prepared. I issued instructions for your bags to be placed there as soon as I began to see that your inquiries would delay you in the abbey a while. Do you want to see the abbot again now?'

'Eadulf and I will go directly to Abbot Cuán and discuss matters. Perhaps you can take Enda to show him his quarters? I believe the abbot's chamber is at the top of these stone stairs on the next floor?'

While Brother Mac Raith accepted to escort Enda, it was clear that he was being asked to do so because Fidelma wanted to see Abbot Cuán alone and his expression was one of suspicion as he watched her and Eadulf mount the stairs to the abbot's chamber.

chapter four

Abbot Cuán did not appear to be in his chambers. Not having an answer to her knock, Fidelma had decided to open the door to peer into the room. While there was no sign of the abbot, a shadowy movement to one side of the abbot's desk stayed her. She recalled an open door in a recess led to a flat roof area, which she knew the late Abbot Ségdae had used as a private garden. She moved across the chamber, followed by Eadulf, and looked out of the open door. It was a small area to which the only access was from the abbot's chambers. The flat roof was enclosed by a little stone wall. The moment she stood at the entrance of this little open-air sanctuary, Fidelma was aware of the almost overpowering odour of lavender. The lavender shrubs made up almost the entire garden. Their evergreen foliage was everywhere but the flowers, which had begun to emerge in late spring, were creating coloured highlights to the plants.

'I find lavender soothing and relaxing, especially when I am faced with problems.' Abbot Cuán's voice, close by, startled her.

He was seated just by the entrance on a wooden stool so that she had not noticed him as her gaze had immediately been drawn into the garden. She turned to him apologetically but he smiled.

'I use this as a small sanctuary to sit and refresh myself. I understand my predecessor did the same.'

'Abbot Ségdae used to sit here,' Fidelma confirmed. She remembered the late abbot had long held an interest in herbs and flowers.

Abbot Cuán indicated the garden with a wave of his hand.

'Ségdae liked a more practical choice of herbs. He grew basil and rosemary, and he even cultivated wild garlic and other herbs. I am now reminded that it is the season for a little clipping of the lavender growth. Left alone, the shrubs become woody and with a grain that is hard to manage. You must never clip the flowering parts back to the more grainy stalks.'

'I was always taught that many used the lavender flowers to create oils that could be used for relieving flatulence,' Fidelma volunteered. 'Otherwise, I know little of the plant.'

'Well, I think the aroma helps relax the mind,' the abbot replied with a grave humorous expression. 'I do not suffer from flatulence so I accept its calming properties. However, I think that you have come to tell me to relax myself in preparation for some serious news and not to talk about the efficacies of plants.'

She was about to frown in annoyance but then she pursed her lips thoughtfully.

'You have a good intuition, Abbot Cuán. That is the purpose for which Eadulf and I have come to speak with you. The death of this bishop may not be a simple matter to resolve.'

'The problem being how to explain Bishop Brodulf's death to those who sent him here? Obviously, under our laws, the abbey is responsible for any accident that has befallen him while being our guest and under our hospitality.'

'I am afraid things are more complicated than a simple accident.'

'More complicated?' the abbot queried. There was a look of anxiety in his eyes as he raised them to gaze at her.

'Having made initial enquiries of your physician, Brother Anlón, and then talking with Brother Áedh, who is an expert on fires, the indisputable conclusion is that Bishop Brodulf was murdered. He was dead before the fire even started, having been stabbed, and then the fire was laid deliberately to disguise that murder.'

There was a silence for some time and then Abbot Cuán rose slowly from his seat and took his stick, motioning her to precede him out of the herb garden back into his study. Inside he indicated Fidelma and Eadulf to be seated before laying aside his stick and limping to a cupboard. From it he took an ornate bronze jug and three drinking vessels. With careful deliberation he poured the amber-coloured liquid from the jug into the vessels and offered them one each in turn with the explanatory word 'corma'. He took his to his chair, behind the wooden desk, sat down and sipped appreciatively at the strong spirit.

'The great blessing in our abbey is that we have a brewer who can perform miracles distilling apples,' he sighed. They did not respond. 'There is no mistake in what you tell me, Fidelma?' he then demanded in a soft tone. 'We can be absolutely certain that this matter was no accident?'

'Absolutely,' she replied shortly.

There was a long pause before the abbot spoke again.

'Then I must ask you to advise me as to what I should do.'

'You realise that although I am my brother's legal adviser, I am not the Chief Brehon of this kingdom? I would have to defer to Brehon Fíthel. It may be that if Bishop Brodulf was a bishop of high status from the kingdom of Burgundia, then it could result in a negotiation between that kingdom and this one. I would have to know more details about the bishop's legal status, the reason why he was here and other matters. I need to know all this before I even begin to look for a culprit.'

At her side, Eadulf looked surprised.

'Surely the one does not exclude the other?' he asked softly.

'It can have that effect,' Fidelma replied. 'Unless an inquiry is made in proper form, then it can be made invalid. If there are negotiations between two kingdoms, then, even worse, words can become disagreements and disagreements lead to conflict. Remember, Eadulf, you and I were delegates to the Council of Autun a few years ago. We had the opportunity to observe those people and meet King Clotaire. The Franks are an aggressive, warlike people. They will demand a full explanation of this death.'

Abbot Cuán raised both hands in a despairing gesture. 'I understand, I understand. But can't you start preparing the ground, even if you feel that you have to hand the matter over to Brehon Fíthel, as your brother's Chief Brehon?'

'If that is your official request, then I can do so,' she replied without hesitation. 'But there is a small legal point.'

'Which is?' Abbot Cuán was puzzled.

'This abbey is a *conhospitae*, a mixed house. As abbot you are also regarded as Chief Bishop of the kingdom, in accordance with being the *comarbae,* the heir, of the Blessed Ailbe, who first brought the New Faith to the kingdom. The abbey consists of both brethren and sisterhood, and its governance within these walls is surely shared?'

'Ah, I see what you imply. In this matter, I have sole authority. We are a mixed house, as you say, like many of the abbeys, but because of certain traditions here we do not have an *abatissa* as co-equal. But we have a *prioressa*. Prioress Suanach was one of our leading scholars many years ago and she has now taken charge of the sisterhood of the abbey. She also looks after the students here as well as being one of our leading teachers. She is a remarkable woman.'

'So you have sole authority to make this legal request of me?'

'I do, but I shall, of course, consult and seek her opinion. Accept this as an official request from me.' The abbot paused, adding clearly, 'As I am *comarbae* of Ailbe, this is an official request from this abbey.'

Fidelma was reflective for a moment. 'Obviously, Eadulf will assist me, and Enda, as a member of my brother's bodyguard, will stand ready for any help that he may have to render. Overall then, I must have free access and authority over all in the abbey, regardless of their origins.'

'Surely that is understood?' the abbot queried in a tired voice.

'It may be understood between us, but sometimes visitors from other kingdoms can fall back on a refusal to co-operate because the law here is not the way of the kingdoms they come from. Do you have many students from other kingdoms here?'

'Not such large groups as they have at the abbeys such as Darú. I am told they have students from eighteen countries studying there. Here, we have only nine different countries represented by students and scholars.'

'In which case I suggest that you should make an announcement at evening prayers or the evening meal to point out that they should co-operate in my inquiries.' When the abbot agreed, Fidelma straightened her shoulders as if preparing for the task. 'Perhaps we should start immediately? Firstly, this bishop, Bishop Brodulf, was from the Frankish kingdom of Burgundia. But why was he here . . . here in this kingdom and in this abbey?'

Abbot Cuán stretched back in his chair and seemed to give the matter some thought before he spoke.

'His reason, so he said, was that he was travelling for information about why the church here, and in particularly its scholars, were not obeying the decisions of the various church councils of the East when others were beginning to accept them. You mentioned the Council of Autun, which you attended. Bishop Brodulf being from that kingdom, he said that he had arrived here to discuss matters of liturgy with our chief scholar, the Venerable Breas. As you may know, Breas is considered one of the authorities of the Faith as it has developed in these western islands. He is our *fer-leginn*, our chief professor. His has been a leading voice in arguing against many changes in the Faith enacted by the various councils held under the jurisdiction of Rome and Constantinople.'

'I have heard of him but never met him,' Fidelma admitted. 'I thought that he was the *Saoi Canóine,* the professor of the sixth grade of Orders of Divine Wisdom at the Abbey of Mungairit?'

Abbot Cuán actually seemed to preen himself with self-satisfaction.

'Recently, the heads of the ecclesiastical colleges of the kingdom declared him a *Drunmclí,* of the seventh grade of Divine Wisdom, thereby holding perfect knowledge. As such he felt there was no other place but this abbey that he should be appointed as chief scholar.'

'So he left the Abbey of Mungairit and came here to instruct your students?'

'To be more accurate, he came back here to instruct.'

'He was here before?'

'He was not only a scholar here when he was a youth. He was a student and rose to instructing students here many years ago. He was a *Rosai* even then – a professor of such knowledge that he could sit on the level of a king in the feasting hall. In fact, just as you can, by virtue of your holding the degree of *Anruth* in legal studies.'

'So when did the Venerable Breas leave here and go to the Abbey of Mungairit?'

'He left here when Abbot Conaing died, well over ten years ago.'

'And exactly when did he come back?'

'That was just over a year ago,' confirmed the abbot. 'He has a good reputation in the Five Kingdoms of Éireann, but why Bishop Brodulf wanted to come here to listen to him instructing our students, I am not sure. It seemed that Bishop Brodulf considered the Venerable Breas' teachings as heretical. They certainly provoked the bishop to anger.'

'Provoked?' Fidelma asked sharply.

'The bishop did not like to be challenged on the facts he

maintained. There were several discussions, which the Venerable Breas allowed his students to attend and contribute to. I should add that it did not please the bishop, who believed that students should not question their superiors.'

'Their superiors?' Even Fidelma was shocked.

'His choice of words,' the abbot confirmed. 'He declared that those of lesser rank should obey and not question.'

'How else were they supposed to learn?' Eadulf muttered. 'It is the nature of the student to seek wisdom from the master and thus gather their own knowledge and perspective.'

'That view was put before him but he did not agree with it.'

'We shall have a discussion with the Venerable Breas later then,' Fidelma said. 'From what point of view were these debates acrimonious?'

Abbot Cuán frowned as he considered the question. 'If you mean who became emotional, I am told that it was Bishop Brodulf. When one is expressing personally held arguments, one cannot easily keep hidden the feelings that are provoked by being contradicted.'

'Not everyone is trained as a lawyer,' Fidelma agreed grimly. 'It takes a lifetime to see facts and how they can be interpreted before simply embracing an argument with an overwhelming emotional belief.'

'Just so.'

'You say such emotions came from the bishop, but surely the younger students would be more prone to being emotional?'

'I cannot deny it. However, it is disconcerting to see someone who should possess more wisdom losing his temper.'

'Then we can have no doubt that some of these discussions would have resulted in personal feelings coming to the fore?' Fidelma pointed out.

The abbot shrugged. 'Not all members of the Faith have the same tolerance as that which the Christ taught we should have.'

'Those followers of the Faith could be counted on the fingers of one hand,' Eadulf muttered.

Fidelma turned back to the abbot. 'When did the Bishop arrive here?' she asked.

'Nine days ago.'

'He was not alone when he arrived?'

'He came with two brothers of the Faith from his own land. One was Deacon Landric, and the other was a simple attendant, Brother Charibert.'

'*Deacon* Landric? Remind me of that role, as it is not a title we use here as yet.'

'It is from the Greek *diakonos* – which was more or less the bishop's steward. It means a servant or a messenger.'

'Then I should next speak with this Deacon Landric as I need to know more about Bishop Brodulf, where exactly he comes from and why he decided to come here. Where might I find him?'

CHAPTER FIVE

Deacon Landric was easily found in one of the guest chambers, which had earlier been pointed out to them by Brother Mac Raith. Fidelma and Eadulf were surprised by his appearance. Far from the idea of an elderly and scholarly man befitting the role of steward to a bishop, the man who invited them into his chamber was young, handsome and more the build of a warrior than someone following a religious calling. He was fair of skin, with a shock of flaxen hair around the tonsure of St Peter, piercing eyes of extreme blue and a ready smile. However, Fidelma thought there was something cruel about his thin red lips, which seemed to curl at one corner with cynicism. He appeared to be in his early twenties.

'*Bonum est te iterum vidēre*,' he greeted in Latin, causing Fidelma even more surprise for the words meant: 'It is good to see you again.'

After a hesitation she replied in the same language with some perplexity: 'Have we met before?'

Deacon Landric's smile broadened, showing white, well-cared-for teeth. 'You would scarcely remember me but I recall you well enough. I was a young member of the brethren at the Council of Autun when you came there.'

'Were you a delegate at Autun?' Eadulf asked, also trying to place the young man.

'*Salve, Frater Eadulf.*' The young man turned to greet him. 'I was not so elevated then but only standing in the shadows of Abbot Leodegar. I was there when Sister Fidelma presented her case about the murder of Abbot Dabhóc before our King Clotaire and Abbot Leodegar. You would not have noticed me.'

They both remembered the King and his Bishop of Autun, who had organised the council that was to have such an impact on those who followed the Faith of the Western lands.

'Was Bishop Brodulf attending that council?' Eadulf asked quickly.

'He was not.'

'So you did not serve him then?'

'I joined the service of Bishop Brodulf less than half a year ago.'

'We are commissioned to investigate his death,' Fidelma explained.

Deacon Landric motioned them to enter and take available seats in his room, closing the door behind them.

'I would hazard that one of your reputation for being learned in your native law would not have made an idle visit to me. How can I help?'

Deacon Landric seemed totally at ease as he sat on the edge of his bed, that being the only remaining seat in the room.

'Perhaps you could tell us something about the bishop first?' Fidelma invited.

'He is from the Abbey of Luxovium, whose abbot is currently Ingofind. Bishop Brodulf was appointed bishop of the surrounding territory in order to travel the area on behalf of the abbey.'

'Then I presume, like we in the insular churches, you rank an abbot above a bishop?'

'That is so, although we are now beginning to follow Rome and place a bishop above an abbot.'

'I have naturally heard of Luxovium, for it was an abbey

established by one of our own great teachers, Columbán, the "fair dove",' Fidelma commented. 'He moved on to establish an even greater abbey called Bobium, where I received hospitality when I was shipwrecked on my return from Rome.'

Brother Landric's smile became sardonic. 'Columbán? He and his followers were chased out of Luxovium long ago by King Theuderic because Columbán refused to accept the Rules of Rome. It was found that he was still celebrating Paschal rituals by the old dating of your Western churches. His followers still wore the tonsure of John instead of Peter, and that—'

'I have heard,' interrupted Fidelma firmly, keeping a serious expression, 'that it was more to do with the fact that Columbán criticised this King Theuderic for living openly with his mistress. That was what was spoken of in Bobium.'

An expression of annoyance crossed the deacon's features.

'Even Pope Boniface condemned Columbán for following the rituals of your culture and not following Rome. Columbán was arrested and imprisoned and then he contrived to escape and even returned to Luxovium . . .'

'That shows the courage of his belief,' Eadulf pointed out with an ironical smile.

'I do not think this conversation is constructive in resolving the present matter. These events happened generations ago,' Fidelma said, trying to bring humour back into the discussion.

Deacon Landric still seemed annoyed.

'The difference between our churches does have a bearing on the reason why Bishop Brodulf came here. That was for the purpose of debating our differences. You will remember the decision of the Council at Autun?'

'Naturally,' Fidelma replied.

'The decision was that all religious houses must accept and obey the Rule of Benedict, the dating of the Paschal ceremonies, and that the tonsure of John should no longer be worn, but only that of Peter.'

'And so?'

'Many Western churches in Gaul, even in the Frankish king-doms, but especially in these western islands, have ignored these rulings from Rome. Even their philosophies stand in defiance of the decisions of the major councils of both Rome and Constantinople on the beliefs and rituals of the Faith.'

'All this is understood,' Fidelma sighed. 'Sometimes, however, even these councils are in conflict with each other. Anyway, let us get back to basics because I have already said, we are not here to discuss ecclesiastical law.'

'As I have said,' Deacon Landric said, 'it was my honour to be appointed Bishop Brodulf's deacon, serving as his steward . . .'

'I gather he came here with another member of the Abbey of Luxovium?'

'Brother Charibert?' The tone was immediately dismissive. 'He is just a servant to the bishop.'

'A servant? I thought all the brethren considered themselves servants to Christ?' Eadulf muttered.

'On whose authority did Bishop Brodulf make the journey here?' Fidelma interposed quickly in case they were about to enter another argument that would lead them away from what she wanted to find out.

'The bishop came on his own authority.' The answer came hastily, causing Fidelma's eyes to narrow slightly. 'Anyway, he was a noble of our people, as are many prelates of the church. He needed no other authority. Having seen that the scholars of the churches in this island were refusing to obey the decisions of the councils, Bishop Brodulf decided to come here to listen to their arguments.'

'Why here especially? I mean, why come to the Abbey of Imleach Iubhair?' she pressed.

'Because he had heard of the twisted ideas of the Venerable Breas and sought to confront him in argument,' Deacon Landric almost snapped.

'In debate one should use logic to make points and not insults,' Eadulf observed heavily.

Fidelma intervened quietly again. 'He chose this abbey because he had heard of its principal teacher? Why choose the Venerable Breas when there are so many scholars in all the Five Kingdoms of this island who would willingly discourse with the bishop?'

'It is claimed that the Blessed Ailbe was teaching the Faith here before Patricius, who was appointed by Rome to become bishop to those who had already accepted the Faith in this island. So the Bishop Brodulf believed that this was the strongest of all the abbeys in this island.' Suddenly, the deacon turned interrogatively to Eadulf. 'Even having seen you in Autun, Brother Eadulf, I find it difficult to understand that you have become so involved here when your own people, in the kingdoms of the Angles, are now mostly accepting the authority of Rome after the Council of Streonshalh.'

Eadulf was not put out.

'It is true that, having been converted by missionaries from this island, I came here and studied before I went to Rome. It was my decision, even before the Council at Streonshalh, when Oswy decided his kingdom of Northumbria would follow Rome. I am not a blind follower. There is much to think about, much to discuss. In a way, it is good to see such discussions as the one Bishop Brodulf proposed here. I agree with discussion, if debated logically and seriously. One can learn much and not accept a decision when it is made merely by a show of hands.'

There was a silence before Fidelma continued. 'Bishop Brodulf came here because this is one of the oldest abbeys in the Five Kingdoms and he had heard of the scholarship of the Venerable Breas. And there were just three in your party travelling from Burgundia? As I recall, it is a long journey from Autun.'

'It was a similar distance from Luxovium,' agreed the deacon. 'We came by boat down the great river Liger, and then took ship with a Gaulish merchantman, which brought us to Árd Mór where we found a guide to bring us to this abbey.'

'I still do not fully understand why Bishop Brodulf would undertake such a long journey from Burgundia to this abbey. With due respect to the Venerable Breas, there are scholars of even greater renown, and still many scholars of our people in Burgundia.'

'I can only tell you what I know.'

'That I understand. But,' she paused to make an impact, 'so far I am unable to glimpse any reason why this resulted in Bishop Brodulf being murdered.'

The young deacon's eyes rounded, his mouth opened but no words came out. He sat for a moment in an apparent state of shock.

'Murdered?' he eventually said in an aghast tone. 'I had not understood that he was murdered. Are you saying that the fire in his guest house was no accident?'

'The truth is that your bishop was murdered and it is my task to find out why,' Fidelma repeated heavily. She had hoped that her shock announcement would have altered the complacency of the man. 'So I am looking for a motivation behind this deed.'

The young deacon seemed to be thinking rapidly. Various expressions registered on his features.

'Do you have any thoughts?' Eadulf observed sharply.

Deacon Landric hesitated. 'I agree that a murder must have a motive.'

'Naturally,' Fidelma agreed patiently.

'I am told that the laws of hospitality are held as precious in this land, almost sacred. Are they not?'

'They are. Everyone, even the meanest member of society, is obliged under the law to give hospitality to all who seek it. The only exception is that a criminal can be refused. But with that exception anyone who refuses hospitality is guilty of an offence we called *esáin*, that of driving away.'

'So, under your law, Bishop Brodulf was here legally enjoying the hospitality of this abbey?'

'There is surely no question of that? You came here as guests from a foreign country and were given hospitality in this abbey. But what is your point?'

'If someone in the abbey objected to our presence, to us being here, objected to our debating matters, and they attempted to silence us, would that be illegal?'

'It would be the crime of *etech* or "refusal", and in that case this abbey would lose its legal status under the law. But that is not what has happened here. You were not refused hospitality but treated as honoured guests. True, we have a murder and therefore we must now find the culprit.'

'The point I am making is that we were supposed to have been given hospitality here, which, so I am told, includes protection. If these debates caused such anger against my bishop and that anger erupted in such a manner that someone . . . I say someone . . . decided to silence the arguments of the bishop in this cruel manner, that surely could be deemed a crime . . . what you call *esáin* . . . wouldn't it? That requires compensation.'

Fidelma stared at the young deacon in surprise.

'You are correct, Deacon Landric. Have you studied our laws?'

The young man shook his head quickly. 'I am using logic to consider a motive and you have supplied the basis of the claim. If this was the motive – to silence the bishop – then this abbey, indeed, this kingdom, would be guilty of a crime for which it must pay compensation.'

Eadulf summed up, looking thoughtful. 'Deacon Landric seems to be arguing that Bishop Brodulf was killed to silence his arguments. But the arguments that he espoused are the well-known decisions of the numerous councils endorsed by Rome, so why silence them?'

'Moreover, in our system, argument is education,' Fidelma

added. 'Surely argument in debate and education is not a matter that would motivate such an emotion as the wish to kill someone who propounded opposite but well-known arguments?'

There were some moments of silence while this was considered.

'That would seem a logical view,' Deacon Landric admitted. 'But we are strangers in a strange land, who came to discuss our views and learn your views. Since no one knows us here, since there is no personal offence that would cause such hatred as to result in murder, where else should we turn for a motive? I have to say there is only one thing that might ignite such enmity and that is these very discussions, or call them debates, that we have been having.'

'Discussion is considered essential in our culture,' Fidelma pointed out mildly. 'It is considered the only way of education: exchanging views and arguing about them to discover their strengths and weaknesses. Only with such consideration can we progress in knowledge.'

'Yet this progression has led to the murder of my bishop and to the violation of the terms of hospitality,' Landric protested.

'Only if your premise is correct,' Fidelma replied. 'Are you serious in your contention that it is only the differences between your theological interpretations and rituals and those practised here that could have aroused such hatred as to lead to the murder of Bishop Brodulf? So whom do you charge? At the moment, you are speaking in general terms.'

'If I were not serious, I would not voice the charge,' replied the deacon furiously. 'I now do so and shall charge the abbot of this abbey, pending the result of your inquiry.'

Eadulf frowned a warning at Fidelma, whose expression showed what she thought of the young man. He spoke in an ironic tone.

'If we follow Deacon Landric's logic and agree the motive was hatred deriving from the disagreements between Bishop Brodulf and the Venerable Breas, it would mean that anyone voicing opposition to Brodulf could be the murderer. Do you have a specific name, Deacon Landric, or are you claiming the Venerable Breas himself is suspect?'

Fidelma stared at him a little shocked as she considered the interpretation that could be put on the words of the young man.

Deacon Landric had a twisted smile on his thin lips when he replied. 'The Venerable Breas is a scholar, but deeply entrenched in his misleading philosophies.' The comment was made in a neutral tone. 'But, of course, he had his acolytes with him during these discussions and perhaps younger men do not contain their emotions so easily as those with age and experience. Of course,' he added, 'I speak from the experience of my youth.'

'What are you trying to say, Deacon Landric?' Fidelma asked tightly.

'It is not up to me to say anything, lady. I am but a visitor to your country, here to assist my murdered bishop. When I saw you at the Council of Autun and witnessed how you resolved the mysteries there, I admired the way you resolved the murders and conspiracy before King Clotaire and Abbot Leodegar. It was like watching a sorceress suddenly sweeping aside a curtain to uncover the true culprit. I studied your technique. I know you do not dismiss any item of information but you pile them up, piece by piece, and go where they logically lead.'

Fidelma was actually smiling softly at his attempted flattery. 'But, in this case, you are doing your best to lead me to the path you want me to follow.'

'The logical path. The obvious path.'

'You think that Bishop Brodulf had presented his arguments with such irresistible force that a scholar such as the Venerable Breas, being unable to dismiss them by sheer logic, has resorted to the more physical method of silencing the arguments?'

'I did not say it was the Venerable Breas,' Landric corrected.

'But one of his young acolytes might not be so restrained. That is how I see it. I say no more.'

'You have already said much. At the moment, we are only speaking of suspicions and not making accusations, except you claim Abbot Cuán would have ultimate responsibility as the head of this abbey. But I presume you attended these discussions with Bishop Brodulf? Was there anyone other than the Venerable Breas who particularly opposed Bishop Brodulf's arguments?'

'The Venerable Breas allowed each of his acolytes to have their say. Sometimes he would correct them. Other times he would admonish them for their presentation when it verged away from a discussion and into an insult.'

'Ah,' Fidelma smiled triumphantly. 'So insults were given. Was that on both sides? It is so easy to let restraint fall and the emotion of the moment take control.'

It was unclear by his features whether Deacon Landric took on board the point of this remark. She waited a few moments and when he did not respond, she continued.

'So there were times when exchanges became heated?'

'There were times,' he confirmed.

'To the point where insults were given and the speaker had to be rebuked by the Venerable Breas?'

'I admit it.'

'I say again, did you notice anyone in particular at these times? Someone who became animated in the course of the argument?'

Brother Landric clenched his jaw for a moment. 'I wanted to avoid being direct with an accusation because I am sure you would be able to discover a name for yourself.'

'For the time being, let us talk about what you saw at these discussions when they became heated.'

The young man made a motion of his right shoulder as if in submission.

'The Venerable Breas had one student who was very sharp in

59

his arguments with my bishop. He was quite articulate, proficient in thoughtful argument.'

'Did you know who he was?'

'He was addressed as Brother Garb. He was a young man. From some remarks, I am led to believe that he is a senior student in the abbey.'

'If this Brother Garb was articulate, then he surely would have not had recourse to showing loss of temper in a debate? Is that not a contradiction?'

'I would usually agree,' Deacon Landric confirmed, 'but there were occasions so I am told.'

'You were not a witness?'

'The matter was mentioned by my bishop.'

'I think we can leave the matter for the present.' Fidelma felt frustrated. 'I will speak with this Brother Garb or with those who actually witnessed the alleged loss of temper. We shall have to resume this after I have made those inquiries. I shall also have to speak to your other Burgundian companion, Brother Charibert.'

'He only acts as a servant to the bishop; fetching and carrying. Why would you wish to see him?'

'We are all equal as brothers and sisters in the Faith, or is there some new rule from Rome that I have not been made aware of?' Eadulf could not help the ironic thrust.

'Your ways are not ours. I made clear that Bishop Brodulf was a member of the nobility of Burgundia,' replied the deacon. 'We still believe in the temporal differences that must be observed in spite of spiritual aspirations that some try to follow.'

'We shall see this Brother Charibert nevertheless,' Fidelma confirmed, rising, with Eadulf following her example.

The deacon also rose and went with them to the door of his chamber.

'I trust we shall have a speedy conclusion to this matter. I would want to leave for Burgundia as soon as possible.'

Fidelma turned at the door. 'We will give consideration to all you say,' she said dryly.

'You don't like him,' Eadulf observed when the door closed behind them and they stepped along the corridor.

'I am suspicious,' Fidelma confirmed. 'Like or dislike does not come into the matter. However, I do not feel comfortable with Landric's statement. It seems that this young deacon has aspirations to direct me to a decision he wants. He seems determined to place the blame upon the Venerable Breas or his students. Curiously, I felt no regret in him for the death of his bishop.'

Eadulf was thoughtful. 'But he did seem shocked when you told him that the bishop had been murdered.'

'Perhaps shocked because the attempt to disguise the murder by destroying everything by a fire had been seen through so quickly?'

'Perhaps. He certainly showered praise on you about your resolution of the murder of Abbot Dabhóc that time at Autun.'

'You know I dislike false praise and you could hear that clearly in the tone of his voice. That makes me question his motivation by the implications in his statement. There is something more about that young man than just superficial deductions. At the moment I can't quite place it.'

'So, what is the next step?' Eadulf queried. 'Should we speak to the bishop's servant, Brother Charibert, or do you want to have a word with this Brother Garb, after what Deacon Landric says?'

'Neither,' Fidelma replied firmly. 'We shall first have a word with the chief professor of the abbey. I want to see how valid the deacon's views are about the antagonism caused during the debates.'

CHAPTER SIX

The Venerable Breas had a reputation that had certainly spread beyond the walls of the Abbey of Imleach Iubhair. Fidelma had never met this controversial scholar in spite of the fact that her brother, Colgú, had assumed the kingship in Cashel seven years before and she had encountered many of the leading abbots of the kingdom. So far as she knew, the Venerable Breas had no interests outside the confines of the classes where he taught his pupils and acolytes. She knew scholars came to listen to him from all the Five Kingdoms, even from the kingdoms of the Britons, Gauls and Anglo-Saxons.

It was with almost deferential manner that some of the brethren pointed the way to the chamber of the respected scholar. Fidelma and Eadulf found themselves at the end of a short passage, before a door of red yew with intricate little carvings on it that seemed to have no symbolic connection to the Faith. Fidelma halted and nodded to Eadulf, but even as he raised his hand to knock, a deep, humorous baritone called.

'The door is open, Brother Eadulf of Seaxmund's Ham. Enter. Enter also, Fidelma of Cashel. Come freely, safely and in tranquillity.'

Eadulf was startled and remained poised for a moment before glancing round, almost with a shudder, as he tried to reason how they had been recognised through a shut door and stone wall. He tentatively took the handle, pushing the heavy door open. With Fidelma close at his shoulder, he entered the small chamber beyond.

The room was shadowy but lit by several tallow candles and the glow from a wood fire. Heavy curtains hung over what appeared to be the only window, obscuring that as a source of light. The walls were mainly covered with many hooks from which *tiaga liubhair*, book satchels, hung. Other books were displayed on several shelves. A few special book boxes, made to protect certain precious books, were stacked here and there. A table was nearby on which were writing materials. There was a comfortable wooden chair with arm rests placed before the small fire and in it sat a figure, almost indistinguishable in the flickering light.

'The only reason a door should be shut is to keep a place warm,' came the deep humorous voice. 'Other than that, it is an encumbrance and an obstruction to exchanges between people. It impedes knowledge and progress. Alas, as I grow old, the door has become a friend to my ageing flesh and bones, keeping my blood from chill. But, one push of the handle, and it is open to all who seek my company.'

'We come seeking the Venerable Breas,' Eadulf muttered, still nervous as to how they had been recognised before the door was even opened.

'I would venture that you have succeeded into your quest. I was named Breas by my mother as she believed it would signify "beautiful in thought" but, conversely, it can also mean "one who fights and creates uproar". You may take your choice, as I was not always regarded as "venerable".'

'How did you . . .?' began Eadulf.

The Venerable Breas was chuckling. 'You have a question about my recognition before you entered through my door? I thought that Fidelma and Eadulf were of perceptive eyesight. Look above the door. I had that door made by the master carpenter Cú Choille.

See the aperture above and the mirror, angled down to reflect the image of those who stand below? There is no magic in life except that phenomenon which we do not recognise and so misinterpret as such. So come and sit by my poor fire and let us talk.'

As they crossed the room, they saw that there were two wooden stools on either side of the fire on which they could sit like students facing their master. There being no other seating, they lowered themselves down. Now they had to look up at the figure slightly above them.

The Venerable Breas was certainly elderly but it was hard to identify how old. Fidelma accepted that he had been a handsome man in his youth, but age had merely given him a new form of attractiveness. The features were not wrinkled but had aged in a smooth attractive way; the cheeks were full and not sagging, the eyes bright and dark, the lips full and red and wreathed with a smile that appeared part of his permanent expression. His beard and hair were snow white, yet seemed to stir as if alive as the firelight danced over them. His hair was worn long so that it merged with the beard. Unlike other members of the religious that Fidelma and Eadulf had seen, Breas' hair was held in place by a long ribbon, made of silk, judging by the way the light shimmered on it. It was worn like a headband and in the centre of the forehead was a small silver plate in the shape of a crescent moon.

The dark eyes caught Fidelma staring at it.

'You are remarking that this is an emblem once worn by those who were designated as being immersed in knowledge? The *dru* – an immersion – and *uid* – knowledge. I make no such claim for myself. I am the *fer-leginn* of the abbey, the chief professor. Having achieved the title of *Rosai* after my twelve years under the masters, I was entitled to wear the symbol. I continued on with my studies and am acknowledged to have attained the seventh grade of wisdom, which, by some, is stupidly claimed as "perfection in knowledge". Let me tell you, there is no such thing as perfection of knowledge. But I bear this emblem for it was handed to me as recognition of that symbolism. It was said that by the moon knowledge was gathered. It is by the moon that we count the passing of time: the passing of the months; of the periods we name for the motions of the moon. Is not the moon central to our very place in the great void?'

Fidelma grimaced impatiently. 'I understand all this. But much of our old ideas are disappearing . . .'

'Not by the New Faith that came to us from the East, but by the groups of men who sit to discuss it and invent new ways of interpretation, which they decree we must follow until another group of men then create a different way, and so on in never-ending cycles. We have already lost what we were originally taught.'

Even in these words there was no bitterness in the Venerable Breas' voice. He paused a moment before continuing.

'Scholars like Ailbe, Declan, Ciarán and others, when they started to teach the New Faith in this kingdom, realised that many of the ideas were compatible with our ancient beliefs. Even the Briton who liked to call himself "the noble one" in the language of the Latins accepted this; even when it was Rome that sent him to be a bishop to those who had already accepted the Faith here.'

Seeing the perplexed look on Eadulf's face, the scholar appeared amused.

'I refer to the Briton who called himself Patricius, which was the Roman term for a noble; a Patrician. His original name was Maewyn Succat, which means a servant of the old god of war of the Britons . . . Succetus. Patricius was a Briton from the kingdom of Rheged.'

He suddenly smiled at Fidelma. 'But you did not come to me to hear knowledge that is easily obtained elsewhere. Firstly, may I offer you an infusion of mint, a special tea, which I have Brother Anlón, the physician, distil for me. As I am not as sprightly as I once was, I would ask you to pour it.' He pointed to a table on which a jug and mugs were placed. 'There is also a dish of nuts nearby. Those go well with the tea. They are hazelnuts.'

As he gestured towards the table, Fidelma realised that the elderly scholar's hands were slightly misshapen, the knuckles red and blotchy. He noticed her look and his smile broadened. 'Alas, *ailtidu* is a companion of mine. Rheumatism causes a debility that Brother Anlón prescribes various ointments to alleviate.'

Fidelma rose to pour the warm liquid, which had evidently been recently taken from the fire for an aura of steam hung over the cups into which she poured it.

The Venerable Breas nodded approvingly as he took a first sip from the awkwardly held cup. Then he turned once more to his visitors with a serious expression.

'Let me say at once, there is a sorrow in me on learning of the death of Bishop Brodulf. He was here but a short time but his days here were illuminating and instructive for my students.'

'Yet he himself was not the recipient of that illumination?' Eadulf queried dryly.

'That was sadly observed,' the old professor agreed.

'That is precisely why we have come to hear your opinion,' Fidelma murmured.

'Rumour is like the wind. I have heard the cause of his death has been blamed on our differences. So now you have come to see if the discussions that we had on subjects affecting the Faith made us forget that we were just scholars in debate and caused us to resort to emotions that would be inappropriate to intelligence and thus give way to feelings that had no place in these sanctified buildings?'

There was a silence as Fidelma and Eadulf waited, thinking the old scholar would continue, but it was obvious that he was waiting for them.

Finally it was Eadulf who spoke. 'We attended the Council of Autun, which is in the same kingdom as that Bishop Brodulf came from. There we observed the nature of his people, who are called the Franks. We know their manners could be interpreted as being . . . shall we say . . . more impatient than is acceptable in these kingdoms.'

The Venerable Breas actually chuckled.

'Diplomatically put, Eadulf of Seaxmund's Ham. I think you, as an Angle, also find the constraints of our ways of thought difficult?'

Eadulf coloured a little.

'I did not—' he began, but the Venerable Breas silenced him with a slight motion of his hand.

'It is perhaps a fault of ours that we indulge in humour when being serious, and appear serious when we are expressing humour. Humour in manners is our way, and so a sweet voice does not usually result in injury. Here we say, do not bring your reaping-hook to a field without being asked.'

Eadulf sighed. 'It is our duty to search for anything that might have caused some enmity towards Bishop Brodulf; something that would inspire a person to encompass his death. So often it is necessary to use the reaping-hook to clear the weeds.'

The Venerable Breas made a dismissive gesture with one hand. 'Such emotions are usually the reaction of the young or those blindly committed to a cause without reason.'

'Was such emotion visible in your discussions? We were told they took place with your students being allowed to contribute,' Fidelma interrupted.

'How else can students learn?' the old man asked. 'However, I must be truthful and admit that the bishop was always aggressive. Perhaps it was a natural feeling of expression in a language that he was unused to.'

'But this caused arguments?' Fidelma demanded.

'Even among the best of scholars, emotions are not entirely suppressed but only concealed for the sake of deportment. So far as I was concerned, I am now too old to become excited by lack of manners in others or by expressions of error in the heat of arguments. Let me remind you of the saying – do not be breaking your shin on a stool that is not in your way.'

'Are you saying that the arguments presented by Bishop Brodulf were irrelevant to you?'

'Precisely.'

'Perhaps you could tell us the basics of these arguments so we can see how they could be viewed?' Fidelma asked. 'We have spoken to Deacon Landric, who says that many of the arguments against the bishop were heresies.'

'Ah, the Greek word *hairetikos*, which once meant "able to choose" but now *hairesis* means the rejection of doctrines agreed upon in Rome and Constantinople.'

'Would it be possible to clarify some thoughts on these arguments for me,' Eadulf asked, not wishing to get embroiled in linguistics. 'Sometimes it is good to seek an understanding from the point of knowing nothing.'

'That is the start of wisdom, Eadulf,' the scholar agreed in a grave voice, but again there was humour behind it.

'Was there a specific subject that aroused the ire of the bishop?'

'The teachings of Pelagius, for one thing.'

'Pelagius? I thought his teachings were still followed among many Western churches and in many parts of the East?'

'He was excommunicated by the Bishop of Rome for his teaching two centuries ago,' replied the Venerable Breas.

'I know his teachings were rejected by Rome as heretical. Why is that? Who was Pelagius?'

'He was an early convert to the New Faith, born in this island over three centuries ago . . . that is, if we accept the writing of Eusebius of Stridon . . .'

'Eusebius – you mean he who compiled the first Bible into a Latin text?'

'The same. Our tradition is that Pelagius was from this island and named Muirgen, "one born of the sea". He went to Rome and then to the Hellenic world, where he translated his name into the Greek version, Pelagius, by which he is now known. His enemies claimed he was full of Irish porridge,' the Venerable Breas smiled. 'The insult is good enough for me to claim him as my brother.'

'So this Pelagius went to Rome?' Eadulf prompted.

'It was said that he was fluent in Greek and Latin, and he became a leading scholar, a spiritual mentor and moral reformer. This was in the days of Siricius, Bishop of Rome.'

'So why is he so condemned now?'

'He made a great enemy. He strongly disagreed with a contemporary philosopher, Augustine of Hippo Regius. Augustine had converted to the New Faith in his thirties, and written several texts. Among them was *Confessions*. Pelagius saw the moral laxity among Christians in Rome as being supported by Augustine's idea of people having no free will until they achieved "divine grace". Everything had been preordained, whether they did good or evil. Augustine was of a Latinised Berber family with social pretensions. His father even adopted the name Patricius, for the same reason as the Briton who arrived to teach among the Ulaidh in the north of this island; from the idea that Patricians were the nobles of Rome. Pelagius wrote a critique of Augustine's *Confessions*, and from then on Augustine used all his friends and contacts to attack Pelagius.'

Even Fidelma, who felt she had gathered enough knowledge of the history of the Faith, was intrigued by the scholar's reflection.

'So it was just one scholar's opinion or ideas against another's?' she ventured.

'Augustine gathered his followers and friends at councils such as Milevis and Carthage to denounce and destroy Pelagius' ideas in favour of his own concepts. Were it not for Pelagius, Augustine might never have achieved the fame that he did.'

'How is that?' Eadulf frowned uncertainly.

'Augustine was affronted that someone from beyond the end of the known world, as they viewed these islands, could dare to criticise his work. Indeed, ego played a great part. While Pelagius was accepted by many for his scholarship – as I say, he was a scholar in Greek and Latin – Augustine had never learnt Greek, the language by which the Faith came from the Eastern world into our cultures.' The old scholar chuckled. 'Augustine put the blame for his lack of knowledge of Greek on the inability of his teacher rather than accept the fault lay in himself. He could not even read the original documents of the Faith.'

'Friends in powerful places are often better than good scholastic judgement,' Fidelma pointed out in a dry tone.

'Indeed, it did not all go smoothly for Pelagius,' the Venerable Breas continued. 'Augustine was on the verge of persuading Pope Innocent to condemn Pelagius when Innocent died. His successor was a Greek, who had read the earliest texts and was sympathetic to the scholarship. But another powerful friend of Augustine was the Emperor Flavius Honorius, who issued an imperial degree condemning Pelagius. That had nothing to do with the religion but was purely political.'

'That wasn't fair!' Eadulf exclaimed.

'Is life ever fair?' returned the Venerable Breas. 'Pelagius died not long after the Council of Carthage, but it was not until the first Council of Ephesus, nearly twenty years after his death, that he and his teachings were declared a heresy.'

Fidelma was enthralled by the old scholar's tale. She had never been a great student of the development of the Faith, apart from where it affected her role as a lawyer. She had not realised that it was developed by old men discussing philosophies and agreeing dogmatic opinions and winning arguments by votes at given times.

'This is why Rome condemns our insular scholars?'

To Fidelma and Eadulf's surprise, the Venerable Breas shook

his head. 'I cite the facts of the contention but not their basis. Why do some scholars stand for Pelagius' teachings and some for Augustine's?'

'Why?' demanded Eadulf helplessly. 'If Bishop Brodulf was murdered as a result of this argument, we should be clear as to what it was.'

'We, of the New Faith, even in our older moral codes, believe that our future, for good or evil, our very morals, is in our own hands. Whether we choose good or evil in our lives is our own responsibility. We should take our own steps towards living a moral life, and we alone are responsible for that choice.'

'It is a fundamental moral teaching,' Fidelma agreed with a frown. 'It is the basis of our law system.'

'But Augustine of Hippo argued that we are all condemned by the original sin of Adam and Eve, as the ancient Hebrew books on the origins of the world have it. Indeed, Augustine went further. He said that everything in our lives had been preordained. Even before we were born, it was determined whether we would go to heaven or to hell.'

'But that is against all our teaching,' Fidelma pointed out. 'Who else is responsible for how we behave but ourselves?'

'That is exactly what Pelagius argued. He wrote that Augustine's arguments imperilled the entire moral law. If we were not responsible for our good and evil deeds there was nothing to restrain us from murdering, robbing and doing other acts of evil. The basis of all law systems would be abrogated. The defence for evil would be: "I am not responsible. God has willed that I am evil and my fate is already written. Before I was born I was destined to do evil and will go to hell. Nothing will save me even if I try to change my character." In our library we have the text of Augustine's *De Libero Arbitrio*, On Free Will. I suggest you read it.'

'I find this incredible,' Fidelma commented. 'I suppose I have not entirely grasped these arguments before.'

'Well, this is why we, here in these islands, cannot accept that we must abandon our moral behaviour and say it is out of our hands. We reject the argument that whether we are good or evil is ordained by God. We have a text by Pelagius in the library that you will be interested in, *Tractatus de Divitiis*, in which Pelagius sees the world divided between wealth, poverty and sufficiency. Overthrow the rich and you will not find the poor . . . for the few rich are the cause of the many poor. I think the Roman emperors, supporting the Faith as a state religion, saw this as a greater heresy than Pelagius' teaching on Free Will. They felt it would inspire rebellion against them.'

'So this is what the arguments were about?' Fidelma was thoughtful. 'Now I can see how vexed these discussions were.'

'Bishop Brodulf was certainly vexed,' the old man sighed. 'He wanted to know why we in our western islands had not accepted the ruling of the first Council of Ephesus, which declared Pelagius and his following to be heretics. His argument was that we had to obey the ruling of the church councils. Most of the councils held by Rome now accept Augustine and condemn Pelagius. In fact, it was just after Fidelma's father, King Failbe Flann, died that the Bishop of Rome, the fourth bearing the name Ioannes, wrote to the bishops of this island, demanding they turn the people away from the teachings of Pelagius. That has not happened so far.'

Fidelma was now becoming impatient again.

'As interesting as it is, we are not here to continue this debate over theology,' she said stiffly. 'We are here to see whether these debates had any impact on events that have led to Bishop Brodulf's murder.'

'It may be that unless you know the bases of the disputations, what happened here will be obscured. Diversity of opinion, deeply held, can sometimes lead to strong emotions, but there should have been no reason to resort to such hatred that would cause someone to take a life.'

'So, in spite of Bishop Brodulf's provocative arguments, you were not aggravated or goaded and found no real enmity against him among your students?'

'I did not say that. Only that I do not recognise such enmity among my students.'

'I am told that some of your pupils joined in these discussions and, being young men, they were probably less temperate than yourself,' Fidelma said.

'That is the nature of the young,' the Venerable Breas replied sadly. 'They must have their say even though their choice of words may not be the careful concept of older men. I cannot deny it.'

'Perhaps you might recall which of your students challenged the bishop with more emotion than others?'

The Venerable Breas shook his head. 'I am saddened by your question, Fidelma. Reflect. You are asking me to name suspects in your murder investigation. That is not right.'

'Your point is well taken. Yet Deacon Landric has already put forward the name of a young acolyte of yours, whom he claimed seemed more emotional than others in this debate.'

'Deacon Landric is entitled to his opinion. After all,' the old scholar remarked with irony, 'we all have free will, in spite of the teaching of Augustine. So you must follow up this matter with Deacon Landric. I can only speak for myself.'

'I accept that. But you will have no objection if I seek out Brother Garb, who is the young man named by Deacon Landric, in order to question him?'

'You have the authority to do so in your position as a *dálaigh*. I would merely remark that we must remember this was a debate among scholars and students. If all such debates were examined as to the temperance of the language we might all be under suspicion if anything untoward happened to our opponents.'

Fidelma smiled thinly. 'That is understood. But a bishop has been murdered and an attempt made to hide that fact by deliberately setting a building in the abbey on fire. It is serious, apart from the fact that the victim was a visiting bishop and dignitary from a foreign land. I have to explore every avenue to get to the truth.'

The old man sighed. 'So you must, because truth must be the goal; it is the food of the moral soul. Let us hope the old saying is true: that falsehood can last further than truth but will eventually pass away and the truth will remain. You have referred to Brother Garb. He is my finest pupil and I hope that he will become my pre-eminent disciple. I am already planning to appoint him as a teacher in this abbey. I will have a word with him and say that you wish to speak with him and hear his views.'

It seemed, from Breas' tone, that their meeting had ended and they rose.

'I would thank you for your explanations on the arguments about Pelagius,' Eadulf volunteered. 'I had not realised the details. Do you think these councils that have sided with Augustine all these years will come to admit that he was wrong?'

The old scholar assumed his wan smile. 'Man, given a little power, is a contrary fellow. It is possible that some of our brethren will continue to believe that men and women are in charge of their souls and their fate; that nothing is preordained. There are no steps forward unless we take them ourselves. We are continually faced by two paths – the path of good or the path of evil. We must recognise the two and not abandon choice because someone says it is preordained by a divine being. I would also say that it is better to have knowledge of evil than evil without knowledge.'

As they walked along the corridor from the Venerable Breas' chamber, Eadulf was still shaking his head.

'A fascinating man but I am afraid of little help in discovering who killed Bishop Brodulf.'

'I would not say so,' Fidelma responded shortly.

Eadulf glanced at her in surprise. 'You still think that this matter of the differences of decisions made by various councils over hundreds of years would create such personal conflicts that they would really lead to murder?'

'I have not dismissed it, and you yourself have admitted that such squabbles have caused a bishop to be executed and burnt by his fellow Christians in the past.'

'Rome now teaches that every baby is born in sin and is condemned, as Augustine said, unless they are granted divine grace, and this can only be achieved by baptism in water in the name of the Christ.'

'And we are taught that Pelagius declared that all infants are born in innocence and not in sin. I know what I believe,' Fidelma pointed out. 'Anyway, let us go in search of this Brother Garb.'

They had barely taken a few steps when the sharp tones of a distant bell being struck halted them.

'An alarm?' Eadulf asked cautiously.

'The summons to the *praind*, the evening meal. I did not notice how late it had become.'

'A harsh sound for such a summons,' Eadulf commented.

'I remember that it was said the abbey had recently finished erecting a stone bell tower, and until they have installed the bell rope the bell-ringer has to climb all the ladders and strike the bell with a wooden mallet,' Fidelma said.

'No wonder it sounds so harsh. But if we are already summoned to the *praind*, that means we have lost our opportunity not only to question the students but for the bath before the meal.'

'True enough. We will be expected to join Abbot Cuán at the table. Perhaps we can rinse our hands somewhere, and after the meal is ended we can find Brother Garb?'

They were lucky in finding a small fountain by the courtyard and, after a cursory rinse of their hands, they joined hurrying members of the abbey who were obviously heading for the *praintech* or the refectory. It was only when Eadulf saw that the religious were mixed, male and female, that he remembered the abbey was a *conhospitae*. He wondered if there were any different regulations applied to eating together. A thought suddenly struck him. He remembered that there was a growing group of ascetics who were attempting to exclude women from a co-equal role in the Faith and, indeed, to exclude them almost altogether, propounding the idea of chastity among men and women pursuing the religious life.

He turned to Fidelma. 'You don't think that Bishop Brodulf supported the ascetics who believe there is no place in the Faith for women? You know that Augustine also denounced women in having any such role and especially disliked the idea of bishops and priests being married. I remember him writing: "nothing is so powerful in drawing the spirit of man downward as the embrace of a woman."'

Fidelma actually chuckled and playfully punched him on the arm.

'I hope we are proof of the opposite. I know there are attempts to turn some sections of the Faith to celibacy, especially priests. That is found among a few following the Faith: hermits who reject women. As you know, for security I once joined the abbey at Cill Dara, which was a mixed house founded by Brigit, who was ordained a bishop and abbess while Cogitosus was bishop and her male partner. There have been attempts to stop women being ordained as priests. At the council of Laodicea it was declared that women should not be ordained, but no one took any notice. Still, we shall go mad thinking about all the things Bishop Brodulf probably disagreed with the religious of this kingdom about. Anyway, if I remember rightly, even most of the Frankish priests and bishops are married, so I don't think that would be an argument of Bishop Brodulf's.'

A voice called their names and the steward, Brother Mac Raith, emerged from among the throng with a worried expression.

'There you are. I have been sent to bring you to the abbot's table. I thought that I had lost you. You have missed the evening bath,' he added in disapproval. 'Never mind. We are about to start the evening prayer.'

CHAPTER SEVEN

The steward conducted Fidelma and Eadulf through the refectory of the abbey. It was a large hall in which several long tables and benches were crowded with the members of the brethren to one side and the sisterhood to the other. There were, of course, a few tables at which the sexes were mixed. The noise of conversation rose normally. On a slightly raised platform at the far end was a table whose occupants sat facing the rest of the dinners. Abbot Cuán was in the centre, engaged in conversation with a woman religieuse on his right. It was obvious that this table was reserved for the senior members of the abbey. The male members sat on the right of the abbot and female members to the left. Of the males, Fidelma recognised only the Venerable Breas, the physician, Brother Anlón, and, at the far end, Deacon Landric. There were vacant seats clearly meant for Eadulf and herself and the steward.

Brother Mac Raith conducted them through the long tables to this elevated section and brought them behind the diners to the centre where the Abbot Cuán stood to greet them with a tired smile. He turned to the woman at his side.

'This is Prioress Suanach, who is in charge of the sisterhood of this abbey. She also helps with the students and takes some of the classes with the *fer-leginn*, the Venerable Breas.'

The prioress leant forward with both hands held out in friendly greeting, one to each of them.

'*Tu tam grata,*' she welcomed. 'It would have been a joyous occasion to have you visit us but, alas, we are in sad times.'

On closer inspection the prioress looked younger than they had first thought. Fidelma guessed that she was nearer thirty-five and still quite attractive in spite of her rather fleshy features. She had dark hair and inquisitive brown eyes, and a curious, almost mocking, smile.

'Prioress Suanach has been with us six months. She returned to the abbey after several years working beyond the seas,' Abbot Cuán explained.

'Isn't a prioress usually appointed from one of the sisterhood who has been long serving in the same abbey?' Eadulf enquired.

Prioress Suanach did not seem disturbed by the question.

'I trained here as a young novice even before Abbot Ségdae became abbot. I then spent a short time teaching here before I elected to join a group of missionaries going beyond the seas. I was nearly ten years in the Abbey of Latiniacum before returning here.'

Eadulf's eyes widened in recognition of the name. 'Latiniacum is the abbey founded by the Blessed Fursa, is it not?'

Prioress Suanach smiled indulgently. 'He was long dead by the time I went there. What do you know of it? You are surely not old enough to have known Fursa, though I am told you are from the land of the East Angles and he spent much time in missionary work in that kingdom.'

'Fursa and his brothers brought the Faith to my land,' Eadulf agreed. 'I am from Seaxmund's Ham, in the land of the South Folk, and was converted to the Faith when I was quite young by one of his brethren who inspired me to come to this land to follow my education. I know Fursa went on to the land of the Franks and established a new foundation in Latiniacum.'

Abbot Cuán coughed to attract attention. 'If you will be seated on my right, Fidelma, and Eadulf to my left, next to the prioress, we can begin.' He indicated the vacant seats. Brother Mac Raith, the steward, took his place to the right of Fidelma. Then the abbot signalled to someone in a small gallery above the main entrance of the refectory. A small handbell sounded. A hush descended on the crowded hall and everyone rose with bowed head.

The abbot began to intone: *'Pater noster, qui es in caelis . . .'*

After the opening ritual prayers everyone automatically sat down, but Abbot Cuán remained standing.

'I have one announcement and, knowing how rumours and hearsay spread, I have to confirm that Bishop Brodulf, our guest from Burgundia, met an unlawful death in the old wooden guest house last night. The remains of his body will lie, albeit covered for obvious reasons, in our chapel until his burial. The interment will be at midnight tomorrow. This is to allow a reasonable period for our traditional *aire* or "watching" of the body in the chapel. Any who wish to do so may attend.' He paused as if to allow those gathered to digest this news before adding: 'I must also announce that we have been joined by Fidelma of Cashel, the prominent *dálaigh*, and her husband, Eadulf. At my invitation they will investigate this unfortunate event and I would urge all to co-operate with them in their inquiries.'

The abbot resumed his seat and once again the noise of voices rose as the servers started to bring the main dishes to each table. It seemed there was no restriction to exchanging news or discussion after the initial prayers. It was also clear what the main subject of the discussions was, as many glances were cast in the direction of Fidelma and Eadulf.

As the meal was being served, Abbot Cuán leant towards Fidelma and whispered, 'I do not suppose there is further news? The Venerable Breas,' he nodded along the table to where the scholar sat picking at his plate, 'mentioned that he has had a discussion with you.'

'It was something that Deacon Landric raised that we wanted clarification on,' Fidelma agreed. 'The deacon told us that there was some enmity in the exchanges that Bishop Brodulf had with your chief professor and his students.'

'He did?' The abbot seemed suddenly weary. 'I was given to understand that the deacon barely attended those discussions. He spent most of his time in our *scriptorium* . . . our library.'

'Perhaps the bishop mentioned such enmity to him,' Fidelma replied. However, she was surprised that, being the bishop's steward, Deacon Landric had not been in attendance during the discussions. 'I have let your chief professor know that I will need to question some of his students and one in particular, a Brother Garb. I will keep you informed of any significant development.'

'Brother Garb? A remarkable young man and very knowledge-able. The Venerable Breas speaks highly of him and intends to propose him as one of the junior professors here. I hope your questioning will not disturb the students?'

'I doubt that it should.'

Abbot Cuán sighed deeply and indicated the hall generally with a movement of his head. 'You will see that your presence and the news of the death of the bishop has created much interest. They probably expect me to make an announcement on the results of the investigation soon.'

'It is to be expected, but they must deal with their curiosity in their own way,' Fidelma replied coldly. 'There is little I can say until I have knowledge enough to say it, and only then shall I report to you as we have agreed.'

Fidelma realised that arranging a gathering with the Venerable Breas' students to question them would not be an option today, for it was already late. She wondered who the senior members of the abbey were at the far ends of the table: on her side, beyond

Brother Mac Raith, and on Prioress Suanach's side beyond Eadulf. While on her side they smiled and inclined their heads as they caught her eye, it was not possible to conduct introductions. They all seemed to be on friendly terms, judging by the exchanges and conversation between one another. She did glimpse the scowling features of Deacon Landric at the far end. He gave the impression of isolation, in spite of sitting with the leading members of the abbey.

She had expected to see the master builder Sítae and his leading overseers sitting in the refectory. She was about to turn to put a query to the steward, but found that Brother Mac Raith had disappeared on some errand. She turned to Abbot Cuán instead, asking if any of the builders usually ate in the refectory.

'Not usually,' he replied. 'They have their own camp a short distance from the abbey and prefer to eat there. They cater for their own meals because they cannot commit to regular times, as we do. And they have their own accommodation there as well – tents, wagons and such like. Basically, it suits both our purposes to keep ourselves separate unless we need to discuss problems affecting the building.'

'I suppose your architect is in constant consultation with the master builder.'

The abbot frowned at her use of the word 'architect'. 'The person who has designed the new buildings and their layout on behalf of the abbey? That will be the Venerable Lugán, who serves us in many roles. He is our *leabhar coimedach*, our librarian, as well as master of all students. You will meet him shortly.'

'I thought the Venerable Breas was in charge of your students?' queried Fidelma, puzzled.

'Breas is our *fer-leginn*, our chief professor, while Lugán organises the students on a more practical level. He is supported by the prioress, whose concern is mainly for the female students. She also takes some of the classes of instruction. But, as I was saying, co-operation with the builders is harmonious. You may not know that the master builder came to me just before the evening meal to volunteer the services of his men to dig the grave for the bishop's funeral for tomorrow night, as well as to act as pallbearers. The men usually assigned for this work also served under Brother Áedh and suffered burns last night, which made it difficult for them to use their skills at digging. It was very laudable of Sítae to make that gesture and demonstrates our good relationship.'

'This, I know,' Fidelma admitted quickly. 'But how can a librarian also be an architect?'

'The Venerable Lugán knows much of the history of this abbey and has access to all the plans that were compiled for the rebuilding going back decades.'

Fidelma sat back and glanced around the refectory. Then she had a sudden pang of guilt when her eyes fell upon Enda, seated at the corner of a table among a small group. She had almost forgotten the warrior and mentally chastised herself that she had neglected to enquire after his wellbeing.

On the other side of Abbot Cuán, Prioress Suanach seemed deep in conversation with Eadulf, and Fidelma wondered what the subject could be that kept them engrossed. She presumed it was probably a discussion about the abbey of Latiniacum, of which Eadulf seemed to have some knowledge.

As the meal continued Fidelma and Abbot Cuán avoided further mention of the death of Bishop Brodulf and began talking about the domestic problems of the kingdom and the church. Time drifted until a bell sounded, bringing the meal to an end. Abbot Cuán rose, leading the assembly with the final *'gratias'* – the thanks for the meal.

Fidelma realised that most of the others were dispersing, some with a smile and nod in her direction. Abbot Cuán caught her attention with an apology.

'If you will wait here, I will get Brother Mac Raith to return to show you and Eadulf to your quarters for the night. Your bags were sent there but I understood from the steward earlier that he had been unable to find time to show you where the chambers are situated.'

'Eadulf and I will wait over there by the main doors for Brother Mac Raith's return. I see Enda is already waiting for us there.'

The abbot bowed his head in acknowledgement and then turned to speak with Prioress Suanach. Eadulf had come to join Fidelma and so crossed with her to join Enda, making their way through the dispersing groups to join him. As they did so, Fidelma caught sight of the Venerable Breas talking to a young man on the far side of the refectory. The older scholar appeared strangely animated. He was unlike the relaxed theologian that they had previously questioned. Then the two vanished behind one of the groups. Fidelma turned back to face the young warrior, who stood waiting for her.

'Enda, I am sorry that we didn't see one another before. Is all well?'

The young man grinned. 'The steward passed me into the care of Brother Sígeal, the *echaire*; the master of the stables. He has provided me with a bed as I presume that we are all staying the night. We played a few games of Wooden Wisdom, which he seems pretty good at. I think he was pleased to have someone to gamble with. I thought that if you needed my help you would have sent for me.'

'We will probably have need of your help tomorrow,' Fidelma assured him, momentarily unsure whether she should condemn his confession of gambling in the abbey stables. 'There may be much to do then. You have been well attended to?'

'As you saw, lady,' Enda returned. 'I was sitting with Brother Sígeal. He seems to have a special relationship with the servers so the meal was plentiful.'

'I suppose that you were not able to learn anything that would be pertinent to what happened to the bishop?'

'Only that Bishop Brodulf was much disliked. When I asked about that, it seemed that he was an arrogant man and treated everyone like servants. There did not seem to be much sorrow when the abbot made his announcement that the death had been unlawful. That very choice of phrase indicates that it was a murder. I suppose I will face questions from the stable master and his lads when I return there.'

'Say as little as possible,' Fidelma advised. 'The fewer people know of the state of our investigations, the better.'

Enda was about to turn away when he glanced back at Eadulf. 'Forgive my curiosity, friend Eadulf. Who was the woman that you were sitting next to and talking with?'

'You meant the prioress? That was Prioress Suanach. Why do you ask?'

'On my way here I saw her in one of the courtyards arguing with a rather attractive young girl. I presume that she is one of the students here. It looked like a fierce argument. I thought they were coming to blows.'

'Coming to blows?' Fidelma intervened in astonishment. 'The prioress and a young female student, you say?'

'That was what attracted my attention in the first place,' the warrior confirmed. 'It was the fact they were almost screaming to each other in some foreign language.'

'A foreign language?'

'Well, a bit like the one that friend Eadulf here speaks. I just thought that they were very emotional. If she is the prioress, I suppose the young girl is a student guilty of some misdemeanour.'

'And they were both speaking the same language?' Fidelma pressed.

'The bell summoning those to the *praintech* interrupted them and they parted, but not in amity.'

Fidelma was quiet for a moment and then glanced in query at Eadulf.

'Latiniacum is in the territory of the Franks,' he explained. 'I suppose that the argument was in the language of the Franks.' Eadulf actually smiled as if he was pleased with himself.

'I should have known,' Fidelma said tightly. 'I wonder if she knew Bishop Brodulf or if the student was one of the Frankish students . . . I hope you did not speak much about our inquiry.'

'On the contrary, I was able to get some relevant information from her. At least, I think it may well prove of interest.'

'How so?'

'Latiniacum is at a little place beside the river once called by the Gauls Dea Matrona, the Divine Goddess. Importantly the area was recently conquered and occupied by the Franks, and is part of the kingdom they now call Burgundia, where Bishop Brodulf came from.'

Fidelma stared at him blankly. She had not known.

Eadulf grinned, satisfied at her reaction. 'In other words, Prioress Suanach lived in Burgundia for nearly ten years before returning here. Perhaps it raises questions.'

'It raises only the need to clarify if she knew the bishop before he came here and if he came here because she was here?' she agreed, but did not seem unduly excited.

'I would have said it raised more questions than that,' Eadulf responded, disappointed by her lack of enthusiasm. 'It seems too much of a coincidence. Perhaps she knew Bishop Brodulf before she left Burgundia. Was there collusion? How did she become prioress here so quickly? Why, shortly after she arrived, did a Burgundian bishop turn up here and then was killed? What is the connection?'

Fidelma shook her head with a smile. 'You are seeking answers to speculative questions, Eadulf. You know my teaching – no speculation without information. Anyway, our abbeys have many connections with Gaul and Burgundia and such places. Some of our leading abbots and bishops have attended councils in those countries.'

'I still think we should press the prioress on this point,' Eadulf grumbled. 'I think that I have a valid reason to be suspicious.'

'Perhaps. But there is nothing unusual in travels between these kingdoms.'

Eadulf was about to respond when Enda interrupted with a cough. The steward, Brother Mac Raith, was approaching. He had a lantern already lit in one hand.

'I came to show you to your accommodation,' he announced as he halted before them. 'Most of the abbey is lit but some areas are still in darkness so take care as you follow me.'

'I will leave you here,' Enda announced. 'You need have no concerns for I know the way back to the stables where Brother Sígeal has arranged for me to sleep in the dormitory with the stable hands.'

He wished them both a good night and soon disappeared along the corridors.

Brother Mc Raith now led the way back into one of the main stone buildings. Fidelma and Eadulf followed him up a circular flight of steps, as if climbing a tower, although these led only to the first floor where a long, broad corridor ran, opened on the one side to a pillared walkway looking out on the darkened countryside and forest areas to one side of the abbey buildings.

'Isn't this where we came to the chamber of the Venerable Breas?' enquired Eadulf as they paused at the top of the stairway.

'His personal chamber is just along there,' Brother Mac Raith confirmed. 'The classes are still housed in the remaining wooden buildings nearby. The rebuilding of the abbey is taking a while and—'

He was interrupted by the slap of sandals along the corridor ahead of them, which intersected the one in which they stood. The stone tiles and this being night increased the echoing of the foot-falls. A figure emerged with a lamp and crossed their path, apparently not noticing them, and vanished.

The steward motioned them to continue to follow him, turning along another corridor until they came to one of several doors of yew wood. As the steward opened the door, they could see a lamp and a fire had already been lit, revealing a square, almost bare room, devoid of anything but two wooden beds, a table and two chairs. There was a chest on which their bags had been placed and several pegs to hang things on.

'It is sparse but there are warm blankets there.' The steward pointed to the beds. 'A jug of water for drink and another for the *indult*, the morning wash. I regret that you have missed the evening bath, because the water is only heated for bathing before the evening meal and will not be heated again until tomorrow evening.'

Fidelma had been going to enquire about the evening bath. She knew that it was her legal right to demand that a *dabach*, a bathing vat of water, should be heated, because it was stipulated by law that a host had to provide a bath for all guests. Bathing was a tradition in society and the full body had to be made clean before the evening meal. The washing of hands and feet was made upon awakening. She turned the matter over in her mind and then gave a resigned sigh.

'I have suggested an extra jug of water be left for your convenience tonight,' Brother Mac Raith said hastily, watching her expression. 'My apologies that there is little more I can do until tomorrow. Soap, and towels have been placed there,' he added, as if reading her mind.

'Very well,' Fidelma finally conceded. Perhaps missing one bath would not matter.

Thankfully Brother Mac Raith bade them a good night and hurried away.

'Well, a busy day and not the one that I was expecting when we rode up to the inn at Ara's Well this lunchtime,' Eadulf said, almost falling on to one of the beds. 'If I had known then what I know now I would have ridden straight on to Cashel and not even stopped for Aona's cooking.'

Fidelma shook her head in rebuke. 'It is not given to us to foretell the future, in spite of the soothsayers and mystics. For most people things are revealed by the passing of time.'

'There are some who have it that the events of the day have to be helped along,' pointed out Eadulf. 'I would rather not have helped today's events. I was looking forward to getting back to our son and the comforts of Cashel. You must not forget that it will soon be the day of your brother's wedding.'

'Finally,' Fidelma replied in humour. 'In truth, I thought that Colgú's marriage to Gelgéis of Osraige would never happen. Conflict, her abduction and then the deferment because of the panic created by news of the arrival of a pestilence have all contributed to its delay.'

'That latter reason turned out to be a part of the plot to over-throw your brother.'

'Indeed. It has been a turbulent romance for them. But I hope they soon will be settled.'

'Speaking of which, you realise who that small, familiar figure was, with the candle, who crossed this corridor without apparently noticing us?'

'Of course. It was the prioress. But what do you mean in linking that with romance?'

'That corridor she entered leads to one door. It was that short passage to the door of the chamber in which we met the Venerable Breas. She was a late visitor to the old scholar.'

Fidelma sniffed disapprovingly. 'Since when have you become prudish and shocked by the fact that women can visit men late at night for reasons other than their sexuality?'

Eadulf yawned. 'It was a thought. Anyway, we have matters to resolve that will not be achieved without sleep,' he observed.

He had barely spoken when there came a timid knock on the

door. Eadulf groaned and glanced at Fidelma. 'What now?' he muttered, swinging himself off the bed and moving to the door. He reached it as there came a second soft knock.

He lifted the latch and opened it while Fidelma held the lamp up.

A tall figure stood framed in the darkness of the doorway just out of the flickering light of the lamp.

'Who are you?' Eadulf demanded. 'What do you seek?'

'I seek the lawgiver,' the figure announced in heavily accented Latin.

CHAPTER EIGHT

Fidelma crossed the room with the lamp held high. The newcomer was dressed in the simple white wool robes of a religieux. He was a well-built man in his late twenties. He was dark of skin, as if used to a life in the open, and with heavy-set features, dark hazel eyes and long and well-combed hair that was bordering on auburn. This seemed to be the only noteworthy aspect about him. The attention to cleanliness; the precise cut of his hair and the careful way his tonsure had been shaven spoke of a precise and careful personality.

'Who are you?' she demanded.

He ignored her question.

'Are you the lawgiver? The one called Fidelma?' he questioned again in a stilted Latin in an accent that did not help the articulation. 'You will forgive me if the language I use is not fluently spoken. I have no knowledge of your language in this place.'

'I am a *dálaigh*, not a lawgiver but one who judges events by the law,' she replied, correcting him.

The man seemed to have difficulty comprehending this.

'I ask again, who are you?' Fidelma demanded.

'I am Brother Charibert, lady,' he announced. 'I was in the service of Bishop Brodulf. Therefore I must give testimony.'

'You mean that you want to state what you know about the

murder of the bishop?' she deduced. 'This could have waited until the morning.'

'I am here to give testimony,' the man repeated stubbornly. 'I served the bishop.'

Fidelma glanced at Eadulf and shrugged. 'If the man is keen to tell us something we might as well listen. We could ask Deacon Landric to translate if Brother Charibert can't speak Latin.'

'But that might compromise any testimony,' Eadulf pointed out. 'There are others who can speak his Frankish tongue.'

Fidelma thought a moment and suddenly an idea occurred to her. She turned back to the man.

'Do you understand this language?' she asked, resorting to Eadulf's language, that of the Angles, of which he had taught her some rudiments. She had realised that the sounds and origins bore a close resemblance to the language of the Franks and it had helped them both when they were visiting Eadulf's homeland and when they had attended the council in Autun.

'I think I can understand, lady,' the man was hesitant.

'Enter, Brother Charibert, and we will hear what you have to say.' She turned to Eadulf as the man entered and sat in the chair that she indicated. 'Your accent will probably be better than mine in dealing with this matter. I will be able to follow you.'

Eadulf regarded the man for a moment. 'Are you comfortable answering in my language?'

Brother Charibert listened, head to one side with a frown, but replied in a more guttural tone, which was the language of the Franks.

'I have heard this dialect before for it is the language they speak to the west of the Frankish kingdoms. Do not the ancients claim that two centuries ago, before the coming of the Faith, our ancestors invaded the island to the west, called Britannia, and, by their swords and battleaxes, began to carve out kingdoms among the Britons who lived there and whom they conquered? Ah, yes; hence we speak a similar language.'

Eadulf looked embarrassed as he was always uncomfortable when reminded of the origin of his own people.

'Suffice that you can understand me,' he answered shortly. 'I have heard that the kings of my people of East Anglia were the Wuffingas, descendant of Wuffa, who led the first Angles out of the east.'

'Your people and mine were the same,' Brother Charibert agreed. 'But our kings do not claim to be descendants of Woden or other gods. They claim they are all the sons of the long-haired warrior Merovech, who defeated the Gauls, the Romans and Alemanni and so created our kingdoms.'

'We seem to understand each other. So you came here in the service of Bishop Brodulf?'

'I was born into the service of Wulfoald of Burgundia who, withdrawing from any temporal rule, freed his slaves so that they could take service in the local abbey. The abbey was that of Luxovium, and thus I came into the service of Bishop Brodulf, who served that territory.'

Eadulf sat down on the edge of his bed, facing the man.

'What did you do in the service of the bishop?' Eadulf queried. 'We have seen Deacon Landric. We understand that he acted as Brodulf's steward.'

'What did I do?' The man was frowning. 'Why, I served my lord as his servant. I served his personal needs. I prepared his meals and his clothes. I attended his general wants.'

'Did you say you were a slave in the house of Wulfoald?' queried Fidelma quickly, 'and he freed you to join the abbey? Who is this Wulfoald?'

Brother Charibert looked surprised.

'Why, Wulfoald was mayor to the late King Sigebert. When Sigebert was deposed, Wulfoald was allowed to retire to his castle and obscurity.'

'Remind me of the meaning of this term "mayor",' Fidelma asked patiently of Eadulf.

'It is a rank given to a noble who runs the royal household,' Eadulf said. 'He would be the first of nobles serving a Frankish king.' He turned back to Brother Charibert. 'You said that you served Wulfoald before the bishop?'

'I and my family before me,' Brother Charibert confirmed.

'There is a question in our minds, which I believe that the lady Fidelma was going to put to you – you say that you were brought up as a slave of this noble called Wulfoald? He set you free and you then joined the Abbey of Luxovium?'

'This is so. But as long as my family can remember we were always thralls in the house of the family of the noble Wulfoald.' The man sounded quite proud of the fact.

'What is that?' Fidelma interrupted, aiming her query at Eadulf. 'What is a thrall?'

'Basically, it is the same as a slave,' Eadulf explained. 'It is the same in my language. You don't have such a precise meaning here but one would say it was like *daer-fuidir* in the law here. One who is not entitled to bear arms or have any rights within the tribe or clan.'

'So you say this man, Charibert, was simply property?' Fidelma said. 'It is, indeed, a different society from ours.'

Eadulf turned back to the Burgundian, who had sat looking bewildered through this quick exchange. 'You say that you were freed but made the choice to serve Bishop Brodulf?'

'There was no choice,' replied the man with a shrug. 'I was told that I was free of the bondage to the house of Wulfoald but should go to serve in the Abbey of Luxovium under the tutelage of Bishop Brodulf. I did not have any clever ways of making my own way in life. I know of no other language save my own. I know of nothing other than being a servant to a master.'

Fidelma shook her head with a frown. 'So you were a servant to the bishop? You were no more than that?'

'I was his personal servant,' Brother Charibert agreed.

'Having gained your freedom from this noble, you joined the Abbey of Luxovium and found yourself as servant to the bishop? How was that?'

'My lord Wulfoald intervened with the prince on my behalf and secured my position.'

'The prince?' Fidelma frowned.

'I meant Bishop Brodulf,' Brother Charibert corrected himself.

Fidelma's eyes widened. 'Are you saying that Bishop Brodulf is . . . was . . . a prince of the Franks?'

'He is cousin to our King Clotaire,' confirmed the young servant quickly. 'Clotaire is King of all the Franks.'

'Who knew in this abbey that Bishop Brodulf was a prince as well as a bishop?' Fidelma demanded.

'I would hardly know that, lady. But I do not think my master would neglect to hide his rank from any of those he was meeting. He was not an unassertive man.'

'And in the capacity of a personal servant, you have accompanied him to this abbey?' Fidelma intervened, repeating the point. 'It is my understanding that the bishop stayed alone in the guest house. My next question would be: how were you able to attend to him as a personal servant when your accommodation was not close to his? A personal servant is supposed to remain near his master to attend to his wants without being called from afar.'

The man seemed puzzled and was obviously trying to translate her meaning. Eadulf repeated her question more clearly for him, adding: 'As a personal servant, how could you perform your service to the bishop if you were excluded from his accommodation?'

Brother Charibert still seemed bewildered by the question.

'The bishop liked solitude. That is true. But this habit of isolation at night only arose recently, just before we left Luxovium. In the abbey there, my room was next to the bishop's bedchamber. But I was asked to remove from it so that he could isolate himself in the quarters where he slept.'

'That is curious,' Fidelma commented. 'This habit of isolation continued when you came here?'

'Deacon Landric and I were given separate accommodation at the request of the bishop. Each day I had to cross that area of the building works to get to the guest house, which was his accommodation. I still had to ensure there was water for his morning wash and for the evening. I had to make ready his clothes. But, after prayers in the chapel, he would take his first meal of the day in the refectory. He took all his meals in the refectory alongside the Abbot Cuán and the senior members of this abbey. He has not eaten alone since he came here.'

'Was that something that concerned you?' Eadulf asked, seeing a slight frown on the other's forehead when he was talking.

'Only that he always seemed suspicious of the food and watched closely when it was served to others, and only when they began eating did he start to eat.'

'Yet he always returned to the guest house each night and slept in isolation? If he was afraid of harm from someone or something, it does not seem consistent. What reason had he for staying isolated during the sleeping hours?'

'It was not my place to question the habits of my lord,' replied the other.

'What would you think if it were in your capacity to question?' Eadulf pressed cynically. 'After all, you are supposed to be a free man and no one can legally abuse you for stating what is in your mind.'

'Abuse me?'

Eadulf restrained his irritation. 'Were you afraid that he would punish you without reason or justification? You don't consider that you have just supplanted one slavery for another?'

'It is not my place to question my master's behaviour.'

Eadulf was about to give up pursuing the point when a further idea occurred to him.

'You have told us that this practice of the bishop's solitude, of retiring alone during the night, is of recent occurrence. I think you said that this started when you left Luxovium or just before.'

'That is so,' Brother Charibert confirmed.

Eadulf shot a meaningful glance at Fidelma before turning back to the young man just to make absolutely sure.

'Are you saying that he did not always follow this habit but only preferred to be alone shortly before he started out on his journey to this country?'

The man grimaced indifferently. 'It is a fact. You asked the question and all I can do is answer truthfully.'

'Did anything occur, to your knowledge, that would account for this change of behaviour?'

Brother Charibert shook his head.

Fidelma now intervened, asking Eadulf to clarify her questions if she did not express them clearly enough.

'Brother Charibert, let us go back to last evening. The evening before the fire. Can you recall when Bishop Brodulf returned to the guest house?'

'Every night it was at the same time,' the man answered. 'After we emerged from the refectory or chapel and the final prayer was given, I would accompany the bishop to the door of the guest house.'

'Just to the door?' queried Fidelma.

'He would wait by the door until I had searched to make sure that no one else was in the guest house,' Brother Charibert confirmed.

'Tell us exactly what used to happen.'

'It was often dark after the last meal of the day. I would prepare myself with a lantern to guide him through the darkness. And then I had to make a search of the building.'

'This is curious, if the man preferred solitude,' Eadulf made a quick aside.

Fidelma waved Brother Charibert to continue. 'Last night, before the fire, you accompanied him?'

'I took the lantern and we went to the guest house. Before he entered, I had to go inside and make a search. As I say, this was usual. When I had concluded the search and lit the lamps, he entered. I left after I heard him putting the bolt on the door into place.'

Fidelma glanced at him in astonishment. 'You say this was a usual practice?'

'It was.'

'Did Brother Landric ever take turns to go through this ritual?'

'Ritual?' queried the man.

'I can think of no better word,' Eadulf agreed. 'Did you not find this a curious procedure? A man who preferred solitude but needed to be accompanied by a companion with a lantern in the evening, that before he entered an empty guest house he needed to have the lamps lit and have it searched. Then the doors had to be locked before he retired? I say this is more than curious.'

Brother Charibert did not respond to either of them.

'Did you feel that the bishop was frightened of something or someone in spite of his desire to be alone?' pressed Fidelma. 'Did you never ask why he had to secure himself alone in the guest house when he retired?'

'Me? Ask him why?' Brother Charibert seemed astonished at the idea. 'I was just a servant. My master, the bishop, was also a royal prince and therefore afraid of nobody,' he asserted.

'Yet what you have described to us is to the contrary,' pointed out Fidelma. 'He was fearful, but of what and whom?' She paused and then continued. 'Let us get back to last night's procedure at the guest house. When you came away, having accompanied him there, did Bishop Brodulf secure the door behind you as usual?'

'It was his usual practice,' confirmed the other.

'He always locked the door? He never left the doors unlocked?'

'Never, and he waited until I went in the morning and identified myself before he unlocked them. After his wash and dressing we accompanied him to the chapel for prayers and then to the refectory for the first meal.'

'Did you have to accompany him everywhere during the course of the day?'

To her surprise Brother Charibert shook his head.

'No, he was happy to be left to his own devices during the day. Sometimes Deacon Landric accompanied him to the debates with the professors and their students, or the bishop spent time alone in the library.'

Eadulf was thoughtful. 'Alone? I would imagine someone was always in the library. So he was never really alone. He was always within some company.'

'Whether he was or not, we are dealing with a very nervous person,' Fidelma sighed.

'And one whose fears have now been confirmed,' Eadulf agreed.

Fidelma was frowning, going over the words of the bishop's servant. 'You said that Deacon Landric even went with you in the evening when you escorted the bishop to and from the guest house?'

'That is correct. Sometimes Deacon Landric would accompany me in the morning. It was my task to do all else as Bishop Brodulf's personal servant.'

'Did you ever notice, or attend, when the bishop had private discussions with the deacon as to the purpose of this visit?'

'The purpose?' The man seemed bewildered.

'There must have been a purpose to this visit or discussion on the debates.'

'I think they did so in the library or in Deacon Landric's chamber.'

'As far as you know, were there any tensions between the two of them? I mean, were they friends?'

'Deacon Landric was the bishop's steward.' Brother Charibert seemed puzzled at the concept of the bishop and his steward as friends. 'There were no disagreements between them, if that is what is meant.'

Fidelma grimaced almost in resignation at Eadulf.

'Truly the bishop was in great fear about something,' she said quickly, resorting to her own language. 'There is much here to consider. He was afraid for his life and that fear has proved to have a valid basis. I was wondering why Deacon Landric did not tell us any of these fears or concerns.'

'We will have to have further words with him,' Eadulf conceded. 'It appears that Bishop Brodulf was really scared of something . . . or a particular someone. I was wondering whether this fear was the cause of the bishop leaving Burgundia. We are told his fears started just before he left the Abbey of Luxovium. But why did he come here, of all places? This idea of his being here simply to learn and engage in the theology or philosophy, or different ways in the practice of the churches of the Five Kingdoms, seems very questionable.'

'Especially in view of the reports of his arrogant behaviour during these debates,' Fidelma concurred. 'This servant has certainly pointed to an intriguing area of behaviour. Even if Brodulf was not safe in Luxovium, why undertake this perilous journal from Burgundia all the way here? And why to this particular abbey? Was he following Prioress Suanach? We can get lost in speculations.'

Eadulf realised what she had said. 'So perhaps the reason that Prioress Suanach is here is not merely a coincidence but might be connected? She could have been the link that brought him here.'

'Perhaps.' Fidelma was suddenly unenthusiastic. 'We cannot make any presumptions yet. At least, we must question Deacon Landric more thoroughly and find out why he did not mention these strange fears of Bishop Brodulf before.'

The Burgundian servant was sitting looking at them as if trying to follow their exchange. Fidelma smiled reassuringly at him.

'Don't worry, my friend,' she said, resorting to Eadulf's language. 'You have been of great help, so far.'

Eadulf, also in his own language, explained. 'We have just a few more questions for you at the moment. We'd like to know a little more about the personal details of Bishop Brodulf. You have told us that he was a prince . . .'

'There is little more I can say about him,' Brother Charibert said with a shrug. 'I was a servant. What would I know of the personal affairs of a prince?'

'You have already told us a lot,' Eadulf responded dryly. 'Let us see what we can expand on. Firstly, you were a slave in the household of a noble called Wulfoald. You were a *thrall*. But he apparently released you from bondage and told you to go to join the religious at the Abbey of Luxovium. You say that he even gave you an introduction to Bishop Brodulf and recommended you as a servant into his personal service. Isn't that unusual for anyone joining an abbey, let alone a bond servant suddenly freed? Do you know why he did that? Was Wulfoald related to Bishop Brodulf?'

Brother Charibert considered this in silence for a moment or two as if summing up what more he should say.

'I think most bishops and abbots are high nobles and princes,' he finally replied, 'otherwise they would not be appointed to their high status. I have never heard of a bishop who is of a background imbued with poverty or had started life as a mere keeper of pigs for a noble. No peasant could afford an education to make them such, at least not in the lands of the Franks. Wulfoald and Brodulf were not related. Wulfoald was a high noble and steward and adviser to kings, but he was not directly of the royal line. However, I think the royal princes respected him. Even when King Sigebert was overthrown and killed, Sigebert's successors felt it would be wrong to kill Wulfoald and therefore they let him retire to his fortress in peace.'

Fidelma regarded Eadulf seriously for a moment, then resorted to her own language again. 'There is a saying that one cannot see the wood because one is looking at the tree. At this moment there seems a preponderance of trees springing up with unpronounceable names. I need to find out a little more about the noble families of the Franks.'

Eadulf considered. 'We are told that we have enough Franks here among the students, and we have the prioress. If Brother Charibert does not feel his education sufficient to tell us the details of what we need to know, there are surely people who can instruct us.' Eadulf paused for a moment and then added: 'Could it be that Bishop Brodulf met his death because he was a prince and not because he was a bishop?'

'You may well be right. It makes more sense than the bishop coming here to engage with our scholars who, according to what we hear, he did not consider worthy of exchanging ideas with. I was also thinking that there are many of our teaching abbeys that serve students from many lands. Among them are refugee princes who have fled from their countries, some bearing ill will to those who have forced them into exile. My cousin, Abbot Lauran of Dare, boasts that he had students from no fewer than eighteen kingdoms, many from the kingdoms of the Angles and Saxons. And I recall being involved in a case involving the murder of a Saxon student called Wolfsan in Dare. That was done to insure a hereditary line of kingship. I wish I could recall the details.'

There was a cough from Brother Charibert, which brought her attention back to him. The young man was clearly growing impatient as he apparently was not able to follow the exchanges between Fidelma and Eadulf.

'Do you want to speak to him further?' Eadulf asked Fidelma quickly.

'He will need to remain in the abbey with Deacon Landric until we finish completing our investigation . . .' She stopped as a thought struck her. 'One thing does occur to me . . .'

Again she asked Eadulf to translate as she tried to form the idea.

'You have clearly told us that the bishop was afraid of something or someone. You told us that he took some elaborate precautions regarding his security at night. At the same time, he had no such fears during daylight and wandered freely on his own.'

Brother Charibert did not say anything but stood awaiting her question with a cautious expression.

'Did he have enemies or rivals in Burgundia?'

'Surely enemies are natural to princes?' the man shrugged.

'So he did have some?'

'I am a servant, lady. What would I know of the family of princes?'

Fidelma sighed deeply. 'Then, speaking of enemies, you probably heard that he had arguments with the scholars and students here? Could you identify anyone whom he argued with and for whom he expressed any dislike or hatred?'

'I know nothing of these arguments. They were in Latin and one of them in a strange language, which I was later told was the language of the Hellenes.'

'You never witnessed these arguments, or saw any threats to the bishop in such circumstances?'

'I would not understand even if I had been allowed to accompany the bishop to such discourses with the professors and students.'

'But outside of them,' went on Fidelma, 'did you not see any threats made to him? Say, threats or even bad behaviour towards him either in the refectory or in the chapel?'

'I should not speak of such things.'

'Better to speak of evil,' Fidelma declared in exasperation, 'than to see it.'

A curious look spread over the servant's features. It was as if he were going to smile and then changed his mind. He became almost confidential.

'I did see the bishop in argument in which I was left in fear of the outcome.'

'Tell us where and whom with.'

'Outside the *scriptorium*, the library. It was early in the morning of the day before he perished.'

'Outside the *scriptorium*? Whom was he arguing with?'

'I think it was one of the senior clerics. The one they call "the keeper of books".'

'You mean the librarian?'

Fidelma tried to remember the name the abbot had given her, but the young man answered before it came to her.

'He is named the Venerable Lugán.'

'Do you know what this argument was about?'

'I only knew that there was anger in their words.'

Fidelma sighed impatiently. 'Yet another person to question,' she said in an aside to Eadulf.

'There was another argument,' Brother Charibert suddenly volunteered, seemingly pleased at their reaction. 'That happened a short time later and perhaps it was the continuance of the same argument.'

'And was that with the librarian as well?'

'It was with the prioress . . . the lady called Suanach.'

Fidelma stared at him for a moment. 'Prioress Suanach? She seems to be having a lot of arguments in this abbey,' she said in an aside to Eadulf, remembering the disagreement that Enda had witnessed.

'Then you must know what the argument was about,' Eadulf pointed out almost triumphantly. 'Prioress Suanach spoke your language and so she would have argued with the bishop in your own language.'

'I did not hear much. She seemed very angry and her voice was raised so that it almost affronted the ears. It was discordant in the extreme. There were evil things said.'

'But you understood?'

'Only a few words, not much. It was just the voices raised in curses.'

There was a few moments' silence.

'Even though it was in your own language you cannot remember what this argument was about?' Eadulf pressed, disappointed.

Brother Charibert raised his shoulders and let them fall as if to dismiss any knowledge. 'I was more concerned with the manner of the prioress. It was as if she were going to launch herself on my lord, the bishop. Her face was so red that it was almost as if she would explode with the blood that was coursing through her.'

'And Bishop Brodulf?' Eadulf asked. 'Was he equally angry?'

'He was of a similar disposition.'

'And you do not know why?' Fidelma's voice was almost raised a tone in exasperation.

'I do not know,' Brother Charibert said stubbornly. 'I am a mere servant.'

Fidelma almost groaned. 'Being a servant does not make you deaf and dumb. The argument was in the language of your people. It was loud. How can you not know what was being said?'

Brother Charibert was quiet for a moment.

'It is clear that you have never been a servant. A servant is there only to obey the orders that are given and not to listen to their betters. If you walk into a room where people are engaged in a rapid and heated conversation, even if they speak the same language that you do, you do not necessarily know what is being said until you have stood for a while and tried to follow what the argument is all about. Is this not so? With a servant, it is more restrictive for they would be punished if they were caught listening.'

Fidelma actually found herself on the point of grinding her teeth.

'But you are supposed to be a free man and not a slave. Your bishop is dead. Is there nothing you can say?'

They did not think he was going to speak again, but then he said: 'I remember this from the exchange. The bishop declared, "You think that you can stop it?" His manner was almost sneering and he told her to attend to her distaff. I do not know what he meant but she replied with a curse and in such a manner I shuddered to hear it.'

'A curse such as . . .?'

'She cried, "A curse on all your dead ones!" That, in my language, is an ultimate curse, lady.'

'There is no argument with that,' Fidelma agreed softly. Then she glanced at Eadulf and spoke in her own language in a more determined tone: 'So we have a few paths to follow. That will be enough for the moment. There is a possibility that we will need to question Brother Charibert further. Tell him he can go for the moment, but emphasise that he has been of great help in our inquiries.'

When the door closed on the strange former servant, Fidelma sank on to the bed with a deep exhalation of breath. She lay a moment staring at the ceiling before turning with a moody expression at Eadulf. He was still sitting on the edge of the bed with his head in his hands. There was a silence for a while.

'I should thank you for your knowledge, Eadulf,' she finally said. 'It was useful that you could communicate with the Frank in your language. I know it sounds a little the same, but it would have taken me a long time to gather the information as you did.'

'You have learnt the basics of my tongue well, Fidelma,' he said with a smile. 'But Brother Charibert's information either misdirects us down a wrong path or it has given us several paths that we will have to spend time exploring. I find it curious that a servant, one who has been a former slave, has the individuality of character to come forward of his own volition to give us this testimony and at such a late hour. I find it difficult to believe he was once a slave.'

'Perhaps he was ordered to come by Deacon Landric? He gives us certain information while using his social standing as a convenient means to deny knowledge. I find it worrying.'

'I am still thinking about the reason why Bishop Brodulf came from the Abbey of Luxovium all the way to this abbey. And now we must not lose sight of the fact that he was a prince of Burgundia as well as a bishop.'

'Brother Charibert was right when he said that most prelates of the church are also nobles. They are usually the only people with the education to take that role.' Fidelma sighed deeply. 'I can't help remembering a student called Wulfstan who was in my cousin's abbey. You remember my cousin Abbot Laisran?'

'Of course.'

'Well, Wulfstan was a Saxon prince who was studying in the Abbey of Darú. When Wulfstan's father died of the Yellow Plague, under your law of primogeniture he should have succeeded to be King of the South Saxons. But he was assassinated. I was able to track down the assassin, who turned out to be a cousin of his, who killed him to ensure that his own father, some prince called Aelle, succeeded to the kingship. Thus are the dangers of inheritance by primogeniture and not by the election of the *derbfine*, the generations of the family meeting together and deciding who is the best man to become their chief.'

Eadulf smiled. It was a favourite topic of Fidelma's to compare the differences in inheritance law.

'I doubt if the Burgundians would send someone all the way here to find and eliminate the bishop, just because he was a rival prince. I am beginning to think it is more plausible that Bishop

Brodulf was killed in bad temper because of his arrogance over the differences of the Faith.'

'That would be one reason,' Fidelma agreed. 'But I do find it a weak one. I am sure there is something more sinister here.'

CHAPTER NINE

The next morning, rising late, they washed, and then ate a hasty first meal of the day in the almost deserted refectory. Neither of them expressed any regret for missing the morning prayers in the chapel. As they were leaving the refectory they encountered the steward, Brother Mac Raith, at the exit. It was the steward who acknowledged them first. His tone was disapproving.

'Abbot Cuán wondered if you had any further concerns relating to the interment of Bishop Brodulf's remains at midnight tonight. He was going to ask you at morning prayers but we noticed that you were both absent.'

'We were late retiring as some unexpected matters arose requiring our attention until the late hours,' Fidelma replied coldly. 'We have no objections about the performance of the rituals tonight.'

'Then all is acceptable to you? There will be a *fled-cro-lige*, the feast of the deathbed, before the ceremony. However, this will be taken as part of the usual evening meal. I have sought Deacon Landric's approval for this. He seems to require no special arrangements other than a simple interment.'

'We presume Brother Anlón is also satisfied? As physician, he must also approve.'

'He approved that the remains were released to mourners at

midnight last night so they could complete the *aire* – the watching – by midnight tonight. Apart from you, as *dálaigh*, it was in the hands of Deacon Landric, but the Franks do not follow the same traditions as we do. Prioress Susanach organised a group of the sisterhood to sit with the corpse in the chapel for the traditional watch until the ceremonies begin. The body will be taken from the chapel at the sounding of the *clog-estechtae* – the death bell. That will mark the body being taken to the burial ground on Cnoc Carron.'

Fidelma felt the urge to tell the steward that she had attended funeral rites before, but resisted.

When she made no comment, the steward continued: 'All is now prepared. As you know, Sítae, the master builder, has agreed with Abbot Cuán that his men will dig the grave and act as pall-bearers. Apparently, his men excavated the grave last night so that it is ready now. I think the *claide*, the grave diggers, in their part of the country observe such a tradition of preparing the grave on the night before the burial. They have even volunteered to carry the body to the burial ground.'

'Abbot Cuán announced that last night,' Fidelma replied, trying not to sound wearied by these details.

'Sítae seems a paragon of the virtues,' Eadulf muttered cynically. 'I thought the matter of attitude to the *fé* was deeply entrenched? Were there no objections?'

The *fé* was the measuring rod by which graves were measured and was regarded with some revulsion and dread by those who were not qualified morticians.

'The abbot certainly blessed the *fé* and the whole business. Sítae and his men were happy with the arrangement,' the steward assured him. 'At least it has saved us a problem until our normal *claide* have recovered from the burns their hands suffered quenching the fire yesterday.'

'We will come to the chapel and pay our respects in order that Deacon Landric has no cause to return to Burgundia with a critical

report of our respect and hospitality for the late bishop,' Fidelma
assured him. 'And now, as it happens, you are the very man I want
to speak with in order that you might answer a few questions.'

'What can I do for you, lady?'

'As steward of this abbey you are probably the best person to
consult about the scholars who come here to study.'

'I am not sure that I am permitted to pass on any personal
details. Are you asking as a *dálaigh*?'

'For the future, you should know that when a *dálaigh,* or judge
of my rank, asks a question, then the onus is upon you to answer,
or receive a fine.'

The steward flushed. 'I am sorry. I was not aware of the precise
rule. I am always at your service and if it is something that is
beyond my knowledge, then I shall recommend the appropriate
authority. Of course, the ultimate authority is the abbot.'

'The abbot did tell us that he had authority over Prioress
Suanach,' Eadulf said.

Brother Mac Raith sniffed disapprovingly. 'The abbot does not
normally interfere in matters affecting the prioress's role. He speaks
for the abbey.'

'Who presides over those who are married? I am told there are
married couples here, raising their children in the service of the
Faith.'

'The married among the brethren and sisterhood, while abiding
by the marriage laws of the Brehons, must also be obedient to the
rules of the community. Both Abbot Cuán and Prioress Suanach
have regular conference to discuss how any problems arising among
the men and women of the abbey may be resolved. There is little
that cannot be resolved, for there is hardly any matter within the
community that requires the extreme of divorce or separation.
Most separations are made on equitable terms, as in our law.
Anyway, nothing has ever arisen that requires the abbot to overrule
the view of the prioress.'

'So there are no restrictions on the development of normal emotions between the sexes in this abbey any more than elsewhere?' Eadulf pressed.

'Our religious communities were formed so that men and women could live together in the New Faith. It is only recently that ascetics and celibates have started to devise philosophies and laws within the Faith to justify their own lifestyles. Some of our prelates, whose tendencies were to that celibate way, have begun to find support from those who try to suppress human desires and make the excuse that it is the route to a union with their deity.'

'I judge from your speech that you are not one of them?' Fidelma observed.

'Not I,' Brother Mac Raith declared almost fiercely. 'I am a man of flesh and blood. So were the first disciples who followed the teachings of the Christ, who taught marriage was a natural condition of men and women. His disciples married, among them Peter, who is accepted as leader of the Faith after Christ was executed. These new philosophies are nothing more than ideas put forward by those who want to fulfil their own purpose.'

'So there are no rules that apply in this abbey that would prevent relationships between its inhabitants?' Fidelma pressed, not wishing to go down the path of the history of the New Faith.

'None, according to the Faith, but only those punishable when such extra-marital relationships hurt a third person and contravenes the *Cain Lánamnus* – the law of marriages, divorce and separation.'

The steward was regarding them with a suspicious expression and so Fidelma felt obliged to comment.

'There is no prurient motive in our asking about this matter, Brother Mac Raith. Let us just say that we are thinking aloud about the law and the relationships in this abbey.'

A grim smile suddenly crossed the steward's features.

'I suppose that you are thinking about last night when we witnessed Prioress Suanach going into the chamber of the Venerable

Breas? Prioress Suanach makes it her practice to call on the Venerable Breas at that hour to ensure that all is well with him. We tend to forget that he is our most elderly scholar. I told you that she attends the scholar each evening without fail. Are you reflecting that the prioress would be twenty years the junior to the Venerable Breas? She was once his student here. Now she has returned, she teaches many of his classes, so it is natural they have a close relationship.'

'What happens between her and the Venerable Breas is not of any general concern,' Fidelma replied. 'Both are equals under law. Speaking of students, this abbey still attracts a large number of scholars from many kingdoms?'

The steward made a motion with his shoulder as if implying it was obvious before answering verbally.

'We do not attract as many as the Abbey of Darú, where it is claimed that scholars from eighteen different kingdoms are studying.'

'My cousin Laisran is given to boasting of this fact,' Fidelma agreed. 'So how many students do you have here?'

Brother Mac Raith made a mental calculation.

'Perhaps about one hundred, and a third of them are from beyond the seas. They probably represent ten kingdoms. After the Council of Streonshalh, we had a large number of Angles and Saxons coming here. They refused to accept the decision of the King of Northumbria, who abandoned our teachings to follow the new Roman ones.'

'There are some from Burgundia. How many?'

'We have three female students from Burgundia, but they certainly did not arrive with Bishop Brodulf or were connected with his party. We also have a few of the brethren who have remained here during the last decade or so.'

'So you have already considered whether there are any links?' Fidelma asked sharply. 'You did not tell me.'

'It was a matter of natural interest when the bishop and his companions arrived. Prioress Suanach spent some years in Burgundia. Missionaries have gone from here to many lands and established communities there over the last century. We probably have several missionaries in Burgundia.'

'We were aware of it,' Eadulf murmured.

'Among these regular members of the abbey, aside from students, were there any links with the bishop?' Fidelma asked.

'To my knowledge – none. As I say, they have been with us many years.'

'You pointed out to me the abbey's students' quarters when we arrived,' Fidelma said.

'Yes, it was the first large wooden building to the right as you pass the library.'

'Remind us of the names of those Burgundian students?'

The steward hesitated a moment in thought.

'These foreign names,' he complained with a sigh. 'There is the eldest, Sister Fastrude. Then two younger girls – Sister Ingund and a Sister Haldetrude. I hope I pronounce these names correctly. Those are the only students. If you want the names of the elderly brethren then I shall have to check the ledgers.'

'Thank you, that would be helpful.'

Leaving the steward looking slightly perplexed, Fidelma and Eadulf walked through the abbey in the direction they remembered.

'I thought that we were going to question the student called Brother Garb,' Eadulf protested once they were out of earshot.

'So we are,' Fidelma confirmed shortly. 'Where else would a student usually be but in the students' quarters? We might also learn something from the Burgundian students as well as Garb. I want to get as much accurate information as possible.'

'So our intention is still to question Brother Garb?'

'That is my intention,' she confirmed gravely.

They had no difficulty finding the students' quarters. Nearby the stone workers and carpenters were already busy with their tasks under the direction of a burly-looking overseer. Another group was involved in clearing the most blackened remains of the burnt-out guest house. As they turned into the students' house, they were greeted by a tall, thin man whose parchment-like skin seemed to be drawn so tightly over his features that he seemed more of a skeleton than a man of flesh and blood. Fidelma recognised him as being among the senior members of the high table in the refectory the previous night.

She recalled that the Venerable Lugán was not only the *leabhar coimedach*, or librarian of the abbey, but held the title of master of all students. The latter role was merely to ensure they attended the right studies, kept a regular attendance and to provide any additional wants. Outside of these academic functions he and the prioress would inspect the students' living quarters to make sure each student not only kept his or her accommodation clean but also performed their toilets regularly and otherwise obeyed the rules of the abbey community.

The Venerable Lugán came forward, showing his yellowing teeth in what was meant as a smile. He was elderly, although not as old as the Venerable Breas. He did not seem as careful about his physical appearance, appearing stooped and frail.

'I am glad you have come this morning, lady, as I did not have a chance to greet you last evening,' he addressed her, forestalling her opening question. 'I first wanted to say that I regret the death of Bishop Brodulf.'

'You wished to speak with me?' Fidelma frowned, slightly annoyed at the distraction from her main purpose.

She waited for the man to continue without comment. It would be natural to expect one to feel regret for the death of a fellow religious, but she wondered why it was being made a point of.

'I regret the death of any human,' went on the Venerable Lugán, breaking the silence as if the expression of regret needed clarification. Apparently, it did. 'I will confess to you that I did not like Bishop Brodulf.'

Fidelma and Eadulf remained silent, wondering if he was going to volunteer a more specific reason.

'I thought I should tell you this before you started encountering any gossip in the abbey.'

'Gossip? Something specific about animosity to Bishop Brodulf?' Fidelma queried in a neutral tone.

'Doesn't the poet Virgil say: "*Fama, malum qua non aliud velocius ullum*"?'

'"Nothing travels faster than scandal",' Fidelma agreed. 'In this case, it has travelled slowly and therefore, Venerable Lugán, you must elucidate, for we have no idea of what you speak.'

The librarian grimaced wryly. He pointed to a bench outside the door of the students' quarters.

'Let us sit there to talk of this,' he said, taking a seat himself. When they seated themselves, he went on: 'Close communities being what they are, I am sure eventually that you will hear talk of my argument with the bishop.'

'So you argued with Bishop Brodulf? At this moment we are at a loss. So perhaps you should explain more?' Fidelma encouraged. 'We know that Bishop Brodulf was engaged in some contentious debate with the Venerable Breas and his students. I did not realise that he had also debated with you.'

'We did not debate, although I once attended and observed one such debate with my good friend and brother, Breas. So I know the abuse that Breas had to endure from the bishop. I would say that Bishop Brodulf was a man lacking in logic and basing his arguments on learning by rote. It was in a different sphere that I encountered him and emotional words were exchanged.'

'Explain,' Fidelma frowned, wondering what different sphere he could mean.

'I am, as you know, the librarian of this abbey. Our library is highly regarded. It ranks among the best in the kingdom. We have volumes in Hebrew, Aramaic, Greek and Latin, as well as in our own mother tongue. We pride ourselves on keeping local records from the time when the Blessed Ailbe founded this abbey. I have been librarian here since the time when Conaing was abbot, before Ségdae. I am proud of my task. Have you visited our magnificent library? I am sure that you must have.'

'I have,' Fidelma agreed patiently, 'although my brother, the King, maintains a sufficient library for my wants in Cashel.'

'Our library here is becoming second to none in the kingdom. And our small band of copyists are highly regarded, both for their calligraphy and their illustrations. We are now constantly receiving gifts of texts from many places. Why, when the Prioress Suanach returned to this abbey following the many years that she spent preaching the Faith in Burgundia, she brought as a gift to the Venerable Breas a copy of the Blessed Gregory of Tours' work *Historia Francorum* . . .'

'A History of the Franks? That must be very scarce and valuable, since Gregory is now many decades dead.'

'Our annals place the worthy teacher's death nearly eighty years ago. The Venerable Breas immediately donated it for the service of our library.'

'It must be of great use, since you now have students from that very kingdom coming here to study,' Eadulf observed.

'It helps our reputation as a source of scholarship.' The librarian was clearly enthusiastic. 'The Venerable Breas has instructed our copyists to transcribe the work so that we have two copies of it. In fact, one of the new students, Sister Fastrude, has recently brought a gift from her abbey, which is an additional text to that of Gregory's text. This is a continuation called *Liber Historiae Francorum*, said to be written by a scribe called Fedegar, which brings the history of the Franks up to the current king of that country. It even has an outline of the various branches of the family of the king.'

Fidelma sighed impatiently, although she could understand the undoubted enthusiasm of the librarian for his library. The librarian interpreted her controlled expression.

'Sometimes, in such works, we can pick up matters of interest to our own land,' he explained.

'In what way?' Eadulf asked, interested.

'One I found of interest. Twenty years ago there was a king called Sigebert who was assassinated by a noble called Grimoald. This Grimoald made himself King. Sigebert's young son, Dagobert, the heir, was secreted away and hidden in the Abbey of Pictavia before Grimoald could have him killed. However, the assassins were close to finding the boy. Abbot Dido of Pictavia sent him here to be hidden and raised in secret.'

In spite of herself, Fidelma was interested.

'Here? To this abbey?'

The Venerable Lugán shook his head. 'It is not known into which abbey the boy was sent, let alone which of the Five Kingdoms. It is probably irrelevant now as this was twenty years ago or more. Grimoald and the other assassins were eventually overthrown. Clotaire, who is related to Dagobert, is now King.'

'Does this book by Fedegar say what happened to Dagobert?' Fidelma asked.

'That is the frustrating thing. We don't even know if Dagobert is still alive. But the important thing is, knowledge emerges in the most unlikely places.'

'I understand that you are justly proud of the library, Venerable Lugán, but may I remind you that we were talking about an argument that you had with Bishop Brodulf?'

It took a few moments for the elderly librarian to bring his mind back to the original discussion.

'When visitors, whether they are of high rank or whether they are acclaimed scholars or lowly students, want to consult the books and scripts that we have here, they are expected to seek permission first. Depending who they are and what they want to consult, I am asked, for not even one of my assistant librarians would be allowed to extend permission without my authority. Therefore, one evening I came to the library and was astonished . . . no, shocked. Yes, shocked, indeed, to find there was someone in the library and certain texts were in disarray. It was evening, a time when the library should have been deserted.'

'Are you going to tell us that it was the bishop?' Eadulf asked, cutting short the librarian's dramatic opening.

The Venerable Lugán seemed oblivious to his slightly sarcastic tone.

'I found this Bishop Brodulf among a pile of scattered documents and with a lighted candle! A lighted candle, of all things! It was not even a more protective lantern. The documents were distorted and scattered before him.'

'Did he offer you an explanation?'

'He did not. He was arrogant and even criticised me for interrupting him.'

'So what did you do?'

'Do? I berated him for disobeying the rules; for disobeying common sense by using a lighted candle in the library and especially where papers were scattered, and scattered by him in such a manner.'

'He did not defend himself?'

'Not at all. He was, as I have said, belligerent towards me. He even told me that he was a bishop and that I had no authority to question him.'

'He did not explain what he was looking for?'

'Not even that. I told him I would report the matter to the abbot and the bishop just laughed in a sneering way.'

'And *did* you report this to the abbot?' Eadulf asked firmly.

'Of course I did.'

'And what did the abbot say?'

'He told me to forget the incident.'

Fidelma was not expecting this retort. 'Did he explain why?' she asked.

'He said that Bishop Brodulf would not be staying much longer at the abbey and that he wanted the remaining days to pass more tranquilly. I had the impression that the abbot was totally exhausted by the tension the bishop had brought here and that he simply wanted to be rid of him.'

'Him or the tension?' Eadulf murmured.

'The abbot did concede that Bishop Brodulf was arrogant and conceited in his opinions. He even accepted that he had created dissensions among the students. However, he urged me just to tidy the library after the bishop had left, and not to pursue the matter further.'

'So you accepted that without further explanation?'

'Cuán is the abbot. What more could I have done? I had realised that while I had been arguing with Bishop Brodulf our voices might have attracted attention. I am afraid that I was guilty of the sin of anger. When I learnt that Bishop Brodulf's death was no accident and that you, as a *dálaigh*, are investigating his death, I thought I should tell you this in case the matter was reported to you by someone else and might be misinterpreted.'

Fidelma sniffed slightly. She did not like anyone second guessing her thoughts or her reactions.

'Another question,' Eadulf interrupted as she was about to respond. 'You say these documents and texts that the bishop was looking through were scattered in the library? What were these papers?'

The librarian shrugged. 'The bishop had tried to put the texts back in place. I suppose he did not want others to identify his interests . . .' He paused. 'I did see the area of papers for he had put them back in a hurried manner. I am most particular in this regard and make sure my assistants meet my standards. I check that everything is left in order before I leave each evening when the library is supposed to be closed. If it is not . . .'

Fidelma's lips compressed slightly as she again attempted to disguise her impatience. Why was it, she asked herself, that people, instead of replying to a simple question with a simple answer, had to go off at a tangent and embroider it with another story? She waited in silence before the Venerable Lugán realised they were waiting for him to answer the question he had been asked.

'I had to sort and replace several of the papers that were not put back in the correct order,' he finished.

'And what were these papers?' pressed Eadulf.

'They were actually a series of loose pages from annals and ledgers to do with the history of this abbey. We keep records and events of the abbey back to the years of the Blessed Ailbe. We have the principal names and deeds affecting all the *comarbae*, the heirs, of Ailbe.'

'So what you are saying is that the bishop was trying to look up some historical records of this abbey?'

'It would seem so,' the Venerable Lugán acknowledged. 'Do not ask me why Bishop Brodulf would be interested in the history of our abbey. It might well be that it was because Ailbe has become regarded as the founder of the Faith in our southern kingdom. As you know, he taught the Faith here long before Patricius in the north of this island. But judging by the texts I saw, the bishop was interested with more modern years.'

'You mean during the time of Abbot Ségdae?'

The Venerable Lugán shook his head. 'The documents most disordered were those from the time of Abbot Conaing Ua Daint. Abbot Conaing died before you left the abbey of Cill Dara and came back to us. That was before you undertook to advise our delegation to the Council at Streonshalh in the kingdom of Northumbria.'

'That was almost a decade ago.' Eadulf recalled that it had been when he had first met Fidelma.

'About that time. Abbot Conaing had served this abbey for many years.'

'Why would Bishop Brodulf have been interested in records or papers relating to that time?'

The librarian shrugged. 'I have no idea, but that was the area he was searching.'

'And, apart from the row you think someone might have over-heard, you have spoken to no one else about this incident except Abbot Cuán?'

'I have mentioned it to no one. I did not want you hearing about the argument, the raised voices, and thinking that I might be suspect for holding some grudge against the bishop.'

'You have confessed a dislike of him,' Eadulf pointed out. 'Do you maintain that you have no malignancy towards him?'

'There is no grudge that would lead me to commit murder,' the librarian replied.

'We thank you for your honesty,' Fidelma intervened in case Eadulf took things further. 'Of course, had we heard any such story we would have consulted you. And you are quite certain about the nature of the documents that he was searching?'

The Venerable Lugán drew himself up with an expression of dignity.

'I am most particular about my library and know exactly where all documents are kept and in what order. The bishop seemed clearly interested in the period Abbot Conaing was here. That included the lists of the brethren, of the sisterhood and the lists of the students who were studying here.'

'Was there anyone well known here in the abbey at that time? Anyone the bishop might have been interested in?'

The librarian shrugged. 'I can look through the papers myself and see if there is any name that catches the eye. Obviously, Breas would have been a teacher here at that time. I was, too. Suanach had just joined as a student.'

'A list might be helpful. If you could also check the names of students attending at that time – students, like Suanach, who is now prioress. Perhaps there might have been others who went on missionaries abroad.'

'Several went abroad. Perhaps he was looking for someone who went to Burgundia.'

'Very well. Tell me what you find and pay close attention to any records like those of the prioress.'

'There is a lot of supposition in relating those documents to this matter,' Eadulf commented softly. 'It might just be a coincidence that those records were disturbed and he was looking for something else.'

'It does no harm to check,' Fidelma replied. She turned back to the librarian. 'We actually came to see some of the students. Brother Garb in particular.'

'I am afraid he is not here. Most of the students are now in their classes.' The Venerable Lugán suddenly glanced across the courtyard. 'Ah, here is one of our senior scholars and she knows Brother Garb.' He called loudly: 'Sister Fastrude! A moment, please.'

The young woman, who was heading in their direction anyway, halted in surprise at the sight of the people gathered by the door. She hesitated and then came forward. She was in her mid-twenties, a short, thickset young woman, with blue-black hair, striking grey eyes and a prominent nose. The mouth was broad and seemed fixed in a permanent grin. She hesitated a moment before them, examining them each in turn, staring at them with curiosity.

'You wanted to see me, Venerable Lugán?' Even her voice had a suppressed chuckle in it.

'Sister Fastrude, this is Fidelma of Cashel. She is sister to our king but also a *dálaigh*. A *dálaigh* is—'

'I know well what the office is,' the young woman interrupted. 'I saw the lady Fidelma at the meal last night and I also saw Brother Eadulf. After the words spoken by the abbot, I made it my priority to speak with Prioress Suanach and learn about a *dálaigh* and her powers.'

'Excellent,' Fidelma smiled at her. 'Then, if you have a moment, we would talk with you.'

'I have a class to attend and I am already late for it,' the young woman replied. 'I shall use you, lady, as my excuse for unpunctuality.'

'You may do so, and I will have a word with your professor, if needs be.' She turned to the Venerable Lugán and asked softly. 'Will you let us know as soon as you can about those papers?' Her tone made it clear that she and Eadulf wanted to speak alone with the Burgundian student.

The librarian inclined his head, turned and almost hurried away.

'There is no one in the general studies room.' Sister Fastrude pointed to a door. 'We can sit in there and talk undisturbed. I presume that you want to talk about Bishop Brodulf?'

'It is a correct presumption but not a difficult one to arrive at,' Fidelma replied gravely as they followed her into the large room where the students would come to do their work after formal classes or to catch up on their reading and writing.

'Do you come from the same area as Bishop Brodulf?' Eadulf asked.

'I *am* a Burgundian,' affirmed the sister, 'but, no. I did not know Bishop Brodulf before he arrived in this abbey.'

'Where in Burgundia do you come from?'

'Do you know my land of Burgundia?' the woman asked in surprise.

'Eadulf and I were at the Council in Autun.'

'Ah, then you will have passed by the little place I come from if you approached Autun from the coast along the great river. It's the river the Romans call Liger because it was the river of silt and sediment. That's what the name means.'

'A great river and a long journey,' Fidelma encouraged her. 'So where is your home along it?'

'The place I come from is called Nevirnum. The great river passes south of it, and beyond, to the east, is where a river that flows from the north passes us to feed it. We are a small community, but already we have a bishop who is the shepherd of our community.'

'But you came here to study. Were you long in this abbey?'

'About nine months. There are two younger students from the same area but I did not know them well until we all set out to be students here. I had heard of this kingdom. Many teachers from this land have come to the Frankish kingdoms of Burgundia, Neustria and Austrasia and even from Aquitaine. You will know that there has been much debate about the future of the Faith, and several communities among the Franks felt scholars should come here to learn more about the ideas and philosophies of this land.'

Fidelma was interested. 'Isn't that what Bishop Brodulf claimed he was doing?'

Sister Fastrude's smile actually broadened. 'That is what he claimed.'

'I was thinking that our missionaries have been able to go to your country and teach, setting up abbeys, without you sending people here in order to learn of our beliefs.'

'It is true. There is much pressure in the kingdoms I come from, especially in view of the decisions at the Council of Autun, when it was ordered that most of the religious houses must accept the Rules of Benedict. However, the Irish ecclesiastical colleges still attract countless scholars from many lands. I had to seek the permission of my bishop to make this journey here as I wanted to judge for myself why Rome seeks to make changes.'

'But you did not know Bishop Brodulf before coming here?' Fidelma asked quickly.

The young woman shook her head. 'I barely even knew of Sister Ingund and Sister Haldetrude before I first met them.'

'Which was where?'

'It was while we were waiting for a ship to bring us to this country. It was at the port at the mouth of the Liger. I had travelled down river from Nevirnum to where it empties at the western ocean by that town that is now named after the Martyr Nazarius. We joined a Gaulish ship and together made the voyage. We came to Árd Mór, the port on your coast here. From there we made our way to this abbey.'

'If you landed on the coast there, did you not know that Árd Mór itself was also one of our earliest teaching abbeys? Declan, another of our earliest teachers, taught the Faith before Patricius. Why didn't you stay there instead of making the further journey here?'

'We were told that Imleach was a blessed spot where the Faith was first proclaimed in this kingdom and even the king of this land chose his Chief Bishop from Imleach. Many also sang the praises of the Venerable Breas as a great teacher.'

'That is a fair enough reason. What do you study?'

'The languages of the Faith: Greek and Latin and some Hebrew. Of course, we also study philosophy and the ancient texts of the founders of the Faith. My companions are even now at such classes where I should be,' she added with her dry smile.

'Then we shall not keep you long. I am thinking that it is odd that you did not know of Bishop Brodulf. After all, he was a leading Burgundian bishop and it seems strange that you came from a fairly close area and are unknown to one another. Did you not talk to him when he arrived here?'

Sister Fastrude chuckled. 'I shall be honest. We all knew Bishop Brodulf by name, due to the fact that he is . . . was . . . related to our king. He was a prince of our people. That does not mean we knew him, but only *of* him. I think all three of us developed a strong dislike of the bishop during the time he was here. I think we would agree that he was arrogant and had a cruel streak. I regret to say it, but I shall not pretend otherwise. He expected us to behave towards him as thralls in his palace. We were expected to be as servants to a prince and not as fellow members of the Faith to their bishop.'

Fidelma made a sympathetic clicking noise with her tongue.

'He was definitely related to Clotaire, the King of Burgundia? Eadulf and I met him once at the Council of Autun. So the bishop *was* related to him? Do you know the exact relationship?'

'Some cousin, I think. Close enough to have been patronised by him.'

'Do you know if this relationship was widely known among the people in this abbey?'

'If they did not know he was a noble, they should have guessed by the arrogance of his behaviour.'

'For example?'

'During those discussions, as example. He did not discuss but stated things as if instructing servants, and he did not engage in explanations,' Sister Fastrude replied. 'If explanations or apologies were needed, he left them to Deacon Landric. Landric should be able to tell you all such details rather than I.'

'As you say, I hear that his discussions with the Venerable Breas, in front of the classes, were often very impassioned.'

The young woman stared at her wide eyed for a moment and then burst out laughing.

'Impassioned? I would say that if such talks had taken place without the restraining authority of the Venerable Breas, then matters might have resulted in physical violence and bloodshed. Only the quiet demeanour of the Venerable Breas caused tempers to draw back from the abyss.'

'Some of scholars and students were extremely upset by his attitude then?' Eadulf asked.

'Yes; they could have respected his differences of opinion but not his arrogance. He did not understand that arguments educate. He saw opposite views only as being a personal defiance to him. But we students knew that he possessed no independent logic or intelligence.'

'I don't understand,' Eadulf admitted.

'Often Bishop Brodulf would say things to which there was no logic, either in religion or in any other philosophy. When he was asked to explain why he stated this or that, or what the origin of it was, he simply declared that we had to accept just because it was the teaching. It was the rule. One had to obey the rule. It was then that Brother Garb would speak up and point out that rules were made for the obedience of fools but only for the guidance of wise men.'

'It has truly been said many times,' Fidelma agreed thoughtfully. 'Virtue and wisdom are inseparable. The mindless ones will follow the rule, even knowing what they are doing is wrong, but, as Aristotle once wrote, the wise men will bend the rule for the service of morality. There is also an ancient saying that necessity is not bound by rules. The sign of wisdom is knowing when such a necessity is for the good or for the evil.'

Sister Fastrude regarded Fidelma with quiet admiration. 'That was along the lines that the Venerable Breas was teaching,' she admitted.

'You mentioned Brother Garb. I am told that this student, Brother Garb, is one who clashed with Bishop Brodulf most often. Is he still in the classes? I would like to talk with him.'

'I presume he is still in class now. But, yes, Brother Garb bested the bishop several times in the debates. It was rare that the Venerable Breas had to intervene or correct anything that Brother Garb said. Garb was especially knowledgeable about the teachings of Pelagius, who is highly regarded in these Western churches but who is denounced as a heretic in Rome. The bishop declared vehemently that he was determined that the instructions agreed at the Council of Autun would be carried out, and that those religious houses who refused would be declared heretical and destroyed.'

Eadulf raised his eyebrows. 'He declared that, did he? I would say that he trespassed on the hospitality and of the law system here.'

'Such arguments, you say, were regular between Brother Garb and Bishop Brodulf?' Fidelma pressed.

'They were regular and most passionate,' Sister Fastrude confirmed. 'Brother Garb has a close friend here named Brother Étaid. I think they supported one another. I almost suspected that they met before the discussions and agreed the best way of inciting the bishop's temper.'

'Say you so?' Fidelma was thoughtful. 'Perhaps you can provide an example for me?'

The young woman frowned as if trying to remember and then nodded. 'Yes, I can recall one discussion when we were examining the argument between Augustine from a place called Hippo, which I believe is in Africa. This Augustine was a sworn enemy of Pelagius. I presume that you will know that Pelagius was from this very island and went to Rome. He was horrified by the state of morality he saw there. Pelagius, having read works by Augustine, blamed lack of moral responsibility on the writings of this theologian.'

Fidelma exchanged a rather wary look with Eadulf in case he pointed out that they knew the teachings and the conflict well. She wanted to let the young woman develop her own thoughts, but hoped she would get to the point quickly.

'Augustine taught that men and woman had no such thing as Free Will. He said that their entire lives were destined even before they were born. It was not their choice but lay in the divine grace.'

'You were going to tell us how this discussion on these philosophies led to violent argument in which Brother Garb and his friend, Brother Étaid, led the attack,' pointed out Fidelma.

'It was like watching bear baiting,' the young woman said. 'First one would attack and, then, before the bishop had recovered, the other would come in. Truly, I did once feel a sympathy for the bishop. Perhaps it was lucky for him that he really did not understand what a ridiculous figure he looked.'

'How did the discussion end?'

'Garb and Étaid would quote first from Pelagius and then from Augustine. Then, as they summed up the arguments, Garb would emphasise Pelagius' point that the teachings of Augustine allowed men and women to indulge in sin because they could argue it was not in their control. Pelagius had argued Augustine imperilled the whole of human morality: there was nothing to restrain them from doing what they wanted in life; nothing to stop them doing evil or to trying to pursue good. It was then the bishop launched a personal attack on Brother Garb and said that the only reason he defended Pelagius was personal pride because Pelagius came from this island. In return Brother Garb said something that I think the bishop took seriously.'

'Which was?' Fidelma pressed.

'Garb said, and said very clearly and forcibly, that as there was nothing to stop him doing evil, it being preordained by Augustine's theory of Original Sin, then it might be preordained for him to conclude the discussion by cutting the bishop's throat.'

There was a few moments' silence as Eadulf exchanged a glance with Fidelma.

'Brother Garb said these words and they were taken seriously?' asked Fidelma.

'Well, that was when Brother Étaid stepped in, for he has a

more humorous way of expressing things. He made a joke that the bishop should not be too alarmed at such threats as he could have a word with God and get Him to change the course of predestination. What was the line he quoted? Because Augustine had argued, "*dabit Deus his quoque finem* . . . God will grant an end to these troubles." So that meant preordained events could be altered. There was much ribald laughter among the students.'

'Did the Venerable Breas disapprove of this?'

'He said it was one means of considering things. That was when the bishop lost it and denounced the Venerable Breas for perpetuating Pelagius' heresy, in expressing beliefs of the Druidic religion.'

'The Venerable Breas taught that point of view?'

'Not as such.'

'So the Venerable Breas disagreed with the Councils of Diospolis and Carthage, which declared Pelagius' teachings heretical, although the bishop upheld the councils' decisions? Did none of the students ever agree with him?'

'None. None accepted that they had no free will. I am afraid there was anger among us because of the paucity of the bishop's arguments and the arrogance in which he tried to thrust them upon us. Brother Garb and Brother Étaid reflected all the young students' views. Often we would sit up all night in the dormitories discussing these matters.'

'From what you say, and from what I have already heard, it was Brother Garb who caused the bishop the most anger? Did Brother Garb display anger as well?'

Sister Fastrude thought for a moment and then nodded her head slowly. 'He was angry when Bishop Brodulf kept referring to all those Eastern councils and their decisions, and asked whether Brother Garb had no respect for the founders of the Faith. Brother Garb turned and shouted angrily, asking him whether he thought the religion of Christ was nothing more than small bands of old men, calling themselves bishops, inventing rules confirmed by a show of hands at these councils. He asked why should he, Garb, care when these groups of old men kept changing their minds from council to council? I think that shocked even the Venerable Breas. When one gets so frustrated, some can have a momentary departure from being calm and collected. That is what happened to Brother Garb. I assure you after the class Brother Garb was back totally at ease with himself.'

Eadulf sighed. 'As Horace said, "*Ira furor brevis est* . . . anger is a brief madness".'

'Are you sure Brother Garb regained his composure after such an outburst?' Fidelma queried. 'He did make a threat on the bishop's life, as you say, whether he was joking or not.'

'Brother Garb became very reflective after that discussion.'

'When was that discussion held?'

'Why, it was . . .' Sister Fastrude suddenly paused and looked nervous. It took a few moments before she said she could not recall.

Fidelma's eyes had narrowed to gimlets, seeming to pierce the woman's mind. 'You said that you knew about the role of a *dálaigh*? You know that you must answer.' Her voice was icy.

It took some time before the woman said: 'It might have been two evenings ago.'

'You mean the day before Bishop Brodulf was found dead?'

There was no need to wait for an answer. The confirmation was on Sister Fastrude's features.

It was Eadulf who broke the silence.

'I believe the classes are over for I see some of the students crossing the courtyard now.'

A moment later and several young men and women burst through the door, chattering and laughing. The moment they saw Fidelma and Eadulf, the sound of their exuberance ceased. One of them, a young male scholar, called out a greeting to Sister Fastrude. She rose slowly and then gestured to Fidelma and Eadulf.

'The lady Fidelma is waiting here to talk with Brother Garb
– where is he?'

The young man who had greeted her answered with a smile.
'We were going to ask you the same question. He did not attend
the Venerable Breas' class this morning. He will be in trouble if
he does not provide a good explanation.'

CHAPTER TEN

'When was Brother Garb last seen?' Fidelma asked the young man who had reported that Garb had not attended his class.

'I saw him making his bed in the dormitory early this morning,' the young man replied, paused and added unnecessarily, 'the brothers sleep in a single dormitory. Males are responsible for keeping their dormitories in order just as the females are.'

'I saw him at the first prayers later,' chimed in another of the youths.

'He was at the *longud,* the first meal of the day,' added one of the girls.

'So has anyone seen him since?' Fidelma asked.

There was some shaking of heads and then another girl said: 'I saw him later but it was shortly after I came out of the refectory. I was coming back here to collect my *ceraculum* and stylus ready for this morning's class.'

A *ceraculum* was a tablet of wood with slightly raised edges containing a surface covered in wax, *cera,* which was written on with a metal stylus. Notes would be made on the wax and afterwards the wax could be rubbed and warmed to be made smooth so that it could be written on again. It was a method used not only by students but by most scholars and copyists before they committed their works to a more permanent form on vellum or parchment.

'So you saw him then? Where was this?' queried Fidelma.

'I was crossing the courtyard to here.'

'Where was he going? Did it look as if he were preparing to go to classes?'

'Not exactly. He was talking to Prioress Suanach. Sister Ingund saw him as well, for she joined me.' The speaker turned to a younger, very attractive girl, as if for confirmation.

Sister Ingund, whose name Fidelma recognised as one of the Burgundian students, seemed reluctant to join in but made a quick affirmative motion of her head.

'Did anyone else see him after that?' Fidelma asked.

There was some shuffling and shaking of heads.

'Thank you,' Fidelma said. 'I am sure we shall soon find him.' She hesitated, and then asked the reluctant young girl: 'So you are Sister Ingund?'

The girl again affirmed with a movement of her head.

Fidelma turned to the first girl who had said she had seen Brother Garb talking with the prioress.

'I presume you are Sister Haldetrude?'

'I am.'

She was a tall, fair-headed girl with piercing, almost violently blue eyes and no more than twenty years of age.

At her side, Ingund was her antithesis: a short, dark and slightly plump young girl, scarcely out of her teens, whose chubby appearance seemed full of vigour. There was something really beautiful about her, Fidelma thought. Something about the crinkling of the corner of her eyes when she smiled, which was not often.

'And I am Ingund,' she confirmed reluctantly.

Fidelma had heard an exacting pronunciation in both girls' voices. It was the same type of accent that was prevalent in Sister Fastrude's voice.

'If it is easier, we can speak in Latin,' Fidelma opened, switching to the language that was universally used, along with Greek, as the language of the Faith.

To her surprise both girls declined.

'We aspire to make ourselves fluent in your language,' replied the elder of the girls, Sister Haldetrude. 'What do you want from us?'

Fidelma realised that if they were students at the abbey, rather than visitors, such as Landric and Charibert, it would be obvious that they would have more than competency in the language.

'Do not look so worried,' Fidelma reassured them. 'Let us have a few words about Bishop Brodulf. I would like your opinions about him.'

'Our opinions about the bishop?' Sister Ingund's eyes widened a little in surprise.

The young man who had first spoken abruptly moved forward. He was of unusual build for a religious scholar: tall and muscular.

'Why do you seek Brother Garb?' he asked, slightly belligerently. 'What do you want with these girls? I am Garb's best friend and his *anam chara*.'

An *anam chara* was a close friend who acted as someone with whom one could discuss all manner of personal problems; an adviser, a companion or even someone who could offer guidance in spiritual matters. Fidelma knew there was a movement from Rome to change this into the official role of a priest, to whom one should confess sins in public and who would then dispense penance and absolution.

Fidelma gave an irritable frown. 'Who are you?'

'I am Étaid, son of Tadgán of Dún Formna of Inis Thiar,' he replied formally.

'Étaid of the ridge islands.' Fidelma was amused by the young man's conceited introduction of himself. 'Brother Étáid would have been sufficient,' she replied softly. 'So you are the soul friend of Brother Garb? I presume you are a student as well? You have the physique of a warrior.'

'I like to keep myself healthy,' the young man answered, not sure whether to accept the observation as a compliment. 'It is not prohibited to take part in *coraidecht* here . . .'

'Wrestling tournaments?' Fidelma was a little surprised. Many ecclesiastical colleges frowned on such physical endeavours. In several places she found they were not approved of, and the death of a famous wrestler by his opponent was often quoted as a reason. However, she was herself an exponent of *troid sciathagid*, an unarmed form of self-defence adopted by missionaries when going to spread the Faith in strange lands.

'I like to indulge in sports,' Brother Étaid admitted.

'And you say you are Brother Garb's friend?'

'Brother Garb and I are the senior scholars here. We have both achieved our degrees of *Freisneidhed* and thus we are allowed to raise questions with all our superiors.'

Fidelma knew well that the youth meant the students had completed four years' instruction and were allowed to debate questions or stand ready to be cross-examined by seniors and their professor to make sure they understood all the obscurities and difficulties.

'If you see your friend before I do, you may tell him that I wish to speak with him.'

Realising the rest of the students, including Brother Étaid, were making no effort to leave, Fidelma turned to the girls and said: 'We shall have a walk. I see seats by the fountain a little way away.' Followed by Eadulf, she ushered them back into the court-yard. Thankfully, the day was pleasant and warm, and they were able to find a bench and table by a small fountain a little way above the students' dormitories where they were sheltered from the noise of the building work.

'Now I understand that you are both from Burgundia?' Fidelma began. 'Sister Fastrude has been telling me that none of you students knew Bishop Brodulf of Luxovium before you arrived here.'

'That is so,' replied Sister Haldetrude, who seemed the more open to talking, 'although his name was well known. He was cousin of our king.'

'I also understood that neither of you knew Sister Fastrude before you met her in the township named Nazarius at the mouth of the Liger on your journey here?'

Sister Haldetrude immediately answered. 'Sister Ingund and I are cousins. Yes, we travelled together to the mouth of the Liger and were waiting for a ship to bring us to this country. It was there we met with Sister Fastrude, whom we actually knew of through our families. Our parents were acquainted by business.'

'So where in Burgundia do you come from?'

'From Bituriga. Our parents were merchants in the town and they sent us to the community established by the Blessed Ursinus. Our mothers were sisters and were close. Our fathers were jointly involved in their merchant business. We were more like sisters of the flesh than cousins. It was from our parents we heard that Fastrude was making the journey to this land because they knew Fastrude's father who was also a merchant.'

'And you had entered the same abbey in Bituriga?'

'We went to an abbey, a double house, founded by Fara, the daughter of a prince at a place called Evoriacum, not far north of our town. It was there we heard story of the great missionaries who came from the West, who maintained the original traditions of the Faith and did not accept the changes being made by Rome and Constantinople. It was fascinating to hear of different ideas from those from the East. When we heard that Sister Fastrude was setting out to come to this land to learn why this was so, we decided to join her. We arranged to meet at Nazarius.'

'So when Bishop Brodulf, with his deacon and servant, arrived here, you neither knew him nor his steward nor his servant? I just want to clarify that.'

'We did not,' Sister Haldetrude said firmly. 'As I said, we knew of him because we had heard that he was Bishop of Luxovium, appointed so by his cousin King Clotaire.'

'Did you like your fellow countryman?' Eadulf asked, picking up a curious distaste in Haldetrude's voice.

'Because someone is from the same country does not mean you are bonded with them. Our family were merchants, trading their wares along the great rivers. We would not have encountered the sort of nobility that Bishop Brodulf claimed was his.'

'Yet you lived not so far from Luxovium,' Eadulf mused, recalling the time he had spent travelling to Autun. 'Even a slow horse puts you hardly less than one or two days from it.'

Sister Haldetrude sniffed. 'And we were scarcely more than a day's ride from Nevirnum but we had never met with Sister Fastrude. A distance measured in metres is not the same as a distance measured in social rank. Bishop Brodulf made clear what he considered his social rank was, and its distance between him and us.'

'I was not questioning your statement, but we need to place everything correctly. It is a habit of mine.' Fidelma was not apologetic. 'I suspect I know the answer to this, but just for clarity's sake, tell us why you had no liking for Bishop Brodulf.'

'When you speak to most of the students who attended the discussions, then you will doubtless know that we could not tolerate him,' Sister Haldetrude replied.

'Not tolerate? That's a strong expression,' Eadulf commented.

It was Sister Ingund who answered. She had been silent for some time, allowing Sister Haldetrude to do all the answering. 'He was not a man to be liked, and being a bishop did not disguise the fact that he was an arrogant man.'

Fidelma was not slow in picking up the implication.

'It is true that he had no respect for woman,' Sister Haldetrude agreed immediately, guessing the question that hovered on Fidelma's lips. 'He even objected to our involvement in the classes with the male students.'

'Did he take advantage of his rank with women?' Fidelma aimed the question at Sister Ingund.

'Not just the bishop, but Deacon Landric also tried to, but without success,' she replied quietly.

'Was this reported?'

'To the prioress,' she confirmed. 'After this, the deacon did keep himself to himself.'

'What of Bishop Brodulf?'

'He said he followed the concepts of the esoteric religious who followed the desert hermits of the East, who believe men should avoid women.'

Fidelma smiled thinly. 'So he was one who believed God created man in His own image and therefore women must defer to men?'

'Exactly so,' Sister Haldetrude rejoined. 'He even claimed it was a basic tenet of the Faith that women should not be allowed to study.'

'That is contrary to all we know,' Eadulf declared, glancing at Fidelma.

'But he quoted the scriptures,' declared Sister Haldetrude. 'He said that it was written by Paul of Tarsus that if women wanted to learn anything then we must ask our husbands in the confines of the home for it was shameful for women to even speak in the church.'

Fidelma sighed deeply. 'I have read the same in the letters of this man, Paul. Sadly, he was a man of his culture although his epistles to the early followers of the Faith are full of the beliefs of the cultures of the East. I know he writes to one follower, Timothy, that women must learn in silence and be subjected to men.'

'It is hard to accept this, lady, as we learn of the Faith in these islands,' Sister Ingund said.

'Indeed,' chimed in Sister Haldetrude. 'We heard the bishop claimed Paul writes that women were created for men and not men for women and therefore we must obey men in all things. He said it says so in the sacred scriptures.' She paused and then quoted solemnly, '"Let women keep silent in the church for it is not permitted for them to speak but they are commended to be under the obedience of men according to the law."'

Fidelma sighed for she had heard the quotation before. 'It is sometimes hard to believe that this cultural prejudice, which is found in the East, has been put forward as an essential teaching of the Faith. We are told we must not dare to challenge it.'

'Bishop Brodulf argued that Pope Gregory was infallible when, less than a hundred years ago, he declared that Mary of Magdala was a prostitute. Before that she was not described as anything other than an apostle of Christ. Now we are told to accept Gregory without question,' declared Sister Haldetrude.

'Yet, Brother Garb told me that he found an ancient text in the library called the *Gospel of Philippos of Bethsaida*, of the Twelve Apostles, which states that this same woman was Christ's constant friend and consort.'

There was a silence while Fidelma and Eadulf digested this.

'We will make enquiries about this text at the library because it is not included in the accepted canon or scripture. However, it is true that some of these new decisions are puzzling in their contradictions,' Fidelma agreed. A thought came to her. 'In what language were the debates conducted when the bishop attended?'

'Greek or Latin were the common languages of learning between the students,' Sister Haldetrude replied.

'The point I was considering was that something in one language does not mean the same in another. We can never be certain of the correctness of a translation. I just wonder what role misinterpretation played.'

'The scholars here pride themselves on the diversity of languages relating to the Faith,' Sister Haldetrude pointed out. 'On the matter of the condemnation of women, we learn no such constraints are placed on women otherwise we would probably not be part of this Faith at all. This is thanks to the freedom of your laws and education. Yet men like Bishop Brodulf would condemn them because they will not support the decisions of the councils who are determined to relegate the position of women.'

Fidelma was impressed at the young woman's knowledge and thinking.

'It is true,' she reflected. 'I attended such an abbey at Cill Dara, the church of the oaks, which was founded by the Blessed Brigit, for both men and women. Women like Ethne and my namesake, Fidelma, were daughters of the High King Loeguire, and were probably among the first converts to the Faith in the north. What would have happened if the noble Abbess Ité had not taught Brendan and others? These women, who have been called Blessed in the early days of the New Faith, are almost uncountable.' Fidelma gave a rueful smile.

It was the quieter Sister Ingund who seemed the more interested in what she had to say.

'The bishop was harsh in his dislike of women and claimed that they were responsible for all the sins of the world. He told us that scripture taught us this was so. He said that any liaison between men and women was sinful. Can it be so sinful?'

'Are you being specific?'

The girl blushed. 'Many men and women come to this *conhospitae* and meet while working here for the first time. They fall in love. Can that be so sinful, as the bishop said, or should one simply forbid such human emotions as love to even exist? That would be to deny a part of our being, and surely God made us so. Therefore, aren't we denying God?'

'A philosopher once pointed out *amor non potest imperari* – love cannot be commanded,' Fidelma responded.

'So the Bishop was wrong to deny that we . . . that those in a *conhospitae*, should not fall in love?' pressed the young girl. 'That even includes a prioress when she pretends to be above such things to students, but is just as human as the rest of us. Therefore, what the bishop was denying is what is normal?'

'It is the way he probably sees his world, for we each see our world in our own perspective, with our own interpretations,' Fidelma replied thoughtfully. 'The secret of living a good life is not to impose our perspective or prejudice as a set of rules that others should obey without question. The same philosopher wrote – *primum non nocere* – first, do no harm. He meant that you live your life without intentionally doing harm to anyone. He added "intentionally" because the best intentions can cause harm.'

Fidelma noticed that Sister Haldetrude was growing a little impatient at her young friend's questions.

'I would have said the matter is clear and we should turn to the law of this country and obey that law rather than the ancient Roman law. Would you not agree as a famous lawyer, lady?'

'Certainly, our Five Kingdoms were never part of the old Roman Empire, which absorbed the Faith and caused its members to accept much of Roman law as part of being Christian.'

'There you are.' Sister Hildetrude turned to her companion in triumph. 'Here we obey the law of this land.'

'In as far as it is accepted by the Faith that has been adopted,' Eadulf added with a frown, slightly worried about the accuracy of the interpretation.

'These youngsters have the right way of interpretation,' Fidelma assured him. 'Under our laws, women have freedom of choice and are heirs to land and property, and even office in their own right. They do not have the constraints that women have in the world where this Faith originated. Perhaps before Christianity was made the official religion of the Roman Empire, the Faith was meant to overturn these silly restrictions on them. Alas, the Roman Empire simply took it over and Christians were made to accept Roman Law as necessary to being accepted as citizens of the empire.'

The two girls were regarding Fidelma in amazement.

'You have given us much knowledge by answering our questions, lady.'

'And it is I who should be questioning you,' Fidelma replied in amusement. She then became serious again. 'I presume that you thought little of Bishop Brodulf's contentions about Faith with the Venerable Breas? So you agreed with Brother Garb, who would often instigate a challenge to the bishop?'

'We supported Brother Garb instinctively although we know we should not have done so,' Sister Haldetrude said firmly. 'We were there to learn and make our own judgements, not to take sides. The Venerable Breas was tolerant and allowed everyone to have their say. For this, Bishop Brodulf often lost his temper with him. I think it was by the tolerance of the Venerable Breas that we learnt more about what we should aspire to in the Faith.'

It was Sister Ingund who added, in a low voice, 'It does not mean to say that we were not sorry to hear of the accident in which the bishop was killed in the fire. A death by accident is always a sad death, even when the person is not likeable.'

Eadulf was frowning until he suddenly understood that the two girls had probably not realised the word by which the abbot had announced the death of the bishop, *duinethaide*, meant a murder.

'There is truth in what you say,' Fidelma said, ignoring Eadulf's meaningful glance. 'Tell me, accepting the bishop was so much disliked, and with reason, do you think there would be any justification in killing him? Would the disagreements that you heard lead dislike to turn into hatred?'

'You mean would we disagree so much with his views that we would have liked to have seen him dead?' Sister Haldetrude asked.

'That is one way of looking at the question,' Fidelma responded gently. 'I suppose that is the ultimate sanction against his views. If it was not his arrogance or attitude to the Faith, is there anything else that Bishop Brodulf said or did to merit such anger as to have him killed?'

'Many would have liked to have seen him humiliated,' Sister Haldetrude replied. 'That is not to say humiliation would have been taken so far as to kill him.'

'But that thought of seeing him humiliated would be one that you and Sister Ingund would share?'

The dark, chubby-faced student compressed her lips thoughtfully for a moment.

'It would,' she affirmed. 'I would like to have seen such an arrogant misogynist dishonoured and degraded by the recognition of his own prejudice . . . but death would be a waste if one dies without coming to terms with one's own prejudice. That way, nothing is ever learnt.'

'You have a wise head on your shoulders,' Fidelma approved.

'His dislike of women was very deep,' Sister Haldetrude added. 'There is one book that is being compiled here that really upset Bishop Brodulf when he found it. I wonder if that is of relevance?'

'What book might that have been?'

'Apparently, a scribe started a history about the time that this abbey was founded. It is called it *An Banshenchus*, *The History of Women*, and it listed many famous women. It was not just the history of Irish women but to it were added some Greek and Hebrew names of famous women. This history, as I understand, has been added to over the years. I know that Brother Mac Raith, the steward of the abbey, had to resort to striking the bishop over an argument about this book.'

Fidelma was shocked and her surprise was mirrored by Eadulf.

'You are not confusing it with an argument the bishop had with the librarian, the Venerable Lugán?' he asked.

'No, with the steward,' Sister Haldetrude said firmly.

'The steward actually struck the bishop?' Fidelma finally asked.

'But the bishop was a guest in this abbey. The laws on treating a guest under hospitality are strict.'

This was something beyond the laws of hospitality, even if the guest was a dislikeable and discourteous one. Why hadn't this matter been mentioned before? The librarian had admitted to an argument, but for the steward to strike a foreign bishop was unthinkable.

'The argument was witnessed by Brother Garb,' Sister Haldetrude pointed out. 'I don't think it was reported to anyone. Bishop Brodulf certainly did not complain to the abbot or we would have heard something.'

Sister Ingund glanced nervously at her companion. 'If we told you what Brother Garb told us, would he get into trouble?'

'We should hear the story from Brother Mac Raith, or be told by Brother Garb what he witnessed. However, we will treat the matter in confidence unless it has some direct bearing on the death that we are investigating,' Fidelma assured her. 'If the matter was some fight between Bishop Brodulf and Brother Mac Raith, then there is no need for Brother Garb to be named unless a complaint was made and he witnessed this. So what led to the striking of the bishop?'

'The bishop was in the *scriptorium* looking through some books. He was often in the library searching,' Sister Ingund begun.

'He was often there? Do you know what he was searching for?' Eadulf interrupted.

'Maybe the Venerable Lugán would know that. Anyway, when the bishop came upon this *History of Women* and started to read the opening lines, he erupted in an evil temper. It spoke of things that were the reverse of what Bishop Brodulf had argued before us. It spoke of Eve as 'generous and wise' and being 'full of vivid merit without meanness'. At that he became very angry. So angry that the steward, Brother Mac Raith, came to see why the bishop had turned apoplectic. The bishop would not control his temper.

He began to tear at the vellum of the book, to try to destroy it. It seemed the bishop had no control. He was screaming that the book was sacrilegious for describing the wife of Adam as benign, generous and wise, when she had condemned men into a world of sin for disobeying God.'

'So what happened?' Fidelma encouraged after the girl paused.

'Brother Garb, who was behind a stand of book satchels hanging from hooks in a corner, saw the bishop take his knife from its sheath and was about to stab it into the copy of the book he was holding. It was then that Brother Mac Raith struck him across the cheek, causing him to step backwards, dropping the knife and book in surprise. Brother Garb thought it was the shock of the thing rather than the hurt. The steward quickly retrieved the book and the dagger. He told the bishop to go and calm himself, to go and take a swim in one of the streams. Only when he had done so would the knife be returned to him. However, from then on, the book would be safeguarded because it was a heinous crime to destroy books – any book being the vehicle of knowledge.'

Fidelma and Eadulf were unable to hide their expressions of astonishment.

'That a senior member of an abbey could strike a bishop in the face, even if the bishop was out of control, is considered a serious assault; even more so when the bishop was protected under the laws of hospitality.'

'Brother Garb told us that the bishop just stood there with his hand to his cheek, staring at the steward, not moving for a moment. Brother Garb thought he was preparing himself to leap upon the steward but he appeared to be controlling himself. Then he said something in Latin . . .'

'Did Brother Garb know what was said?'

'He said it sounded like – "*Mea est ultio et ego retribuam*" . . . I think it was some quotation but neither he nor we knew where it came from.'

'I do,' Fidelma's voice was heavy. 'It is from scripture, Deuteronomy. "Revenge is mine. I will repay".'

'And then?' Eadulf prompted.

'The bishop turned and walked out. The steward stood for a moment and then collected some things, together with the book the bishop had nearly destroyed, and left the *scriptorium*.'

'When did this confrontation happen?'

'Three days ago,' Sister Hildetrude answered.

'Something happened the next morning during the discussion with the Venerable Breas,' Sister Hildetrude said reflectively. 'It was Brother Garb who said it arose from a question by the bishop, which was obviously provoked by the incident in the *scriptorium*.'

'Explain,' encouraged Fidelma.

'Bishop Brodulf suddenly asked the Venerable Breas whether the students paid much attention to the lives of those who first brought the Faith into this country. He then asked if the students had read the recent text *Vita sancti Patricii*, a life of the Blessed Patrick. The Venerable Breas replied the library was open to all students. At first it was thought that the bishop meant a text that had been written by Muirchú maccu Machtheni in the Abbey of Slébhte. However, the Bishop said he was referring to an earlier life written by Benen mac Sesenen, who was called, in Latin, Benignus, a contemporary of Patrick.'

'I have heard of Benignus,' Eadulf remarked. 'My understanding is that the scholars of this kingdom do not agree with those in the north as to who first brought the Faith to this country.'

'The bishop found that out during the subsequent exchanges,' Sister Ingund said cynically.

'I am not sure that I understand the point you are making here,' Fidelma said.

'Apparently it was from the text written by this Benignus that it is told how Patrick began to stamp out the old beliefs and their teachings. It is said that Patrick destroyed, by burning, one hundred and eighty books of the Druids. He then explained why he was raising this point.'

'Which was?' Eadulf was puzzled.

'That it was right to destroy the religion of the pagans whenever and wherever it was found. Patrick destroyed these books and it was our duty to continue to destroy the pagan and heretical books whenever they were found,' explained Sister Ingund.

'In other words,' Sister Hildetrude added, 'he was seeking justification for his attempt to destroy the *History of Women* in the library here.'

'Did he find any sympathy with that argument?' Fidelma asked.

'He did not. The Venerable Breas compared the burning of books with the obliteration of memory, the destruction of intellect and death of human spirit. At that the bishop was angry again and said that this was a sin before Christ, for Christ himself agreed with such destruction.'

'Did the bishop cite an authority for such a statement?' Fidelma asked, mildly surprised at the assertion.

'He quoted from scripture; from the Acts of the Apostles, that when Paul of Tarsus went to Ephesus, the local people became so afraid of the Christians that they were encouraged to bring forth all their pagan books and burn them. It is recorded that they were destroying books worth fifty thousand pieces of silver. Paul is quoted as having written thereafter, "so mightily grew the Word of God and prevailed". So by destroying books, the Faith prevailed.'

Fidelma shook her head sadly. 'His fanaticism would leave no area for progress,' she muttered.

'I think that fact was made clear to him. It was Brother Garb who commented – first one consigns books to immolation, and then the next step such fanaticism would engender would be to consign human beings to the same fate to stop them reinventing or rewriting such texts,' Sister Haldetrude said softly.

'What happened then?' Fidelma pressed.

'That was the last debate we had,' Sister Ingund confirmed. 'That was the day before yesterday when the guest house had burnt and the bishop perished.'

They fell silent for a short time. Then Fidelma sighed. 'Maybe there is an irony there, or the motive of Brodulf's killing.'

Fidelma rose and thanked the two Burgundian girls for spending their time answering the questions. After the two young students had left them, Fidelma and Eadulf sat for some time in thought. It was Eadulf who finally broke the silence by drawing a long whistling breath.

'It seems that we do not have to look far for motives nor suspects. I would say that it is hard not to meet anyone in this abbey who did not have a reason to hate the bishop. It all comes down to the character of this Burgundian.'

'The bishop does not sound a nice person, that is true,' Fidelma agreed. 'But his not being nice is no justification for killing him. Unless we find out who did this and are able to present the facts to both Abbot Cuán and to Chief Brehon Fíthel, this very kingdom could be in much trouble. There is a matter of recompense. Don't forget that we are told that the bishop is related to King Clotaire of the Franks. We must avoid stirring the enmity of that king.'

'But the Franks are a long way from this island,' pointed out Eadulf.

Fidelma couldn't help remarking on the irony. 'I suppose that was what the Britons might have said about the Romans many centuries ago, or what they said about the Angles and Saxons two centuries ago. How much of the island remains in the hands of the Britons?'

Eadulf flushed. 'But that was different!' Then he realised her amusement as he struggled to find an excuse for his people's invasion and conquest of the land of the Britons.

'I suppose it does depend on how you look at things,' he conceded reluctantly.

'If we can't find Brother Garb, let us find Prioress Suanach,' Fidelma decided. 'She was seen talking with Garb so maybe she would know where he is.'

Before they could move they became aware of a figure approaching. It was Enda. The young warrior came into the court-yard, glancing round. He saw them by the fountain and hurried towards them with a serious expression.

'You look worried,' Eadulf greeted.

'Nothing for us to worry about,' Enda replied with a grimace. 'I've just come from Brother Sígeal. You know, he is the master of the stables. He's the one who is worried.'

'What is he worried about?' Fidelma asked.

'He thinks there was an attempt to steal one of his horses during the night. The animal was in its stall last night and this morning the gatekeeper was awoken by passing warriors who found it deserted on the track by Cnoc Carron.' Enda's bleak features brightened a moment. 'At least it wasn't one of our horses. I made sure of that.'

'So whose horse was it?' Eadulf asked.

'It belonged to Brother Anlón, the physician.'

CHAPTER ELEVEN

A voice was calling Fidelma by name at that moment, distracting her from Enda's news. She looked up and found the Venerable Lugán walking towards them with a hurried gait from the direction of the *scriptorium*.

'I thought you might still be here,' he greeted with a quick acknowledgement of his head towards Eadulf and Enda. 'I have checked on the records.'

'And?' Fidelma prompted when he did not proceed.

The librarian assumed a concerned expression. 'It did not take me long,' he admitted. 'I soon found the page that mentioned Prioress Suanach. It was just an entry recording her return to the abbey in the autumn of last year and her election as prioress by the sisterhood.'

'Only that? No earlier mentions of her time here?'

'Little more. It just said she had returned to the abbey after a decade beyond the seas serving in the Abbey of Latiniacum; that she had arrived back in the autumn, arriving at Árd Mór.'

'So there is nothing there that we did not know?' Fidelma was disappointed. 'Why would Bishop Brodulf be so interested? I would have thought that, as a Bishop of Luxovium, he would have had no need to search in your library for such information about her.'

'If that was his intention – just to find that information,' Eadulf pointed out. 'We don't know for sure what he was really looking for.'

Fidelma sighed. Then she remembered that she had other questions for the librarian.

'I hear that you have a copy of *An Banshenchus*, *The History of Women*, which the bishop took strong exception to the other night. Are you sure it was not that the bishop was looking for?'

The librarian looked surprised. 'How did you hear of it?'

'Is what I have been told, true?'

'Brother Mac Raith reported the incident to the abbot and I was called. The book was handed back to me for safekeeping. It was decided to say nothing about the incident.'

'Are you sure it has remained safe?'

'When it was handed back to me, I ensured it was placed in a secure location where the bishop could not attempt to destroy it again.' The librarian hesitated. 'And you heard how the steward obtained the book after the bishop attempted to destroy it?'

'I did,' replied Fidelma grimly.

'I have to say that the bishop made no formal complaint against Brother Mac Raith. That was why the abbot considered it best to let the matter drop.'

'It can only be dropped if it is discovered that it has no bearing on the bishop's death. I will inform Abbot Cuán that I know of the incident,' Fidelma said.

The Venerable Lugán showed his bad teeth in an attempt to smile. 'It was, in my opinion, the best thing the steward has done – smacking the bishop across the cheek. I don't think I would be alone in applauding that action.'

'If the bishop wasn't looking for this book, to which he took exception, and he was not looking for any details about the prioress, what do you imagine he *was* looking for in the library?' Fidelma asked, changing the subject.

The Venerable Lugán shrugged. 'Among the section of texts he was looking through, there were many records relating to the abbey. And, in tidying the papers, I found that a small number had been removed from the archive.'

'Removed?' Fidelma snapped. 'You did not mention this before.'

'I only noticed them missing while I was looking just now. No other word can come to my mind unless we call the bishop a thief. The missing papers were records. Some were on parchment bound in a ledger and I found they had been cut out of it with a sharp knife. The sort of blade it seemed that one uses for sharpening quills. Those records were intact before I had the argument with the bishop. I would say that the culprit could only have been Bishop Brodulf.'

'What were the missing papers about? Do you know generally, even if you can't be specific, what the bishop was looking for?' Fidelma demanded sharply.

'They were pages listing the names of events at the abbey, names of those who joined the abbey during specific years.'

'Which years?'

'Mainly the final years when Conaing Ua Daint was abbot. It was when your cousin Máenach, son of Fingin, ruled from Cashel.'

'Máenach? He was a cousin that holds no attachment in my heart.' Fidelma made the observation almost to herself. 'But I know what years you mean . . . troubled years for me, some ten years or so ago. Wouldn't that have been about the time when Suanach left here for Latiniacum? Would those pages have contained reference to anything else?'

'Only the list of names of the others that entered the religious life here, and the students, with their ages and the places they came from. Of course, this was also the period of the Yellow Plague so there were many deaths, many who fled to the western islands thinking to avoid the pestilence. So who knows if the records were properly kept? It was not a good time for record keeping.'

A second question suddenly occurred to her.

'I have just been told of a text in your library that is called the Gospel of Philip. I have never heard of it.'

The Venerable Lugán pursed his lips for a moment. 'It is not one of the twenty-seven texts that were finally approved at the Council of Rome when Hieronymus of Stridon was commissioned to translate them into Latin as the New Testament.'

'But it exists? And wasn't Philip one of the original Twelve Apostles?'

'True enough. Of course, the four Gospels that were included as the canon were just named after some of the Apostles, but none was written by them.'

'And this one?'

'The text we have has some sections in Coptic and is four centuries old. We have a later Greek translation attached. Odd that you should mention it, as Brother Garb has been doing some translation work on it from the Greek.'

'I will delay you no more,' Fidelma sighed after some thought. 'Thanks for your help. I now want to have a word with the prioress.'

The Venerable Lugán was just turning away when Fidelma called him back.

'My apologies, I meant to report a matter to you as master of scholars. I have been told that Brother Garb did not attend classes this morning and has not been seen since after the first meal. I do want to speak with him so, if you find him, would you send him in my direction?'

'I'll have a word with the Venerable Breas in case he was told the reason why the young man was absent. The Venerable Breas does not like his students, even senior ones, missing classes without a good reason. Brother Garb is his favourite student. He intends to appoint the boy one of his assistant professors when he qualifies.'

'So we have heard,' Fidelma replied. 'Thank you so much for

checking those records. I will keep this matter strictly between ourselves, especially the incident of smacking the bishop.'

The Venerable Lugán was hesitant and looked anxious. 'I am concerned by the loss of the abbey records. Am I allowed to report this to the abbot immediately? The value of these records could be immeasurable, and if the bishop took them we would have to assume that they perished in the fire.'

'I have no objection. Oh, and do you know where I may find the Prioress Suanach at this time?'

As they walked in the direction that the Venerable Lugán indicated, Fidelma quickly brought Enda up to date on what had been happening.

The young warrior shook his head slowly. 'I am afraid I am not much help in these circumstances,' he admitted. 'A warrior's training and weapons are of little use within the walls of an abbey or any religious foundation.'

It was Eadulf who gave him practical reassurance coated in humour.

'How long have you served in the King's bodyguard, Enda? And more specifically, how long have you served Fidelma and myself?' When Enda hesitated, he went on. 'I'll tell you. Seven years; seven years since you rode with Fidelma to rescue me from the Abbey of Fearna, where I was about to be executed by that fanatic Abbess Fainder. What do you think would have happened to me on that occasion, or on many subsequent occasions that I could cite?'

'What is the point that you are making, friend Eadulf?' frowned the young warrior.

'The point is that you have been an indispensable part of our company over those years, so now is not the time to doubt the part you play in our investigations.'

'Eadulf is right, Enda,' Fidelma agreed encouragingly. 'And remember that we are here to find out someone who has committed a violent crime – the murder of a bishop in circumstances where a warrior's training would seem more essential than us asking mere questions.'

The young warrior seemed a little pleased at this acknowledgement and his features dissolved into a relaxed expression.

'We will have a word with the prioress first and then you can tell us all about the attempt to steal this horse that you mentioned. Meanwhile, I have a task for you while we talk with the prioress.'

'By your command, lady,' Enda smiled.

'You might like to wander among the builders and see what gossip you can pick up. It is more than likely they had encounters with the bishop. Do not make things obvious but often gossip bears berries of truth in it. Also, we are looking for a student named Brother Garb. If you hear anything as to where he is, we just want to talk with him.'

Enda seemed pleased to be given a task to fulfil and left them, arranging to meet them in a short while.

The place to which the Venerable Lugán directed them was one of the wooden buildings of the abbey set apart, beyond the boundary fence, in a clearing among a copse of fruit trees. Here, the librarian had told them, Prioress Suanach would be found at this time of the morning instructing in the art of mixing ink or *dubh*. There was a fire burning outside the hut. It was surrounded by stones built to a height as if it were a well head. Instead of the means of lowering a bucket into its depths there was a metal grill on which a cauldron was sitting. The fire was causing the contents of the cauldron to bubble with a noxious odour. Not far away were piles of thick branches chopped and piled up. Inside the wooden building, behind a closed door, they could hear the penetrating tones of Prioress Suanach raised in instruction to her students.

Sister Fidelma bade Eadulf wait, and approached the door to knock on it.

It was Prioress Suanach herself who opened it.

'Ah, Fidelma, I thought that you might wish to see me,' she greeted without waiting for Fidelma to speak. 'I will join you outside, for the aromas within this hut are not of the best if you are unused to them.'

She closed the door and Fidelma and Eadulf moved away from it, passing the bubbling cauldron to a spot where the strong-smelling odours were not blown in that direction. It was a few moments before the prioress came to join them.

'What is that aroma?' Eadulf could not help asking.

The prioress chuckled. 'I gather that it is not to your liking?'

'I have enjoyed better smells,' Eadulf admitted.

'But without it we would have no civilisation,' Prioress Suanach told them with a smile. 'We are making ink. Perhaps you would like me to explain?'

Eadulf had never thought about it before. His only contact with *dubh* was by placing it in a cow's horn, in which to dip a quill in order to write.

The prioress pointed to the pile of short branches.

'You know something of herbs and plants,' she addressed Eadulf. 'You should have enough forest learning to identify that wood.'

Eadulf shrugged. 'All I know is that the wood is a variety of *scé* . . . thorn bushes. Maybe whitethorn or hawthorn.'

'Exactly. We gather these branches in early spring. In fact, these were gathered just a few weeks ago. They are left to dry. Then we strip the bark from these branches and soak them in water for eight days. They are drained and the water is then boiled until it turns black. It is left until it is a thick liquid. After a while it is boiled again with a little *corma,* or any strong alcohol, mixed. Not too much; just a little. Then it is left to stand and, as soon as cool, it is ready for use.'

Fidelma was impressed. 'And this is what you are doing?'

'The abbey demands quantities of ink for its scribes as well as its students. I have told you only how to get the black ink, which is produced for its intensity and durability. But there are other methods to achieve colours for our calligraphers to produce great illustrated works.'

'Alas, we do not have much time, fascinating as this instruction would be,' Fidelma pointed out shortly.

Prioress Suanach simply pursed her lips for a moment at the implied rebuke.

'I do not forget that you have an important role here. You merely want to discuss the business of Bishop Brodulf. I did not know him when I was in Latiniacum, which is in Neustria and not Burgundia, as everyone here seems to think. Nor, after meeting him here, did I wish to know him. There is not much I can tell you. I have already discussed him with Brother Eadulf, who has doubtless informed you of my opinions.'

'Neustria?'

'It is one of four petty kingdoms that make up the kingdom of the Frankish people.' Prioress Suanach adopted an indulgent manner. 'The once-powerful kingdom of the Franks emerged after the last of the Roman armies in Gaul was destroyed. The Franks were united, but when Clovis, their king, died he left the kingdom to his four sons. They divided the kingdom into Neustria, Austrasia, Burgundia and Aquitania.'

'So there is no central kingship now?' Fidelma asked.

'Sixty years ago, a king called Clotaire, the first of several to bear that name, brought them back into unity, calling himself King of the Franks. However, there are always petty squabbles between the princes of the four areas.'

'All in good time,' Fidelma smiled. 'I was just thinking that, as you have spent so long in the kingdom of the Franks, you must have knowledge of the Frankish people. It is background that I seek. For example, I have heard a curious reference that they are ruled by "people with long hair".'

Prioress Suanach laughed with genuine amusement.

'That is because the ruling family are nicknamed as such. They are the Merovingians, the sons of Merovech. And that name means "long haired".'

'Bishop Brodulf is related to this king of the Franks who is also called Clotaire, whom we met at Autun?'

'Clotaire is the third of his name; a descendant of a son of Merovech. Brodulf was, indeed, his cousin.'

'Do you think that this relationship would cause the bishop to have concerns about his security? You say there are squabbles among the Frankish princes.'

'I think all Merovingian nobles rest uneasy in their beds.'

'Explain.'

'All four kingdoms are supposed to pay the current Clotaire tribute. But the squabbles continue. Austrasia and Aquitania claim independence. The descendants of Merovech's sons are ambitious for themselves and anyone who attempts to better themselves is seen as a threat by them.'

'I can follow family ambitions when there is no law of succession and anyone is free to pick up the crown,' Fidelma commented. 'But I do not see the significance of how Bishop Brodulf would be as fearful unless he was a direct heir and in contention with the current king?'

'The significance is that it is the descendants of Merovech's sons who are arrogant princes and have no compunction to assert their claims in violence, even against their own fathers, to remove them and claim their positions. Many members of the family have been assassinated in this way.'

'Because Bishop Brodulf was related to . . .?'

'By all accounts, Brodulf is a vehement supporter of his cousin, Clotaire. He would not be immune from such actions. If, as you say, he was fearful of his own safety, then perhaps he felt that he was in danger of assassination and went through precautions automatically? There was, indeed, some chatter among the younger ones here about his curious behaviour. His fear of assassination might explain it.'

'Would he really be so fearful of his family ambitions?' Eadulf was not persuaded. 'Fearful, even here in this abbey, miles away from his own country?'

'A lot of people from the Frankish kingdoms have come here to study at the great ecclesiastical colleges,' the prioress confirmed. 'Many are descendants of those assassinated, or are in the same danger. Many have fled here for refuge and many have come with thoughts of vengeance in their hearts.'

Fidelma exchanged a quick glance with Eadulf.

'You are suggesting that this may have been the motif for the murder of Bishop Brodulf? That his death might have nothing to do with the arguments with the Venerable Breas and his students?'

'It might well be,' the prioress agreed. 'There was talk, I remember, among the religious at Luxovium that the bishop was actually a descendant of King Sigebert of Austrasia, with a good claim to be King of the Franks.' .

Fidelma made a gesture of despair with her hands. 'Austrasia? I am confused with these kingdoms. This is one of the four kingdoms . . .?'

The prioress interrupted to reassure her. 'Austrasia means "the eastern kingdom", while Neustria is "the western kingdom". Burgundia is "the land of the highlanders". Then to the south we have a kingdom whose name remains the name of the original Gauls . . . the Aquitani.'

'So accepting that Bishop Brodulf was somehow related to one of the kings of the Frankish kingdoms, you think his behaviour, as described by his servant, about being fearful of going at night to his guest house, has a bearing? That the bishop was fearful of assassination and, moreover, that he feared someone here?'

'The enemies of the Merovingians are widespread,' Suanach confirmed.

'But he would have been more secure if he had not gone to that particular building and insisted on being isolated each night. He should have stayed within the abbey, with his steward and servant at his side.'

'Perhaps he was even afraid of his steward and servant. Members of the family have been assassinated by those they thought were serving them,' Prioress Suanach suggested.

'You are indicating that a war of vengeance exists within his family, which has resulted in the assassination of Bishop Brodulf?'

The prioress shrugged. 'It's as good a reason as any other. A logical one, if you know the history of the Merovingians.'

'I know little of them although I am told that this abbey has two histories of the family in its library,' Fidelma said.

'Ah, yes. I, myself, brought the history of the kingdom written by the Blessed Gregory of Tours as a gift to the abbey when I returned here.'

Eadulf heaved an exasperated sigh. 'So we should discount the theory that the immediate cause of Bishop Brodulf's murder might be anger arising from the arguments that he had with the students of the Venerable Breas?'

'It is not for me to suggest anything,' Prioress Suanach replied.

Fidelma thought for a moment. 'It is too early to discount any possibility. I suppose we must bear in mind that if Bishop Brodulf was of the bloodline of these Merovingians, he did not have to be closely related to the kings. He could have been chosen for assassination simply because he was a member of the family and might be in the way. It could be some act of vengeance. That could have a bearing on matters.'

'It is sometimes hard making the right deductions when one does not know the background,' Prioress Suanach observed wearily.

'You have obviously learnt much of the history and culture of the ruling family of the Franks,' Eadulf commented.

'Of the history, I know only what I have read in the text of Gregory of Tours.'

'But Gregory died nearly a hundred years ago,' Fidelma reflected. 'Do you know recent history? Didn't one of the students, Sister Fastrude, bring a more updated history to the library here?'

'She did. It was a text that extended Gregory's text. I have not examined it closely.'

'But it is available in the *scriptorium*?'

'It should be. The Venerable Lugán should know.'

Eadulf frowned abruptly. 'Did you ever hear of a noble called Wulfoald, who decided to give his former slaves their freedom?'

The prioress thought for a moment and then gave a shake of her head.

'It's not something usually associated with Frankish nobility,' she smiled. 'Did I not say that these Frankish princes were incestuous, killing each other off to attain power and position?'

Eadulf turned to Fidelma with a helpless shrug. 'It's like some disease. A family killing each other for the sake of power. I am glad I was not born into such a nest of vipers.'

Prioress Suanach smiled sympathetically. 'I confess I was happy to return here. We must utter praise that our culture is different,' she declared solemnly. 'If I were not of the Faith, I would give thanks to Ecne, our old goddess of wisdom, that our laws and our system of succession of governance is so different.'

'At least our rulers do not rely on who is best able to assassinate all rivals or survive the blood lust of their relatives,' Fidelma agreed with quiet humour.

'I am sorry there is nothing more positive I can say,' Prioress Suanach said. 'Are you making no progress?'

'I have to admit that this matter, which I thought might be more or less simple, grows darker and more complicated by the hour.'

Eadulf was thoughtful. 'It still might be simple. We are only considering possibilities at the moment. One possibility still might be enmity caused by the arguments that Bishop Brodulf indulged in. Another might be the family background of the bishop. Indeed, as we go on, we might find many more possibilities. Yet this family feud as a reason cannot be discarded. If a prince from a Frankish kingdom was sent for safety to an abbey here for fear that he would be assassinated, and that many years ago, he could have remained here in safety. What if his relatives sought to eliminate him as you said happened to Wulfstan at the Abbey of Darú?'

Fidelma grimaced without humour.

'And what part does Brodulf play in this? Did he come here to protect this prince or come here to assassinate him and was himself assassinated?'

Prioress Suanach suddenly rose with an apologetic motion of her hand.

'You have your work to do,' she announced, 'and I have a mine. Some of these girls are learning these crafts for the first time and so I must keep a careful eye on them.'

Fidelma and Eadulf rose as well.

'We thank you for your time, Prioress Suanach. You have given us much to think about.' Fidelma hesitated. 'Oh, just one thing more. We still want to talk to that young student Brother Garb. So far we have not been able to find him.'

'Brother Garb?' she frowned. 'Is he not in the students' quarters?'

'When we went in search of him, the Venerable Lugán told us he was not there. Then we were told that he did not attend this morning's classes with the Venerable Breas along with the other students. We were told that you saw him after the first meal, the *longud*. Did he mention to you that he would be absent from the scholastic work?'

To their surprise the prioress confirmed that he had.

'He said that he was not feeling well,' she replied without hesitation. 'I thought he was going to the scholars' dormitory to lie down.'

'What sort of malady did he say he had?'

'He said he felt a disorder of the stomach, a feeling of biliousness.'

'So he just went to lie down in the scholars' dormitory?'

'I told him that, before he did so, he first should go to see Brother Anlón.'

'Did he do so?'

'I expect that he would take that advice because he did look in a bad condition. Stomach aches are sometimes not to be taken lightly and Brother Anlón is adept at performing many healing tasks.'

'In that case we will see if Brother Anlón knows where Brother Garb is.'

After they left her, they walked back to the main abbey complex.

'An interesting woman,' Eadulf opened. 'And although we spent that time at the Council of Autun, and even met King Clotaire, I knew nothing of the history and the rapacious family who rules the Franks. Could it really be that this bishop was afraid of assassination?'

Fidelma immediately gave a shake of her head. 'Based on the story the prioress told us, I would say it was unlikely. Unless he was more closely related to an inheritance of title and power, there would be no reason to assassinate him. Nevertheless, he was afraid. We shall bear in mind that he could have been killed in vengeance or hate.'

'And he made himself hated by many here,' Eadulf sighed. 'So do not abandon the theory that his death was due to someone's dislike of his arrogance, his manners or some other reason.'

'That is why we must see this Brother Garb,' Fidelma pointed out. 'He would certainly have cause to hate the bishop.'

chapter twelve

Fidelma and Eadulf did not have to look far for the abbey's physician. Brother Anlón was walking towards them from the sections of the old wooden buildings where the artisans, forges and distillery were sited. After a brief exchange of greeting, Fidelma remembered that Enda had said that it was Brother Anlón's horse that had gone missing from the stables during the night. When she asked the physician about it, the man shook his head and seemed reluctant to entertain the subject.

'It was some mistake. I have just seen Brother Sítae about it and the horse is back in the stables.'

Fidelma and Eadulf were surprised. It was unusual for Enda to have reported something inaccurately. However, Fidelma felt she should get on with the more urgent business and lost no time in asking if the physician had seen Brother Garb.

'He came to me complaining of some disorder of the stomach,' Brother Anlón confirmed. 'It was not long after the first meal.'

'Biliousness?' Eadulf queried.

The physician scowled at him. 'I believe that is what I said,' he replied coldly. 'After Brother Garb described his symptoms to me, I gave him an infusion prepared from *lem* and told him to go to lie down.'

'Infusion of *lem* – that's elm bark?' Eadulf could not help explaining to Fidelma before the physician did. 'This is a good time of year to prepare it. You take the inner bark of the elm, removing the layer that is a bit like cork, and pulp and mix it until it resembles a milk-like quality and then you drink it.'

'It is a demulcent, serving to soothe the stomach,' Brother Anlón interposed, seemingly a little sour at having Eadulf impose on his sphere of knowledge.

'So having taken this medicine you would have expected him to return to his dormitory to lie down?' Fidelma asked.

'Only for a short while, that is if he abided by my instructions and took the medication as I recommended. You are not the first to ask after him so I am sure that he is being well attended to.'

'Who else has been asking after him?' Fidelma was curious.

'One of the little foreign girls,' the physician replied. 'The girl called Sister Ingund. I directed her to the dormitory, as I do you.'

'He did not appear to be in his dormitory when we spoke with the students earlier. Is there anywhere else he might be?'

'If he has not followed my instructions, then I wash my hands of him. These senior students often believe they know more than those who have spent a lifetime in the practice of medicine.'

It was clear they would get no other information from the physician so they allowed him to go on his way. Once he was out of earshot Eadulf said quietly: 'Odd about the horse, but maybe we did not allow Enda time to tell his story properly.'

'We were interrupted by the Venerable Lugán,' Fidelma conceded. 'Anyway, we'd better concentrate on finding Brother Garb.'

'If Brother Garb had taken that infusion, he would certainly need to rest awhile. With stomach pains that need such medication, he would not wander far. Should we go back to the students' dormitories to make sure that he is not there?'

'If it is most likely that Brother Garb has obeyed the physician, we can leave him for a moment. I want another word with the abbot before we do anything else.'

They had reached the foot of the stairs leading up to Abbot Cuán's chamber when they spotted Enda again. He immediately approached them with an expression that told them that he had not been successful in finding out news about Brother Garb.

'Not much gossip, I'm afraid. Seems there are two sorts of builders employed here: the craftsmen and the labourers without skills. I found out that there are a lot of people employed here who are of the *daer-fuidir* class, who are without rights and will work in the most dangerous positions for a *screpall* or two. Most of them are not worth talking to, I'm afraid. They hardly know that they are working in an abbey. They just do what they are told and drink too much ale in the evening.'

'It's not unusual,' Fidelma admitted. 'On building projects like this you often find such men who have lost most of their rights in their clans and this is the only work they can find. This is why injuries and even deaths among the manual labourers are prevalent. Master builders have just a small group of high-paid craftsmen whose honour prices, if they are injured or even killed, are relatively high. Therefore, master builders do not have to pay compensation for the majority when accidents happen, unless, out of the goodness of his heart, a master builder will give a widow something. It is not obligatory.'

'Is it similar to the use of slave labour?' Eadulf queried. He knew that, among the Angles and the Saxons, slaves were used not only by kings and nobles to build their fortifications, but also by abbots and bishops to erect their ecclesiastical buildings.

'Well, the subject is irrelevant in this case,' Fidelma pointed out. 'There is something I wanted to ask you, Enda, when we were interrupted earlier. What was it you were saying about a missing horse?'

'It was Brother Sígeal, the *echaire*, who mentioned it this morning when I awoke,' Enda replied. 'He said that one of his horses had gone missing during the night.'

'And you said it was the physician's horse?' Eadulf said.

'Of all the senior brethren in the abbey, the physician is allowed a good horse,' Enda reminded Eadulf. 'The curious thing is how and why the beast escaped from the stables as well as how it was returned.'

'Curious?'

'That's right. It was secured in the stable last night, but this morning the gatekeeper was aroused about first light by passing warriors who had found it abandoned outside the abbey.'

'So this was why Brother Anlón was not concerned?' Eadulf commented immediately.

'The concern would surely have been, how did it get out in the first place?' Fidelma replied. 'Aren't the stables small and enclosed?'

'Mostly,' Enda agreed. 'They are within the main walls of the abbey, as you have seen. Next to the stables, on the far side from the main gates, is a small paddock where horses are exercised and scrubbed down. There is an alternative gateway here so that the horses don't have to use the main gate.'

'It's not a big stable. Our horses are kept there, aren't they?'

'When I first heard the news, I checked immediately. That's when I was told it was the physician's horse and not one of our horses that was involved.'

Enda knew how fond Fidelma was of her own horse. It was an ancient breed of Gaulish pony, which her brother Colgú had given her when he had become King. She had named it Aonbarr, 'the supreme one', after the mythical horse of the ocean god Manannán Mac Lir, which could gallop across seas as well as land, and travel to the ends of the world without tiring.

'The stables are small, no more than half a dozen horses, including the three that belong to us,' Enda said. 'Each animal is kept secure in its stall. A horse left to its own devices could certainly not leave the stables without human assistance. That is why Brother Sígeal was sure an attempt was made to steal the animal. The one used by the physician is a fine animal.'

'Well, it was probably one of the stable lads who left the stall open or forgot to close a gate,' Fidelma suggested. 'Forgetfulness is part of the human condition.'

However, Enda seemed to be treating the matter seriously.

'I'd be surprised if the stable boys were so remiss in their duties. Brother Sígeal is very precise and the stable boys were both questioned immediately. Sígeal is one of those folk who do not like mysteries and would gnaw at it like a dog with a bone until he obtained a resolution. His training is strict, and both boys denied responsibility for negligence. Besides, they would not only have left the stall unbolted, but the side door of the stable into the paddock open, then the gate on to the highway.'

'You say the animal was found just outside the abbey gates by a passing group of warriors – who were these warriors?'

'A company of Warriors of the Golden Collar on a mission from your brother the King, lady,' Enda replied. 'It was first light and they were passing along the highway that leads past the main gates of the abbey.'

'On a mission from my brother?' Fidelma was interested. 'What were they doing here?'

'According to the gatekeeper, a company of nine were on their way to the community further west. The one on a hill set up by a local religieux called Mocheallóg. They saw the horse loose on the road and realised it was no wild beast. It was bridled and had a *dillat*, a riding blanket, on its back. Their commander stopped, took the horse in hand, and roused the gatekeeper. The gatekeeper recognised the animal as being that used by Brother Anlón and took it in. The warriors could not stop, but passed on. All they could say was the animal was loose outside the abbey.'

'From what you describe, it seems the suspicion of Brother

Sígeal is well founded,' Fidelma observed. 'It sounds as if it were some mischief by the stable lads, otherwise why would this animal have been taken?'

'As it is Brother Anlón's horse, and a good one, we might have another word with him. He didn't seem unduly concerned about it. Even if it was returned, I would have been worried as to who had released it.'

Fidelma turned to the young warrior. 'Enda, go back to the stables and see what else you can find out, if anything. Check with the stable boys in case they are trying to hide something.'

They left Enda trotting off to the stables.

'Had the horse not been returned I would have suggested an obvious connection to our mystery,' Eadulf offered. 'Brother Garb was seen at the early morning prayers and then the *longud*, the first meal. He was seen talking to the prioress and complaining of a stomach disorder, after which he saw Brother Anlón to get an herbal demulcent for it. The horse that went missing belonged to the physician.'

'You are suggesting a link between the horse and Brother Garb?'

Eadulf sniffed defensively. 'I did say, had the horse continued to be missing . . .'

'But it came back. It went missing and was returned before Brother Garb went missing,' Fidelma pointed out. 'He has been seen this morning in the abbey. This is not to say there might not be some connection, but not the one you think.'

'Do you think there might be a connection?'

'When a violent death takes place, and one in a confined abbey, it is an unusual occurrence. Therefore, if a horse goes missing for a while . . . if it just vanishes from a secure stall in a stable during the night but is then found outside the abbey, and there is no explanation . . . it is so unusual that it must be considered.'

Eadulf was thoughtful for a moment. 'So shall we have another word with Brother Anlón?'

'We must first see Abbot Cuán. Then we must see if Brother Garb is now in the students' dormitory.'

They had ascended the flight of stone stairs to the shadowy passage that led to Abbot Cuán's chamber when they almost collided with a familiar small, slightly rotund figure, who gave a curious squeal of protest and then stood back.

'Why, Sister Ingund,' Fidelma recognised her. 'This is opportune. I wanted another word with you.'

'But we have not long finished speaking.' She sounded defensive.

'You neglected to tell me how you found Brother Garb.'

Her frown deepened. 'How I found him?'

'I understand that Brother Anlón directed you to the scholars' dormitory where Brother Garb had gone to rest after taking one of the physician's potions. Why didn't you tell me that you had seen him there?'

The girl's raised her chin pugnaciously. 'Garb was sleeping. He looked exhausted and so I left him. I felt it better that he was not disturbed. I had hoped you would not pursue matters. I shall go back to the dormitory shortly when he wakes.'

'We shall also go to see him shortly,' Fidelma agreed. 'Meanwhile, it is fortunate that we met because I wanted to ask you a question while you are on your own.'

'I don't understand.'

'You made a reference to the prioress being in love and denying it. I did not have a chance to follow up on that in front of your friend, Sister Haldetrude. What do you know about the matter?'

The girl flushed, thought for a moment and then brought up her jaw defiantly again.

'I cannot say that I like the prioress and I know that is a grievous fault.'

'Would you be willing to share your reasons for your dislike and what you mean by her being in love?'

'I am entitled to keep my personal thoughts private.'

Fidelma smiled coaxingly. 'Sometimes even the *arcanum arcanorum*, the secret of secrets, is worth giving away for the sake of the greater good.'

'I don't understand.'

'Let me put it this way. If the prioress has done you a wrong, then it must be accounted for, especially if it leads us to establishing the truth of a greater wrong.'

'I don't know what you mean.' The girl was still defiant.

'I would be interested to know the cause of the argument that you and the prioress had the other day. You were witnessed having an animated argument in the Frankish tongue and the witness believed it was one consumed in emotion.'

The girl flushed. 'It was a personal matter.'

'I am a *dálaigh* pursuing the death of a bishop from your country in this abbey. There is no such thing as a personal matter. I think you realise enough about my position to know that when I ask for information you are bound by law to respond.'

There was a silence while the girl wrestled with the question. Finally she muttered: 'She was accusing me of behaving wrongly.'

'How so?'

'Of having inappropriate emotions about Brother Garb.'

'Inappropriate? In what way?'

'Of the very thing we were talking about.'

'You mean that she realised that you are in love with Brother Garb?'

'I admit it,' the girl replied defiantly after a short hesitation. 'It is not wrong.'

'It is not wrong,' echoed Fidelma in agreement. 'Was she upset because she was in charge of the welfare of the students and thought the affair might be inappropriate in that matter?'

Sister Ingund shook her head. 'I fear it is even worse. I aroused her anger when I said that being in love with Garb was no worse than the prioress being in love with the Venerable Breas.'

'Ah. Is it obvious?' Fidelma sighed.

'Garb told me once that he was sometimes embarrassed at how she behaved in front of the Venerable Breas and him.'

'I suppose this was why you were asking questions about Bishop Brodulf's views on celibacy among the religious?'

Sister Ingund answered with a sniff. 'I would not believe that a man or woman of their age had such passions. But to accuse me of inappropriate emotions . . .'

'This is what your argument was about outside the refectory?'

'That argument was in my language, which the prioress speaks fluently, and I thought no one would understand, otherwise I would not have mentioned it as justification for my relationship with Garb.'

'It was the voice and language of the body more than the meaning of words,' Fidelma explained. 'Words can disguise true meanings where often the movement of a body can betray the true thoughts.'

'All I would say is that her attitude showed she took a dislike to me.'

'One further question; did this matter arise suddenly?'

'Arise suddenly?' she repeated, not understanding.

'Had it been raised before? Was there any hint that this was in the prioress's mind?'

'So far as I was aware, it occurred suddenly. Although now one looks back it was clear that both the Venerable Breas and she were almost worshipping Brother Garb as rising to great influence in the Faith. They would have objected to anything that would have deflected him from his studies.'

Fidelma was thoughtful for a moment.

'Has Brother Garb expressed his thoughts on this?'

The girl raised a shoulder and let it fall. 'I doubt that he knows truly how I feel about him. He sees me only as a friend.'

'Thank you for your honesty, Sister Ingund. I will have to see

Brother Garb soon to ask him about his feelings about the bishop. We must remember that someone killed him out of hate. That might lead on to other relationship matters. But I will try not to say anything about this conversation. It does not seem relevant.'

The girl inclined her head and then, without a further word, turned and hurried off down the corridor.

Eadulf was standing with a surprised look on his features.

'I suppose one should take into account that human behaviour always has its most immediate basis in emotion, even when there is no logic to it. Poor little girl.'

Fidelma did not reply but turned towards the abbot's study, pausing before the heavy door with its yew panels and brass fitments. It was only then it struck her that there was a pattern to the new rebuilding of the abbey. It had originally been constructed in keeping with the materials of the area. Having emerged from the surrounding yew forests, it had been an excellent idea to utilise the local material, hence its name 'borderland of the yew trees'. Now the new abbey was re-emerging in limestone excavated from the nearby hills but still using much of the original yew trees.

Fidelma rapped on the door, which, to her surprise, swung open immediately. The steward, Brother Mac Raith, stood just inside. He took a step backwards, ushering them both in with an unusually cheerful expression.

The abbot sat behind his desk with a concerned frown. His expression brightened as he saw his visitors enter and he rose and waved them to seats.

'Ah, Fidelma – Eadulf, I was going to ask if I could see you to find out how your investigation was progressing.'

'Shall I remain?' the steward asked.

'I would appreciate it,' Fidelma confirmed before the abbot dismissed him. 'There is a matter that I want to clarify.'

The steward took a stand to one side of the chamber.

'And so?' prompted the abbot. 'What news?'

Fidelma was honest. 'There is nothing positive as yet. The fact is, we are only at the early stages. It seems that Bishop Brodulf was such a dislikeable man that, for some reason or another, one could say that most people have cause to dislike him, while it would not be beyond reason to say that some might develop an enmity with him.' She smiled up at the steward at her side. 'I understand that even you were provoked into striking him.'

Brother Mac Raith flushed and shifted his weight uncomfortably. He began to mutter something but Fidelma held up her hand.

'I know. I have heard he was about to destroy one of the valuable books in the library.'

'The details were reported to me,' Abbot Cuán intervened defensively. 'Brother Mac Raith saved that book, even if the action to do so seems extreme.'

'I was a *scriptor* in this abbey for many years, as you know.' The steward apparently wanted to deflect criticism. 'That I, whose life has been devoted to preserving books, should stand by to see such a valuable text destroyed by bigotry? Yet I have done penance in the chapel for striking a bishop.'

'As I have said, I understand the action,' Fidelma repeated. 'Perhaps I might have done the same. But it seems that this bishop's intolerant actions were extreme. That the book was saved was the main thing. But the librarian, the Venerable Lugán, has informed me that other texts were not so lucky.'

Abbot Cuán's mouth compressed into a thin disapproving line.

'I heard that the librarian had cause to have harsh words with Bishop Brodulf. I presumed he was hunting for some book he wanted to destroy? You may have heard that three centuries ago the Patriach of Alexandria, Athanasius, was the first Christian prelate to devise a list of twenty-seven texts that he felt would be acceptable to all members of the Faith. Many texts not on his list were destroyed or burnt at his instigation, especially after he wrote his Festal Letter, naming texts that he said should be ignored. The twenty-seven books were accepted at a council of Rome called by Pope Damascus. By then, this abbey had acquired several such excluded texts, brought mainly from the East, where they have remained in our safekeeping. I am sure that, if the bishop knew of them, he would have sought to destroy them.'

'We keep them in a special artificially constructed souterrain, where they are safe in a chest to which no one, not even our senior scholars, is allowed access to examine them.'

'Why should anyone want these books to be destroyed?'

'Because when the council in Rome did not choose them to be part of the canon, Athanasius ordered that they be burnt. As simple as that. The twenty-seven approved texts were to be translated into Latin and they have been the basis of the Faith for the last three centuries.'

'As it is not among the twenty-seven texts, I gather the Gospel of Philip was one not chosen?'

The abbot looked shocked. 'How do you know of that work?'

'I have heard of it,' Fidelma said lightly.

'God forbid that Bishop Brodulf would have even known it was in our *scriptorium*,' declared the abbot. 'If he did, it were better he was dead.'

CHAPTER THIRTEEN

'That is a harsh judgement,' Fidelma commented in surprise.

'I am no theologian, lady, but then neither was Bishop Brodulf. I simply believe those who burn books are equally as guilty as princes who preside over massacres of entire peoples. As people are the living embodiment of an identity of a culture and history, so are books. From books, knowledge can be transmitted. If they are destroyed we descend into ignorance.'

'I am in sympathy with your concept,' Fidelma replied. 'But I don't think that was the bishop's purpose to come here in search of such books. I do not think, by the sound of his contribution to the debates, that he was possessed of the intellect necessary to assess such ancient texts.'

'Then what was he doing in the *scriptorium*?'

'I expect the librarian will report that to you shortly, but it seems that a ledger has gone missing. It was a ledger written during the time of Abbot Conaing Ua Daint.'

Abbot Cuán's eyes widened. 'That was about fifteen or twenty years ago,' he said.

'Indeed, it was. There is little doubt that Bishop Brodulf took it from the library. The Venerable Lugán presumes that it perished when the guest house was destroyed by the fire.'

The abbot was shaking his head in bewilderment. 'Such a record would be irreplaceable to us, although not valuable to the Faith unless one was writing a history of this abbey and its influence.'

The steward seemed astonished. 'Why have we not been informed of this?'

'I think it was because the librarian has only just realised the fact,' Eadulf observed, speaking for the first time. 'We don't know why the bishop was looking for it, and certainly it would not be for writing a history. This might be a motive behind his murder.'

Abbot Cuán exchanged a bewildered glance with his steward.

'Are you saying that he came to this abbey for an explicit purpose and not just because we are the oldest abbey of this kingdom?'

Fidelma did not hide her impatience. 'I do not feel it was a matter of chance, as Deacon Landric would have us believe. Why should Bishop Brodulf spend much time looking at records in your *scriptorium*? I do not believe it was for proscribed books to destroy.'

'I can only repeat what the bishop told us,' the steward replied. 'He came to debate theological matters with the Venerable Breas, our leading scholar.'

Fidelma glanced at Abbot Cuán. 'To make it absolutely clear, he was definitely not invited to come to this abbey?'

Abbot Cuán looked indignant. 'I certainly did not invite him. I did not even know him.' He glanced at his steward, who also shook his head.

'The first we knew of this Bishop Brodulf was when he arrived at our gates,' Brother Mac Raith confirmed.

'You are suggesting that it was no accident as to why he came to this abbey and that it was something to do with examining the abbey's records?' Abbot Cuán asked suspiciously.

'It is a logical supposition,' Fidelma confirmed. 'But there must be some specific reason why a bishop leaves his territory to travel such distances across the seas to arrive by chance at the gates of an abbey in a foreign land. Coincidences do happen. Even if it is coincidence that he came here, it is more logical to assume that he had some prior knowledge of the abbey. Maybe I will be proved wrong about the ancient texts. Who knows of them? However, it just does not sound plausible that he travelled so far to listen to debates that were at odds with his philosophies. The fact that he was prepared to destroy any texts that he disagreed with could provide an answer.'

'Not many early Christian writings survived after the fourth or fifth centuries. As I say, all texts not in accordance with those approved by Athanasius, and then by Rome, were destroyed. That is why we kept those we had a secret.'

'But you think that Bishop Brodulf was truly attracted to debating with the Venerable Breas?'

'It is the only other logical reason I can see. Breas is certainly known among the scholars. His argument on Paschal dating with Abbot Cummian is even now quoted by many. It is the Venerable Breas who has argued that, for simplicity's sake, we should now follow the calendrical computations worked out by Dionysius Exiguus, dating our years from the birth of Christ. Many have argued saying we must either follow the *Anno Mundi* system, borrowed from the Hebraic teaching, while others claim we should accept the *Anno Urbis Conditae*, dating from the foundation of the city of Rome. We have students come here from many places to debate this.'

'I doubt if that is what prompted the bishop,' Fidelma pointed out. 'Once more I say that I have heard that his intellect was lacking in this field.'

'Anything is possible,' the abbot observed with a shrug, as if trying to dismiss the matter. 'I agree, though, that he was not an intelligent scholar.'

'Remember the prioress lived in his country for ten years,' the steward added. 'She was a student of the Venerable Breas before she went there. Perhaps she encouraged the bishop to come here.'

'Except that she told us that she had never met the bishop until he arrived here. One of the students could have informed him about Breas' reputation. Other than that, I do think the bishop had known that this was the abbey he wanted to come to before he arrived outside your gates.'

'You sound as if it was a very important matter, Fidelma,' the abbot frowned.

'I am simply not content to accept that, out of the blue, a Burgundian bishop travels all this way across inhospitable lands and tempestuous seas to come to an abbey to discuss theological matters that he was vehemently opposed to. I think there is more to this.'

'I still can't see why you dismissed arguments during the debates as a reason for stirring hatred?'

'Let us be logical. He is based in the Abbey of Luxovium. There are still enough abbeys – many *conhospitae* – that exist in those Frankish lands that were founded by our missionaries and are still governed by those of our culture and beliefs. There are many that have not yet accepted the Rules of Benedict, as decreed they must do so by the decision at Autun. There are many in Gaul who have not abandoned the philosophies of Pelagius. So why does this Bishop of Luxovium make this long journey here? If one needed to travel in search of such arguments or discussions, why not go to the nearer kingdoms that border Frankish lands? Why not go to the Abbey of Gildas, where Eadulf and I spent time after being ship-wrecked on the way back from Autun? What was Brodulf's purpose in coming here? I am sure it was not masochism, for he must have heard all the arguments before, even though he could only use dogma to contest logic?'

There was a silence as they considered her almost frustrated questions.

'Put like that, it is a puzzle,' the abbot admitted. 'Could it not be simply that this abbey is famous for being founded by Ailbe, who was one of the first to bring the Faith to these southern lands? Did *that* attract Bishop Brodulf to make the journey here?'

Fidelma gave a small dismissive gesture with one hand. 'With due respect, it seems a weak reason. What would many in the kingdom of the Franks know about Ailbe? Great teachers like Ailbe, Declan, Ciarán, Ibar and others who taught the Faith in this land long before the Briton called Patricius are almost forgotten. There has been much activity in recent years from Árd Magh, not only extolling the virtues of Patricius but campaigning for recognition from Rome as the premier church of the Five Kingdoms. There are now factions that intend to make it appear that Patricius was the only person who brought the Faith to this island. So the great teachers of the south are all ignored.'

'So what are you saying?' Brother Mac Raith asked.

'It is because those in the north kingdom, the Ulaid, are gaining influence with Rome that the name of their teacher resonates now. That is why I find it hard to believe that the Bishop of Luxovium would be inspired to make the voyage here simply because he has heard of the founder of this abbey of Ailbe's or even the reputation of the Venerable Breas.'

There was a long silence.

'I think the lady Fidelma may be correct,' Brother Mac Raith finally admitted in a low voice. 'If Bishop Brodulf's idea were to simply engage in debates, it was certainly not with the purpose of learning anything. If he wanted to know the teachings of Pelagius, then there are copies of his writings still existing in the abbeys as far east as Anatolia and as far south as Africa. In fact, Pelagius is known in all parts of the world. Even at this late time, two centuries after Ephesus made Pelagius a heretic, many eastern communities still claim support for his teachings.'

Fidelma glanced at the steward approvingly. 'Exactly so.'

'So it once more comes down to the question. What purpose do you think the bishop came here to achieve?' Abbot Cuán demanded.

'If I knew that, I would know the key to many things that have disturbed me about this matter. You have supplied me with another motive. If it was known your library held some old heretical texts . . . My next step probably should be to have another word with Deacon Landric.'

'I thought that you had questioned Brother Landric last night?' Brother Mac Raith frowned.

'Last night I was not in possession of any facts other than the bishop had been murdered. Now I know some of his actions and how he was disliked here, I think we should try to elicit some more information about his behaviour.'

'Fidelma, now that you know our *scriptorium* holds certain texts that are not approved of, and condemned, by certain people in Christendom, I must place you under a *géis* not to reveal this in your discussions with Deacon Landric.'

Fidelma thought for a moment. A *géis* was a sacred prohibition.

'I accept the *géis* that I will not refer to this unless the fact is already known.'

'We still have to find and question Brother Garb,' Eadulf reminded her.

This brought a sharp reaction from Abbot Cuán.

'Have you still not found him?' he exclaimed. 'I heard from one of the students that Garb had not attended the first class of the day.'

'We will speak with Brother Garb later. Since we are here, it might be advisable to question Deacon Landric in your presence, Abbot. That way you will be satisfied the *géis* is kept.'

There being no objection, it did not take Brother Mac Raith long to locate Deacon Landric and bring the suspicious Burgundian to the abbot's chamber.

In the intervening period Fidelma had suggested to Abbot Cuán a line of questioning he could take with the deacon on her behalf, as she felt that the abbot's authority would be more likely to elicit

responses than if she were to attempt to extract them. So she and
Eadulf sat to one side of the chamber and allowed the abbot to
motion the man to be seated before him.

'As abbot,' he began almost pompously, 'I have to compile a
report on the tragic death of your bishop and, because of his
princely rank, of which I am now officially informed, I also must
make this report to Colgú, the King of Cashel. He will have to
recount the facts to your king.'

Deacon Landric seemed surprised and he stirred a little uncomfortably in his seat.

'I am sure there is no need for all this protocol.'

'I would be neglecting in my duty if I did not fulfil all the
conventions,' replied the abbot. 'You can confirm that Bishop
Brodulf of Luxovium is of a princely family in your kingdom?'

Deacon Landric hesitated before giving a slight shrug. 'He is
a cousin to our king, Clotaire.'

'Then it is my duty to ensure news of his death is reported to
King Clotaire accurately and with any resolutions about the cause
of it.'

The bishop's steward made a small motion as if in acceptance.

'Now there is only one small matter we must resolve before
any other. That is: the reason he came to this kingdom and, more
specifically, to this abbey.'

'The reason?'

'It is a long journey from Luxovium to here and could be fraught
with many dangers to the traveller.'

'We encountered none.'

'For which the Lord be praised. But I have used a conditional
term. That it was not hindered by dangers was not a foregone
certainty when you set out,' Abbot Cuán pointed out. 'So I ask
again, what was imperative to this journey?'

'Why, perhaps you will recall that the bishop told you when
we arrived. As I subsequently told the Lady Fidelma last night,

the bishop came here to hear the views and discuss matters of theology with the Venerable Breas, he being a leading scholar in your abbey.'

'Are you saying that his reputation spreads into Burgundia?'

'Of course,' the deacon answered confidently.

'When did you first hear of his name and teachings?' the abbot asked.

There was only a slight blink to indicate that the steward had to think. Later Fidelma had to admit that Deacon Landric had a quick mind.

'The then abbot of this place, Abbot Ségdae, came to Autun for the great council. He was attended by both Fidelma and Eadulf so that they will know the circumstances. One presumes that knowledge about the Venerable Breas could easily be spread by him.'

Abbot Cuán glanced quickly at Fidelma.

'So you were told about the Venerable Breas by Abbot Ségdae, even though he was not teaching here at that time?'

Deacon Landric looked puzzled.

'The Venerable Breas had left here to go to another abbey and only returned here very recently.'

Deacon Landric was not put out. 'We are talking of a scholar's reputation and not personal knowledge,' he pointed out. 'All I can say is that the bishop was intrigued by the reputation of the Venerable Breas and doubtless was inspired to have the exchanges.'

'So when he heard the Venerable Breas was instructing the students of this abbey, he made up his mind to come here, having heard of his reputation?'

'That is so,' Deacon Landric agreed.

Eadulf was about to interrupt but Fidelma silenced him with a fierce glance. It seemed neither Abbot Cuán nor Brother Mac Raith had picked up on anything.

'Are you sure there was no other reason for his coming here?' Fidelma smiled innocently.

'What other reason could there be?' Deacon Landric was now confident again.

'I was wondering,' Fidelma replied softly.

She was prepared to let the silence continue, but Brother Mac Raith interjected, not realising the path she was leading to.

'Was the reason to search for something in our archives?' His voice crackled so suddenly that the Burgundian almost jumped.

'I do not know what you mean,' he muttered after a pause.

'Why did the bishop feel that he had to steal some of our records and what has he done with them?'

Brother Mac Raith's outburst was too late to control. Fidelma heaved a sigh of resignation. What was it Caesar had said? '*Alea iacta est* – The dice have been cast!' She had wanted to use this information later. Too late. She just hoped that he avoided mentioning the ancient prohibited texts and referred only to the abbey ledgers.

'Bishop Brodulf was in the library where he was discovered hunting through some records. In fact, in his agitation he was making such a mess of the papers and ledgers that the librarian rebuked him. It has now been discovered that there is a volume of records missing, which only Bishop Brodulf could have taken.'

'I have no idea what you mean,' Deacon Landric declared.

It was clear to Fidelma that the news came as a surprise to him, but he recovered quickly.

'Are you calling the bishop a thief?' He turned with a stern look to the abbot. 'I should caution the lady Fidelma. It is a dangerous path to call a bishop a thief. I would also remind you that he was a guest from a foreign land and was of royal blood.'

'It is only dangerous if the accusation cannot be proved,' observed the abbot quietly.

'Then it is best to prove it immediately,' declared the Deacon, rising from his seat in anger.

'In good time,' the abbot assured him without responding to his emotional outburst. 'Until we do so, I still have to continue to make inquiries. You and Brother Charibert should remain within the boundaries of the abbey until this matter is resolved. We will take cognisance of the fact that you have denied all knowledge of the bishop's actions in this matter. Should you wish to amend any statement you are free to do so.'

Deacon Landric merely scowled and made his exit from the abbot's chamber without another word.

'Be careful, Fidelma,' Abbot Cuán advised her quietly. 'He is clever and I believe he has a ruthless, vengeful streak in him.'

'If one needs to have a care, perhaps it should be the steward.'

Brother Mac Raith was taken aback. 'What have I done that I should have a care of that Burgundian?'

'You are the one who smacked the bishop across the face,' Fidelma pointed out in grim humour. Only Eadulf noticed the quiver at the corner of her mouth.

chapter fourteen

Leaving the abbot and his steward, Fidelma and Eadulf made a fruitless search of the student dormitory for the missing Brother Garb. Enquiries only confirmed that no one had seen him since Sister Ingund had seen him asleep in the dormitory. Finally, they decided to retire to their own guest chamber for a short break in order to discuss matters, but they had barely begun when there was a soft tapping at the door. It was Enda.

'I hope I am not disturbing you,' the young warrior apologised, 'but I thought you would want to know more about the horse that left the stables.'

Fidelma bid him enter and take a seat.

'We were just discussing things to see how far we have progressed in this case, Enda. Did you find out the mystery of what happened to this animal? How did it become loose from its stable?'

'The physician, whose horse it is, seems adamant that it must have been one or other of the stable lads. But both stable lads deny having let it loose. They say they were both undisturbed during the night.'

'Do you think they both, or one of them, lied?'

'I have to say that their denial is not unreasonable,' Enda admitted, 'as I was sleeping nearby and also lay undisturbed. When the horse was found next morning, it had a blanket still on it, a *dillat*, with a single rein bridle.'

Fidelma knew that religious often used a *dillat* or thick woollen blanket as it was easier and cheaper to use than investing in a leather saddle.

'So someone saddled this horse?'

'It was clear to me that someone saddled and put a single rein on the horse and then led it outside by a side gate. I checked the stall where the horse was usually kept and confirmed that the only way the animal could get out was if someone released it. If the person taking the animal was of sufficient dexterity it could be done without disturbing anyone sleeping at the other end of the building. I mentioned that there is a way of taking it out of the stables without going through the main gates and so avoid disturbing the gatekeeper.'

'I remember. You said there is a side gate from the stables through a yard where horses are given a rub down, and from there it could have been led to the main track outside.'

'I asked to see the *dillat* and reins. Thankfully, they had been left in the stable.'

'Why do you say "thankfully"?' Fidelma asked.

'Because when I examined the *dillat*, I saw there were blood stains on it and they were very recent stains.'

Enda allowed a moment for them to consider this before continuing.

'I could find neither wound nor injury at all on the animal.'

'You checked thoroughly?' Eadulf pressed.

The glance the warrior gave Eadulf was enough to indicate such a question to a warrior of his standing and equestrian knowledge was not worth an answer.

'Therefore?' Fidelma prompted.

'While Bother Sígeal, the stable master, was in the middle of berating his stable lads, for he is sure one or other of them had a hand in releasing the beast, I examined the hoofs of the horse so that I knew what impressions it would have made. Then I saddled my own horse and went out through the side gate. Outside I could follow the initial tracks without too much trouble. As you know, lady, I am not without skill as a tracker.'

'So you decided to track where the animal had been taken, if we follow the assumption it was taken anywhere? But there must have been many tracks on that highway, not to mention the tracks of the warriors who discovered the animal outside the abbey,' Fidelma pointed out.

'But I succeeded in tracing most of the route of the animal.' The young warrior was confident. 'It was obvious that someone had taken the animal.'

'So you were able to follow the tracks?' Eadulf prompted.

'They led westward to the front boundary wall of the abbey.'

'Did anyone observe what you were doing?'

'There was no one about except a couple of men who were clearly not of the brethren. They were in the burial ground opposite the abbey, looking at some grave or other.'

'Abbot Cuán gave the master builder permission for his men to dig a grave for tonight,' Fidelma said. 'They were probably checking on the work. Go on.'

'I followed the tracks beyond that western corner of the abbey. The tracks turned northwards up the incline, almost parallel with the western wall, right along the stone-built section and then along the more open wooden wall where the rebuilding work is going on. They went on a hill rise to the yew woods. They seemed to cross a broad track that led out of the woods into the abbey grounds. I lost the tracks here. There were too many tracks on this: horses, oxen, wagons. I realised the track must lead westward into the woods where we were told the builders had their major camp.'

'I remember. It is also where their artisans prepare their materials for the rebuilding of the abbey,' Fidelma said.

'Did you lose the tracks there?' Eadulf asked.

Enda made a negative gesture. 'I did not lose them totally. Even though the northern side was covered in woodland, I crossed the track and eventually found traces of the same animal's hoofprints again.'

'So where did these take you?'

'I found the horse's tracks were also mixed with human footprints. It was quite muddling. I could not find that they led much further on, but turned back down towards the main highway fronting the abbey.'

Fidelma frowned at his hesitation. 'And so?'

'Back on the highway I found the mixed tracks. It was as if the animal had stood in the same spot for a while. A restless animal that is forced to stand still will sometimes stamp its fore hoofs up and down impatiently. This apparently had happened. Yet there was something odd about it.'

'Odd? How so?' Fidelma asked.

'I realised that the imprint of the horse's tracks had sunk deeper into the ground coming down the rise to the highway than going up.'

'The ground there had become softer than before?' Eadulf hazarded.

'No, it was not softer ground. The horse had merely become heavier.'

Fidelma smiled as she guessed what Enda was going to say. 'You mean that it was suddenly carrying a heavier weight on its back?'

'Perhaps whatever it was carrying might have been the cause of the blood produced on the *dillat*? The horse had returned to the main highway heavier than it went. Knowing that the horse had not been injured I returned up the incline briefly to check if I could see any spots of blood on the ground. I could not.'

'When the horse was discovered on that track by the passing warriors, nothing was loaded on its back?'

'Nothing.'

'It is intriguing. Why does someone even go to the risk of breaking into the stables to take a horse, to bring it round to that part of the abbey, load it with something, bring it back to the main track, unload it and apparently just leave it there?' Fidelma was thoughtful for a while.

'I can offer no explanation, lady,' Enda confessed.

'Perhaps armed with this knowledge we should now have another word with Brother Anlón, he being the owner of the horse.

'You did good work, Enda.' Fidelma smiled quickly at the warrior. 'You did not spot anywhere that the horse had been stopped, where the weight became heavier? You halted at that main track between the builders' camp and the track to the abbey building site? Could the tracks not have continued around the back of the abbey and down along the eastern walls? Could the horse have been led to complete the full circle around the abbey, arriving back on the track at the other side?'

'That route was not borne out by the evidence, lady,' Enda pointed out.

'But did you check it?'

'I did not, lady. Should you wish it, I will return immediately and check it.'

'Not at the moment,' she told him. 'I might wish to follow these tracks myself, but later. Meanwhile there are other things to consider. Let us first see if there is any further news about Brother Garb. The boy cannot just have vanished.'

They found the steward discussing matters with two members of the brethren in the main courtyard. He was not happy. Before she could speak, he greeted her.

'I have to confirm that Brother Garb has not been found in the abbey in spite of a wide search. We have looked everywhere at the insistence of the Venerable Lugán, he being in charge of the students.'

Fidelma's lips compressed into a thin line of annoyance. 'Are you sure everywhere has been searched?'

'Everywhere that I can think of,' the steward replied. 'If he is purposely hiding then the need for food will surely make him reappear.'

'I am sure that we cannot just wait for him to reappear,' Fidelma chided dryly.

'The one who is waiting always thinks the time is too long,' muttered the steward piously.

'It is not my intention to wait,' Fidelma snapped. 'You don't catch a wolf by sitting outside its lair and pleading for it to emerge. Sometimes a wolf has to be goaded. We will talk about this later, as I see one of the students wishes to have a word with me.'

She had noticed one of the young students crossing the courtyard and heading directly towards her.

It was Brother Étaid, whom she had met earlier.

'I am come from the Venerable Breas,' the young man greeted. 'He sent me to ask if you could attend him at your convenience, lady. He is in his chamber at this moment now that the classes are over.'

'Then I shall not keep him waiting long,' Fidelma replied solemnly.

Brother Étaid hesitated. 'I was wondering if there is any news of Brother Garb? I am told that he has not been seen since he went to rest in the dormitory.'

'This is true. He told Brother Anlón that he had a stomach ache and received some medication before going to lie down in the students' dormitory.'

The young man grimaced. 'I think it was one of the Burgundian female students who told me that he was supposed to be in the dormitory resting. I did not see him there.'

Fidelma gazed at the youth thoughtfully. 'Does he have any other special friends that he might go to confide in if he thought he was in trouble?'

Brother Étaid's eyes narrowed. 'You mean someone to discuss whether he should take advice over the death of Bishop Brodulf?'

The phraseology of the young man's question immediately interested Fidelma.

'Why do you say that? What advice would he need about the bishop?'

'The bishop is dead. Last night, at the *praind*, the evening meal, the abbot clearly said he had been murdered. I am not slow witted, lady. Brother Garb was always arguing with the bishop. To be honest, so was I. But Brother Garb was often very forceful in his arguments. It is more than likely that some suspicion would be voiced against him. Especially when the bishop responded with such antagonism and threats of revenge.'

Fidelma stared thoughtfully at the student for a moment or two.

'This is the first time I have actually heard that the bishop uttered threats of revenge. Revenge for Brother Garb arguing? Did no one specifically inform the bishop that senior students are expected to argue with their teachers and professors, all the better to obtain knowledge?'

The young student simply shrugged. 'I suppose we all took that for granted. I was merely thinking of the intensity of those arguments and wondered if Brother Garb felt that some might consider it a reason for suspecting that he was involved in perpetrating violence on the bishop.'

'Are you saying that Brother Garb, if he felt this concern, would have no person in the abbey to whom he might have gone to discuss such a matter?'

'Other than myself, I can think of no one.'

'And you consider yourself his friend?'

'Not just a friend, lady, but, as I have told you, I am his *anam chara*. Garb and I have been soul friends since we came to this abbey to study,' Brother Étaid confirmed.

'So did he talk about his concerns with you? That is what a soul friend is for.'

'Only about the way his arguments might be misinterpreted to foreign ears and eyes.'

'But he had said nothing that was censured by the Venerable Breas?'

'He had not. He had said nothing that any sane scholar would take as a personal affront. I do not think the bishop understood that scholastic arguments are to be left behind within the class.'

'So, other than you, there was no one Brother Garb would go to in order to seek advice? What about one of the female students?'

'Ah, you mean Sister Ingund? I think he liked to relax on walks with her but certainly not confide in any intellectual discussion.'

'So you know of no one else?'

'Unless it was the Venerable Breas himself,' the youth replied confidently. 'As far as I saw, and I took part in our scholastic debate, there was no need to seek any advice over the way the arguments were put.'

Fidelma was quiet for a moment and then she shrugged.

'I must not keep the Venerable Breas waiting. Come, Eadulf, let us see what is on his mind.' She turned to Enda and added: 'We will meet you in the refectory as it approaches time for the *etar-shod*, the midday meal.'

They found the Venerable Breas in his chamber almost in the same position as when they had first encountered him. He smiled and gestured for them to be seated on the stools before him.

For a long while the old scholar remained quiet. It seemed that he was intent on moving his weight into a more comfortable position. It was Fidelma who realised this was a gambit to establish dominance and she recognised it because it was an old trick of her own. As a *dálaigh* she also tried to open questions before the other was ready. It seemed the Venerable Breas was adroit at such conversational gambits. He waited awhile, staring at her with a long thoughtful expression.

'I sent one of my students to find you,' he opened.

'Brother Étaid found us,' Fidelma's tone showed a slight irritation. 'Otherwise we would not be here.'

'That lad has a good mind.' The words were spoken reflectively as if the old scholar chose to ignore her tone. 'It is good that he and Garb are such friends and, as you probably know, *anam chara*. Were it not for Brother Garb, then Brother Étaid would have been my leading scholar and the one I might have chosen to become my assistant in this school. But as it is, I am allowed only one position. Brother Garb is one possessed of a fine analytical mind, who should one day become a great scholar of the Faith. I have foretold he will do great things. It is good that the boys do not resent each other or have petty jealousies.'

'Is there some matter that we could help you with?' Fidelma pressed sharply as the Venerable Breas again fell into a thoughtful silence.

A shadow of a smile spread over the lips of the old scholar. 'You will forgive an old man if I sometimes reflect before I speak. Sometimes thoughts are not always obvious and need to be phrased carefully.'

Fidelma and Eadulf both waited. After a moment the Venerable Breas seemed to make up his mind.

'I wanted to say that even the largest of communities is still a community. Things are known even when they are not said. We are like a family inside the abbey, each learning the assets of the others, their weaknesses as well as their strength.'

'I have served in an abbey,' Fidelma asserted, assuring the old scholar that she was not ignorant of life in such a community.

'Indeed,' he sighed. 'The abbey at Cill Dara. It was your relative, who is an old friend of mine, Laisren of Darú, who advised you to join that abbey as legal adviser to the prioress. It was at a time when your brother had no claim to the kingship and the king was your cousin, Máenach, who had scant respect for your brother or for you. Alas, the Prioress Íta at Cill Dara was a frail woman whose frailty you eventually discovered. That was why you left the abbey and eventually left the religious life to concentrate on your legal work. I know you did not enter the abbey for the sake of religion anyway. You entered for the morality of the law. Is that not so?'

Fidelma was taken aback by the old man's summation of that sore point in her life.

'So Laisren told you this?' She did not like her motives to be revealed to strangers and kept certain points of her life even from Eadulf.

The Venerable Breas allowed another shadow of a smile on his thin lips.

'You made a wise decision in leaving the abbey as soon as you started to gain a reputation as a *dálaigh*, although you had the patronage of many religious prelates to secure your path. It is still noteworthy that you remain generally recognised as "Sister" Fidelma, rather than by the noble title of "Fidelma of Cashel".'

Eadulf, who had remained still, now stirred uncomfortably. He was about to speak when the Venerable Breas held up his hand as if to silence him, having noticed his action.

'Do not fret, Eadulf of Saexmund's Ham, in the land of the South Folk, among the East Angles. I say these things only to illustrate that in communities like this, knowledge does not always remain secret.'

'Having made that observation, and knowing it is accepted, it would then seem a contradiction that this community still whispers secrets as the ones you have called us to explain,' Fidelma observed dryly.

Not by any altering of his facial expression did the old scholar react.

'I have called you hither merely to add to your knowledge so that a matter you hear is not distorted in any fashion.'

'Ah,' Fidelma suddenly smiled. So the old man had a human weakness after all when he was trying to present an atmosphere of omnipotence.

'Much meaning in that "ah",' the Venerable Breas observed. 'I shall try not to disappoint you.'

She was thinking rapidly over the conversations she had had that might have brought about this interview with the scholar.

'All I have heard is that your students revere you,' she finally said.

'That is good,' agreed the old man. 'However, it is not the good that intrigues me.'

'We were told last night that the prioress is in the habit of visiting your chamber last thing at night, and usually every night,' Eadulf offered. 'It is such gossip as that which bothers you?'

The old man's reaction was unexpected. He burst out in a chuckle of amusement, which subsided into a cough so that he had to reach for some water.

'You think that fact and such speculations about the relationship between Prioress Suanach and myself would be of concern?' He shook his head with mirthful features.

'It was of no concern of ours unless it was inconsistent with the law,' Fidelma sighed. 'Instead of playing the master and indulging in student games with us, I suggested we get immediately to the point.'

'Ah, Fidelma, the colleges have lost a great professor in you,' the Venerable Breas observed, still amused. 'But very well. As you know, in my classes I have several young girls among the scholars. Young girls sometimes have a reaction to their teachers.'

Fidelma reflected on her own schooling.

'Sometimes admiration of a teacher gets mistranslated into some emotional experience, depending on the maturity of the young girl,' she commented.

'Just so,' the old man agreed. 'I have known teachers take

advantage of it, some willingly and cynically accepting the advantage of their position and some mistaking their own emotions. Shame is their portion.'

'It is inevitable in the human condition,' she conceded, wishing he would get to the point.

'It becomes a problem when there are people about who try to use gossip for their own ends.'

'Very well; are you saying that someone will use the story to make trouble . . . but for whom? For the elderly teacher or for the young girl.'

'In this case, for the old teacher.'

'Are you saying that this is someone wanting to destroy your reputation?'

'Exactly so.'

'So what rumours would damage your reputation?'

The Venerable Breas grimaced sourly. 'Bishop Brodulf was merely an irritant. However, his steward, Deacon Landric, goes beyond the bounds of acceptable behaviour.'

'In what way?' Fidelma asked.

'He makes it known that he suspects that I, or my students, such as Brother Garb, were responsible for Bishop Brodulf's death.'

'There will be speculation until the matter is resolved,' Eadulf pointed out. 'Of course, we could act more resolutely if we could find Brother Garb.'

'Garb is not the only one he cites,' the old man sighed. 'He names another of my students and says I influenced them with sexual favours to take part in the assassination.'

Fidelma compressed her lips for a moment. 'Would that be Sister Ingund?'

The Venerable Breas barely twitched the muscle at the corner of his mouth.

Fidelma went on: 'I believe that the Prioress Suanach was told this story and has remonstrated with Sister Ingund, believing her involvement with Garb to be true. It upset the young girl very much. If the source of this story is Deacon Landric then we will put a stop to it and the prioress can be reassured of the truth. Anyway, I am surprised Prioress Suanach felt she should have words with Sister Ingund.'

'Have you spoken to the prioress on this matter?' the Venerable Breas asked.

'It should not even have been a matter worthy of being raised. As I say, Sister Ingund was upset.'

'Is it possible that Prioress Suanach might believe there is something in Deacon Landric's claims?' Eadulf interposed.

'That I manipulated young Sister Ingund to entice Garb to enact physical violence on the bishop? You think at my age it is possible I could persuade a young girl's emotions? Come, lady, I am flattered but it is not possible.'

'Age might have little to do with it,' Fidelma replied solemnly. 'Age does not exclude a male from the human function.'

For a moment the Venerable Breas stared at her as if trying to gauge her seriousness. The shadow of a smile again formed on his thin lips.

'Lady, since you are direct, I shall be so also. The last time I was able to engage in that function was many years ago. Fifteen years or maybe twenty years ago, if you want precision. It was just before I went to Mungairit as a teacher. I did have a relationship with Suanach and we have found, despite the years apart, we have still that relationship . . . but not a physical one.'

'Very well, I accept your word.'

Eadulf suddenly interrupted with an exclamation: 'Of course! Mint tea and hazelnuts. I should have known before.'

Fidelma regarded him with a puzzled frown.

The Venerable Breas was chuckling again.

'I was wondering how long it would be before you, who have studied the healing arts, realised my malady.'

'What malady?' Fidelma demanded, looking from one to the other, puzzled.

'The condition is called *dibreith*,' Eadulf pointed out.

Fidelma, who guessed it was some medical term, was yet no wiser as she searched Eadulf for elucidation.

'The Venerable Breas is sexually impotent,' Eadulf explained, with an apologetic look at the old scholar.

'Therefore,' the Venerable Breas went on, 'in spite of what Brother Landric, or others, may say, or accuse me of, such intimate claims against me are impossible. I am in a state called *dichumaic* and totally incapable.'

'How did you say that you knew this, Eadulf?' Fidelma asked, turning to him. 'You said you should have known something about mint tea and hazelnuts.'

'Any physician, even the like of Brother Anlón, will treat the lack of having any sexual stimulation by prescribing mint tea and hazelnuts,' Eadulf explained. 'I had noticed when we first came here that the Venerable Breas was indulging in mint tea and hazelnuts.'

The old man grinned. 'I can assure you that the physician has been a failure in trying to restore even the memory of my youthful times. Anyway, having heard such stories being whispered, thanks to Deacon Landric, in view of the circumstances, I thought I should bring this matter to your attention.'

Fidelma regarded the old man for a moment. 'But surely the prioress would have known this? So why would she have taken it up so aggressively with Sister Ingund?'

The Venerable Breas thought for a moment and shrugged. 'You mistake what is meant here. She sought to stop Sister Ingund from being too closely associated with Brother Garb, should it transpire that he killed the bishop as a result of mutual hatred.'

'We shall take that into consideration, should the matter arise,' Fidelma assured him. 'But since we are discussing relationships, I wanted to ask you about your relationship with the Venerable

Lugán. You are both senior members of the abbey and in some respects your roles in the abbey are similar.'

'The Venerable Lugán? I have known him for many years for we were also young together here in the years before I left this abbey to go to teach at Mungairit. We are good friends.'

'In your positions as the keeper of the books in the library or, indeed, as master of the students, there is no conflict between you?'

'None that I find worthy of the term "conflict". He is, perhaps, a little too free with some who use our library and archives, but withal, he is a good archivist and astute keeper of the books.'

'He has told you about the problems in the archive with Bishop Brodulf and Brother Mac Raith?'

'He has. It is regrettable. He particularly told me of the strange searches the bishop was engaged in.'

'What do you think the bishop could have been looking for at that period? A period twenty years ago?'

'That, I am afraid, we may never know, seeing that the Venerable Lugán believes the documents, some ledgers, were stolen by the bishop and perished in the fire with him. It is exceptionally frustrating for me because there are texts that members of this abbey would need to consult for history's sake.'

'That I understand,' Fidelma agreed.

'It would have been good to compare the dates and references to a text he was also consulting. That is, of course, the *Liber Historiae Francorum*. Lugán has informed me that it is one thing that is missing.'

'*The History of the Franks* written by Gregory of Tours?' Eadulf asked.

The Venerable Breas shook his head. 'Not the old text, which I think we might have been well acquainted with. No, the text that Lugán saw him making references to was the more recent one by the scribe Fedegar, which brings the history up to date. It is the one young Sister Fastrude brought as a gift to this abbey from her own Abbey of Nevirnum.'

'The Venerable Lugán did not mention the bishop was using that volume. Has it gone missing? I thought it was only the records of the abbey that were supposed to have been taken?'

'It seemed Lugán had overlooked this matter, which was not discovered until I asked Sister Fastrude to fetch me the book and she immediately returned to say it was one of the items that was now missing from the library.'

Fidelma was silent, considering this news. Finally, after a few more exchanges, she rose and Eadulf followed her example.

'I'll confirm the manuscript is missing with the Venerable Lugán. You may also leave the other matter in my hands. We shall have a word with Deacon Landric.'

The Venerable Breas smiled softly. 'I leave it to you because a destructive tongue is sharper than a knife in the back.'

CHAPTER FIFTEEN

T he Venerable Lugán looked up from where he was apparently checking a catalogue as they entered the *scriptorium*. His pale face expressed exhaustion. He put down his quill neatly and set the text aside before he gazed expectantly at them.

'I understand from the Venerable Breas that you have found another work missing since we spoke,' Fidelma opened.

The *leabhar coimedach* raised his shoulders slightly and let them fall.

'Another sad loss. I found the copy of *Liber Historiae Francorum*, a recent acquisition to the library, is missing. It is a text by a scribe called Fedegar, and given to us by the Abbey of Nevirnum.'

'When did you discover it was missing?'

'Not long after I spoke to you about the other matter. The book was brought to us by Sister Fastrude when she came as a student here. The Venerable Breas had asked her to take him the text for some research and when she asked me, I discovered it was missing from the shelves.' He paused, pointing to the far side of the library. 'Actually, Sister Fastrude is doing some work there now.'

Fidelma glanced to Eadulf. 'Ask Sister Fastrude if she would join us for a moment.' Then she turned back to the Venerable Lugán.

'And that was when you realised it was missing?'

'I made a thorough search just in case it had been placed elsewhere. I had to admit to the Venerable Breas that certain items had gone missing and that there could be no one other than Bishop Brodulf who could be the culprit.'

'How can we be sure that the bishop was responsible for the removal of this text?'

'It was placed nearby where the bishop had been rummaging among the other texts. I say "rummaging", for he was clearly no scholar. His mistreatment of books was—'

'I understand,' Fidelma said shortly. 'So, this text by Fedegar was near where he was going through some other texts?'

'Among the books in that section were works by Gregory of Tours. Nearby had been the text of *An Banshenchus*, *The History of Women*, which our steward managed to save from destruction.'

'Do you think that the bishop destroyed this text by Fedegar? He had tried to destroy *An Banshenchus*.'

'Fedegar's text was a history of the bishop's own people. Why would he destroy that?'

'Perhaps because he disagreed with it, and when it comes to a history of one's own people that can be the most contentious of all to those who do not agree with it. Can you remember what was in this history by Fedegar?'

The Venerable Lugán grimaced a negative expression. 'Alas, I have never read it. We have so many texts sent to us in recent times.' He waved his hand around the room. 'It is hard to keep up with everything.'

A female voice interrupted. 'It was a history of my people, the Franks. More particularly of our princes. I am appalled that Brodulf has taken it.'

Fidelma turned to find Sister Fastrude had joined them with Eadulf.

'Was this history of your people any different from the text of Gregory of Tours?'

'It was a continuation of the text that Gregory of Tours started and repeated some of it. Gregory ended his history nearly one hundred years ago. Fedegar wrote later and merely updated the history.'

'Apart from the recent history, was there anything remarkable about it?'

A faint smile crossed Sister Fastrude's features. 'I am sure the Venerable Lugán here would agree with me that one should find all history remarkable, ancient or modern. It reveals the nature of men and that nature never changes.'

Fidelma pursed her lips for a moment. 'I presume you refer to Bishop Brodulf's attitude to women? However, you say that this was just a straightforward history?'

'Is any history straightforward?'

'You are possibly more qualified than I to discuss this philosophy in one of the Venerable Breas' classes,' Fidelma replied dryly. 'What I am seeking to discover is whether there might be something that would be of particular interest to the bishop?'

'I would not have said so,' replied the girl. 'There was, as part of the text, a family tree of the line of the royal family of the Salian Franks.' She caught the perplexed look on Fidelma's face and added, 'That is the family of the Frankish kings from Merovech. That might be valuable.'

'Why valuable? I would imagine the generations are well known by the historians and lawgivers in your country.'

'Only to some. Our people know who their rulers are. What they don't know is who their rulers *should* be.'

'I don't understand.' Fidelma was perplexed at the inflection.

'It is also interesting to have such documents for those wishing to understand Salic Law. It was Clovis who ordered the Law of the Salian Franks to be written, especially the law on inheritance.'

'I thought that was simple,' Eadulf intervened. 'Like my people, the Angles, it is surely the first born who inherits.'

to inherit, what then?'

...er still lives, then the

...e eldest son, then his

...arest male relative on

...od is exhausted will a

...rpose of the Salic Law

...le?' Fidelma's features

...stem.

...en in this kingdom, I

...re more conducive to

...ble as it indicates the

...red.'

...have been assassinated

...d about a King Sigebert

...also assassinated.'

...Law,' Sister Fastrude

...ces who should have

...when the bell for the

...to the refectory when

...a's path. It was Sister

...at is the bell for the

...ed nervous so Fidelma

...n us in a walk to the

...ntain. But for only a

...meal today.'

...ister Ingund.

...e.

'I did not mean that, but . .

something but I do not want it t

the information . . . at least no t

'That is direct enough.' Fi

gestured for the girl to do the

bishop's death? If so, you have

The girl began to speak hurr

as if checking if anyone was a

'You know Brother Garb has

'We knew,' Fidelma replied.

'I found out a short time ago

out of the building I heard a n

of the building is a small woo

from the outside. In fact, you

around the back of our buildin

'I don't think we have notice

behind the house of students the

purpose does it serve?'

'It's a small storage house

put bags and other items that are

'Why do you bring this to o

'I heard a noise and I thou

there.' Sister Ingund looked

searched it earlier. But I thou

went to the corner of the build

I could see anything.'

'And could you?'

'I did see someone come o

'And you are going to descri

'A male religieux, tall but,

over his head and long indisti

see. Luckily, he went to the op

I was.'

'I made a thorough search just in case it had been placed elsewhere. I had to admit to the Venerable Breas that certain items had gone missing and that there could be no one other than Bishop Brodulf who could be the culprit.'

'How can we be sure that the bishop was responsible for the removal of this text?'

'It was placed nearby where the bishop had been rummaging among the other texts. I say "rummaging", for he was clearly no scholar. His mistreatment of books was—'

'I understand,' Fidelma said shortly. 'So, this text by Fedegar was near where he was going through some other texts?'

'Among the books in that section were works by Gregory of Tours. Nearby had been the text of *An Banshenchus*, *The History of Women*, which our steward managed to save from destruction.'

'Do you think that the bishop destroyed this text by Fedegar? He had tried to destroy *An Banshenchus*.'

'Fedegar's text was a history of the bishop's own people. Why would he destroy that?'

'Perhaps because he disagreed with it, and when it comes to a history of one's own people that can be the most contentious of all to those who do not agree with it. Can you remember what was in this history by Fedegar?'

The Venerable Lugán grimaced a negative expression. 'Alas, I have never read it. We have so many texts sent to us in recent times.' He waved his hand around the room. 'It is hard to keep up with everything.'

A female voice interrupted. 'It was a history of my people, the Franks. More particularly of our princes. I am appalled that Brodulf has taken it.'

Fidelma turned to find Sister Fastrude had joined them with Eadulf.

'Was this history of your people any different from the text of Gregory of Tours?'

'It was a continuation of the text that Gregory of Tours started and repeated some of it. Gregory ended his history nearly one hundred years ago. Fedegar wrote later and merely updated the history.'

'Apart from the recent history, was there anything remarkable about it?'

A faint smile crossed Sister Fastrude's features. 'I am sure the Venerable Lugán here would agree with me that one should find all history remarkable, ancient or modern. It reveals the nature of men and that nature never changes.'

Fidelma pursed her lips for a moment. 'I presume you refer to Bishop Brodulf's attitude to women? However, you say that this was just a straightforward history?'

'Is any history straightforward?'

'You are possibly more qualified than I to discuss this philosophy in one of the Venerable Breas' classes,' Fidelma replied dryly. 'What I am seeking to discover is whether there might be something that would be of particular interest to the bishop?'

'I would not have said so,' replied the girl. 'There was, as part of the text, a family tree of the line of the royal family of the Salian Franks.' She caught the perplexed look on Fidelma's face and added, 'That is the family of the Frankish kings from Merovech. That might be valuable.'

'Why valuable? I would imagine the generations are well known by the historians and lawgivers in your country.'

'Only to some. Our people know who their rulers are. What they don't know is who their rulers *should* be.'

'I don't understand.' Fidelma was perplexed at the inflection.

'It is also interesting to have such documents for those wishing to understand Salic Law. It was Clovis who ordered the Law of the Salian Franks to be written, especially the law on inheritance.'

'I thought that was simple,' Eadulf intervened. 'Like my people, the Angles, it is surely the first born who inherits.'

'But if a man does not have any sons to inherit, what then?' Sister Fastrude countered. 'If a man's father still lives, then the father inherits. If the father is dead and the eldest son, then his brothers inherit. If no brothers then the nearest male relative on the father's side inherits. Only if this method is exhausted will a female be able to claim inheritance. The purpose of the Salic Law is the exclusion of any female inheriting.'

'But why should you say this text is valuable?' Fidelma's features formed an expression of distaste for the system.

Sister Fastrude smiled. 'Since I have been in this kingdom, I have come to appreciate your laws. They are more conducive to my way of thinking. But I say this is valuable as it indicates the number of rightful heirs that have disappeared.'

'Disappeared? Ah, you mean the rulers who have been assassinated and other relatives put in their place? I was told about a King Sigebert who was assassinated, and his successor was also assassinated.'

'All while claiming to abide by the Salic Law,' Sister Fastrude agreed. 'Fedegar reminds us of those princes who should have succeeded and did not.'

They were just leaving the *scriptorium* when the bell for the *etar-shod* began to sound.

They were turning across the courtyard to the refectory when one of the female students blocked Fidelma's path. It was Sister Ingund. She was slightly breathless.

'What do you want, Sister Ingund? That is the bell for the midday meal. Can't it wait?'

'I would like to speak immediately.'

'Then you may speak freely.' The girl seemed nervous so Fidelma gave her an encouraging smile. 'Either join us in a walk to the refectory or let us sit a moment by that fountain. But for only a moment or two as I do not want to miss a meal today.'

'I don't wish to be seen . . .' muttered Sister Ingund.

'With us?' Eadulf asked in a cynical tone.

'I did not mean that, but . . . but, it is true. I need to tell you something but I do not want it traced back to me as the source of the information . . . at least not until this matter is resolved.'

'That is direct enough.' Fidelma sat on the stone wall and gestured for the girl to do the same. 'Is this the matter of the bishop's death? If so, you have our attention.'

The girl began to speak hurriedly and kept glancing about her as if checking if anyone was aware of her.

'You know Brother Garb has disappeared from the dormitory?'

'We knew,' Fidelma replied.

'I found out a short time ago when I went to see. When I came out of the building I heard a noise at the back of it. At the back of the building is a small wooden shed with a separate entrance from the outside. In fact, you cannot get into it unless you go around the back of our building.'

'I don't think we have noticed it. As you say, if it is a structure behind the house of students then we would not have seen it. What purpose does it serve?'

'It's a small storage house where the students who come here put bags and other items that are not wanted during their residency.'

'Why do you bring this to our attention?'

'I heard a noise and I thought Garb might have been hiding there.' Sister Ingund looked worried. 'I knew the steward had searched it earlier. But I thought Garb might have come back. I went to the corner of the building to peer along the wall to see if I could see anything.'

'And could you?'

'I did see someone come out and replace the latch.'

'And you are going to describe this person?' prompted Fidelma.

'A male religieux, tall but, as to anything else, he had a hood over his head and long indistinguishable robes. That's all I could see. Luckily, he went to the opposite corner of the building where I was.'

'So you did not recognise him? You did not see in what direction he vanished?'

The girl shook her head.

'If it was not Brother Garb, why do you think we would be interested?' Fidelma asked with curiosity.

'Because, after the figure had vanished, I went to the door of this storehouse and lifted the latch.'

'It was not locked, of course?'

The girl shook her head. 'It never is. Everyone knows that. It's just a wooden latch and there are no keys, for who would want to take anything from it? What worth are the empty bags of students?'

'You lifted the latch and what did you find?' Fidelma encouraged.

'Inside is a shadowy place if you do not have a lamp. But there was light enough from the door to see the piles of bags on lower shelves. One thing I noticed immediately, for it had been hastily placed not far inside the door. It was a leather bag. It was large, of the type carried by men on long journeys. You fix it on your shoulders by straps.'

'Why did this particular bag attract your attention?'

'Because I recognised it. It belonged to Brother Garb and the person who placed it there was not Garb.'

'How do you know it was the property of Brother Garb?' Fidelma queried immediately.

'Because I once saw him using it to carry some heavy things. It was when we were asked to move materials that we used in our classes from one of the wooden buildings. This was due to be demolished and we were asked to take them to a new stone building. Brother Garb volunteered to carry some heavy items in this bag. I remarked on it.'

'Just because it was of heavy leather?' Eadulf asked.

'No. On one side of the leather were a number of weird marks that had been burnt into it with a poker.'

'Weird marks?'

'Just groups of lines. I have seen them before but do not understand their meaning.'

'We will go and examine this, Eadulf. Will you join us?'

Sister Ingund shook her head. 'I do not want Brother Garb to get into more trouble. I only tell you this because someone other than he has used that bag. I think it might be of help to him.'

The girl sprang up, a redness on her cheeks She opened her mouth as if to say something and then she turned and hurried away.

'We'd better have a look right away,' Fidelma said, rising and making her way to the students' quarters. They had no trouble in finding themselves around the back of the building to where the small solitary shed stood. It was just as the girl had described it. It was a rough wooden shed without any metal locks or bars. Once the latch was lifted the door swung open.

It was almost impossible to miss the leather bag lying almost immediately inside.

Fidelma reached forward and picked it up by the leather strap. The name on it was clear. Although Sister Ingund had not known the ancient Ogam lettering, Fidelma did. The letters were burnt on the side of the leather bag. They proclaimed the name 'Garb'.

'Anything in it?' Eadulf asked hopefully.

'I doubt it,' Fidelma replied, carrying it out into the full daylight before she began to open the fastening and peer into it. 'Empty . . .' she began. Then she suddenly reached down, wet her finger with her tongue and put it to the bottom of the bag. Then she brought it back to eye level and examined the powder that was attached.

'What is it?' Eadulf asked.

'What would you make of it, Eadulf?' She held out her finger for him to inspect. He did so and then he, too, bent to peer into the bag.

'Fine grains, but the remains are enough . . .' He smiled trium-phantly. 'That's sulphur dust, right enough.'

Fidelma examined the bag critically, smiling agreement.

'So now we know how the sulphur dust was transported from the builders' camp, if this is what ignited the fire in the bishop's guest house. Whoever used this to transport the quantity here should have cleaned this bag more thoroughly.'

'This is Garb's bag. But Sister Ingund says he was not carrying it when she saw someone place it there. So who was it who used it?'

'Well, first we must check Brother Áedh's assertion that the sulphur dust was the very ignition means for the fire,' Fidelma decided. 'Once we know this sulphur dust was used in the fire, let us see where it came from. Meanwhile, let us replace this with the other bags until we are ready.'

They were crossing the courtyard again, Fidelma striding out with Eadulf trotting bewilderedly after her. He was more confused when she hailed one of the brethren and asked him to send their excuses to the abbot for missing the midday meal. Before he could ask her why they were not going for the meal, Enda appeared, heading for the refectory. She hailed him.

'Come, Enda, we have to go for a ride. Immediately. Let us get our horses and retrace the journey you made after the horse's tracks this morning.'

He exchanged a perplexed glance with Eadulf as Fidelma headed off towards the stables. They left the stables through the side gates, without Fidelma explaining anything. They turned west along the track, passing the front of the abbey. Opposite, on the southern side of the track, rose Cnoc Carron, the abbey cemetery.

A movement in the cemetery caught Fidelma's eye.

'I see a man still working on a newly dug grave,' she remarked.

'That's where I saw the builders this morning,' Enda told her. 'He's not exactly working, though. More like standing guard.'

Eadulf glanced across. 'I suppose it is the bishop's grave, or will be after tonight. Conscientious fellows, probably making sure there is no slippage of soil before the ceremony tonight.'

Fidelma halted at the edge of the western walls of the abbey.

'So you turned up this rise, following the walls of the abbey up to where the yew forest starts?' she asked Enda. 'I am not checking on your report about the horse, Enda,' she added to assure him. 'I seek something different.'

It was clear that Enda was not mollified, but he began to move on, leading the way along a barely discernible path.

'I found the tracks of the horse moving in this direction,' he said, pointing to the north-west. As Enda had previously said, the way followed in an almost parallel path to the outer walls of the abbey.

'This is where I lost the tracks for a while,' he said after they had ridden a little distance. He pointed down to where the ground was suddenly devoid of grass and shrubs and covered as if in dust. It was obvious to see why. It was as if a new track or roadway crossed this part, continuing down into the open abbey grounds where the building work was taking place.

'Where did you pick up the tracks after this?' Fidelma asked Enda.

'Much further along, where the undergrowth and grasses start again.'

Fidelma looked carefully around. 'I presume that this crossing path is from the builders' camp to the west. In the other direction is where they are at work on the abbey buildings?'

Enda agreed with a motion of his head.

'And if we follow that path west, away from the abbey, I will find the main builders' encampment there?' Fidelma asked.

Enda pursed his lips, still with an expression of perplexity. 'Beyond those trees is a clearing with several makeshift huts and open fires. That provides accommodation for the builders. There are work places, forges for smiths and carpenters' works. Piles of tools and other material are stacked around.'

'Is that where they keep the oxen and asses they use for transporting materials to and from the abbey buildings? I noticed Sítae, the master builder, had eight oxen and two asses working on the building site.'

Enda shook his head. 'Apparently the oxen are kept on the eastern side of the abbey, in an open field. They are looked after from sunset to sunrise, and be careful if you go there during that period for the herd is guarded by a *dam conchaid.*'

Eadulf looked startled for he had not heard the expression before. 'Are you saying a "wolf-fighting ox"? What in the name of the devil is that?'

'At night the ox herd are turned loose with an aggressive bull that will even charge and maim a fox,' Enda explained. 'There's no need to tell you that there are plenty of wolves in these parts. But I have also heard stories of various *búabell,* wild oxen, who will attack unprotected herds.'

'So the animals are taken to this field, an open enclosure, overnight and put in with this animal who protects them? Do they not have a *bóare*, a herdsman, to keep an eye on things? It seems a bit excessive,' remarked Fidelma.

Enda smiled thinly. 'Apparently the master builder values his eight oxen highly so he tends them himself like prize milch cows.'

Fidelma was thoughtful. 'They are kept on the eastern side of the abbey and if anyone disturbs them at night they would have to contend with a fighting bull ox and a *bóare*?'

'Exactly.'

Fidelma put her head to one side for a moment and then grimaced. 'Then it makes sense.' She left them puzzled, then said: 'I want to look at the builders' camp before we follow the tracks back again.'

They followed her lead along the track and found it was a short distance beyond the area of forest, which was dominant in local yew but mixed with oak and elm. The ground opened into a fairly substantial man-made clearing in which there were several well-constructed wooden huts. They were not sophisticated buildings but just strong enough to make comfortable sleeping quarters for the various workers of master builder Sítae. At one end of the camp there were a couple of forges with smiths attending the fires or working at some metal on their anvils. Beyond that, Fidelma recognised a lime kiln. She had seen the like before. Again, a worker was attending it and there was a great pile of limestone nearby. In this area there were also piles of different stones, and a wagon was standing with two patient oxen, being loaded with large rocks by a couple of men stripped to the waist in spite of the chill of the midday spring. There were also several artisans at work, as well as the smiths: carpenters, stone cutters and metal workers preparing various items to be taken down to the abbey building site.

As Fidelma and her companions sat on their horses regarding the scene with interest, a man approached and touched his knuckled hand to his forehead.

'Greetings, lady. Is it Sítae that you are seeking?'

She glanced down at the man and realised he was one of the workers she had seen at work in the abbey the previous day. She acknowledged his greeting.

'I was just interested in looking at your camp. What is your name?'

'I am called Patu, lady.'

'The quiet one?'

'Most people render the meaning of my name as a "hare", for it is said that when the hare runs, it runs quietly,' replied the man with a grin. He reached forward to pet the nose of Fidelma's pony, Aonbarr. 'You have a nice animal there. Even a better breed than that owned by the abbey's physician. It's a Gaulish breed, if I'm not mistaken?'

Fidelma was surprised. 'That is true. You know something about horses then, Patu?'

'Although my trade is in carpentry and joinery, my father bred horses in the valley just south of the Humps of Cliú. Maybe one day I will return and continue the breeding of them instead of risking my life building abbeys. Now,' he drew himself up briskly, 'what is it I can do for you? Sítae is not here at this time.'

'Well, we were just exercising our horses,' Fidelma responded. 'Therefore we are looking for nothing in particular. Tell me, is this where much of the work is done preparing items that need to be crafted before you take them to the building site at the abbey?'

'It is, lady, but, as I say, the master builder is down in the abbey. He would be much better at explaining things to you than I am. I am not even a master carpenter. Even our master mason is down at the site.'

'No matter,' she replied. 'I can understand more or less what is happening.' She pointed towards the lime kiln. 'I see you have many piles of different stone piled there, not just limestone.'

The man eased his stance, moving from one foot to the other to balance more comfortably, and nodded agreement.

'We use many different types of stone. As we work with dry stone, it has to be carefully dressed so that it is watertight when one block sits on another. However, Sítae has started to follow those who have adopted the binding ideas of the Greeks and Romans.'

'Which are?' Fidelma promoted.

'A crushed mixture of limestone and sand, as well as certain types of crushed stone or dust as aggregates. It is usually mixed with animal fat or even milk. When hardened, it makes a strong binding.'

'Can you use it to bind with any stone?'

'With limestone and sandstone, and in certain buildings we have even used it with granite. But what granite we use is from Laigin, so here we are using white and red limestone, which we find easy to quarry. In fact, we get the red sandstone from near where my father's place is. Those mountains where I grew up, the Humps of Cliú, are red sandstone and shale.'

Eadulf suddenly interrupted. 'I noticed you call the stone buildings *derthech* . . . why is that? It means an "oak house", but these are stone houses.'

Patu grinned. 'Technical words only, my friend, but such words often pass from one concept to another so the original meaning is lost. Time was when the buildings were mostly constructed in wood and an important building was made from oak. So *derthech* was, indeed, an oak-made house. Now we use the word for most of the important buildings, like chapels and churches and even abbeys, whether they are of stone or oak.'

Eadulf had touched Fidelma's elbow to silently indicate an angular stone box standing nearby. It was carved without joins, but covered with a lid secured by a heavy flat stone. There was a lot of yellow staining on it. It was obvious what it contained. Fidelma turned to the man called Patu, who had now become at ease with them.

'I think that is sulphur dust in that stone box. Isn't that used to cause a small explosion to help break pieces of rock?'

The man regarded her with some amazement. 'You know much of our trade.'

'Not all that much,' Fidelma countered. 'Just enough to know that you sometimes need to break up rocks. Sometimes you need to heat the rock to split it. Do you use much of this sulphur dust here?'

'Not that much. We keep a small amount to help when we need it. As you see from the weight of this container, no one is going to lift it up and take it away.'

'Is it secure and safe?' Eadulf asked. 'One could lift the lid and scoop out what they wanted to put in a bucket and take away.'

'Believe me, it is secure. There is always someone nearby in the camp so that the idea of someone just helping themselves is absurd. Only a few people here know how to use it to break stones.'

'Or to use it for any other purposes?' Eadulf asked quietly.

'In which case they would not need an entire bucket,' the man laughed. 'I suppose you are thinking about what Sítae told us. He said that it was claimed that a bucket of sulphur dust was used to set fire to that guest building. Well, it would have to be proved that it came from here.'

'I think, in the circumstances, it would have come from nowhere else,' pointed out Eadulf.

'I am told that it is claimed by someone called Brother Áedh that a bucket would have been needed. If someone took it from here, it would not have been easy to remove such a quantity and carry it off in the right container. Certainly it would be noticed if they tried to take it in an open bucket.'

'But you don't keep a special watch on dangerous materials like sulphur dust?' Fidelma asked.

'You see where it is. You see our camp is remote and there is always someone about. I saw you enter some time ago and recognised you as the *dálaigh* from the abbey. You would have been challenged had I not done so.'

'So you keep it guarded because it is dangerous?' Fidelma pressed.

'No one is going to steal it from this site. If they tried, they would have to be very clever. Also, we are made to account for all materials. There are regulations under law that things must be compensated for. If things are missing, we must compensate the overseer; if he can't account for it, he has to compensate the master builder, and so on.'

Fidelma was thoughtful.

'We have learnt much and must thank you.' She straightened herself and glanced round as if in appreciation. 'I see that you work at carpentry.' She nodded to the bench that the man had left to come forward to greet them.

'I am what is called a *saor denma tighi*, lady.'

'A house-building woodworker,' she explained quickly, when Eadulf asked what it meant.

'You have some fine tools. Are you not a master carpenter?' Enda asked. 'The one responsible for all the red yew carving?'

'I am not. The master carpenter had to leave us the other day. He left the very day before that foreign bishop was caught in that terrible fire.'

'Ah, yes,' Fidelma said. 'His work was the subject of much praise in the abbey. He did some beautiful work in yew. I remember his name was Cú Choille. So, you worked under him?'

'He was second only to the master builder. Watching his carving technique was a lesson in woodworking itself. I have often seen him at work at his table here, shaping a piece of wood with a press, or turning wood on the lathe. Anyway, Sítae has put the word out that we are badly in need of a new master carpenter.'

'But that would not be you?' Eadulf enquired.

'Bless you, my friend, but that would be someone who has obtained the degree of professor in all the arts of cutting and shaping wood.'

'I recall the master builder mentioned your name as someone who knew how to shape a *fé* and use it for the burial of the bishop.'

The man seemed hesitant. 'I have carved a *fé* before, lady,' he confirmed.

'Well, you seem to have done well enough to acquire all these tools of your crafts,' Fidelma pointed out.

The carpenter shook his head. 'Things like the *tornaire*, the lathe, the press, and the grindstone all belong to the master builder.'

'Wouldn't it be more appropriate that the master carpenter would own such things?' Enda questioned, swinging down from his horse as if to examine the structure of the lathe. 'It is as valuable an instrument as I have seen. I saw a similar one in my village. They called it a *deil*.'

'I have heard it called both *tornaire* and *deil*,' affirmed the carpenter. 'Each carpenter has his own special tools with which he travels.' He turned to Enda's other point. 'Such items are too heavy for one person to carry. But with regard to certain smaller, special items, the master carpenter always carried his instruments with him.' He smiled at Eadulf. 'I see you do the same, my friend, for you have a *lés* attached to your horse . . . a medical bag, which proclaims you to be a doctor of sorts and without which your worth to be able to practise the healing arts would be in question.'

Eadulf was almost uncomfortable. Although he had studied the healing arts at Tuam Brecan, he had never qualified but knew enough to retain his *lés*, which had been useful in many of the cases he and Fidelma had been involved with.

'We understand,' Fidelma said hurriedly. 'So each carpenter would have his own bag for his personal hand tools? A carpenter comes to know his tools well, and so he guards them carefully.'

'Just so, lady. You could not have expressed it better.'

'So he would always keep his own tools, such as chisels, hammers, mallets and so on?'

'You have the right of it, lady,' Patu agreed. 'But heavy objects such as lathes, presses and grindstones would be brought by wagon and remain on the site until the work is finished.'

Enda turned and was about to climb back on his horse, but as he did so, he seemed to recognise one of the instruments on the bench he had been examining and quickly bent and scooped it up.

'Now this is a wicked-looking thing. I think it is called a "fork point".' He handed it up to Fidelma. 'It is by these that carpenters can get some perfect circles in their work.'

Fidelma took the item carefully for the name fork point described it perfectly. Eadulf glanced quickly and saw they were handling a pair of compasses, designed to set out a circle. The length of the arms of the compasses, from the hinge of the two stout oak arms inserted on to metal points, was about thirty centimetres. Fidelma, who must have seen similar instruments, held them for a moment as if studying them in awe. Then she handed them back with a look of solemn approval.

'Well, thank you again, my friend, for showing us your fascinating camp. We must return, but we shall doubtless see you at work in the abbey.'

Following her lead, Eadulf and Enda turned their horses and made their way back to where they had halted at the cross tracks.

Fidelma turned to Enda. 'What made you pick up the compasses?' she asked.

'I noticed some writing on them and thought you might be interested.'

'Some writing?' Eadulf was puzzled. 'Why would that be important?'

'There were marks in the ancient alphabet on one of the oak arms,' Enda explained.

'More than just alphabet marks,' Fidelma confirmed. 'But I did not have time to read it.'

'It was a name inscribed in the old alphabet.'

'What name?' Eadulf asked puzzled.

'The name was Cú Choille.'

Eadulf gave an exclamation as he realised what he meant. 'That was the master carpenter, who had to leave the abbey the day before the bishop was killed. Which means . . .?'

'You heard what Patu, the assistant carpenter, was saying about personal tools?'

'Are you saying that the master carpenter would not have left behind those tools when he went, and this man, Patu, robbed him of them?' Eadulf shook his head with a small cynical grimace. 'Come, we have enough mysteries to resolve without creating one of our own.'

Fidelma did not react. 'It is a point to be borne in mind. Anyway, I am convinced that the sulphur dust came from the builders' camp. That is why I went to see their encampment. The sulphur was in the bag we found. The flammable material was taken, then hidden behind the guest house in readiness for its use that night. It shows the murder of the bishop was planned well in advance.'

'By Brother Garb?' Eadulf demanded.

'The only matter we can confirm is that the burning of the guest house was a planned action,' she repeated. 'We still have to find this young man.'

'But if not Garb, then who? Do you suspect that the killer was one of the builders?'

'What would be their motive?' Fidelma shook her head. 'No, the motive remains among the people in this abbey. We have investigations still to do.'

She turned to Enda. 'Come, my friend, now show us where you followed the horse tracks back to the main trackway.'

It was not long before Enda pointed to some deep impressions of hoof marks.

'As I said, it looks as if the horse was taken further up and then acquired a heavy burden.'

'I see where the impression of the hoofprints looks deeper than before,' Eadulf agreed. 'It does imply that something was loaded on to the beast. But certainly it was much heavier than a bag of sulphur dust.'

From Fidelma's disapproving glance, Eadulf realised he had made the wrong assumption.

'Whoever took the sulphur dust from the builders' camp in Garb's bag did not go through the problems associated with taking a horse from the stable and making the night ride.'

'So someone took the horse, went up to the yew forest at the back, took something heavy and loaded it on the animal before returning with it down to the main trackway that runs in front of the abbey,' Eadulf said slowly. 'Maybe they went somewhere else first?'

'Roughly it,' Fidelma conceded.

'Then, having reached the track, the horse was left to its own devices outside the abbey gates?' Eadulf shook his head. 'It just doesn't make sense.'

Fidelma said nothing for a moment, examining the area around them. Then she shrugged. 'Well, whoever took the beast, they took it during the night, used it to transport something and, when they had finished, released it in the early light where it was discovered by passing warriors who, thankfully, returned it to the abbey.'

'Are you saying that makes sense?' Eadulf asked cynically.

Fidelma shrugged expressively. 'At the moment it does not have to make sense because we don't have enough information. Meanwhile, we have much to accomplish. Perhaps we can persuade the kitchens to let us have something to compensate for the midday meal we have missed.'

chapter sixteen

While Enda was taking their horses back to the stables, Fidelma went to see if she could persuade the abbey cooks to provide something to sustain them until the evening meal. Eadulf felt he should retrieve the bag with Garb's name from the back of the students' house. He had begun to cross the courtyard towards the students' house when he saw, further down from the wooden buildings beyond the blackened ruins of the former guest house, a group of builders. They were standing in a group outside another building, which had clearly been marked for demolition before the rebuilding scheme. The odd thing was that they were just standing there, silent and uneasy. Then one of them caught sight of Eadulf, turned and came towards him in a loping stride. It was a curious ungainly trot as if the man were trying not to break into a run. On an impulse Eadulf halted.

'Brother Eadulf!' The burly man was slightly breathless as he came to a halt before him. His face was red and the expression anxious.

Eadulf now saw that the man was Sítae, the master builder.

'I recognise you, Master Builder,' Eadulf replied lightly. 'What can I do for you?'

'You can come with me, if you would. I need to show you something.'

Eadulf frowned. 'I don't understand.'

'It is urgent. I hear that you are looking for a young scholar named Garb. I suggest that you come with me now.'

Eadulf hesitated before he started to follow the master builder. The man hurriedly led him to the building outside of which the group of workers had been standing. Sítae waved them aside and led Eadulf into the building. The old wooden structure was empty, stripped ready for demolition. He did not hesitate but led the way up the unstable rotting stairs to the upper floor. There was then no need for an explanation.

The upper floor was a single room contained by a sloping roof, like an attic. From one of the roof's support beams, the body of a young man was swaying slightly. He was held tight with a hemp rope around his neck. He wore tattered and soiled religious robes. A discarded chair was on its side nearby. From the angle of the head and the discoloration of the skin, Eadulf didn't have to ask if the youth was dead or, indeed, how he came by his death.

Eadulf glanced at Sítae, who interpreted the unasked question.

'We were due to start demolishing this building when one of the carpenters came here to check that we knew what wood could be saved for any reconstruction.'

'We have been searching for a missing youth, one of the students,' Eadulf admitted. 'Didn't the steward, Brother Mac Raith, search this area?'

'He certainly came searching the area for someone,' replied Sítae. 'But I can assure you that the body was not here earlier.'

'What do you mean?'

'Exactly what I say,' replied Sítae, defensively. 'The place had been searched earlier. The body was not here then. This young man, whoever he is, must have come in and hanged himself while we were resting during the midday meal. We have only just discovered it and I was going to report it when I saw you crossing the courtyard. Is it the person that you were seeking?'

'I believe it might be,' Eadulf replied. 'I have not seen the young person myself so I need someone to identify the body. Can you go and fetch the steward, Brother Mac Raith? Oh, and also get someone to fetch the lady Fidelma, and you had better fetch the physician, Brother Anlón. Have one of your men bring me a ladder and a sharp knife so that I may climb up and loosen the knot of the rope on the beam.'

Sítae looked nervously at the still-swinging body. 'This is not good, Brother. The second death of a religious on this site is a bad sign. My men often encounter death by accidents but this is something else.'

He hesitated a few moments more before turning to fulfil Eadulf's instructions.

It did not take long for Eadulf, with the help of one of the workmen and a ladder, to cut the rope and lower the body of the young man to the floor. There was hardly a reason to examine it. The young man was beyond all help; the body was deathly white and cold. Nevertheless, Eadulf spent some time, frowning, as he scrutinised it.

It did not seem long before the dour features of Brother Anlón emerged from the floor below and looked at the body and then at the beam from which it had been cut.

'It seems that you don't require my services,' he said. 'Death by hanging is clear enough.'

He had barely made his pronouncement when Fidelma, accompanied by Brother Ma Raith, climbed up into the room.

'*Sta coram Deo et omni mala!*' Brother Mac Raith muttered as he performed the sign of the cross.

'Is this Brother Garb?' Fidelma demanded without wasting time.

'It is,' the steward affirmed, clearly distressed.

'A simple case,' Brother Anlón intervened airily. 'I thought the boy did not look well when he came to me earlier this morning to complain of stomach pains. It seemed there was probably something worse going on in his mind.'

'Not such a simple case,' Eadulf observed dryly.

The physician turned to him with a scowl but before he could speak, Eadulf went on: 'There are a few matters to be considered. You will have noticed the coldness of the body?' He asked the question of Brother Anlón.

'What temperature do you expect a dead body to be after a hanging?' the physician demanded in cynical tone.

It was Fidelma who bent to touch the skin.

'It is very cold, as might be expected,' she said.

'As might be expected?' Eadulf turned to Sítae, who had rejoined them. 'Correct me if I am wrong, Master Builder, but this building, both floors, was cleared ready to start disassembling it after lunch?'

'That is correct.'

'It was empty when your workers left for their midday meal? When that was over, one of your men came in and found the body and immediately informed you?'

'Exactly so.'

'How long would you say that the building was left empty? Do you allow your workers to take very long breaks?'

'Not at all. Time is money.'

'So in that short time, this young man is supposed to have come in here with a rope and chair. Then set it up and hanged himself. Is that correct?'

'What else could have happened?' Brother Anlón cut in, a sneer in his voice.

'When have you ever known a body go ice cold in the short time he was hanging there?' Eadulf queried.

Brother Anlón turned defensively to the master builder. 'Your workmen must have left the place empty for a longer period.'

The master builder shook his head immediately. 'Time is difficult to be precise about, but no more than it takes to eat a bannock and drink ale. Then we returned to work. Not long at all.'

'Yet in this period,' Eadulf spoke slowly and sarcastically, 'this young man comes here, with a rope and chair, ties the rope . . . By the way, the chair does not reach where the rope is tied on the beam, so where is the ladder that he must have used? Then he climbs on the chair, puts the rope around his neck, kicks the chair away and strangles himself because his neck is not broken.'

'Awkward, but possible,' Brother Anlón countered determinedly.

'Awkward? Impossible! And in the short time left, the body grows exceedingly cold. Also feel the stiffness of the facial muscles . . . that occurs sometime after death. The boy has been dead some time.'

Fidelma faced Eadulf grimly as his meaning struck her. 'I think you have made your point, Eadulf. You are saying that the body was already dead when it was placed there. That the youth was killed earlier this morning?'

'The boy had been dead some time to grow so cold. I would say he had been killed elsewhere. While the builders were having their break, someone came with a ladder, rope and chair, and the body, and put that body in position.'

'Anything else?' Fidelma asked.

'It seems a lot of work for a single person to do all this,' Eadulf replied. 'Indeed, at least two people to carry the body and the ladder, chair and rope.'

'Anything more?' Fidelma encouraged.

'Examine the neck. There are two separate wounds, which I think were made on two separate occasions.'

'You now say that he was hanged twice?' Bother Anlón snorted in derision. 'Now you are descending into fantasy.'

'Am I? You will find bruising on the neck that still shows indentations of the thumb. That is ante-mortem bruising, for the boy was strangled. That was what caused his death. Now over this bruising are the marks of the rope. The roughness of the hemp has cut here and there, leaving the strands of hemp, and it has started the discoloration.'

Brother Anlón was still disparaging. 'As a physician used to dealing with death, I would say that discoloration can appear after death and for a short time.'

'Used to dealing with death?' Fidelma was struck by a thought. 'I suppose you must have observed several deaths due to accidents during the building work here?'

The master builder glanced anxiously at the physician. 'The physician has agreed that my men and I have a good safety record.'

'Doubtless, but I wish the physician to answer,' Fidelma replied firmly.

'There have been one or two injuries, usually falls from the stone works. My experience of death—'

'Does not seem adequate in this matter,' Fidelma snapped, before turning back to Eadulf with an apology.

'I was about to point out the most important thing of all,' he continued. 'What is being missed here by Brother Anlón is that we have two different sets of bruising on the neck. The young man was strangled and sometime later was brought here, and the murderer or murderers attempted to disguise the murder by making it seem that he took his own life.'

There was a silence while Brother Anlón was apparently trying to think of a different explanation but could not do so.

'In the same way, the bishop was killed and then the guest house set afire to disguise the real cause.'

After Eadulf agreed, Fidelma uttered a sigh.

'So Brother Garb was attacked and strangled this morning. Unless we find another witness, the last person who saw him alive was Brother Anlón here, when he gave him medicine for his stomach and told him to go to the dormitory to lie down.'

The physician started to say something, but Eadulf intervened to remind Fidelma: 'Sister Ingund was the last to see him asleep in the students' dormitory.'

Fidelma acknowledged his correction. 'She saw him lying

asleep. So what we are saying is that he was attacked and strangled to death just after he had taken the physician's potion and gone to lie down. Would that medication have caused sleepiness?'

There was no disguising the anger of the physician's denial.

'Very well,' Fidelma continued. 'He was then strangled to death and his body hidden until it was transferred here in an attempt to mislead us into believing the boy had hanged himself.'

'Are you saying that the killer of Garb is the same person who killed Bishop Brodulf?' Brother Mac Raith asked, picking up on her earlier comment.

'As Eadulf has observed, we are not looking for one murderer now,' Fidelma replied.

'Two murderers?' Brother Mac Raith frowned.

'Think about it,' Eadulf reflected. 'Think of the work involved in trying to make the killing of Brother Garb look like a suicide. Much concerted work was needed to place the body where it was, especially hoisting it into position. We are looking for two murderers, with one of them needing the strength to strangle a relatively fit young man. I would say that one is possessed of strong hands and strength.'

There was a few moments' pause and then Fidelma instructed Brother Mac Raith to oversee the removal of the body to the chapel, having assured herself that Eadulf could cast no further details by physical examination. The steward agreed to report to the abbot and make further arrangements in accordance with his wishes.

It was the master builder who gave a sarcastic grin as he turned to leave.

'I expect the abbot will want another grave dug, Brother Mac Raith? You had better ask him. It won't take my men long.'

Brother Mac Raith regarded him in disapproval. 'I'll raise it with him. In normal circumstances, once the physician gives his report, we should have at least a night and a day of the *aire*, or waking the body, in the chapel. I will let you know.'

As he left, Fidelma turned to Brother Anlón. 'Do the builders have their own physician or do you take care of them?'

'The builders have a man who looks after minor cuts, bruises and even some broken bones. He is no more than a bone setter or doctor for cattle. I have only had to deal with the usual injuries. I would say that Sítae takes very good care of his men.'

Accompanied by Eadulf, Fidelma found Sister Ingund alone in the deserted dormitory and it was obvious that the news of the discovery of the body of Brother Garb had already been brought to her. She had been sobbing. Her eyes were still watery, red and discoloured around the lids. She looked up at their entry with a sound as if she were trying to swallow something.

'We are sorry to come to you at this time,' Fidelma opened as sympathetically as she could, sitting down beside the girl. Eadulf stood discreetly to one side.

'Garb could not have committed *fingal*!' the girl declared in a tight voice, wiping the tears from her eyes. The legal term for 'kin-slaying' was the same as used for a suicide.

'We think that he was murdered,' Eadulf said softly.

'I loved Garb,' the girl said brokenly. 'We had plans.'

'That much is obvious,' Fidelma told her gently.

The young girl lowered her head with another sniff.

'Prioress Suanach warned me against it,' she said.

'She was misled by someone. She was told you tried to coerce Garb into some plot against the bishop.'

The girl shuddered. 'How could she think such a thing?'

'It is not inconceivable.'

'I was in love with Garb,' she repeated in a voice now drained of emotion. 'The prioress was insane.'

'Only with the insanity that love can bring,' Fidelma explained.

Sister Ingund looked hesitant. 'I don't understand.'

'You should know that the Prioress Suanach has been in love with the Venerable Breas since the time she was a young student here.'

230

'In love? But she is older than I.'

'Perhaps that proves the point?' Fidelma smiled grimly. 'If no one knew their age, would they shackle themselves with the emotional constraints that it imposes? Love is a timeless emotion while age is just a number. Love comes from emotion, not from how we perceive the condition of our skin. It was simply that what emotion Suanach experienced, she could believe could happen to others.'

Sister Ingund compressed her lips. 'Yet it was not so with me. I was in love.'

'Suanach was in love and felt she was protecting the Venerable Breas from the accusations of some plot to kill the bishop. Now I just want to know what your relationship was with the Deacon Landric.'

'Deacon Landric?' Sister Ingund was shocked. 'I had no relationship with him. I did not know him until he appeared at the abbey with Bishop Brodulf. We have barely spoken. Who says I had a relationship with him?'

'I just wanted your reassurance,' Fidelma said.

'Was he the one who told the prioress the lie about me? Why did Suanach believe him?'

'Sadly, as I have said, because of her own love for Breas.'

'Then let us tell the Venerable Breas to make sure it is not so.'

Fidelma reached forward and patted the girl's arm.

'He has already been told. We must now consider why Deacon Landric would tell such lies.'

'He hated Brother Garb, of course,' came the immediate response. 'That is probably reason enough.'

'Why would he hate Garb? Because of the arguments he had with the bishop?'

The girl shook her head vehemently. 'I don't think that was the real cause of his hatred. Although I believe Deacon Landric supported the bishop in such matters.'

'Then why should he hate Brother Garb enough to stir enmity in this petty manner?'

'Brother Garb was one of the Venerable Breas' best students. We all admired him. He followed all those arguments about the various interpretations of the Faith. He once told me that there were dozens of interpretations of the Faith and often there were conflicts between one sect and another. Like there was between the Venerable Breas and Bishop Brodulf.'

'So he studied all these different interpretations?'

'He was working in the library here more times than out of it,' the girl commented.

'What sort of things was he interested in?'

'He once told me that long before Rome accepted the Faith, a teacher called Theodotus of Byzantium arrived in Rome teaching the Faith. He taught that Jesus was only a man who was very virtuous and spiritual. That idea was accepted by many groups. A hundred years later there was a council in Antioch at which it was argued, but the idea was condemned by the majority of those attending. In spite of that, the concept continued to be accepted among many groups.'

'Brother Garb used this in his arguments with Bishop Brodulf?'

'Brother Garb said that in the early days of the foundation of the Faith, the leaders often taught that Jesus was a mortal man and some even taught that he had a wife who followed him and his mother and sister during the time he taught in Galilee and Judaea. Garb said his teachings were sound and moral, and that "Son of God" was an acknowledgement of his mortality, not of his deity. That caused the greatest argument of all with Bishop Brodulf. There was one . . .'

The girl suddenly paused; uncertain whether she was now speaking out of turn.

'Go on,' urged Fidelma, thinking it was a way to get the girl to open up to her.

'Well, he told me about a man called Apollinaris, who was Bishop of Laodicea, who was declared a heretic at the first Council of Constantinople – that was about three centuries ago.'

'And what did this Bishop Apollinaris teach?'

'That Jesus was a human being and not divine, but that he inspired others with his thoughts and thus it was his thoughts that were divine and such thoughts were the mirror of souls, which could inspire fellows. But Apollinaris was not the first follower of Christ to see things in this way, nor was he the last to do so.'

'That was a teaching that must have sat uncomfortably with the likes of Bishop Brodulf,' observed Eadulf. 'I must admit, it also sits uncomfortably with me. It is against the Faith that I have come to accept, for is it not recorded in scripture that Christ himself proclaimed His divinity?'

'One is asked to believe that the scripture accurately records the words even though written after a century had passed since those times,' confirmed the girl. 'Even with the passing of years, and translating from one language to another, with many interpretations, we still have an accurate recording of things said and done. Garb studied these things. He once told me that he was beginning not to accept the Faith at all, because he discovered that far from a deity coming to earth and declaring himself, a man had appeared, taught good and moral things based on the religion and culture of his people. That he was executed and thereafter people from many diverse cultures set up movements in this man's name. Centuries passed and, in these different cultures, ideas were agreed at meetings until they came close to finding some basics that a majority would agree to. Anyone who did not subscribe to these central ideas was called a heretic or unbeliever. Garb declared to me that he found it unacceptable to rely on the inventions of old men as the basis for a religion.'

Fidelma was quiet for a while and then she glanced uneasily at Eadulf.

'It is a strange reasoning for one studying theology. That declaration might be the motive for his death,' she commented thoughtfully.

Sister Ingund stared at her. 'You mean that Garb was killed because of his arguments?'

'If these were the arguments he took, it would not only anger the bishop but anyone else subscribing to the Faith because most interpretations accept Christ as divine. Garb's arguments were obviously fierce. It is evident that the bishop would have returned that anger threefold. Do you think that Garb killed Bishop Brodulf?'

'He would not kill anyone,' asserted the girl immediately. 'He was of such a gentle disposition. Sometimes he would leave his books and his arguments aside and we would go walking in the forests. He would point out flowers and other plants. He would point to fungi and tell me what his mother used to prepare, and with herbs and roots dishes that I had never heard of before. Once we found a small fox that was trapped in thorn bushes and, in spite of the snapping and clawing from the little creature, Garb was able to extricate it from the bush and set it free to run back to its mother.'

'Well, it sounds as if he had a gentle nature,' Fidelma agreed. 'But that is not conclusive to claim a man or woman could never commit a murder. I have known several men who loved all manner of creatures, but who would ride off to battle and be seized by the bloody battle frenzy.'

'Would you say he would refuse a conflict if forced on him?' Eadulf asked.

'I am not sure that I understand. He would defend himself verbally against Bishop Brodulf and his arguments.'

'That is a conflict in words. What would be his reaction if Bishop Brodulf had gone up to him and struck him?'

'Ah, I see what you mean. Isn't it supposed to be one of the teachings of the Faith not to respond to violence? It is written:

"He that strike you on the right cheek, turn to him the left." Is that not so?'

'How would Garb respond to that? Would he turn the other cheek?'

Sister Ingund thought for a moment or two. 'We talked about it, Garb and I. He said that it was the hardest concept of all to respond to because he felt that instead of preventing violence it was an invitation to more violence. He felt that one should stand up against violence and prevent the attacker from doing further violence. He felt this idea of turning the other cheek merely displayed a lack of spirit. That it would entice bullies to abuse you further. Bishop Brodulf was a proud and haughty man and ready to take advantage of anyone who did not stand up to him. Garb argued that one should show spirit instead of subservience.'

'Did Garb ever have to physically stand up to Deacon Landric, for it seems that the deacon was just as proud and haughty as the bishop he served?'

'It was true that Deacon Landric was arrogant, and it would seem that he was also provoking violence at times. But Garb was never a violent man.'

'Garb was never violent?'

'As I have said, he would never be provoked physically. He was more concerned with verbal argument.'

Fidelma sighed. 'One can lead to the other.'

'Not with Garb,' Sister Ingund assured her firmly.

'Cast your mind back to the day before the fire in the guest house. Did anything unusual happen on that day? Do you remember the events of the day?'

'Unusual? We students awoke and washed as usual and went to the first service of the day. Then we went to the *longud*. After that we went to have our usual classes with the Venerable Breas.'

'Was Garb there?'

'For part of the time.'

'How do you mean, part of the time?'

'He left soon after we started. It was a very quiet session.' Sister Ingund frowned as a thought struck her. 'Bishop Brodulf was not in attendance . . . It was later that we heard that the Venerable Lugán had gone to the abbot to complain about the bishop's behaviour in the library.'

'When did you hear that?' Fidelma asked sharply.

The girl frowned, thinking about the question.

'Just after the midday meal. We were seated near the Prioress Suanach, finishing our meal, when the Venerable Lugán came and spoke rapidly with her. Although they spoke fast in their own language, I am a good student and was able to hear that the bishop had been in the library. He had put some of the texts that he was looking at in disarray. The librarian had complained to the abbot, but on his return to the library he found some texts missing. I could not hear exactly what it was about, but I knew the Venerable Lugán was saying the bishop had removed them without permission.'

'You said that Garb had also left the class. When did you see him next?'

'That evening.'

'Did he tell you where he had gone?'

'He admitted that he had spent most of the time in the library.'

'Did he see the bishop there?'

'It was after the bishop left that Garb went to see what it was that had infuriated Bishop Brodulf so much and led to the argument with the librarian.'

'Did he know what text had gone missing?' Eadulf asked.

'If he did, he did not tell me. I later learnt from Garb that Bishop Brodulf had been infuriated by a book called *An Banshenchus* because of the praise it gave to Eve as the mother of humankind. I was told it described her as generous and wise and of great virtue and accomplishment.'

'What did Garb think of that?'

'Garb was a son of his people of which you yourself are a product. Women are considered the co-equal and companions of men, just as men are the co-equal and companions of women. Garb learnt that Bishop Brodulf regarded this as sacrilege and a betrayal of the Faith. For Bishop Brodulf, Eve was to blame for the woes of man in order that women could be relegated in society.'

'So this was another matter that made Garb angry?'

'It was a point that confirmed why he was now questioning his role as the advocate of the Faith.'

There was a silence as Fidelma and Eadulf considered matters.

'I want to get this clear,' Fidelma said sharply. 'Are you saying that Garb was rejecting the Faith and even returning to the old religion or was he choosing another path?'

'Another path?'

'When the Roman emperors decided to legalise the religion of Christ as the State religion of the empire, there were many different ideas, theologies and concepts, so something had to be done to unify them all into one concept. Here, we still follow some of the teachings of Arius, the Bishop of Alexandria, who was declared a heretic at the first Council of Nicaea. That was one such attempt to form a united faith. Arius did not believe that Christ was divine, but that the title "Son of God" was a courtesy one. Many other groups believed that. The important thing was that although Arius was condemned as a heretic, he still had the support of the emperor and Arius' teachings continued to spread and be influential.'

'All I know is that Garb was possessed of a brilliant mind,' the girl continued. 'He argued things I do not completely understand. I have to say, he was both excited and appalled at where his thoughts were leading him.'

'Did Garb attend the main meal the evening that the guest house caught fire?' asked Fidelma.

'He did.'

'And nothing unusual happened? There was no sign of the stomach upset he had the next morning?'

'Garb did not eat much. He said he felt slightly nervous. I told him off as we had been due to meet that afternoon but he did not show up.'

'Where were you supposed to be going?'

'It was a period for the students to find some quiet spot to practise what Garb called *dercad*.'

Fidelma was momentarily surprised, but then felt she should not have been.

'You students practise the ancient art of meditation?' she asked. Some abbots and bishops condemned meditation as being a pagan practice inherited from the Druids. For Fidelma it had been essential at times in her life when the ancient art had so often helped her calm extraneous thoughts, soothing fears and irritations, and leading to a state of *sitcháin*, or peace, in order that her mind was clear enough to make a correct decision.

'The Prioress Suanach told us about this meditation almost the first day we arrived here. It was unusual for us as it was not part of philosophy. We were told to go to an isolated spot and concentrate on nothing. It was an impossible process for most of us.'

'So that afternoon, you did not see Garb. When you saw him at the evening meal and told him off, did he explain where he had been? You say he was nervous. Did he say he was not feeling well?'

The girl looked uncomfortable. 'I knew something was on Garb's mind, but he said that he had been discussing the debates with the Venerable Breas. It was felt, following events in the library, that had been quite confrontational.'

'So, if someone claimed to have seen Garb walking from the builders' camp with a heavy bag on his back that would have been contrary to what he told you?'

'Impossible,' the girl replied in surprise. 'Who says this?'

'Don't worry. It was not a specific identification. Just one of the builders who saw a religious on that path,' Fidelma said. 'When was it that you talked about Garb's study of the Faith and his growing unease at the confusion of the teachings?'

'On several occasions, especially after the debates with the bishop.'

'And that evening, did you and Garb walk together from the refectory to the students' dormitory?' questioned Eadulf.

'Yes, but we each went to our separate dormitories.'

'Were you roused when the fire broke out?'

'Some of us were woken by the noise and shouting. From the door we saw Brother Áedh galvanising his men to action. We students were told to stay back so as not to impede the attempts to put out the flames.'

'Did you see Garb then?'

'Of course. He came out of the male dormitory with the others and we all stood together watching from a distance until the flames were brought under control but by then it was too late and the entire building had become a shell of charred and blackened wood. We did not learn the bishop had perished in it until later on . . . in fact, that was when you and Brother Eadulf arrived.'

'You did not see Garb the next morning, even though he had been seen at morning prayer and attending the first meal. Why was this?'

'I had chores to attend to and I missed him.'

'You spoke to those who had been with Garb in the dormitory? Did all of them remain there during the night?'

Sister Ingund showed her anger. 'If you are implying that Garb burnt down the guest house and killed Bishop Brodulf, I swear to you that he did not.'

'It is my task to ensure that I have all the evidence in this matter,' Fidelma assured her. 'Tell me, what do you think of Brother Étaid?'

At the apparent change of subject, Sister Ingund looked uncertain.

'You must know he came here with the party that included Brother Garb. He was from the same area of your country.'

'Yes, but what do you think of him?' Fidelma insisted.

'He's just an ordinary boy. He has no doubts about what he believes in, unlike Garb. After leaving here he plans to emulate the Venerable Breas and become a great teacher. I think he is ambitious in that. He is certainly the opposite in character to Garb. While he joined in the arguments, I had the impression he did so for effect rather than from belief. In fact, Garb used to smile and say that he was the son of a fisherman from an island to the south-west of here and so he should know that while a boat is safe in the harbour, it was not what a boat was built for.'

'Did he mean that Étaid was not intellectually curious in spite of his ambition?'

'He accepted all that the Venerable Breas taught.'

'Whereas, Garb, at the same time as arguing the teachings of the Venerable Breas, nursed doubts and questioned them. I suppose I see the point,' Fidelma admitted. 'However, did you know that Étaid told me that he was Brother Garb's *anam chara*?'

Sister Ingund's reaction was a sad smile. 'If Garb needed a soul friend then I do not think that he would have settled for Étaid.'

'Do you mean Étaid would be lying if he made such a claim?' Fidelma demanded.

'Not necessarily so,' the girl reflected. 'During some of the early days here, the Prioress Suanach suggested that we get to know one another. If we struck up a good relationship, we were advised to see if that could continue to develop into the intimacy that is required of a soul friend. I recall that Garb and Étaid did try the experiment at first. I don't think it worked. Étaid was too conservative and Garb too full of questions and doubts. That is why Garb made an excellent scholar; always asking questions but, moreover, always retaining the answers.'

'So, what happened?'

Sister Ingund produced a wan smile. 'Garb and I became true friends of body and soul.'

'Who knew the reality of this?'

'We tried to retain it as a secret. You have told me that Deacon Landric noticed and distorted it.'

'You feel that you had become a friend until death.'

'That has proved true,' she stifled a note of emotion but her expression dissembled.

Fidelma rose. 'I am sorry for your loss, Ingund, and it would be indelicate for me to suggest that you are young. Love will find you again for you have an open heart and goodwill. When you love again, you will remember these words.'

'How can I feel trust again, until I know who killed Garb?' the girl replied tightly. 'Garb will always be by my side until his murder is explained and avenged.'

'I will try my best to fulfil this task. If it cannot be done, don't become a prisoner to the task. Remember this, Ingund, when the storm winds begin to rise, some people will start building walls. Others will see the opportunity to set up wind mills.'

CHAPTER SEVENTEEN

The news of Brother Garb's death had spread rapidly through the abbey. Groups of nervous-looking members of the brethren and the sisterhood stood in whispered conversation here and there. Fidelma and Eadulf crossed the courtyard back to the main building, passing some who gave them almost fearful glances. As they turned towards the abbot's chambers, Brother Mac Raith met them coming down the stairway.

'I am just come from Abbot Cuán,' he greeted them, his expression full of anxiety. 'The master builder was there and has persuaded the abbot to give his permission for his men to dig a second grave on Cnoc Carron.'

'I thought the custom was for at least a night and a day of the watching before the burial?' Eadulf commented.

'That does not prevent the grave being dug once the *fé* has measured the body. The body will remain in the chapel until tomorrow and thus follow the custom. The bishop's remains will still be buried as planned, at midnight tonight. Sítae insisted there is some nervousness among his workers. He wanted no delays over the burial.'

Fidelma regarded him in curiosity.

'The deaths were not related to accidents among the builders. Brother Anlón says Sítae has a good record in this respect. Why would the builders now be nervous?'

'Probably it is superstition among his men,' Brother Mac Raith replied. 'Deaths on a building site remind them of their own mortality.'

'Especially deaths in an abbey, it being concerned with the afterlife,' Eadulf observed whimsically.

'Burial at midnight is an ancient custom, but superstition associated with it remains. This is why Sítae put it to the abbot that his men would be happier if he could see a way of burying both remains this night,' the steward said, ignoring him. 'Sítae insists his men are nervous.'

Fidelma was suddenly reflective. 'It has been many years since I have considered the law as regards the work of builders. Is the master builder responsible for all accidents amongst his men? I mean, in terms of medical costs and compensation for those injured during their work. Or is that the responsibility of the abbey?'

Brother Mac Raith was confused for a moment as he tried to see a connection between Fidelma's question and the burials.

'The master builder knows his trade and craft too well to put himself, or his workers, in harm's way.'

'But is he responsible if any of his men are injured or killed by accident? He has to pay the compensation, not the abbey?'

'As he is the master builder, then his agreement is with the abbey. But his men are employed by him. He is responsible for them. The abbey is responsible to him if he is injured and he can show the abbey is at fault. The abbey would then have to compensate his honour price of twenty *séds*.'

'That is the equivalent honour price of a noble in a territorial chieftain's household,' Fidelma commented slowly.

The steward smiled grimly. 'As steward of the abbey and ultimately of its finances, I have much responsibility. The master builder has many craftsmen ranging from those skilled in mixing materials, to smiths, carvers, painters, engravers . . .

all manner of skills and arts connected with the construction of great buildings.'

'However, if anything happens to his workers, he is responsible for their honour prices – that is, the responsibility for compensation in death, serious injury?'

'That is so.'

'So he is responsible under the law for such maintenance, curative treatment, attendance of a physician and food to sustain them until they are well. There is no discrimination? It is the *Book of Aicill* in which it is so written. It says in the Law of Torts that full sick maintenance must be paid to the worker who is injured for the sake of unnecessary profit. He has followed the law and ensured his workers are tended to by the best medical care available?'

'That is so also. But these matters are irrelevant because the deaths are not those of builders,' Brother Mac Raith pointed out. 'We have yet to determine who is responsible for the bishop and the boy's deaths.'

They watched Brother Mac Raith scurry away before Eadulf turned to Fidelma, puzzled.

'I hardly think it is the right time to start thinking about building works and carpentry,' he reproved.

'There is never a wrong time to pick up information,' she replied without taking umbrage.

At that moment the Prioress Suanach came down the staircase from the upper floors.

'Is it true?' she greeted them in a shocked voice. 'I hear the boy Garb was murdered. I cannot believe it. It is not true!'

'I am afraid the boy was murdered, although whoever did it made an attempt to make it look like suicide,' Eadulf confirmed.

The prioress looked grim and her voice was vehement.

'The boy was young and full of life. Moreover, he was our leading student, whom the Venerable Breas championed as someone to join the leading academics in this abbey. He was admired by the group of students who debated under the tutelage of the Venerable Breas. It is impossible to think that such a young talent could be destroyed. For what reason? There is no doubt about the cause of his death?'

'There is no doubt,' Fidelma confirmed.

'Do you think there is a connection with Bishop Brodulf's death?'

'Unfortunately, we were never able to question Brother Garb. So we were not able to assess either his state of mind or whether people might harbour hatred against him. Since you are here, let me ask you a few questions. How was Brother Garb regarded among his fellow students?'

Prioress Suanach paused, thinking rapidly at Fidelma's change of subject.

'Although he was young, he was looked upon as a leader. The Venerable Breas will confirm that all the students admired him. Certainly, as I say, the Venerable Breas had the greatest respect for him and I believe it was his intention to make him a teacher here.'

'In this matter, you admired the opinions of the Venerable Breas?'

Fidelma could have sworn the woman's cheeks coloured a little. 'I have long admired the Venerable Breas. He is our leading scholar. He taught me at this abbey before he left to go to Mungairit, returning as chief scholar before I went abroad. As you know, I returned here after a decade or so in Burgundy. Therefore it has only been in these last months that I got to know him again.'

'Brother Garb had no animosity with any of his fellow students?'

'None. He was not that sort of youth.'

'So, as far as you know, he had no enemies among the students, including the Burgundian students?'

The prioress frowned. 'Why do you ask about them particularly?'

'Isn't it logical? According to reports, Garb was the one who was leading the arguments with Bishop Brodulf. Did they not feel that Bishop Brodulf should command their allegiance when being so vehemently denounced by a student from this land?'

Prioress Suanach shook her head. 'Students have to argue, else how should they learn?' She repeated the phrase automatically. 'Tutors and students understand the process of education.'

'And among the relationships between the students there was no enmity?'

'Of course not.'

'Everyone was good friends?' Eadulf pressed. 'None more so than others?'

Prioress Suanach raised her face towards him with an almost defiant look. 'What are you implying, Brother Eadulf?'

'Implying? Nothing. Merely asking. You have a group of young men and women who are studying and living in close quarters. So far as I am aware this is a *conhospitae* and not governed as some esoteric groups who form themselves into the type of celebrant assemblies they claim are derived from the teachings of the desert hermits. You have healthy young groups here. You, yourself, have never had to chastise any of the students for inappropriate behaviour? So I merely ask and do not imply.'

The prioress stood silent for a moment, perhaps wondering how much Eadulf knew or wanted to pursue about her arguments with Sister Ingund.

'Brother Garb seemed to get on well with everyone. I have said as much before.'

'Yet you had cause to rebuke Sister Ingund for her relationship with Garb. However, was there no one else in the group who seemed a little closer to him than the rest? We were told you encouraged the tradition of each student to have an *anam chara*.'

'I believe in that tradition,' confirmed the prioress. 'Among all the religious of the Western churches, and even among those not of the religious, each individual is encouraged to have a soul friend – an *anam chara*. They need someone with whom they can discuss their most intimate secrets and problems. It was a concept of the Old Faith, helping one another with problems in life.'

'There is a movement now from Rome that says we must adopt the idea of confessing sins in public, because it was claimed it had been started by John the Baptist. Then he would immerse believers in rivers of lakes to wash clean their sins. Wasn't that idea part of the original Faith?'

'The Venerable Breas says that we have adapted much into our Faith. We can follow our own path. Public confession and speaking to an *anam chara* is not the same thing. Talking over a problem with a close friend, seeking advice on spiritual and temporal matters is not what they do in Rome. Now I hear that public confession is being changed to confession to an ordained priest in private.'

'So, as I asked, there was no one in the group that you knew who was in that relationship to Brother Garb?' Eadulf asked.

'I believe it was Brother Étaid that was his *anam chara*,' she replied at last, her voice distant.

'And no one else?'

'You must know that an *anam chara* is a specialist position, and the secrets that pass between one and another are sacred between them.'

Fidelma spoke hurriedly in case Eadulf pursued the matter. 'Yet we have heard that Brother Étaid was no longer his soul friend. Are you sure he had no other special friends?'

Prioress Suanach sniffed as if in disapproval. 'I suppose you have been listening to gossip?'

'We have to judge who is spreading the gossip and why. Especially when it is spread by Deacon Landric.'

The prioress flushed; her lips tightened. 'It was noticed that he always seemed to be in conversation with Sister Ingund. They often met together. I did hear them having a fierce argument.'

Fidelma and Eadulf exchanged surprised glances.

'When was this?' Fidelma asked.

'I heard them arguing when they thought no one was about.'

'I thought you said argument was a way of learning among students?' Eadulf pointed out rather cynically.

'It depends on the nature of the argument and of its subject matter.'

'But you are saying that you overheard an argument between Garb and Ingund that was not merely students testing theories?'

'Do I need to spell it out? It was an argument of some private nature between them.'

'Why were they unaware of your presence during this argument?' Fidelma asked.

'I remained silent behind the door when I heard their voices.'

'So you were listening in? How long were you there?'

'Long enough.'

'For what?'

'To hear their voices raised against one another.'

'During this time you neither saw them nor identified yourself?' Fidelma pressed.

'I heard their voices plainly.'

'A wise *dálaigh* might claim this as *fianaise clostráchta* – hearsay evidence – in that you were not a physical witness. For example, they might have been arguing a text. It could be suggested as supposition. In law, presumptive conclusions can be many, as was the evidence suggested by Deacon Landric.'

The prioress flushed again but her face was distorted in anger.

'I will leave you with my remarks,' she almost spat through clenched teeth. 'If there is anything that needs amplification, I am sure that Sister Ingund will tell you. Anyway, Brother Garb is dead. His death seems to have cast a pall of unease over the students here. In fact, it has left an uneasy feeling among the builders as well as the brethren. The master builder has consulted the abbot, suggesting that rituals should be terminated so that both bodies can be buried tonight. Of course, I can think of no specific laws that would prevent it. But I am not in favour of abandoning our rituals just to alleviate the tension that is now spreading. I think the abbot is right to refuse permission to have Brother Garb buried at this time.'

The prioress stood as if waiting for an answer and so Fidelma nodded.

'In that respect, I think you are correct. We need that period for further investigation. The boy's body cannot be interred tonight.'

Prioress Suanach pursed her lips for a moment. 'It will be announced in the refectory this evening.'

She swung round abruptly and left without another word.

'Well,' Eadulf sighed, 'I am not sure whether that was a help or not. Is there anyone else we can talk to?'

'I must ask Abbot Cuán whether Sítae put forward legal reasons not to adhere to the rituals of the usual obsequies. After that, I want to reconsider a few things.'

'Reconsider?'

'To reconsider the evidence as we now have it.'

'At first we had a simple mystery,' Eadulf replied. 'A foreign bishop is killed and then the body burnt in his guest chambers, presumably to disguise the reality of his death. There are too many possibilities as to why anyone would like to dispose of him. So consideration of that is just guesswork.'

'But we get down to a suspect who had had more arguments with the bishop than most. This person disappears. Unlike the first victim, this person is well liked, so it appears no one hates him.'

'No one except Deacon Landric, the bishop's assistant,' pointed out Eadulf.

'So it seems. Anyway, Brother Garb was generally well liked

and admired. Yet he too is murdered and the body taken and so placed to point to suicide and disguise the fact of the murder.'

'You have summed it up: we have two murders that seem to have some connection,' Eadulf sighed. 'No wonder both Sítae and now Prioress Suanach say there is an ominous gloom among the builders and among the students in this abbey.'

'And presumably among the general brethren and sisterhood,' Fidelma smiled dryly, as they climbed the stone steps to the abbot's chambers.

It did not take long to assure the abbot that he was correct in delaying the burial of Brother Garb for the traditional period, even if an earlier burial might alleviate the tensions. After that, Fidelma and Eadulf retired to their chamber.

The previous evening and that morning they had to make do with a brief wash. It was only in the evening that water was heated in the *dabach*, the large tub prepared for visitors in the guest houses of every abbey or fortress. In fact, when they made their way to their chamber, they found one of the sisters already laying linen towels and bars of scented soap with other items. The bathing room was on the floor below, where a sister had heated the *dabach* for them to take the ritual bath.

'At last –the evening bath. I feel uncomfortable, having missed it last night,' Fidelma complained as she gathered the toiletries.

Hardly any time passed before Eadulf was relaxing after his own steaming bath, perched on the end of their bed, watching Fidelma comb her long, flowing locks of red hair with the aid of a *scathán*, a mirror of highly polished metal, and a *cíor* or bone comb.

The same sister who had prepared the baths knocked on the door to collect used towels and to tidy the room.

'That is the initial bell for the *praind,* the evening meal,' she advised.

'Do we go straight to the evening meal?' Eadulf asked. 'Is there no gathering for prayers in the chapel seeing that . . . that . . .'

The sister shook her head. 'The abbot says that matters for the funerals will be announced before the meal,' she replied nervously. 'It is my understanding that prayers will be taken in the chapel afterwards as part of the services. There is much speculation that the abbot has given his authority for the young Brother Garb to be interred tonight as well.'

'Who says that?' Fidelma demanded at once.

'The story is prevalent among the students, and it is reported that the builders are digging a new grave on Cnoc Carron.'

Just then the bell began to ring again, this time with a harsher and more urgent sound. Fidelma raised her eyes skyward with a resigned expression.

'The evening meal already? One is not given much time to prepare.'

The young sister had withdrawn and Eadulf looked troubled.

'Do you think it is true? The steward seemed positive that the master builder's suggestion had been refused. I am surprised that the age-old rituals on burials could not be bypassed for the bishop, but they could for the young student,' Eadulf observed as they left their guest room to go towards the main refectory.

Fidelma grimaced. 'No need to be surprised. Rituals and customs can be changed in cases of expedience. In this case I do recall reference to a law about funeral customs, and Abbot Cuán has to make decisions and ask for the approval of the prioress or senior members of the *conhospitae*. As I said, they are not laws in themselves but customs protected by law. And remember that the abbot is part of the Eóghanacht kindred.'

'But as the abbey comes under the law of the kingdom, as you have always told me, then you, as a *dálaigh*, should be instructing it in law.'

'There is truth in what you say, but the laws of these kingdoms are now being influenced by the Faith. It is even being discussed whether the swearing of oaths on legal matters before a Druid should be removed from the law system and their status denigrated. I think even the Druids will finally disappear by the next century.'

'I don't understand.'

'When Christianity was made the state religion of the Roman Empire it followed that any Christians had to obey Roman law. Christianity had been a belief that was secretly passed on through slaves and the poor without property. It was regarded with distrust by the Romans. Now it seems that it has become a religion of the Emperor, of kings, princes and nobles.'

'Which means?' Eadulf asked. 'I thought old law texts, like the *Crith Gablach,* ask: what is higher than a king? The answer being given that the King does not ordain the people, but the people ordain the King, so he is only given authority to carry out the will of the people.'

Fidelma smiled sadly. 'No, the new text is being amended – who is higher, the King or the bishop? As the King now has to rise before the bishop, on account of the Faith, the new answer is obvious. We are now told that the honour price of an abbot, such as Abbot Cuán, is fourteen *cumal.* That is the same honour price as that of a king of one of the Five Kingdoms.'

'How can this be a progressive development from the original laws?' Eadulf sighed.

'Very simply, as I said. The founders of the main religious communities and subsequent abbots are of the royal lineages. Indeed, some of them were even kings themselves. So they were endowed with land rights and now the land on which the abbeys are built have become like royal centres, with the abbots usually succeeded by the election of their *derbfine,* the family council, just like kings and princes.'

'But Abbot Cuán – surely he is not prince?'

'Even Abbot Cuán,' she confirmed. 'He was nephew of Cuán Mac Amalgado of the Eóganacht Áine, who succeeded my father briefly as King of Muman. What I am trying to explain is that he is my very distant cousin. I can only advise him in these matters but I have to defer to my brother's Chief Brehon. I cannot give an order to anyone unless I have the authority of the Chief Brehon.'

CHAPTER EIGHTEEN

There was a sombre feeling among those who filled the refectory that evening. Fidelma and Eadulf took their places alongside the abbot and the prioress. The steward, Brother Mac Raith, was much in evidence, ensuring everyone was in the right seats. The bell summoning them to the *praind*, the evening meal, had just ceased when Abbot Cuán rose and waited for the assembly to be silent. There were certainly more people in the refectory than on the previous evening. Indeed, the long tables were so tightly packed that some of the gathering were still standing, waiting for an opportunity to squeeze on to the benches. Not even the death of Bishop Brodulf had caused such an atmosphere of curiosity and even tension. Was it the gathering in expectation of learning about the event, or was it in respect of the death of a popular young student? Was it the news of the murder or the victim that attracted attention?

Fidelma was peering round the refectory when Eadulf, with his usual uncanny perceptiveness, leant forward and whispered to her, 'The students' tables are those to your right, just in that corner.'

She had not noticed the table previously, but now she realised there were a lot of young people seated there, and with the master of the students, the Venerable Lugán. She could see the Burgundian students among them. That the Venerable Lugán was seated there this evening was curious; he had previously sat with the senior members of the abbey.

Abbot Cuán, after clearing his throat, began to speak.

'It is my sad duty to confirm that the burial of Bishop Brodulf, a visitor and guest of this abbey, who perished in the fire of the guest house, will take place at midnight.'

To Fidelma's surprise, the Venerable Lugán had risen from his seat among the students.

'As master of the students I am requested by the students here to raise a matter.'

Abbot Cuán did not look pleased at the interruption. Watching him, however, Fidelma felt he had been forewarned of it.

'What is their concern?'

'It is now common knowledge that one of our leading students, Brother Garb, has been found dead.'

'I was about to announce that,' the abbot replied sharply.

'I have been asked to say that the students expect a proper respect for their fellow in that they insist on a full day's *aire*, the watching by the body of Brother Garb, before the burial takes place. That the watching should take place in the chapel with all due respect and the proper procedure of lamentations should follow.'

'Why would they not think this would be done?' Abbot Cuán demanded.

'There has been a growing rumour that this custom might be changed. It is said that Brother Garb might be hurried to his grave tonight. It has been reported that the *fé* has already been measured and that his grave is already being dug on Cnoc Carron. The rumour has it that this has been requested by those not of the religious of this abbey. The students would consider this a lack of respect.'

Fidelma wondered if she would be called upon if legal precedents were needed. Thankfully, she had gone through those she knew earlier when she had advised the abbot not to accept the master builder's advice.

'The customs and rituals will be met,' Abbot Cuán declared in a strong voice. 'In both cases, we are dealing with a matter of unlawful killing. So long as medical and matters of evidence have been secured, the burial of the bishop will be tonight and the burial of Brother Garb will be tomorrow night. Had you consulted me before this meal, this matter would have been made clear for you to inform the students. The matter should no longer provide a distraction.'

'The customs and rituals will be followed in so far as they apply,' the Venerable Lugán repeated, with emphasis. 'What does that mean? The activities of Sítae's men have led the students to believe otherwise.'

'I have said what I have said,' snapped Abbot Cuán. Then he bent as Prioress Suanach whispered something to him. He straightened up and continued. 'If there is any misapprehension it may be on the part of those who do not fully understand our rituals and of the circumstances in which permission was given to members of Sítae's workmen to prepare the grave in advance for tomorrow.'

Watching him, it was clear to Fidelma that the Venerable Lugán's heart was not in any further protest, and that he had raised his comments only at the request of the students, who had doubtless heard of the master builder's plea to the abbot. He sat down among the murmuring youth.

Abbot Cuán gave a palpable sigh of relief and decided to carry on.

'Just before midnight you will hear the death bell sounding, upon which you will all gather at the chapel to commence the processions to the tombs of the blest on Cnoc Carron where the body of Bishop Brodulf will be interred.'

The pause was met with silence.

'Very well,' the abbot continued. 'The full days of lamentation have been curtailed for the reasons I have stated. However, we will dedicate this evening's *praind*, the main meal, as a *fled cro-lige*, the feast of the deathbed, to Bishop Brodulf. With that in mind, I so dedicate this feast.'

Indicating with a motion of his hand for those gathered to rise, the abbot intoned a short *gratias*, a thanks, blessing and dedication of the meal.

Fidelma was impressed by the dishes the abbey had made. It was clear the choices had been made especially. She already knew that the Abbey of Imleach was not one of those frugal communities that accepted the new fasting concepts of the Desert Fathers.

In fact, there were several choices. There was *sercol-tarsain* or salted venison, which was very popular due to the large herds that wandered the country. A second meat dish was *caer-fheóil*, sheep flesh or mutton. It was considered a more popular delicacy than beef. For those who did not desire meat there were various forms of river fish, nuts and fruits. The abbot seemed to make his kitchens provide as well as the cooks of any powerful noble. Unlike the previous evening, this meal was eaten in silence; almost a reverent silence, the dining a little hurried, and everyone was thankful when the abbot rose to intone the final *gratias*.

Later, during the tolling of the *clog-estechtae*, the death bell, the brethren and the sisterhood began to gather outside the chapel, but the solemn tones of the bell drew only a small fraction of the abbey's inhabitants. There appeared as many builders as religious. Fidelma remembered that the abbot had given the master builder permission for his men to dig both graves, due to the fact that the abbey's grave measurer and the burial party had been injured in the flames. Truly, it did save considerable time, energy and effort. There had also been the problem that it would be hard to find someone willing to handle the *fé*, the grave measuring rod, because of its occult symbolism.

At a signal, the lanterns were held high on staffs to light the way of the procession and, from the chapel, the remains wrapped in the linen *racholl*, or shroud, were brought out, ready to be placed on the *fuat*, or bier. This was done by volunteers from the builders. The *fuat* was to be wheeled on a *carreus* to the Port na Fert Failtech, the burial place or tombs of the blest, which was the name for the abbey's burial ground on the adjacent Cnoc Carron. It was an unusually silent ceremony, for there was no *lámh comairt*, the clapping of hands, or *caoine*, weeping aloud, or other outward signs of showing affection for the dead that was usual at funerals. Neither did anyone come forward to sing the traditional *écnaire* or requiem at the graveside. It was curious that Deacon Landric and Brother Charibert followed the process but did not engage in it.

Even Fidelma was surprised when it was a group of the builders, led by Sítae, who carried the *fuat* of the bishop to the grave, which had been dug in a far corner rather than beside members of the religious. It was no wonder that rumours among the students had been rife and caused them to make the Venerable Lugán raise a protest on their behalf. Fidelma learnt afterwards that Abbot Cuán had agreed to the argument from the master builder that this should be allowed as a special tribute, as the bishop had technically met his death on their building site. It was unusual, but Fidelma understood the symbolism.

It seemed natural, however, that this particular bishop was buried with only a brief ceremony and blessing. There was no testimony for Abbot Cuán to declare, as was the custom. Curiously, the bishop's steward, Deacon Landric, had declined to deliver the customary *amra*, or elegy. It was almost as if there was a profound feeling of relief when the *strophaiss*, or branches of broom, were laid over the body and the group of builders began to fill in the grave.

As they began to walk back into the abbey Fidelma turned to

Abbot Cuán: 'I observed that Brother Landric did not accept the opportunity to give the *amra* by Bishop Brodulf's grave?' It was delivered as a question.

'I had presumed the customs in Burgundia were different from those here, but Prioress Suanach informed me that something similar to our rituals is expected. It is odd and I was surprised that neither of the bishop's companions wanted to play any role in the burial rituals,' admitted the abbot.

Brother Mac Raith, who was walking with them, added: 'As Deacon Landric was the bishop's steward, I was also surprised. He seemed to know something about the bishop and also the family connection to their king, so there was enough information for some words to be said. But he did not volunteer.'

'Did he give the impression he was not marking the occasion for any particular reason?' Fidelma asked.

The response was negative. Fidelma was thoughtful until she saw Prioress Suanach on the far side of the courtyard and swiftly excused herself, turning to join her.

'I am told that Deacon Landric claimed he could not contribute an elegy over the body of Bishop Brodulf. I was surprised to hear it. I saw that your young Burgundian students were attending the funeral. I was wondering why a prayer was not said by them or even Brother Charibert, as Deacon Landric declined.'

Prioress Suanach sounded disapproving in the gloom. 'I think the plain and simple fact is that no one liked Bishop Brodulf, or cared sufficiently about him to be concerned whether he went to his grave with a prayer or a curse to mark his life.'

Fidelma grimaced sadly. 'That is certainly a woeful judgement on a human being. He was a Christian, as we are.'

'Not exactly as we are. Brodulf was a law unto himself,' the prioress responded. 'Deacon Landric, even though he was Bishop Brodulf's steward, probably disliked the bishop as much as most people came to do so after they met him.'

'You think Deacon Landric disliked him?' Fidelma asked with a frown.

'At times it was almost as if Deacon Landric purposely distanced himself from the bishop. Anyway, I am sure the students were not so much concerned with the bishop as with avoiding him.'

'Well, he was a Christian bishop, and even if we disagreed with him we should have some sympathy,' Eadulf sighed. 'A sad word or two does not go amiss in the circumstances.'

'I am afraid, Eadulf, you are an idealist,' Prioress Suanach said dryly.

She left them to go towards her own chambers. Fidelma and Eadulf turned to find most of the crowd had dispersed, although Enda stood waiting for them at a respectful distance.

It was now after the moon's zenith, but it was pale, hardly noticeable behind dark scudding clouds, which were seen only because of the faint light of the moon itself.

The tall figure of Enda came forward. 'I was wondering if there was anything else you wanted from me before I went to bed.'

'I don't think so, Enda.'

The warrior hesitated and then suddenly produced a roll of papyrus from under his shirt.

'While we were at the funeral one of the students gave me this. I think it was the one called Sister Ingund.'

'What is it?' Fidelma asked. It was too dark to see anything.

'I wouldn't know,' Enda shrugged. 'She said to hand it to you as she found it under Brother Garb's bed. She didn't want to be seen giving it to you.'

'She said nothing else?'

Enda thought for a moment before replying. 'I couldn't fathom this but she said something about understanding the mind.'

Fidelma took the scroll. Then she and Eadulf bade Enda to sleep well. In their chamber, Fidelma lit a candle and sank onto the bed with the papyrus.

'If you wish to be abroad at first light, then we best get to our bed at once,' Eadulf said. 'Remember it is now well after midnight and the sun rises early at this time of year. I can't see us even getting closer to resolving this mystery.'

'I am well aware of that,' Fidelma snapped. Then she heaved a sigh. 'I am sorry, Eadulf. That was uncalled for. I am a little out of temper. I would not admit to anyone else that I am not in the easiest of moods.'

'I would be a bad companion if I did not know that,' Eadulf replied. 'Don't worry, I know the workings of your mind. Things will all come together soon.'

'For the first time I cannot see a way forward. That's what causes me frustration. I am confronted by a blank wall.' She suddenly hesitated. 'What did you say?'

Eadulf was perplexed.

'I didn't say anything.'

'It was something about things coming together soon.'

'All I said was that I know the workings of your mind.'

'The understanding of the mind,' Fidelma said firmly. She smoothed out the scroll of papyrus.

'What is it?'

'It is some notes in Latin with some passages in Greek, but it references things in a language I am not familiar with.'

It did not surprise Eadulf, for the great ecclesiastical college of the Five Kingdoms had made a point of teaching the languages from which the New Faith derived. These were languages taught to students.

'It seems to be some notes and references written by Brother Garb, for he signs his name at the top of the page.' Fidelma peered closely at the papyrus by the flickering light of the candle.

'What does it say?' Eadulf urged.

'A line in Latin . . . it says: "I will sin to even ask the question!" The line is underscored.'

'What question?'

'There are references in Hebrew and some lines. I recognise little but the titles of some of the ancient texts. The Talmud, Zohar Leviticus, Book of Adam and Eve and something called the *Alphabet of Sirach*.'

Eadulf shrugged. 'I know little of such works.'

'There is a short text given or translated into Greek and then Latin.'

'Which says?'

'It is like a quote from Genesis. It says: "It is not good for man to be alone. So God created a woman from the earth, as he created Adam himself, and called her Lilith. Adam and Lilith immediately began to fight. She said: 'I will not be below,' and he said: 'I will not be beneath you, but only on top. For you are fit only to be in the bottom position, while I am to be the superior one.' Lilith responded: 'We are equal to each other inasmuch as we were both created from the same earth.'" Then it says she left the Garden of Eden to live with the Archangel Samael. Adam pleaded with God to find him another companion who was subservient to him and thus God created Eve.'

Fidelma and Eadulf sat staring at each other, shocked by the text.

'Is there anything else?' Eadulf finally whispered.

'A note in Latin, which seems to be in Brother Garb's hand. It says "... the *Alphabet of Sirach* took this from the earliest Hebrew texts." Then he puts a question: "... our teachers deny there was a woman before Eve. That woman demanded that she was equal to man. It is an ancient text of the Hebrews. How can such ancient texts be ignored or rewritten?"'

Eadulf grimaced after a little thought. 'Thank God I am no scholar. That is a question that I would not like to attempt to find an answer to.'

Fidelma rerolled the papyrus and put it into her bag before

undressing and getting into the bed. After a moment she extinguished the candle.

'Initially, I thought there was an overabundance of paths to be taken. So many people hated Bishop Brodulf, so there was no lack of suspects. And now there are other mysteries that are confusing. What was Bishop Brodulf really here for? What was he looking for in the library? Where are the records that he took and what did they mean for him? Is there a connection with the prioress? Would simple prejudice against women really have caused such loss of temper over that book, *A History of Women*, and how the image of Eve is perceived? What we now learn is opposed to how Eusebius, who you will remember produced the first Bible text in Latin, interpreted the scriptures.'

Eadulf gave a groan in the dark. 'I implore you to stop, Fidelma. You sound just like the oral rotation of my mind, and I, too, am getting frustrated.'

'Well, it is the first time I have heard that the ancient Hebrew teachings say that Adam had a first wife called Lilith and that she refused to accept that women should be held as subservient to men.'

'The trouble is that you are right, Fidelma,' he sighed. 'There are too many questions and not one approaching an answer. There is no easy path.'

Fidelma suddenly heard him chuckle.

'Doesn't one of your favourite Latin writers say: "*suspectum semper facilis uia*"?' he suddenly asked.

'I am not sure that is exactly what was said but it is a good reminder that an easy path is always to be suspected. Well, we will see if there is anything that catches the suspicious eye on this path tomorrow.'

It seemed that they had barely gone to sleep when there came a rapid knocking at the door and the voice of the steward, Brother Mac Raith, came urgently calling their names. Eadulf groaned but he was the first to roll out of the bed and make his way towards the door to open it. The steward stood there in an agitated state, holding a lamp in one hand.

'What is it?' Eadulf yawned, hardly awake.

'Forgive me, forgive me,' the steward exclaimed. 'I need you and the lady Fidelma to come with me.'

Fidelma was throwing on a warm cloak while also stifling a yawn.

'What is the problem?' She looked towards the window to try to guess what hour of the night it could be. It was still dark.

'If you could come with me, please.' The steward was clearly anxious. He turned to Eadulf. 'I have noticed you usually carry a *lés*. Bring it.'

Eadulf reluctantly picked up his robe, slipped into his sandals and picked up the medical bag it was his custom to carry. With a quick glance at each other, he and Fidelma joined the steward at the door.

'This way,' Brother Mac Raith urged.

He hurried away along the corridor and down the stone steps to the lower floor. As they followed his quick figure they realised he was heading for the *scriptorium*. The steward paused outside the door for a moment before opening it. He motioned them through and shut the door behind them. Aside from the steward's own lamp there was another giving a faint light at the far end of the room. In the flickering gloom of this, there was a figure in a half-sitting position on the floor, learning back against the wall at the far end.

Eadulf immediately hurried forward as the figure stirred and groaned.

Fidelma felt a moment of relief that they were not being shown another body. The figure was the Venerable Lugán. Even in the poor light, Eadulf saw there was blood on the man's head. He knelt down beside the elderly librarian, who groaned again and tried to open his eyes.

'Can you hear me?' Eadulf asked, reaching forward and taking the man's wrist in his hand, feeling for a pulse. He noticed a cut on Lugán's temple.

The old librarian coughed a little and then groaned. Then he grimaced painfully but with a gesture of assent.

'Do you know who I am?' Eadulf pressed.

There was a pause before the librarian answered: 'Eadulf.'

Eadulf turned to the steward. 'Can you bring some water in a basin, and a cloth to bathe his wound?'

The steward turned without a word and hurried away.

Fidelma dropped down beside Eadulf. She had taken the lamp that had been in the library, holding it up to illuminate the man's injuries for Eadulf.

'Stay still,' Eadulf instructed the librarian, as he tried to move. 'Let's see what injuries you have first.'

By the time he had examined the man and found only the blow to the head, which had cut the skin, the steward was back with the basin of water and a cloth. The steward also produced a flask, from whose aroma Eadulf deduced it contained a strong cider. Eadulf first allowed the old librarian to take a few sips from the flask and then set about cleaning his face and head of the blood.

'Now let us hear what happened,' Fidelma asked of the steward, while Eadulf finished cleaning up and assisting the old librarian into a proper chair.

'I was making my final inspection of this part of the abbey . . .' began the steward.

'You were making an inspection at this time of night?' she queried. 'Isn't that unusual?'

'It is late because of the funeral. I thought it prudent in the light of recent events. I am not usually about this late but there were also a number of accounts to finish.'

'Go on.'

'I was passing the *scriptorium* when I noticed the door was ajar

265

and there was a faint light coming through the opening. I pushed it open and came in. It was then I saw the Venerable Lugán stretched out on the floor. I was not then able to arouse him. So I came to get Brother Eadulf, knowing he had once studied the healing arts and I have seen him about with his *lés*, his medical bag.'

Fidelma frowned slightly. 'Why did you come for Eadulf and not for your own physician, Brother Anlón?'

'For two reasons,' the steward replied immediately. 'You are close to the *scriptorium*. You know where Brother Anlón's apothecary is – at the far end of the abbey, which has not yet been rebuilt. The second one is that you are investigating the deaths in this abbey. I was not sure whether the librarian was alive or dead. Better to come to get Brother Eadulf and yourself, for I know there are some things connected with events in this library.'

'Reasons enough,' Fidelma agreed, turning to look at the Venerable Lugán. 'How is he?' she asked Eadulf. 'Well enough to speak?'

The old librarian responded a little peevishly before Eadulf could reply.

'The blow on the head knocked me unconscious and split my skin, but has not left me bereft me of my senses. I shall doubtless have a bruise across the temple for a while. But I survive.'

'Are you able to tell us how you came in this state?' Fidelma asked.

'That I am.' He eased himself into a better sitting position and waved back Eadulf to give him a little more space. The Venerable Lugán massaged the back of his neck slowly with one hand and exhaled deeply.

'I was thinking much about those missing ledgers,' he began thoughtfully.

'The ones that you said Bishop Brodulf must have removed from this library?'

'What else?' he replied testily. 'I kept seeking an explanation.

Why would Bishop Brodulf be so interested in the archives of that time?'

'Did any ideas come to you?'

'None. Anyway, I felt a compulsion to come and take a look at one or two places on the shelves that might have been overlooked as hiding places. I came to the *scriptorium* and entered. It then happened very quickly.'

He paused and they waited expectantly for a reaction.

'What happened?' Fidelma finally prompted.

'There was a figure crouching in the shadows. The back was towards me and they were examining the records here.'

Eadulf made a soft whistling sound, receiving a disapproving look from Fidelma.

'Did you recognise the figure?' Eadulf asked.

'The back was towards me, as I said. Immediately they heard me, they extinguished their candle . . .'

'Isn't this the same area that you saw Bishop Brodulf searching the records?' demanded Fidelma.

'It is the same area.'

'So what happened? Presumably you had a light even though the figure extinguished their light?'

'I gave a cry and started forward. The figure turned and seemed to have a stick or cudgel in the hand. They struck me and I was knocked unconscious by the blow.'

'You had a moment when they turned. Did you recognise who it was?'

'I had no time. The figure was clad in robes with the hood over its head. But I am sure it was a male. It was tall enough, and I am not sure if a girl or woman would have had strength enough to strike so hard.'

'It was certainly a blow to the side of the head from which you are lucky not to have sustained worse injuries,' Eadulf agreed. 'I am not sure a woman could have hit so hard. You must take things easy for a time. I would prefer it if Brother Anlón were consulted and took over your treatment. I would not wish to cause enmity by interfering as he is the physician of this abbey.'

Fidelma had risen and was now looking about the area.

'You say that the figure was here when you spotted him?'

The elderly librarian was now asking Eadulf to help him to his feet so that he could indicate the spot where the attack happened.

'If I remember correctly, that was also the shelf where Bishop Brodulf was examining the ledgers, which you showed us?' Fidelma was thoughtful.

'It is,' the librarian confirmed. 'You can see the empty space from which the ledgers went missing. At that time none but Bishop Brodulf could have taken them.'

'So Bishop Brodulf was here and you are sure that there was no one else that used this area? That only Brodulf could have done so? If he took them, you felt they must have been incinerated in the fire.'

'That is true.'

'Then I wonder what this mysterious figure was doing looking in this area. What else is here?'

She glanced along the leather-bound volumes on the shelf. Then an idea came to her. She turned to the steward.

'The abbot and you once spoke of certain ancient books now considered contrary to the agreed texts of the Faith. You said they were here in the library, hidden in a souterrain. Is it near here?'

Brother Mac Raith looked uncomfortable. 'Not far but the entrance is hidden. No one would be able to access it. However, the students have researched from the texts along here from time to time.'

'Texts such as . . .?' Fidelma encouraged.

'Texts from the languages of the East – Hebrew, Aramaic, Greek . . . we have a few such texts there. Brother Garb was a frequent user of the library, as was Sister Fastrude and Brother

Étaid . . . oh, all of them at some time or another. Even some of the visitors came and read the texts on the shelves here – Brother Landric and Brother Charibert and—'

'Just a moment,' Eadulf said sharply, 'did you say Brother Charibert used the library?'

The Venerable Lugán seemed to have recovered something of his sharp sarcastic tone. His reply was almost defensive. 'I only saw Brother Charibert here once or twice, in the corner over there. I know he was regarded as a servant but we are not as prejudiced as his master was. He was welcome here along with scholars.'

'What was he looking at?' Eadulf asked.

'I've no idea,' the librarian admitted. 'He was so intensely occupied that I did not wish to interrupt his study. After a while I went back and he was gone and the text he was reading had been replaced so I have no way of knowing what it was.'

'Can you recall, was this before or after you had the problem with Bishop Brodulf?'

The Venerable Lugán rubbed his chin thoughtfully as he considered. 'I think afterwards. Though it might have been earlier on that same day.'

'You maintain that the bishop took the text and we can only presume those he took perished in the fire?' Eadulf said.

'Remind us again of what the ledgers stored here contained?' Fidelma asked.

'They were the lists of names and achievements of all those students and scholars and even general communities in this abbey from the time of Abbot Conaing until the time of Abbot Ségdae.'

'Are you sure that these were what disappeared after you found that Bishop Brodulf had been searching here?'

The Venerable Lugán seemed affronted by the question. 'I have said so before and I will repeat it once again,' he said sharply.

'Perhaps this person who attacked you just now did not know

they had disappeared or that they had possibly been destroyed in the fire,' Eadulf pointed out with a frown.

'Possibly,' Fidelma replied slowly. 'However, there are other possibilities. Venerable Lugán, I know you have been injured and that this is a bad time. Can you just look here and see if there is anything further missing other than what you have identified following the visit of the bishop?'

'My mind is not fully functional,' the librarian protested.

'But I am afraid it is important.'

With a protesting sound, the librarian moved forward with the help of a curious Brother Mac Raith, who was now holding his lamp high. The Venerable Lugán began to shuffle through the ledgers and papers on the shelf.

'There is nothing I can see missing other than what I believe Bishop Brodulf took with him.'

'I think you said that what he took with him was unique?' Fidelma queried.

'In my eyes, as well as in the eyes of the abbey, yes, they were unique.'

'So no matching records cover that period of the abbey at all? There are no copies or other references.'

'There is no copy, to my knowledge. I speak as the archivist of this ancient abbey. That,' he added in a slightly mocking tone, 'is the meaning of unique.'

Brother Mac Raith intervened. 'I have confirmed with Abbot Cuán that these ledgers have gone missing and that they have become a great loss to the abbey.'

'Very well,' Fidelma accepted. 'Then we can do no more for the moment. The attacker, whoever it was, has gone. There is much to be done tomorrow, and there is another funeral in the evening, which I presume will be more significant than the last one.'

Brother Mac Raith seemed puzzled.

'As it is the funeral of a leading young student of the abbey,' she explained patiently. 'Brother Mac Raith, I suggest you escort the Venerable Lugán to his chambers and assure he retires to a good night's repose.'

Once back inside their own chamber Fidelma flung herself on the bed in annoyance.

'You have something on your mind?' Eadulf asked as he joined her.

'It looks as though there is some sort of key in those records. First, Bishop Brodulf is searching for them. Then another stranger to this abbey and its history starts searching, is interrupted and thus attacks the librarian. For what reason? We are told by the librarian that certain documents have been taken by the bishop and we presumed they have been destroyed in the fire. Now we hear there were several people researching manuscripts in that area of the library. But there is only one person that interests me.'

Eadulf tried to recollect the name but gave up guessing and thus earned a look of disapproval from Fidelma.

'Who would you say was the least likely person to be in a library researching texts?'

Eadulf shrugged but then a thought came to mind.

'An illiterate servant who could not speak more than his own language? A servant who had been a slave? The servant to Bishop Brodulf?'

'Exactly,' Fidelma exclaimed. 'Brother Charibert. He who could not muster sufficient Latin to have a conversation with us. Who claimed not to be literate but was able to be appointed as a servant to Bishop Brodulf.'

Eadulf pursed his lips in a silent whistle.

'And literate enough to go to the library and become engrossed in reading a text. But which text, and was it one of those that disappeared?'

Fidelma rose from the bed.

'The hour is late but we will go and have a word with our illiterate Brother Charibert,' she declared determinedly.

'There is a problem,' Eadulf pointed out. 'Doesn't Brother Charibert share quarters with Deacon Landric?'

Fidelma hesitated, staring thoughtfully at the early light in the sky.

'I think Brother Mac Raith said they were in the same quarters but perhaps they are not in the same chamber,' she finally said. 'I think Deacon Landric is just as conceited and pretentious as the bishop was. Perhaps Landric would have insisted he had a chamber to himself rather than share it. Let's chance it.'

Reluctantly, Eadulf followed her along the corridor and down to the courtyard again, crossing to where they had gone to see Deacon Landric. They had halted in the corridor leading to the chambers assigned to Deacon Landric, which were at one end of the corridor. They stood undecided just as one of the brethren appeared, pursuing some early morning duty in the abbey.

'Brother Charibert? The Burgundian?' the religieux frowned. He pointed to an arched gate, which opened into a very small yard, beyond which was an old wooden building. It was still dark as the glint of the upcoming dawn had not yet penetrated these darkened reaches of the abbey. Eadulf had assumed the day would grow light sooner than expected and he regretted leaving the lamp behind. But he moved confidently across the intervening space to the old wooden door, wondering how best to open it without disturbing the occupant.

Even as they stood there, about to enter, they heard a slight noise on the other side door. It was being opened. By instinct Fidelma seized Eadulf's arm and indicated a dark alcove nearby. They crossed the intervening space in one stride and squeezed into the protective darkness. It was pure instinct but it was one of those curious moments that Fidelma had that worked to her advantage.

The dark figure exited from the door. It carried no lamp but did not even pause to find a candle to ignite as it moved into the small yard. It came abreast of the alcove and paused to check the archway into the main area of the abbey where there was enough faint light to cause some illumination in the passage. Fidelma drew in a soft breath as she recognised Brother Charibert. She moved quietly out of the alcove and was two paces behind him.

'*State!*' she hissed dramatically. '*Ne circum vestere, si vitam tuum diligemus!*'

Brother Charibert came to halt immediately in answer to her order to halt and not to turn if he valued his life.

CHAPTER NINETEEN

Fidelma felt Eadulf come up to stand behind her ready for any reaction, but Brother Charibert stood quite still. She continued quietly in Latin, ordering Brother Charibert to return to his own chamber. He turned obediently, without a word, and went back through the door, with both of them following closely behind. He opened another door on the far side of an antechamber and went through into a small bedchamber and halted at the end of the bed in the semi-gloom of the early morning light. Fidelma and Eadulf followed, with Eadulf closing the door behind them. Brother Charibert made no attempt to turn but waited patiently for further instructions.

Still speaking in Latin, Fidelma said: 'You may now sit down, Brother Charibert, and we can have a serious and truthful talk.'

The Burgundian obeyed without a word.

'I have to say your knowledge of Latin has vastly improved since we last spoke,' Eadulf observed humorously, as he bent to light a lamp near the bed.

'*Sic loqueris omnic cum Latin,*' Fidelma added with a cynical smile.

Brother Charibert shrugged indifferently. 'Even a slave can learn to read and write Latin.'

She sat down on a chair opposite him while Eadulf stood with folded arms as if to keep sentinel over the man.

'It would best if you were able to expand your memory a little. You can speak Latin as well, and probably better.'

Brother Charibert did not reply for a moment or two and then shrugged. 'I will not deny it. And therefore . . .?'

'Therefore, you can explain the meaning of your performance when you were questioned.'

'Sometimes it is useful to claim a lack of knowledge when you are out to gain knowledge.'

'What knowledge were you seeking?'

'If I knew, I would not be seeking it.'

Eadulf had noticed something and suddenly took a step forward to a shelf. There was something almost hidden under a folded piece of linen. It was a small leather-bound text. He glanced at it. He made out the title to be *Western Sayings*. It was a Latin text, but there was a loose leaf in it. He glanced at it and then handed it to Fidelma. Someone had been trying to copy old Irish letters on it. She took it, said nothing but placed the leaf in her *marsupium*.

'So you are interested in scholarship? We have little time to play with the use or meaning of words in any language. So let us return to some basic questions. Do you still claim that you were a former slave of a noble who was freed to serve Bishop Brodulf at Luxovium?'

'I do.'

'Is it true that the bishop was a prince of the royal house of the Franks? Because I doubt if he would employ a former slave as a secretary.'

'I must presume that you have never heard of the freed Greek slave Narcissus, who became private secretary to the Roman Emperor Claudius? He achieved great power and wealth.'

'I was more interested in why neither you nor Deacon Landric came forward to give an elegy at the funeral last night.'

Brother Charibert smiled thinly. 'That was the decision of Deacon Landric. Who am I to stand against him?'

'Who you are is what we must now try to discover,' Fidelma replied grimly. 'So you maintain that you were a slave in the house of this noble Wulfoald before joining the Abbey of Luxovium?'

'That is the truth, as I told you. My lord Wulfoald liked to ensure his senior slaves had some knowledge. I was taught grammar and literature in my own language . . .' He glanced at Eadulf with a smile. 'I was interested in our exchanges in your language, Eadulf. I had not realised that our dialects were so closely associated.'

'Very well. You learnt Latin and literature. Go on.'

'I also learnt some of the language of the Hellenes, enough to serve in the abbey.'

'Did you also learn Hebrew?' Fidelma asked sharply.

Brother Charibert hesitated and then shook his head. 'No more than to construe a few lines of the sacred texts.'

'Did Bishop Brodulf know this?'

'He knew I had some passable Latin but he was one of those nobles who is too arrogant to notice the talents of a mere servant. You were correct that such a noble as Brodulf would not employ an illiterate slave.'

'You said that your former master, Wulfoald, freed you on condition that you went to the abbey,' Eadulf observed. 'Is that now true, and wasn't that a curious thing for him to do?'

'Wulfoald thought I would have a better future as a member of the religious in Luxovium.'

'It doesn't sound likely,' Fidelma commented dryly. 'How did you find yourself serving the bishop on this trip to what must be an alien country to you?'

'When I went to the abbey, I took a vow of services as many do to the Faith. I am fulfilling that vow.'

'So what interested you in the library of this abbey?' she asked without raising her voice.

That produced a reaction, although Charibert's nervous jerk of the head was so quick as to be barely perceptible.

'I like to improve my knowledge.'

'It seems many people, including the bishop, sought to improve their knowledge among the texts in that particular area of the library. When were you last in the library?'

Brother Charibert frowned. 'When? I suppose yesterday afternoon.'

'Not sometime after the funeral of the bishop?'

'Why should I go there in the middle of the night?'

'Where were you going just now?'

'It is my practice to rise at dawn and have a walk for exercise.'

'I repeat, what interests you in the library? You have been observed there.'

'There are some interesting texts kept there.'

'Texts that also caught the attention of the bishop?'

'I have no way of knowing what Bishop Brodulf was interested in.'

'So what were you interested in?' Fidelma asked again, sharply.

'Why . . .' Brother Charibert, glanced quickly from one to another, 'I saw that the library had the great work on Salic Law, which had been ordered to be gathered by King Clovis over a hundred years ago. Where else would I see a copy within my hand's reach? It was also a history of my own people, the Salian Franks. Think what fascination that held for me.'

'So you are interested in the origins of your people? Even though you were just a slave among them?' Eadulf was cynical.

'Perhaps it would lead me back to the time when I was not a slave. Who knows how history has scattered the lives and destinies of my family?'

Fidelma examined the young man with appreciative interest.

'An interesting philosophical point,' she admitted. 'But as this Clovis died so long ago wouldn't you say that this has no relevance to your condition today?'

'Better to know something of your origins than nothing,' Brother Charibert responded.

'Well, now that you are no longer in service to Bishop Brodulf, perhaps you are considering moving on to educate yourself further and seek to teach the Faith rather than be a servant to bishops and abbots?'

'It is a wish of mine,' Brother Charibert agreed with a faint smile. 'I have no wish to swap service to Bishop Brodulf to that of Deacon Landric.'

Fidelma shot a meaningful glance at Eadulf and began to rise. 'We will detain you no longer, Brother Charibert. In future, I think it would be best if you were more truthful when being questioned by a *dálaigh* in this country.'

Brother Charibert also rose. 'I will, lady, and thank you for your indulgence.'

By the time Fidelma and Eadulf had entered the courtyard beyond, the dawn had spread a stronger light over the abbey buildings and there was much movement from the religious as well as the builders from the far end of the complex.

Fidelma glanced at Eadulf. 'Well?' she prompted.

'I believe Brother Charibert is a liar,' he said flatly. 'An educated slave freed and finds himself not only in the religious but as secretary to an influential bishop?'

'It is not unknown,' Fidelma pointed out.

Eadulf sniffed. 'I have read Dio Cassius as well. The story of the freedman Narcissus is well known. After Claudius, he had to commit suicide when Nero came to power.'

'The frustrating mystery is trying to identify the exact nature of the missing documents; those Bishop Brodulf was interested in.'

'The history of this abbey? Also a history of his own people. Were these documents consumed in the fire? If they were not, who had them and where are they?' Eadulf shook his head to emphasise his perplexity.

'The Venerable Lugán seemed certain that only the bishop could have taken them. We learnt this morning that others had access to that area of the library. There are now many possibilities. Who was it who attacked the Venerable Lugán? Was this attacker a confederate of Bishop Brodulf or a rival? Was he the one who killed the bishop and burnt the records, or was he unable to find the records because they were not in the bishop's possession, so came to the library to search for them? And if this person was a rival of the bishop, what records could there be that needed the bishop to pay for them with his life?'

Eadulf shrugged. 'Too many questions, and time is running out before Deacon Landric starts creating problems and complaining to your brother, the King. I still say that Brother Charibert is a liar.'

'You are probably right,' Fidelma agreed. 'But we need more information to prise the truth from him.'

The abbey bell started to ring.

'That is already the bell for *longud*?' Eadulf sighed. 'I am exhausted and the day has hardly begun.'

'Eat sparsely then, Eadulf.' Fidelma allowed herself a smile. 'A full belly is a great aid to sleep and we want our wits about us this day.'

It seemed several people were missing from the refectory during the first meal, including the abbot and the prioress. The librarian was also missing, but this was expected after the affair of the night. Only Brother Mac Raith, looking pale and wan, had put in an appearance among the senior members of the abbey. Deacon Landric was talking to him, speaking rapidly with quick movements of his hands as if to emphasise points. Brother Charibert sat by himself, seemingly disconnected with his surroundings. There were quiet or whispered exchanges from the students' tables. A general feeling of subdued apprehension appeared to have descended on everyone.

What concerned Fidelma was that Enda had not put in an appearance. She pointed this out to Eadulf, but he was not alarmed.

'If he has sense he has just caught up on his sleep, as we should have done. That is the only criticism I have with your burial rituals. Why hold it at midnight? Is it something to do with the fact that you count the time by this method? Nights followed by days, so midnight would be the start of a time period?'

'Perhaps,' Fidelma dismissed in an irritable tone. 'It is just unusual that Enda would oversleep.'

It was as they were leaving the refectory that Eadulf chuckled. 'What did I say? There is Enda now.'

The warrior was, in fact, walking across the courtyard towards them.

'Where have you been?' Fidelma greeted him sharply before he had a chance to say anything.

Enda did not look perturbed.

'I decided to go for a short ride at first light. I am not used to being cooped up without some activity.'

Eadulf grinned. 'It's true. Not having exercise is not a good sign of a healthy life. Perhaps that is why Brother Charibert was setting off on his pre-dawn walk. Mind you, I still think he was a liar.'

Enda was looking at them in slight irritation. He had obviously wanted to impart some news. He finally broke in: 'I saw something interesting as I rode by the cemetery earlier.'

'What sort of interesting something?'

'There was a group of men at the bishop's grave.'

Fidelma seemed disinterested. 'Often a grave is visited in respect. I see nothing interesting there. Who were they?'

'They were builders. It was Sítae, the master builder, and a couple of his men.'

'They were those who dug the grave and carried the *fuat* to it last night. I suppose Sítae wanted to make sure everything had been done correctly,' Eadulf offered.

'Nothing interesting in that,' Fidelma added. 'As you know, there is sometimes sinkage with a new grave and they are obviously ensuring all is in order. It is a hard task being involved in a burial at night, so it is better to come and inspect things in daylight.'

Enda was clearly trying to conceal his impatience.

'I had only gone for a short ride and on my return I saw only one of the builders had remained and he was just leaving the cemetery. I stopped to have a word with him.'

'Was it anyone we know, Enda?' Fidelma asked.

The warrior glanced about as if he wanted to make sure they were not being overheard.

'You remember the worker we saw up at the builders' camp?'

'The man called Patu? Of course.'

'It was he. He asked if I remembered you raising the point about sulphur dust.'

'Go on.' Fidelma was all attention now.

'He said that he had been speaking with one of the workmen who had mentioned something interesting; something that happened on the day before the fire at the guest house.' He paused as he wanted her full attention. He had now secured it; she was leaning towards him expectantly.

'The worker was walking up the hill from the abbey, back towards the builders' camp. It was late evening with dusk descending. This particular day this worker had been late packing his equipment and was hurrying back to the camp for a wash. The builders usually bathe in the stream there before they have their evening meal.'

'And . . .?' Fidelma prompted.

'The man saw someone walking hurriedly from the camp towards him. That is, walking down towards the abbey.'

'I presume the figure was not a builder?' Eadulf asked cynically.

Enda stared at him. 'How did you know?' he demanded.

'Because Patu would not volunteer any information that cast suspicion on the builders.'

'Go on,' Fidelma pressed.

'The figure wore the robes of the religious. He was youthful in appearance but that could only be told by his build and the way he carried himself, which was not the gait of an old man.'

'He did not recognise him?' Fidelma had already guessed the answer.

'The builder did not recognise the religious.'

'Then the point of this story is?'

'That the builder saw that it was a member of the abbey who took the sulphur dust . . .'

'Does this builder have a name at least?' Fidelma ask shortly.

'I was told it was a stone mason by the name of Mothlach.'

'What did Mothlach say about this figure?'

'The religious was carrying a heavy bag on his shoulder. It was one of those leather bags that you hang from your shoulders by straps. Many travellers use them.'

'How did this Mothlach know the bag was heavy?'

'Oh, that's easy, lady,' the warrior replied. 'You can easily see when a bag someone is carrying is heavy or light. You judge by the position of the body of the person carrying it.'

'So he saw this religious carrying a heavy bag? And so?'

'The description of the person put me in mind of the description that we have been given of the unfortunate Brother Garb,' Enda pointed out.

'Brother Garb?' Fidelma's voice was toneless as if she knew what he was about to say. 'And this . . . er . . . encounter? Patu told you it was on the day before Bishop Brodulf met his death?'

'He did so.'

'And when did this stonemason, Mothlach, remember this incident? That is, according to Patu.'

'It happened after we saw Patu. Patu says they were sitting at their fire last night talking of your visit when Mothlach remembered the incident.'

'There are more questions here than answers,' Fidelma muttered grimly.

'What questions?' Eadulf asked her in surprise. 'I think it clears up some points.'

'Which are?'

'We suspected that Brother Garb might have a reason to do harm to the bishop, due to the arguments they had. We know sulphur dust was an incendiary to set fire to the guest house. Áedh showed how it was used. We saw Brother Garb's leather bag, the type now described, had been used as a means of carrying the sulphur dust. Now we have a description of someone looking like Brother Garb carrying this bag from the builders' camp to the abbey on the day before the fire. It all fits.'

'Very neatly,' Fidelma agreed. 'Too neatly. So who murdered Garb?'

Eadulf opened his mouth, thought for a moment, and then closed it again.

'Why wasn't Mothlach sent immediately to me to tell this story? I don't suppose Patu told you?'

'He did. Patu told Mothlach that this morning he was sent off to attend to the cutting and loading of red limestone in the mountains south of here. That is why Patu passed the story to me instead of sending him.'

Fidelma sniffed sceptically.

'Were no words exchanged between Mothlach and this religious carrying a bag?'

'None,' Enda replied immediately. 'I gather this was due to the fact that before they grew close to each other, the one with the leather bag turned aside on to another path into the woods. When Mothlach came to the place where the man left the path, he looked along it but the man had vanished into the surrounding woods.'

'A very convenient witness,' Fidelma snapped in her frustration.

'But if we accept it,' Eadulf pointed out, 'it is corroborative evidence.'

'In what way?' she countered.

'The confirmation that someone took the sulphur dust from the builders' camp, as we thought. They took the sulphur dust down to the guest house in the leather shoulder bag we now know to be Garb's bag. It was transferred from the bag to the wooden bucket that had been hidden at the back of the house. Leaving the sulphur dust in their personal bag would not only have identified them but would also have been dangerous. A spark . . . an inhalation . . .'

'It is a point that I did not overlook, Eadulf.'

'And the description of this figure?' Eadulf insisted. 'It all confirms Brother Garb as the culprit.'

Fidelma turned back to Enda. 'I do not suppose our friend Patu told you just how long it will be before this stone mason, Mothlach, returns from the quarries in the mountains?'

'I suppose it will be several days. Maybe a week,' Enda replied. 'It is not a far journey but in choosing, cutting and transporting the red limestone . . .' He shrugged.

Fidelma compressed her lips in an expression of annoyance. 'Several days?' she muttered. 'And a principal witness.'

'Do you really need to question him personally?' Enda asked in a slightly tired tone.

'Of course. You must know the role of a *dálaigh* by now, Enda,' she snapped back.

The warrior was not perturbed.

'If that is so, I know where the red limestone quarries are in the Sléibhte na gCoillte, the mountains of the forest. It is but a short ride south. Of little more distance than it is between here and Aona's inn at Ara's Well. I would say, if we left now, we could get there, speak with this man, Mothlach, and return before night-fall. It might even be achieved by the evening meal, and certainly well before the burial of Brother Garb.'

She stared at him in surprise. 'Are you sure? He would not have been sent to any other quarry?'

'I'll wager my gold torque on it, lady,' smiled the warrior

confidently. Even Eadulf knew that the Nasc Niadh, the golden collar, worn by the élite warriors of the King of Muman's bodyguard, was not something to barter lightly.

'Then let's get our horses. We'll leave a message to tell Brother Mac Raith when we hope to return, but not where we have gone.'

'He probably won't like that,' muttered Eadulf with a groan. He was actually expressing his own feelings, as Fidelma knew well. Eadulf disliked travelling by horseback. It was only in recent times that he had grown used to the duty of taking their young son, Alchú, for a morning ride.

'His likes or dislikes are no concern of mine so long as they do not interfere with my investigation,' Fidelma replied sharply.

Eadulf knew that the sharpness was intended as a rebuke to him.

It was only a short time before Enda was leading them at an easy trot beyond the long hill of Cnoc Carron, south to the forest-strewn lower hills of the Mountains of the Forest. These were twenty-four peaks, some of which rose well over nine hundred metres. Cutting through them from west to east was an area Fidelma knew well. It was the long, impressive Gleann Eatherlai, with its winding river marking a passage between hills that rose on both sides. She had travelled and even stayed in the valley.

Enda told them that the quarries were among the trees on the north side of this glen. The sandstone and shale hills rose where deep corrie lakes found natural resting places among the heights. Here and there, between the yews and oaks, were open stretches of gorse, their yellow flowers proclaiming the month, with moss carpeting the area, and where groups of grazing animals, especially deer, did not seem put out by the group of riders.

In this idyllic setting, Fidelma was beginning to grow concerned.

'Are we going the right way?' she finally demanded. 'I have seen no tracks that would be suitable for carts of rock to be taken to the abbey along here.'

'Trust me, lady,' returned Enda. 'The track they use is further to the east. I am taking you a short way to the quarries that they use.'

'How do you know about them?' Eadulf queried.

'I would be a pretty poor commander of the King's bodyguard if I did not make myself conversant with such sites and developments within a distance of twenty-five kilometres from Cashel.'

'Is that where we are?' Eadulf asked in surprise, glancing around. 'It is the mountains that make things seem so distant for me. The land I come from is flat in every direction.'

'There are no mountains at all in the kingdom of the East Angles?' Enda was incredulous.

'A few rises we call hills, but nothing like the peaks here.'

'I see a track!' Fidelma suddenly declared, pointing to the south-east.

'There you have it, lady,' declared Enda with a smile. 'That is the one that leads back to the abbey. We can join it, and a little further south is the first of a couple of quarries that I hear are being used for the red sandstone used in the abbey.'

It was not long before they reached the track and Fidelma had great difficulty in resisting the urge to allow her horse to break into a faster pace. She held back because she knew how uncomfortable Eadulf would be. However, it was not too long a stretch before they came to the mouth of a small basin-type valley with several ravines feeding into it. One of the ravines had not dried, and fresh water splashed and gushed down it to form a substantial stream close by a group of beech. Beyond, in the small quarry, was a section of bare rock faces, almost like cliffs from which all overgrowth had been removed, and where women with picks and shovels were extracting blocks of red sandstone with great dexterity.

At the entrance to the dried little valley, which had obviously been hewn by rushing waters from the peaks, perhaps millennia before, oxen and carts were parked and a line of oxen was carrying lumps of the extracted stone to the carts, the heavier stones in hods strapped on their brawny backs.

A shout from one of the men announced the visitors' arrival had been noted. Work was stopped immediately as the group of about half a dozen men stood watching the newcomers uneasily.

Then, as they swung down from their horses, one of the men began to move to greet them, obviously reassured that no attack was intended by the fact they had dismounted. He came trotting forward towards them. He was a short man, whose lack of height was compensated by a thick muscular torso, which was bare, as he, like his fellows, was stripped to the waist. He was covered in the sandstone dust and a mass of hair. On his head was thick curly hair, which was like a thick bush covered with a fine layer of stone dust. The short man came up and stood, feet wide apart and hands knuckled into fists on his waist. The visitors were unable to observe his chin behind the thick bushy beard, which seemed part of his hair, but they knew it was held in an aggressively challenging pose.

The man's eyes narrowed when he saw the golden collar symbol around Enda's neck.

'We have authority from the Abbot of Imleach to cut stone here for the building work on his abbey,' he announced defiantly as if they were challenging his right to be there.

Fidelma took a step forward with a smile of greeting.

'If you are Mothlach, the stone mason, then we come only to have a word with you,' she smiled. 'I would say that you must be, for the name fits you well.'

There was an audible chuckle from some of the men nearby for the name Mothlach meant a shaggy-haired, rough-looking fellow.

Mothlach scowled at his companions. 'You have the advantage of me,' he declared.

'I am Fidelma, a *dálaigh*. We have been investigating the death of the foreign bishop and of a student in the abbey. We do not seem to have encountered one another before.'

The stone mason relaxed. 'Ah yes. I have heard of you, lady. We have not met. I do a lot of dressing of stone in the encampment outside the abbey, so we have not encountered one another.'

'You were not one of the builders at the funeral of the bishop last night?'

'No. Sítae, the master muilder, wanted some volunteers with knowledge of carpentry to help prepare the *fuat* and dig the grave. But, as you see, I am a stone mason. So the master builder and Patu, the next senior carpenter, undertook the task as a gesture to the abbey.'

'So you were not one of those who dug the grave and attended?'

'That was done by Sítae with Patu and a couple of the *daer-fuidir*, the labourers without skills or rights. Have you ridden all this way just to ask me that?'

'No,' Fidelma replied. 'But since you say it, it has been a thirsty ride. I see you have some logs felled by that stream in a shady quarter. If you have some ale cooling in the stream, then I presume you are not unacquainted with the rules of hospitality? If so, we can go there and discuss what Patu has been saying that you witnessed.'

The man's expression cleared. 'Ah, you mean seeing the young religious carrying the bag?'

'Exactly that,' Fidelma agreed.

Leaving their horses to drink by themselves in the small stream, they seated themselves on the felled logs and Mothlach offered refreshment from jugs of ale Fidelma had noticed had been left cooling in the waters.

'So what do you want to know?' asked the stone mason after a moment or two.

Fidelma turned to Enda and asked him to go through what Patu had told him he and Mothlach had discussed. It did not take the stone mason long to agree on all the points.

'But you did not see the young man who was carrying the bag

close up? You see, your description was like the young scholar who now lies dead,' pointed out Fidelma.

Mothlach ran a hand through his tumble of dirty hair. 'You mean the one who was found hanged yesterday? Well, it might have been him or not. I don't think so because I have seen him in the abbey grounds before. In fact, I am sure it was not him. He was similar but not the same.'

'Why are you sure?' Fidelma demanded.

'There was something about the stature of the body. The person I saw was more thickset, more muscular than the student who died. I am sure of it.'

Fidelma sighed deeply as if she had been banking on the connection.

'You are saying that it was not Brother Garb you saw carrying the bag, which turned out to have sulphur dust in it?'

'If I am told I must make a choice, I would say no; I would say that the young man who died yesterday, Brother Garb, was definitely not the one I saw.'

Fidelma shook her head almost sadly at Eadulf. 'Facts are facts and we cannot change them,' she said softly.

'I am sorry for that, lady. I can only bear testimony to what my eyes perceive.'

'Quite rightly so,' she replied.

'One has to be careful on building projects,' the stone mason went on. 'You are often asked to bear witness in cases where your word is the difference between a worker receiving compensation or not.'

Something stirred in Fidelma's mind.

'I was asking Brother Anlón if there had been many accidents on the abbey site only yesterday,' she said.

'I would say that Sítae is a good master builder,' replied the man immediately. 'He tries to make sure his men work in safety as much as they can. But one cannot guard against every eventuality.

But as the physician probably told you, there have been few deaths and not many injuries since we started this job.'

'Any connected with craftsmen?'

'Only a few slight injuries,' the stone mason answered. 'The two deaths have been of the *daer-fuidir* class, where no honour price had to be paid to family. The injuries among us have been negligible. Compensation is minimal.'

'And so there have been no real injuries then?'

'The only one I heard of was on the day before that on which the bishop died in the fire. That was our master carpenter.'

Fidelma looked at him curiously. 'Are you talking about a man called Cú Choille?' she asked slowly.

'He was the master carpenter,' agreed Mothlach. 'I was told that he was called back home, somewhere in the south-west. I only know that he had a problem because someone told me that they thought they saw the master carpenter being taken into Brother Anlón's.'

'Taken into the physician? By whom?'

'Sítae and Patu accompanied him so that they will tell you. Anyway, it can't have been a bad injury because it was later that evening that we were told that Cú Choille had received a message from his home that needed his attention. He had left immediately. We were told that Patu would take over the duties of Cú Choille until further notice.'

Fidelma was quiet for a moment. 'He left that afternoon? Before the evening meal?'

'We builders never attend the evening meal. But, yes, before that.'

'What about the man who saw Sítae and Patu take the master carpenter into the physician's apothecary? Who was he?'

'He was our coppersmith, a *cérda* called Tassach.'

'A skilled worker?' Fidelma smiled, relaxing. 'So we will find him back at the abbey?'

Mothlach shook his head. 'Not at this time. He was sent to see if he could obtain more copper ore from the merchants at Cluain Meala. There is a brisk trade there when barges come all the way up the great river Suir.'

Fidelma paused, thinking. 'So did anyone else actually see Cú Choille leaving for the south-west after he had this . . . this accident? He seems to have left in a hurry.'

'It was suddenly,' agreed the stone mason. 'Sítae mentioned that it was something to do with his wife. He must have been in a hurry became he left several of his tools behind. He also left his mule and cart behind, which he usually used to transport them.'

Fidelma exchanged a quick glance with Eadulf.

'Exactly,' Eadulf nodded as if she had asked a question.

Fidelma stood up abruptly. 'Well, we must get back to the abbey. I would like to eat before we attend the burial of young Brother Garb.'

chapter twenty

Fidelma and her companions arrived back at the main gates of the abbey later that afternoon. Fidelma and Eadulf had barely handed their horses over to Enda to take to the stables and pressed on him the importance of not stating where they had been that day, when the steward hurried from the abbey buildings. Brother Mac Raith hailed Fidelma in a tone of relief.

'The abbot wanted to see you as soon as you returned.'

It was a usual characteristic for the steward to look and sound agitated so Fidelma was not perturbed at his tone.

'I was about to retire for some contemplation before having the evening bath,' she protested. 'Has something happened?'

'There was a rider from Cashel, lady,' answered the steward. 'The abbot is now most anxious to see you.'

Fidelma glanced at Eadulf. That did concern her, for she was often anxious for the safety of her brother, Colgú. Only a few weeks before, certain princes had conspired in a plot to remove him from the kingship.

'Do you know what news the messenger has brought?' she demanded at once. 'Is all well with my brother?'

'The messenger did say that all was well with the King. But he bore an important legal message for Abbot Cuán.'

For a few moments, Fidelma felt relief. Then she felt unease.

'A legal message? In that case, I had better see the abbot at once.'

As they walked towards the main buildings, Eadulf said: 'If it is some legal matter, I don't think it sounds as if it requires both of us to see the abbot. I'll meet you back in our chamber after you have spoken with him.'

In fact, he was grateful to go to rest after the pace that Enda had set for the return journey from the quarries. So far as he could see, the trip there had only confirmed what Enda had been told by Patu.

When Fidelma entered Abbot Cuán's chamber she found the abbot looking quite distracted. He seemed relieved to see her and motioned her to take a seat.

'Fidelma, I have no wish to press you for a resolution to the mystery of the bishop's death. Tell me, are you near reaching any conclusions?'

Fidelma examined him with puzzled interest. 'These things always take as long as it takes, Abbot Cuán,' she replied seriously. 'Are there problems arising that a resolution has not yet been made?'

'There are concerns about a lack of resolution regarding the bishop. Deacon Landric is pressing for a time to depart back to Burgundia. And now we have another death to confuse us. The students have not been able to settle after the death of Brother Garb. These matters oppress me sorely. Now I have received a rider from your brother's palace . . .'

'From my brother himself?'

'Not from the King,' Abbot Cuán replied with a shake of his head.

'Then who . . .? Fidelma began.

'From the Chief Brehon of the kingdom – Fíthel.'

Fidelma had been expecting the Chief Brehon to become involved as soon as she had heard of the death of the Burgundian bishop.

'Apparently, he is concerned at the manner of the bishop's death, which he believes was an accidental fire,' the abbot went on. 'You told me at the start that the fact the bishop was a foreigner in this land, and of high status, means the Chief Brehon must advise the King as to possible compensation.'

'I presume Brehon Fíthel will be coming here?'

'Brehon Fíthel will be arriving here before midday tomorrow.'

Fidelma did her best to contain both her surprise and her irritation.

'I would not blame Brehon Fíthel,' the abbot said nervously, watching her features.

'Why should I not?' Her response was waspish.

'The rider also brought news of a ship anchoring at Árd Mór. It contained some embassy from the court of Clotaire, King of the Franks. I believe that news of this has prompted Brehon Fíthel's journey here.'

Fidelma's eyes widened. 'Clotaire could not have heard the news of the bishop's death already? What prompted this embassy to set out?' she demanded after a few moments' thought.

'They will know soon enough,' Abbot Cuán replied. 'Your brother wants proper information to greet them with.'

'Who are they?' Fidelma demanded.

'The delegation is led by someone called Prefectus Beobba. I am told he had intended to journey to the High King, Cenn Fáelad mac Blathmaic, at Tara.'

'So why does he come to Cashel?'

'Because it is the nearest sea port to the Gaulish port from the Frankish kingdom. His intention was to travel on to Tara but, doubtless, once he gets news of Bishop Brodulf's death, he will stay and demand explanations.'

'You don't think this journey was planned with Bishop Brodulf in mind?' she asked.

Abbot Cuán frowned. 'How could it be? As you remarked, the

news could not have reached Burgundia yet. I think your brother merely wants to have some answers ready for this Prefectus Beobba once he hears the news.'

'I suppose that is logical,' she admitted.

'Well, it seems Brehon Fíthel will be here early tomorrow because he will be spending the night at Ara's Well. Oh, and do not forget we bury Brother Garb at midnight. So if there is anything – anything at all – that you could tell Brehon Fíthel, it would be useful to prepare it.'

Fidelma thought deeply for a moment. It was in that moment, when several thousand ideas crowded in her mind for her attention, that her decision was made. The more she sought to dismiss one idea, another came to take its place. How the decision happened she was not sure. Instead of dismissing each question she found they all coincided as one in her mind. She smiled grimly.

'Very well. Tomorrow at midday we will hold the *dáil*, a legal court. Perhaps it is best to hold it in the chapel, being more suitable than the refectory. I presume that you and the Prioress Suanach will have no religious scruples about the use of the chapel? Good,' she pressed on, even though the abbot had made no answer. 'As head of the abbey, you should sit in judgment together with Brehon Fíthel. As steward, Brother Mac Raith will have to make all the arrangements. I want everyone to attend, including all the senior builders.'

'The builders?' An expression of anticipation appeared on Abbot Cuán's features. 'Then you know who killed the bishop and the young scholar?'

'Everything will be presented at midday tomorrow, and my interpretation,' she assured him grimly. 'There is to be no work for the builders tomorrow. This will allow the senior builders, including the master builder, to attend the *dáil*. Is that understood?'

'Then they have an involvement? I thought it was decided earlier that the fire was nothing to do with any neglect on their part?'

'All will be explained at the appropriate time,' insisted Fidelma. 'Under my authority, the steward will summon those I ask to the chapel and I will instruct Brother Mac Raith as to how the *dáil* should be constructed.'

'You said that you expect Brehon Fíthel to preside?'

'The Chief Brehon will sit with you. You will sit not only as Abbot of Imleach but as Chief Bishop of the kingdom.'

'All this is very sudden. Are you sure you have the information that you need to uncover who the culprit is?'

Fidelma let a sardonic smile play on her lips. 'I would not commit myself otherwise. Meanwhile, we have the burial of Brother Garb to attend to.'

She rose and then turned towards the door.

'You will be at the interment of Brother Garb?' the abbot called.

'I will be there,' she assured him as she left.

A few moments later Eadulf was staring at Fidelma in horror as she told him of her decision.

'Tomorrow at midday?' He was aghast. 'You think that you can prosecute a case, naming the guilty, by tomorrow? But we know nothing . . .'

'On the contrary,' Fidelma said confidently. 'We have all the facts, it is just the interpretation of the facts that needs to be clarified.'

'I don't see it.'

'I'll explain more in the morning.' She grimaced humorously. 'I'll need until that time to resolve thoughts in my own mind first. The main point is that it was only when I started to separate matters in my mind that they began to make sense.'

Eadulf looked even more concerned. 'You still need to work things out?' He was incredulous.

She ignored him, leaving him to his bewilderment as she picked up her towel and toiletries and left the room to go down to the *dabach* for her bath.

There was a more solemn feeling in the refectory as Fidelma and Eadulf made their way to their seats later. The large hall was crowded. As each took his or her position for the abbot's blessing, there was certainly more of a reverent and respectful atmosphere than before. However, when the abbot made the announcement of the holding of the *dáil* at noon the next day, there was an excited reaction. It took a while for the clamour to subside, after which Abbot Cuán made the expected announcement that this was to be regarded as the *fled-cro-lige*, the traditional feast of the deathbed, for Brother Garb. This caused a respectful calm to return. The abbot then kept the opening *gratias* to the minimum.

This evening, the meal was not consumed with normal conversation. At carefully timed intervals, members of the young scholars who had studied with Brother Garb stepped forward to the lectern to read passages from the scriptures. Once the meal was over, with the final *gratias* or thanks, people seemed to be unwilling to depart but sat around in the refectory, indulging in whispered exchanges and conversations.

The Venerable Breas sat, solemn and white faced, with Prioress Suanach. They were joined by an equally sombre-looking Brother Étaid, Brother Garb's *anam chara*, or soul friend, as he described himself.

Sítae, the master builder, appeared, and immediately came to Fidelma. She wondered if he had heard, by some curious means, of their trip to see Mothlach at the limestone quarry. However, she noticed that the man's face showed some perplexity but not hostility.

'I just wanted to verify this instruction of the steward's for tomorrow, lady,' he opened.

'Which is?'

'He says that you have requested the building work to stop tomorrow because you are going to explain about the deaths in this abbey.'

'Not exactly correct,' she replied dryly. 'A *dáil*, a court, will be held in the chapel tomorrow at noon. This will be presided over by the Chief Brehon of the kingdom jointly with the abbot himself. It is done with their authority under my advice. I have requested your attendance and those of your senior artisans. So that you can attend without concerns, it is wise that all work stops during the hearing.'

'But why?' Sítae demanded. 'We are losing precious time in our working schedules.'

'You will find that this legal matter takes precedence over your concerns, Sítae.'

'I have to object.'

Fidelma was unperturbed. 'It is your prerogative, but you and your senior workers have to make that objection to the Chief Brehon when he opens the court tomorrow.'

Sítae snorted indignantly.

Fidelma carried on with an almost dreamy smile, 'I am sure the Chief Brehon will be in a frame of mind to consider compensation if it is found that your time has been truly wasted.'

Sítae opened his mouth, stared at her, and then snapped it shut, turning away into the hall.

'That's upset him,' Eadulf said softly. 'I think his weakest point is that he is a man who doesn't like to see his profits erased.'

'Exactly my thoughts,' she agreed. 'You have an instinctive way of coming to my conclusions.'

Fidelma continued to watch the master builder on the far side of the refectory as he waylaid the physician, Brother Anlón, and engaged him in a short but intense exchange.

'I wonder what that is about,' Eadulf muttered.

'Don't forget that if one of his workers is seriously injured then he has to pay for any treatment and time lost,' pointed out Fidelma. 'He has to pay even Brother Anlón. As for Brother Anlón, charity only goes as far as members of the abbey. Anyone who needs his services from outside the abbey, and that includes the builders, has to pay the fees as set by law.'

'There is some matter between them? I thought it was accepted that Sítae's reputation is good in that respect?'

'So it is. But I do not think Brother Anlón has a similar reputation. I have told you that the abbot of the religious community, or, indeed, a bishop, is usually of an educated noble family. When they set up their community, they are granted the land by the head of their family. So they are regarded as a noble and a prince in legal terms.'

'Yes, I understand that.'

'Every noble family has its own physician. Therefore the physician in an abbey is regarded in the same legal manner. He is entitled to a tract of land, with other allowances and perquisites, not only to maintain his services and provide his curative medicines, but to maintain himself. Over and above his duties to his "family", in this case the brethren who look upon an abbot as their ruler in law, he is free to practise his art on those who are not of the immediate family. From those not of the immediate family he is allowed to exact payments.'

'It is complicated,' Eadulf sighed. 'So the builders have to pay his fees?'

'All law is complicated,' Fidelma smiled. 'I have studied eight years at Brehon Morann's secular college and achieved the degree of *anruth*. Had I had support I might have studied four more years and become an *ollamh*, a professor of the law. Things were not to be. It was not until my brother was elected as heir apparent to the King and then became King of Muman himself that I had security enough. So I went straight into the practice of that law I knew.'

Eadulf was quiet. He knew Fidelma still harboured a resentment that she had sought to become the Chief Brehon of her brother's kingdom of Muman, but the Council of Brehons had chosen the more qualified Brehon Aillin. He, being frail, had almost immediately succumbed to an ague and been replaced by Brehon Fíthel, a younger though more qualified judge. Moreover, the very person who would arrive in the morning to judge Fidelma's presentation.

Eadulf tried to think of some words of support but, without knowing how Fidelma was going to proceed to unravel the mystery, he was at a loss to say anything that he felt was appropriate. In fact, he was perplexed about her comments about Sítae and Brother Anlón, not seeing how they fitted anywhere in the mystery.

Enda came to join them and, as Fidelma turned to him, he met the question in her eyes with a quick shake of his head.

'I have not mentioned our journey this afternoon,' he said in a low voice. 'Not that I can see how it helps explain away the death of Bishop Brodulf or this young boy we are about to bury. I see that man Patu is already outside with the builders who volunteered to dig the boy's grave as they did the same for the bishop.'

'They don't intend to act as pallbearers, surely?' Eadulf demanded. 'That role I would have thought was the prerogative of the fellow students of Brother Garb.'

'Having dug the grave, they will accompany the *fuat* only to refill the grave when the ceremony is over. The students will carry the body, as they are entitled.'

Eadulf, still perplexed, glanced at Fidelma. 'Perhaps I should amend my words about Sítae being concerned with money. He has to be compassionate to volunteer his workers to fulfil the place of Brother Áedh and the robust men in the abbey who were injured in the fire. His builders even helped quench the fire and they certainly had no responsibility in causing it.'

Fidelma pursed her lips for a moment. 'We do not always see the details of an exchange or know when an exchange is taking place.'

Eadulf and Enda exchanged bewildered glances, but before they could raise further questions the sombre ritual notes of the *clog-estechtae* began to sound – a slow, sad, ceremonial tone.

In small groups the members of the abbey began to gather at the chapel doors. Many of them held lamps high on sticks, giving an atmospheric, eerie flickering light. There suddenly came a single stroke of the bell, the chapel doors opened and the *fuat* was carried out. It was a simple affair of matted reeds. It was carried by young male students who had been companions of Brother Garb. The body had been washed, clothed and 'watched', as was custom, through the previous night and day. Now it had been wrapped in the *recholl*, the customary grave shirt.

As the *fuat* was carried out, the bell began to sound again, this time with a softer, mournful tone. The young students came forward and began to take up their positions behind the *fuat*. Fidelma saw that the pallbearers were led by Brother Étaid. Behind the *fuat* came Sisters Ingund, Haldetrude and Fastrude, then others she did not recognise. Behind the students came the senior members of the abbey, led by the abbot, with the prioress, the steward, Brother Mac Raith, and the Venerable Breas and the Venerable Lugán. As Fidelma and Eadulf took their places, she caught sight of Deacon Landric and Brother Charibert. The faces of the rest of the mourners were lost among the flickering lanterns.

As the procession moved off towards the abbey's burial place, the *caoine*, or cries of lamentation, began to rise as well as the *lámh comairt*, the custom of clapping hands, indicating sorrow. It was an eerie sound whose origins were lost back in the days of the Old Religion and its customs.

In this manner the procession snaked its way through the abbey to the main gates and through them across the track to the entrance to the Hill of the Cairn. Here the grave diggers stood with their lanterns and spades at the ready. Fidelma noticed this new grave had been dug on the opposite side to where they had interred the bishop.

Fidelma was anxious to observe as much as possible, for there was considerable emotion for the young scholar's death, compared to the almost cold silence that had accompanied the bishop's burial. In fact, there was almost no consoling the little Sister Ingund, who had to be supported by her cousin, Sister Haldetrude. They were surrounded and supported by the little group who had been Garb's fellow scholars.

As they gathered at the graveside, the *fuat* was placed at the edge of the grave ready to be lowered. Here the scholars, led by Brother Étaid, began to sing the *nuall-guba*, 'the lamentation of sorrow', the high tenor of the young man's voice joined by the rest of the scholars in chorus.

> Dear the head, dear the head of this soaring star;
> an ascent as rapid as its curving fall down beyond the
>   night's horizon.
> Dear the voice, dear the voice, when raised in defence
>   of Truth;
> not once was shown the frailty of the young mind's
>   uncertainties . . .

The lament went on with its soft cadences, touching those gathered with the sounds rather than the words. Fidelma found the words intriguing, thinking that they were probably written by the young student Étaid himself. As the sound of the sorrowful voice died away across the desolate graveyard, leaving only the sounds of individual grief and sobbing, Abbot Cuán came forward. Fidelma expected him to intone the *amra*, the traditional elegy. But when the abbot held up his hands and the sobs and lamentation died to silence, he began to speak the ritual prayer. Then he addressed the assembled mourners slowly.

'*An Galach* – The Brightness – shines down on this earthly shell, for as the body has ceased to be and the soul goes to judgement, so too, the moon symbolises that the day has ended and now the moon moves across the sky to announce another day.

Another day by which we have the opportunity to gain many things from that we also call The Brightness. *An Aesca* is the place where knowledge is gathered.'

Eadulf realised that the Abbot was using euphemisms for the moon dating from pagan times. It was a traditional prohibition to speak the proper name for the moon, for it was a sacred goddess and anyone who spoke it was cursed. Even such customs had remained, in spite of the coming of the New Faith.

Now the abbot continued: 'Brother Garb was his name but his life was a denial of it, for he was refined, gentle and easy of nature. Only ignorance and illogic disturbed his smoothness. He desired knowledge above all things.'

Fidelma was frowning at this opening until she realised that the name Garb, which was often given to either a male or a female, meant 'rough'.

'As abbot, I would speak of this young man's qualities but this night I will confine myself to say only that I was proud to have been abbot here during the time that Brother Garb was a student. I make this comment briefly, as it falls to his teacher, to his mentor, to the counsellor who had placed such high hopes in him, to deliver the *amra*, the elegy, over this grave.'

He held out his arm and motioned for the Venerable Breas to step forward. The old scholar did so, supported on one side by Prioress Suanach.

'My friends, it is with regret I see the form before me ready to be consigned to the soil whence he came. We thought that he was destined for great things. We thought he would become a great scholar. He came to this monastery from Innis Arkin, one of a hundred islands, in a great inlet to the south. He was a fisherman's son. Fishermen were the first disciples of our Lord and, like them, Brother Garb wanted to become a fisher of souls. At a tender age he was already regarded as a *staruidhe* of the fourth grade of wisdom. He was a master of the lessons of divinity, a *fursaindtidh* or illuminator. He held an ecclesiastical degree by which he could cross-examine his tutor or be cross-examined by him so as to make sure that he understood all difficulties and obscurities and explain them. He is a great loss to the scholarship of this abbey.'

For a moment or two, it was thought the old scholar had ended his elegy but the Venerable Breas seemed only to have paused for reflection, for he straightened his shoulders again.

'Many among you were aware that I had designated him to be my assistant when he achieved his appropriate degree and might even have become my successor as the master of the students. To that end I allowed him to act in debates as my voice. During these last weeks, there came among us a bishop from Burgundia who said he was seeking to learn our ways and teachings. Sadly, this guest from beyond the waves could barely understand the teachings he claimed he represented, much less learn from us. He sought to impose his own half-understood teachings and belief. This led to conflict . . . I should say, verbal conflict. Brother Garb showed in such debates as we had that he was fulfilling my belief in his abilities. He was drawing a reputation among his fellow students. His was a mind that sought knowledge, like a thirsty man seeking water, in the great desert of fabrications where grows the tempting easy flowers of false knowledge that are strewn enticingly along the paths to the Lair of Lucifer.'

The old scholar was speaking with a passion now that seemed to take charge of his shaking frame. He paused only to inhale and to recover the strength of his breath.

'False! Attractive flowers that ensnare us. No flowers are prettier than those that carry poison and thorns. Is not our *moing mhear* attractive as it entices us to mistake it for cow parsley when it comes into flower in the few weeks from now? But it is actually the most deadly of poisonous entrapments – hemlock.

'Our world is spread with such dangerous and attractive plants

that have been set to ensnare us, even as the most careful and
discerning of minds are misled from the true path towards the
dark vales of the evil one.

'So, here, at the graveside of this young scholar, I would remind
you of the sacred scripture of the Blessed Matthew when he pointed
out that knowledge can destroy as well as help. You have heard
that even the Druids, as they disappear into the mystical mists of
their unbelief, ask what is different about this God from the East
that we must believe only in Him? Was He the only one born of
a virgin? Are we not told that Dechtire, the virgin daughter of
Cathbad the Druid, was asleep when the mighty god of light, Lugh
Lamhfada, came and impregnated her so she gave birth to a son
named Sétanta? Did not the child grow to be a spectacular and
wondrous saviour of his people, taking the name Cúchulainn?
When his people were cursed by the goddess Macha to suffer the
debilities of labour pains as her vengeance on all their men, did
he not come alone and save them? And did he not provide the
ultimate sacrifice, being doomed to die chained to the Pillar Stone
for his efforts to save his people?'

The mourners were silent, most clearly puzzled by the parallel
that the old scholar was referring to. Only those who had heard
the ancient stories and legends of the time beyond time knew
anything of the story. Fidelma saw the bemused look on Eadulf's
face, for he had not indulged much in learning about the pantheon
of the Children of Danu, the mother goddess. There was some
nervous shuffling among those gathered.

The Venerable Breas was speaking again.

'I have used the story to show how some have been misled;
some are seduced by such stories when others say, why is this
Christ of the East named as the chosen one, a saviour who will
lead his people to salvation? It is said he was no more of a deity
than was Cúchullain, who was born of a virgin to save his people.
In virgin birth, we all have stories of the ancient heroes. Of how

wondrous heroes rose to defend their people and died in the attempt. Some are so misled. Believe them not.

'I say to you that knowledge of such things is not the only way forward because in your thirst for knowledge of Life, the Evil One will distract you with such poisonous thoughts. With knowledge must come Faith first and foremost. Does not the Blessed Matthew write in scripture the words of Christ? He writes: "If you shall have faith and stagger not . . . and if you shall say to the mountain – take up and throw thyself into the sea, it shall be done!" Your Faith shall move the mountain.'

He stopped again and there was a puzzled quiet. The old scholar glanced round as if realising where he was for the first time. Then he looked down at the *fuat* and the body they were about to consign to the grave.

'I speak with the thoughts and words that young Brother Garb would have doubtless said if his spirit had taken possession of my voice. Faith is first and knowledge comes only in support of Faith. And thus we commit his earthly remains to the clay from which he came.'

As he stepped back, Abbot Cuán came forward to intone the final prayers. The body was lowered into the grave and then covered in green bushy branches of birch and broom as a protection to the body before the earth was shovelled over it.

There was a curious look of triumph on Fidelma's features as she turned to Eadulf.

'So, all the points are now come into focus and the final explanation can be presented,' she murmured.

CHAPTER TWENTY-ONE

'Brehon Fíthel has arrived,' Brother Mac Raith called as Fidelma and Eadulf were leaving the refectory after the first meal of the day.

'Already?' Eadulf muttered. 'He must have been up early.'

Fidelma signalled to Enda to join them as she followed the steward, who was already trotting nervously towards the main abbey gates. As they arrived they were in time to see a group of horsemen entering the gates. At their head was her brother's Chief Brehon. Fíthel was a dark, swarthy man of her own age, with deep-set, dark eyes. He would have been handsome but for his prominent hooked nose and narrow bloodless lips. He was accompanied by a thin, nervous, almost skeletal youth with long, drab mousy hair and small stature. This, Fidelma knew, was Fíthel's secretary and official scribe, whose job was to record all the judge's decisions. She always felt his name was incongruous for it was Urard, which meant one who was very tall. Behind them rode two familiar figures, Warriors of the Golden Collar, her brother's élite bodyguard. They were Aidan and Luan, who, along with Enda, had shared many of her adventures in adversity.

Brehon Fíthel slid from his horse, tossing the reins to one of the stable boys, who had come forward to take charge. No one could say that Fíthel was a modest man. His looks and movements made it clear that he was well aware of his position, for he held the status and right to sit in the presence of the King and interrupt him to correct him on the interpretation of the law.

He turned, to give courteous acknowledgement to Brother Mac Raith, as the abbey's steward. His dark eyes quickly examined the group around the steward.

'Your abbot is indisposed?' he asked, implying censure that Abbot Cuán was not there to greet him in person.

'I have sent him word of your arrival,' the steward replied nervously.

Even before the steward had finished, Fíthel turned to Fidelma with a thin smile. There was a degree of reserved respect between them, for it was not so long ago when Fidelma herself stood before the Council of Brehons to submit herself for appointment as Chief Brehon of Muman. However, the Council had decided that there were others better qualified and Fíthel had inherited the office.

'Salutations, Fidelma. I bring you greetings from your brother, Colgú. I trust you and Eadulf are well?'

'Greetings to you, Fíthel,' Fidelma replied solemnly. 'We are well. I trust your journey here has been without incident?'

'Without incident and moderately comfortable.'

'I trust that you left my brother, the King, in good health and that the concerns of office do not weigh heavily on him.'

For a moment the Chief Brehon pursed his lips but whether the expression was of disapproval or concern, it was hard to tell.

'I have no wish to interfere, Fidelma, but you will know that your brother is under some burden about this matter, which has fallen to your lot to make a report on. We have been informed of the death of the foreign bishop, burnt to death in this abbey's guest house. This has given your brother much alarm, especially when the rumour is that this bishop is also a prince of his people and related to the King of the Franks. Naturally, the King is anxious, as am I. What can you tell me of this matter?'

'I quite realised that this matter had diplomatic proportions,' Fidelma agreed calmly. 'Indeed, the ramification of the death of a relative of the King of the Franks might go beyond this kingdom if not equitably resolved.'

'So how does this matter stand? I trust you will be able to explain it to my . . . to the satisfaction of the law?'

'I have already arranged with Abbot Cuán and his steward here,' she indicated Brother Mac Raith with a nod, 'for a *dáil* to be held in the chapel at midday. All the witnesses will be gathered so that they may listen to my outline and reasoning of this matter. At this hearing they may, and where possible, present any defence or denial of my contentions.'

Brehon Fíthel looked surprised. 'A *dáil*? Are you ready for that?'

'Knowing of your imminent arrival, I have suggested that you sit with Abbot Cuán, the Chief Bishop of the kingdom.'

Brehon Fíthel was hesitant. 'Of course, that is legal etiquette. But are you ready? Whom do you charge with culpability?'

Fidelma allowed the shadow of a smile to form. 'We will let the matters unravel within the proceedings rather than give warning of our accusations beforehand.'

Brehon Fíthel was clearly unhappy.

'Let me emphasise at the beginning, Fidelma, I am not here to interfere in your investigation nor your method of pursuing matters. Certainly, if you can show if anyone is culpable, then, as Chief Brehon, I must make a judgment. I should tell you that this matter now concerns the emissary of the Frankish king, who is currently a guest in your brother's court.'

If he meant to cause concern, Brehon Fíthel was disappointed.

'Ah yes; I have heard of the arrival of a Prefectus Beobba at Árd Mór. I heard he was apparently journeying to the High King's palace but, having learnt of the death of his Bishop Brodulf, he remained at Cashel for a report.'

'You know this already?' The Chief Brehon was clearly surprised.

'I think that, after the *dáil*, you will have a report and resolution to present to my brother and to the Prefectus Beobba,' Fidelma said complacently. 'I will delay you no longer for I am sure you want to announce your presence to the abbot. If I may, I will instruct the warriors that accompanied you as to their duties during the *dáil* as I have only Enda in my service.'

Brehon Fíthel was indifferent, pointing out that as Enda was commander of the King's household guard, he had disposition of its members anyway. However, he added: 'I fail to see the need for warriors to attend your presentation at this *dáil*. It is only an accidental death by fire in the guest house of this abbey.'

Only Eadulf was aware of the malicious humour that played for a moment on Fidelma's lips as she replied.

'Perhaps I should have brought you up to date immediately? The bishop was murdered and the body burnt to disguise the fact. There is also a second death; the murder of a young student, Brother Garb. There is another matter but this will be explained during the *dáil*.'

She spoke without emotion. Eadulf, however, could see that she enjoyed seeing the complacency on the face of the Chief Brehon turn into an expression of shock.

'Two deaths here in the abbey?' Brehon Fíthel's voice was breathless. 'How could this have been kept secret? We have heard no word of this. But we thought—'

'As I said, all will be revealed in the hearing and you shall be judge over it. We can only hope that your judgments, when you return to Cashel, will be enough to satisfy this emissary from the King of the Franks.' She paused and glanced over her shoulder. 'I see Abbot Cuán hurrying, as best he can, to greet you. I fear his leg pains him greatly these days. I would try to save him from too many exertions.'

Brehon Fíthel's mouth was still opening and closing like a fish's as Abbot Cuán joined the group and became voluble in his greeting to the judge.

Fidelma left the group, with Eadulf and Enda following, and strode forward to welcome the two warriors that had accompanied Brehon Fíthel. Aidan and Luan had been with them in many dangerous adventures. They were professional warriors, members of the élite bodyguard of which Enda had risen to be commander. After an exchange of news and gossip, Fidelma and Eadulf joined Enda in instructing them as to how they should be deployed during the *dáil*. Then Fidelma and Eadulf left Enda to see to their accommodation.

'Now, what of us?' Eadulf sighed as he joined Fidelma, turning back into the main abbey buildings.

'For us?' Fidelma smiled. 'There is a little more hard work. Don't worry, I must tell you what I have in mind in my presentation at the *dáil*.'

The abbey chapel had been almost transformed since the morning services had ended. The altar and religious ornaments were covered to show all due respect and to allow for the use of the secular endeavours. The benches had been rearranged in a way more suitable for a court. On the raised area, immediately before the high altar, a table had been set in order that Chief Brehon Fíthel, with Abbot Cuán at his right side, could be seated. At the Chief Brehon's left side sat the harassed, thin scribe, Urard, with his pens, inks and papers, ready to record the details of the presentation and judgments. Next to the abbot was his steward, Brother Mac Raith. He was positioned ready to carry out any physical tasks needed to maintain order in the court.

Just below the raised level of the judges, to the right, was a small table and chairs arranged for Fidelma with Eadulf at her side. Eadulf was allowed to assist by his special adoption into the King's family, as husband to Fidelma, and by recognition of his services. Enda stood behind them. Opposite sat all the senior members of the abbey, led by Prioress Suanach, the Venerable Breas and the Venerable Lugán, with the physician, Brother Anlón, Brother Áedh and Brother Sígeal, with many other leading members of the abbey. Nearby sat the visitors, Deacon Landric with Brother Charibert. There were also the senior students, led by Brother Étaid and Sister Fastrude.

At Fidelma's request, on the seats on her side of the chapel were the master builder, Sítae, and several of the senior artisans, including Patu, the carpenter. There had been murmurs of surprise when the group of builders had entered and been placed as instructed to their prominent seats.

Now, as Brother Mac Raith assumed his seat, it seemed everyone was in the desired position. Chief Brehon Fíthel had cast a glance towards Fidelma, who indicated she was ready. Brother Urard, the scribe, picked up a small silver bell and jerked at it twice so that its sharp tones cut through any conversation in the chapel, which was now a legal court. Stillness fell among those gathered.

Abbot Cuán rose. 'This is a secular court. Nonetheless it is held in an ancient abbey chapel and involves matters pertaining to the abbey. Therefore I invoke the name of our Lord, the Christ, and seek His blessing for truth and justice to prevail on our deliberations. I also invoke the name of the Blessed Ailbe, who first brought the Faith to this kingdom and to this very spot.'

There was a muttered 'Amen' and Brehon Fíthel rose as the abbot resumed his seat. 'I remind those here, as Abbot Cuán has said, that this is now a secular court. There is no need for a preamble to these proceedings, for the law is the law. The procedures are laid down in the *Cóic Conara Fugill*, the Five Paths of Judgement. We will hear the investigation of the *dálaigh* into events that befell here in the last few days. All who are questioned by her must state the truth. It will fall to me, acting with the abbot, as to what charges will be deemed right and proper and what penalties may be incurred.'

There was a soft murmuring among the assembly. At a gesture from Brehon Fíthel, the scribe, Urard, rang his bell again. Brehon Fíthel sat down and looked in invitation towards Fidelma. She rose.

'Before we turn to the matter of the deaths of Bishop Brodulf and that of Brother Garb,' she began, her voice echoing but clear in the chapel, 'I have to deal with a third death in this abbey.'

There were immediate gasps of astonishment. Everyone was looking about in perplexity, trying to identify who was missing and whom the third death related to.

The scribe began ringing his bell in agitation to bring silence again.

Finally some calm was obtained. Brehon Fíthel was looking angrily at Fidelma.

'Lady, I am aware of your penchant for drama on these occasions. I know of no third death. It is only when I arrived here that I discovered that there had been a second death: that of a student named Garb. Now I have to tell you, as Chief Brehon, I am not inclined to indulge you in any dramatics.'

Fidelma turned and her face was without expression. 'I can only say that no dramatics are intended, Brehon Fíthel. If you will recall, I did forewarn you of a third matter on your arrival. I regret that you should think I was seeking an indulgence before listening to my opening statement.'

Brehon Fríthel began to open his mouth and then closed it when he recalled Fidelma's words. He motioned her to continue.

'It is with regret, I have to ask you to order the disinterment of the body of the bishop from its grave.'

She stood ignoring the pandemonium that arose following her statement. Urard, the scribe, was ringing his hand bell without any effect on the uproar.

Abbot Cuán was whispering to the Chief Brehon. He shook his head as if in answer to whatever the comment was. He knew Fidelma's tactics too well to know she did not say anything without a purpose. Once again, Brehon Fíthel, in a harsh tone, cut through the discord and achieved a silence.

'This is now constituted as a court to administer law. There will be respect shown to its officers.' When the exclamations and the muttering subsided, Brehon Fíthel turned to Fidelma, his tone admonishing. 'I will not let it be said that I made a decision before listening to you, Fidelma of Cashel. As an advocate of the law that I am sworn to uphold, I would not do so without cause. For the moment, I accept that you are too good an advocate to engage in drama for the sake of it, and that you will have backing for such a statement. Just tell us in simple language what is intended.'

Fidelma bowed her head towards him. 'My meaning is simple: that if you dig up the grave of the bishop and remove his body you will find another body underneath. This had been placed there in the darkness during the night before the funeral of the bishop. During the attempt to extinguish the fire in the guest house, in which the body of the bishop was found, several of Brother Áedh's men were injured, rendering them not fully fit to carry out their duties as grave diggers and pallbearers. Sítae, the master builder, volunteered some of his men to dig the grave for the bishop and to act as pallbearers. Thanks to them the grave was ready early in the next day. After the period of watching in this chapel, following a short ceremony, the bishop's body was lowered on top of another corpse, which had already been placed at the bottom of the grave.'

There was uneasy movement and muttering where the builders were seated. At their head, Sítae, the master builder, sat suddenly pale like an unmoving effigy. By his side, the carpenter Patu's features showed struggling emotions but he remained as tight lipped as his master.

Once again, Abbot Cuán was whispering to the Chief Brehon. Brehon Fíthel shook his head and addressed Fidelma.

'As the abbot knows of no other death apart from those of the bishop and of the young scholar, I presume that you are prepared to inform us of the identity of this other body?'

'I will,' Fidelma replied immediately. 'But perhaps it would be better for his conscience if Sítae would tell us?'

The master builder continued to sit stone-like. He made no response. By his side, Patu seemed to come to life, turning to whisper anxiously to him. There was no movement.

'Very well,' Fidelma began after a silence, 'if you will not—'

Patu suddenly arose excitedly. 'It was Cú Choille! It was the body of our master carpenter.' He dropped back down as if exhausted amid another outbreak of exclamations of surprise and horror, which echoed through the chamber.

Brehon Fíthel appeared bewildered.

'The master carpenter? One of the builders working on this abbey? Hopefully someone is going to tell us how the master carpenter came by his death and what is the meaning of this act of sacrilege in that he was buried in the same grave as Bishop Brodulf?'

Fidelma looked across to Sítae, but he still sat staring ahead of himself as if he were not part of the proceedings.

'As Patu has become the spokesmen for the builders perhaps he will offer the explanations? I would point out that, as matters stand, it seems that this burial was a conspiracy of Sítae and his artisans who worked in this abbey. That being so, I am sure the Chief Brehon will remind you that all the compensations and fines arising from this matter fall on each and every one of the builders, though not of the *daer-fuidir* class. Over and above that, there is the matter of desecrating the grave of a bishop. You will doubtless be reminded of the law relating to *deochrád*, sacrilege. Aside from what has been done against this abbey and the Faith is the matter of how Cú Choille died and the surreptitious manner of that concealment, which involved a member of this abbey.'

It was clear that Chief Brehon Fíthel disliked being told what his duty was in this matter. By his angry expression he was obviously about to censure Fidelma. Then the carpenter, Patu, arose uncertainly. Although a strong man, he was actually shaking as he tried to form words.

'His death was an accident,' he stuttered.

'What manner of accident?' Fidelma demanded sharply.

'He fell.'

Fidelma raised her brow to express irony. 'Fell?'

'It is the truth that I tell,' Patu declared.

'Then let us hear the completeness of this truth,' Brehon Fíthel snapped angrily.

'It was the day before the guest house burnt down and they found the foreign bishop dead,' Patu began hesitantly. 'It was the time of the midday meal and all the work had stopped except on one of the sections that was to be a bell tower at the back of the buildings. The top floor had not been completed and Cú Choille was working alone on an arch to the doorway in which he wanted to fix some special carvings that would indicate the use of this place where students would gather to study the abode of the blest.'

Brehon Fíthel was puzzled, not understanding the meaning and Abbot Cuán leant forward quickly 'Nemindithib is the study of the heavens, the abode of the blest. It is where the students watch and record the movements of the planets. It is a tradition that many of the abbeys have taken over so that we might continue to gain knowledge from the stars.'

'Continue your testimony,' Fidelma advised Patu quickly. 'Perhaps we should add, at this point, that Cú Choille was not only the master carpenter but a fine artist and wood carver whose work is found in many special places in this abbey.'

'Well, it seemed he wanted to finish the fixing of his work

before coming down for the midday meal. I was there to remind him about the meal when, suddenly, he seemed to slip and fall . . . He fell all the way to the ground almost at my feet.'

'Was he dead?'

'No, he was still just alive but—'

'Who else had seen him fall?' Brehon Fíthel interrupted.

'No one else.'

'What did you do?'

'I ran to find the master builder – Sítae. We decided to carry him to the abbey physician.'

'This is confirmed by a coppersmith called Tassach,' Fidelma pointed out. 'Tassach witnessed Sítae and Patu carrying Cú Choille into the apothecary of Brother Anlón.'

This caused the master builder to stir.

'Tassach is not in the abbey at this time,' he protested angrily, as if finding his voice for the first time. 'How can he be a witness?'

'He has been conveniently sent on an errand to Cluain Meala. Thankfully, he told a stone mason, Mothlach, what he saw. Mothlach will return to the abbey soon, if needed. Is there a need for a challenge?' Fidelma asked. She turned to where the physician was sitting tensed. 'It would make it easy, Brother Anlón, if you confirmed this?'

The physician's mouth tightened a moment and then his body seemed to slump. 'The man was still alive when he was brought to me,' he said softly.

'So the master builder and Patu brought Cú Choille to you. He was still alive. Is that correct?'

The physician made an acknowledgement.

'You examined him?'

'He was still breathing but there was little to be done.'

'So where and when did Cú Choille die?'

'He died in my apothecary within a short time of my examining him.'

'You did not report this matter to the steward, Brother Mac Raith? Why not? Was that not your duty?'

'I . . .' The physician glanced to the granite expression of the master builder. 'I made an agreement with Sítae.'

'What sort of agreement?' Brehon Fíthel demanded. 'What sort of agreement could this have been?'

Fidelma turned towards the master builder. 'Do you still insist on keeping silent, Sítae, or do you wish your companion Patu to continue shouldering all the burden of this sad story?'

'I saw nothing but ruin ahead.' The master builder's voice was barely audible. 'What more could I do in order to save the workmen reliant on me, to save my reputation, my wife and family?'

'By which I understand that you mean, albeit this was a death by accident, you would be liable, as the master builder, for compensation based on the honour price of the master craftsman?'

'I could not descend into the loss of honour, status and being cast to the vagaries of being a *fuidir* . . . one without rights or status,' replied Sítae.

'I thought you said this was an accident?' Brehon Fíthel was perplexed.

'So it was,' Sítae agreed. 'But I was master builder and I am responsible.'

'In what manner did you see it as your responsibility then?' pressed the Chief Brehon. 'I fail to see how you could suddenly be relegated to that position.'

'The contract that I had with Abbot Cuán was to renovate and rebuild and create this abbey, supplying all the craftsmen, labour, equipment and materials. Should I fail to do so within the time we agreed, it was my responsibility and I would suffer a financial penalty. I was responsible for the welfare of all the men. I had taken a chance on the number of injuries and the amount of compensation that would happen during the work. There had been several injuries during the time, but I was able to deal with them for, as usually happens, it was merely labourers, the *daer-fuidir* class, those of no rights, who sustained injuries. Only a few of the higher level of labourers were ever injured. But we did have several injuries in which compensation and medical treatment had to be paid.'

'Cú Choille was your master carpenter, the second in authority to you?' Fidelma made it more like a statement than a question.

'Exactly. His death, though accidental, would have ruined me. His honour price alone, which I would have had to pay above all other considerations, was fifteen *seds* – that would have left me ruined.'

Fidelma glanced at Brother Anlón but addressed her remarks to Sítae.

'So you came to an agreement with the physician to say nothing, but you had to pay him for doing so? I would have thought such payment was substantial? Anyway, as it was a period when everyone was eating and resting, you formulated a plan to hide this death even though the man was not yet dead.'

'He was dying of his injuries,' Sítae exclaimed. 'He was dead in a short space. There was no saving him. Ask the physician.'

'But even though life lingered, Sítae, Patu and Brother Anlón, you all agreed to hide the death to save major compensation, which would have led to a greater loss. You decided to remove the body of Cú Choille from the building site. I presume you put him in one of the barrows but you needed others in your scheme to dig the grave and help bury the body. From what was noticed, it was only a couple of poor *daer-fuidir* that you persuaded to help you bury the body. Maybe you paid them or maybe they worked under duress. We shall find out. But Cú Choille's body was taken . . .'

'He was dead by then,' Patu insisted loudly. 'The physician pronounced that he was dead.'

'Dead or not, the body was put in a barrow, presumably covered or disguised, and taken back to your camp or nearby to hide. The next thing was to get rid of the body in such a way that you would pay no compensation.'

Brehon Fíthel was shaking his head. 'Just so that I am sure in my mind, you claim this death occurred on the day before the bishop was found dead?' he enquired. 'So it has nothing to do with that death?'

'Bishop Brodulf was in the guest house that was set fire to that very night. Thus, when his body was found the next day, it needed burial. That presented the perfect method of disposing of the master carpenter's body,' Fidelma said.

'Are you saying the two things were not connected?' interrupted the Brehon.

'It was a coincidence but it presented Sítae with a cover that he had not foreseen and he took full advantage of it. Sítae and Patu had hidden the body and put out the story that a message had come asking Cú Choille to return to his home at once; that he had left immediately and that would explain his absence and the fact that many of his heavier tools were left behind. It was curious that no one saw Cú Choille leave for home and that he left even the lighter tools that Patu was now using.'

Fidelma paused and took a deep breath before continuing.

'You must have had a sleepless night, Sítae, wondering how next to deal with the most difficult task of hiding the body so that it would never be discovered. You could rest easy that the physician would never reveal anything because he would have had to reveal that he took payment for his silence. Oh, yes, I am sure you paid him well. Patu would also keep silent, for the prospect of being promoted to master carpenter was a great incentive. We have to make an assessment about the two labourers.'

She paused as if expecting an answer but none was forthcoming and so she continued.

'You must have thought that Fate was on your side when that very night the wooden guest house burnt down, the bishop was found dead, and several of Brother Áedh's men, who not only fought the fire and were injured, were the same whose role in the abbey was to dig graves. This meant not only was there a body to be buried in the abbey's burial ground, but the men who usually measured and dug the grave were incapacitated . . . they could not fulfil their office. To you this was Fate that was almost a miracle. The idea came to you that you would volunteer your builders to dig that grave . . . I think it occurred to you when you were speaking to me.'

The master builder made no attempt to deny it.

'You went immediately to the abbot and secured his permission,' Fidelma continued. 'Patu knew the use of the *fé*, and all it needed was a couple of your strong men. No problem, as you still had power over them, especially the *daer-fuidir*, the workers without rights. You lost no time in having that grave dug that very evening and made deeper than usual, so that that night you could remove the body from the place you had hidden it near the camp.'

Eadulf whispered to her: 'What about the matter of the horse? Why did he need the use of the horse when he has all those oxen and mules to move building materials?'

'I am glad you remind me of that,' Fidelma smiled. 'This I found the most bizarre thing. For some reason it was felt necessary to transport the body from its hiding place to the graveyard by horse. Why? Because Sítae did not want to use one of his own mules and oxen? Maybe he thought they were valuable beasts and didn't want them injured in the darkness. Or maybe because he had them penned each night on the far side of the abbey guarded by a herdsman but, more importantly, by what is known as a "wolf-fighting ox". An ox that even attacks wolves. It would have been impossible to extract an ox or mule without raising the alarm.'

There was a deathly hush in the chapel as everyone strained forward to follow the story.

'I think it was the physician who volunteered his own horse. If he was not the one who led the beast out of the stable, knowing exactly how to do so without raising an alarm, then he certainly told Sítae and Patu how to do so. Again, we shall find out. Certainly Patu knew about horses. He demonstrated that when he talked to me at the camp by referring to things that someone who knew about horses would mention.'

'But the physician was in this conspiracy?' Abbot Cuán demanded.

'He was. Perhaps Brother Anlón has never heard the phrase "*Fata obstant* – The gods will otherwise". Whatever man plans, fate will often take a hand, and not to bring them to the desired conclusion. Oh, as we know, the horse was taken from the stables, led to the body and then taken to the burial ground. The master carpenter's blood stained the *dillat,* or blanket, on the animal.

'The rest was simple. The body was put in the open grave with broom and birch covering on it and there awaited the funeral of the bishop. In the dark, on the next evening, no one spotted anything untoward. And here, I believe, is where the Fates did intervene.' She paused and looked at Patu. 'Is there anything you want to correct before I finish my narrative?'

'You have the story, lady,' Patu admitted, resigned. 'We were about to leave the cemetery and return the horse, which had been tied to the gate. But it had not been tied firmly enough. It jerked its head free and, finding freedom, starting to wander down the track. It was just before sun-up and, by coincidence, a band of warriors were coming along the track. Seeing the horse, they stopped. We, of course, had hidden ourselves behind the bushes and trees in the cemetery ground when we saw them.'

'And then what?' the Chief Brehon prompted sharply.

'The leader of these warriors took charge of the horse and rode up to the abbey gates opposite. He roused the gatekeeper, who recognised the horse and took it in. Scarcely a few moments passed before the group of warriors rode on to the west and the abbey gate was shut. At the time I supposed that this was good luck in that it saved me the task of having to sneak it back into the stables myself. We went back to our camp and entered the abbey in our normal way. I had to alert the physician so that he would not betray anything.'

'So you are saying that it was you who took the animal in the first place?' It was Brother Sígeal, the master of the stables, who asked.

'I followed the physician's instructions carefully,' Patu admitted. 'That side yard and entrance is your weakest link and one thing that should be attended to any future building of that area of the abbey is a strengthening of the walls and entrances.'

Brother Sígeal snorted. 'A thief telling me how to keep safe my own horses?'

Fidelma smiled broadly. 'A wise Roman lawyer once advised: "*set fur capere fur* – set a thief to catch a thief".'

Brehon Fíthel turned to Fidelma. 'But the physician told him how to take the horse.'

'The physician had become part of this conspiracy. I think the axiom does not need alternation.'

Brehon Fríthel sighed. 'So this matter is an entirely isolated case not involving murder but one of concealment of a body? This master carpenter was killed in an accident, and to avoid paying the various legal compensations and honour price, the master builder decided to hide the body?'

'That is the essence of the matter,' Fidelma confirmed.

'Obviously an immediate step is digging up the grave, removing the body of the master carpenter and reburying the bishop in a proper manner. The same must also be done for the master carpenter. Sítae, Patu and Brother Anlón will be held until all related matters are considered and the fines and compensation ordered and made. I will have to reflect on punishments affecting the *daer-fuidir*, as they were probably coerced into this.'

The steward, Brother Mac Raith, rose. 'This will be a matter that has to take into consideration the contractual arrangement with the master builder and the compensation he owes for not fulfilling his obligation to us. I will have to examine these contracts to present before you at a later date.'

'Naturally so,' Brehon Fíthel agreed dryly.

'There is, of course, another related matter.' It was the sharp voice of Abbot Cuán. 'The worst offender in this matter is Brother Anlón, who has not only abandoned his duties and obligations to this abbey, but his oath of allegiance to uphold the Faith.'

'And another oath,' Fidelma quickly reminded him. 'An oath that is more important than the others. That is, his oath as a physician; as a healer. Remember, by his own admission, Cú Choille was still alive – even though death was inevitable – when he was carried into Brother Anlón's apothecary. The physician did not fight for that life until the last breath, but abandoned his patient to negotiate a bribe from Sítae to keep silent about him and his death. After that he even helped in the hiding of the body by concealing it in the bishop's grave.'

Eadulf had whispered to Fidelma and she turned back to Brehon Fíthel.

'I am reminded that, in spite of the New Faith, physicians still swear an oath in the name of Dian Cécht, our old god of healing, whose powers are still invoked throughout the kingdom. That oath is they would use all their knowledge to serve the sick without bias, to the best of their abilities, and do them no intentional harm.'

'You are right, Fidelma,' Brehon Fíthel agreed solemnly. 'Brother Anlón shall share the cell along with the others until we decide what manner of penalties his actions entail. Take them—'

Fidelma interrupted him, causing him some surprise.

'An indulgence first, Brehon Fíthel. Before he is incarcerated, we will need Brother Anlón as witness in the next matters before us. He is the physician involved in the deaths of Bishop Brodulf and Brother Garb.'

Brehon Fíthel was irritated. 'One presumes that he is competent to give such evidence? After all, you have already cast enough aspersions on his bias as a physician.'

'On his bias, not his ability,' Fidelma replied solemnly. 'It is his ability that he is called upon to confirm.'

'I presume you are ready to present that case, Fidelma?'

'I am prepared to offer you explanations. Whereas the sad death of Cú Choille, the master carpenter, was an accident but made into a crime by the concealment of his death for profit by Sítae, the deaths of Bishop Brodulf and of Brother Garb are more serious, for they are murders.'

'I shall declare a pause before the court proceeds to the matter of these deaths and then it is your task, Fidelma, to bring the murderers into the open to face retribution.'

chapter twenty-two

When those attending the hearing had reconvened and adjusted from the surprises of the opening session, and when Urard, the scribe, had rung his bell, Brehon Fíthel announced the proceeding were open. Fidelma rose to her feet without prompting.

'We now come to the matter of the deaths of Bishop Brodulf and Brother Garb. We have here two murders which, although we thought them to be related, we found them not related at all.'

This sent more murmurs of surprise through the assembly.

'I will deal with the murder of Bishop Brodulf first. The attempt to disguise the murder by setting fire to the guest house was made so that it was initially thought the bishop perished by accident in the fire. The abbey's physician quickly disabused us of that. Dagger blades are not destroyed by fire.'

Deacon Landric leaned forward as if he were going to speak but then relaxed while Brother Charibert remained still. There was some whispering among the Burgundian students.

'There is no need for me to relate the details about the old guest house fire and the finding of the remains of the bishop. The abbey's physician, Brother Anlón, examined the remains and will testify that the cause of death was either a dagger or knife wound. As I said, the murderer initially hoped that the fire would incinerate the evidence of this. The physician showed that Brodulf had been stabbed through the heart with a single blow. In this matter Brother Anlón did carry out his duties appropriately. The reason for the murder, as we eventually discovered, was, in fact, motivated by matters whose origin was in Brodulf's own country.'

She paused for a moment.

'I will now deal with that motive before coming to the name of the person responsible. You will all know that Bishop Brodulf, of the Abbey of Luxovium in Burgundia, arrived at this abbey with his steward and his servant. The bishop claimed he was here to observe how the Venerable Breas instructed his students and to understand the differences that exist between our theologies. Like many prelates, abbots and bishops, Brodulf was of noble Burgundian birth. In fact, he was a close cousin of Clotaire, the third of his name to claim himself as King of the Franks. That means that Clotaire claims to rule over the four Frankish kingdoms, even though the claim is disputed among his own family. There are many witnesses to the bishop's arrogance. I do not intend to dwell on this unless I am challenged. Bishop Brodulf had the arrogance of a Frankish prince but was a vehement supporter of his cousin.'

She turned to where Deacon Landric was sitting, his face a grim mask.

'As I say, the declared purpose of this visit was that the bishop wished to observe the teaching of young students by the Venerable Breas. The Venerable Breas has achieved a reputation for his learning and the encouragement of his students who have so far honoured him by being appointed to leading positions throughout Western Christendom in spite of the many differences of theological aspects of the Faith we now hold with many churches in other lands. For example, we hold with the theologies of Pelagius, while other churches, even Rome, call him a heretic. So Brodulf declared that he wanted to observe this difference in teachings, rituals and philosophies of our churches.'

She paused for a moment and smiled briefly as if a thought

struck her. 'Our methods of teaching seemed somewhat different from that of the bishop, who several times involved himself in arguments during the debates and went so far as to lose his temper. He especially singled out Brother Garb for the subject of his ire because Brother Garb was presented as the leading student of the group he engaged with. The Venerable Breas, in the tradition of our teaching methods, encouraged Brother Garb to argue forcibly about the matters before them.

'Now this is where we were misled because I am afraid that too much emphasis was placed on the anger shown in these debates. Once the murderer of the bishop realised his ruse of making the death appear to be in an accidental fire, then he began to subtly point us to these debates and arguments. Thus Brother Garb appeared as a suspect, someone who developed a personal hatred of the Bishop Brodulf. He became the centre of visible conflicts with the bishop.'

'Are you saying that the murder of Bishop Brodulf had nothing to do with the tensions provoked by the arguments of theological interpretation?' Abbot Cuán exclaimed as if bewildered.

'Bishop Brodulf came here on the instruction of the King of the Franks, his own cousin, Clotaire,' Fidelma replied. 'He was sent for a single purpose. That purpose was to find and kill someone.'

There was a collective gasp.

'Fidelma,' Brehon Fíthel was horrified, 'you are talking about a bishop of the Faith! Are you accusing a man of the Faith of being an assassin? Of being a killer?'

'I am afraid that the one thing does not exclude the other. Being appointed a prelate does not banish one from being a human being with all the vices that come with it,' she observed mildly. 'Many men and women put on religious robes or claim to observe the philosophies of the Faith but still manage to ignore them when it is to their advantage to do so. I read in Eusebius' translation of the scripture the words "*non occides*" – do not kill. I read no caveats beside that commandment. No words such as "unless", or other qualifications and limitations. Yet still religious leaders, or those claiming to be so, will find such pretexts to justify their private or public slaughters.'

There followed an uncomfortable silence.

'So what was the "pretext", as you call it, that Bishop Brodulf would use?' Brehon Fíthel asked. 'Whom did he want to kill?'

'I will repeat again, Bishop Brodulf did not disguise the fact that he was a prince of the Merovingian family. His personality was too narcissistic to allow any humbleness. He arrived here to find and eliminate the one person who had a superior claim to be King of the Franks over his cousin to whom he was devoted. His intention was to make his cousin's throne secure.'

'To find a rival Frankish prince in the kingdom of Muman?' Abbot Cuán was astounded. 'But there are few Franks settled in the abbey. Or are you saying that one of our young Burgundian students here is such an heir?'

Fidelma was aware of expressions of excitement among the group of students opposite.

'Not among them. Nevertheless, there are many who come to this land in search of safety from death or from a desire to follow our ways. It is not beyond memory when many Britons sought refuge here to escape the conquests of the Angles and the Saxons from the eastern lands who sought to carve out kingdoms in what had previously been the land of the Britons. We welcomed them. As we now welcome the Angles and the Saxons who, having been converted by our missionaries to the Faith, and educated by them, have now come to settle amongst us since their own princes have decided to follow the new ways of the Roman churches and not those as we have taught them.'

The Chief Brehon was looking concerned. His voice now matched the grimness of his expression.

'Fidelma, we know you are a scholar of some reputation and hold the second highest degree that our secular and ecclesiastical colleges can bestow. However, we are faced with a murder here. Perhaps you would address it? So far, I have heard merely assertions, but I should not have to remind you that our law relies on evidence. You have accused Bishop Brodulf of being a murderer. So who murdered him?'

'He was an assassin,' Fidelma went on calmly. 'But he did not get the chance to assassinate his intended victim before he was himself assassinated. He was afraid of assassination himself and by the very people whom he hunted. His companions, Landric and Charibert, will attest to his fears. It explains his curious insistence on not sharing his guest accommodation with anyone else . . . not even with his steward or servant. He felt that kept him safe at night.

'The clues to the reality of this situation were shown by his fixation on investigations in the *scriptorium*. It was the particular texts that gave the clue. Even that would have had no impact on my thoughts until I had some discussion about Frankish history, thanks to Prioress Suanach, and to Sister Fastrude, who had brought to this abbey a most useful history of the Franks as a gift to the library.'

'What was this history?' Brehon Fíthel asked.

'It was written by a Brother Fedegar and was a more recent version of the *Liber Historiae Francorum*, a history of the Franks. The history that we need to know was that of some twenty years ago, during the time of King Sigebert of the Franks. Sigebert was assassinated and his young son, Dagobert, was taken into safety by loyal family members. They eventually took him to safety in this kingdom, to be raised and protected in one of our abbeys. Dagobert was to be raised here until his followers felt it was safe and opportune for him to return and claim the throne. As I say, this happened twenty years ago.'

'You say that this was why Bishop Brodulf came here? After twenty years?' Brehon Fíthel's voice was cynical.

'The Franks have long memories. The evidence is that Brodulf believed, rightly or wrongly, this was the most likely abbey that Dagobert had been taken to. It was certainly well known for its ecclesiastical school and for welcoming students and guests. The Venerable Lugán will tell you, Bishop Brodulf began an assiduous search of the records, particularly the records of twenty years ago. He tried to throw off the curiosity of both the librarian and steward by picking quarrels about other texts in the library, such as *The History of Women*.'

There were affirmative mutterings from Brother Mac Raith and the Venerable Lugán.

'I believe he finally succeeded in finding the reference he wanted. In his arrogance he took the text with him and this was noticed by the Venerable Lugán. But this also alerted the person who was sent to protect Dagobert. The one whose task had been to accompany Bishop Brodulf and either prevent him from finding Dagobert or to stop the assassination. Once this person knew that Brodulf had found the clue to Dagobert's identity and was about to leave for that place where Dagobert was, then he had to act. Bishop Brodulf must die and the knowledge must die with him.'

'How was it known that Bishop Brodulf had not shared this knowledge with his companions?' Brehon Fíthel asked immediately.

Eyes were now turned to where Deacon Landric and Brother Charibert were sitting.

'It will be explained in a moment.' Fidelma assured him. 'Both Deacon Landric and Brother Charibert had tried to mislead me by playing much on the theological arguments that had happened. Both referred to Brother Garb as the antagonist. Oddly, they did not do this in collusion but from entirely different perspectives. One was to hide Bishop Brodulf's real mission in his role as

Brodulf's accomplice. The other was to turn suspicion of Brodulf's death away from himself.'

Brehon Fíthel eyes widened. 'Are you saying that one of the two was Bishop Brodulf's accomplice in trying to find and kill the claimant to the Burgundian throne, and the other was trying to protect that claimant by having killed Brodulf?'

'As simple as that,' Fidelma agreed. 'Brother Charibert admitted he had served in the house of Wulfoald and was sent to Luxovium to ingratiate himself with Bishop Brodulf. Wulfoald, as we learnt, had been King Sigebert's steward. Charibert was successful in becoming servant to Brodulf. When he realised that Brodulf had found Dagobert, exiled in this country, he had to eliminate him. He stabbed him and, to disguise the crime, burnt down the guest house. He had already prepared for this by taking Garb's bag from the shed at the back of the students' quarters, a bag that has Garb's name on in our ancient Ogam letters, so was easily identifiable.'

'Easily identifiable?' Brehon Fíthel queried. 'Only to those who know the ancient letters. They have not been used generally for at least a century or so. But you claim this Burgundian knew the ancient letters and is the culprit?'

'Brother Charibert had been practising the old Irish letters to gain that knowledge. Eadulf found a paper on which Charibert had been copying the letters inserted in the volume *Hesperica Famina*, which we found in his chamber. And while Charibert was not seen taking that bag, he was witnessed by one of the students returning the bag, with a residue of sulphur dust that was used to activate the flames in the guest house. A further witness, a stone mason named Mothlach, had seen a figure in religious garb carrying the bag from the builders' camp but, realising he had been seen, Charibert left the path and concealed himself.'

'So you accuse Brother Charibert?'

'I do,' Fidelma confirmed. 'Brother Charibert was motivated to prevent Bishop Brodulf uncovering where Dagobert, this princely exile, was hiding. He killed him, and then tried to obscure the matter by setting the guest house on fire. I believe he burnt the reference that Brodulf had identified as to where Dagobert was hiding. Thereafter, Deacon Landric, a supporter of the King of Franks, but not entirely privy to the bishop's discovery, tried to continue the search not only for Dagobert's whereabouts but for the assassin of his bishop.'

'What say you to this, Brother Charibert?' the Chief Brehon demanded.

Brother Charibert simply answered with an eloquent shrug.

'Make him say where Dagobert is hiding!' Deacon Landric shouted, rising to his feet and turning as if to strike his companion.

The warrior Luan moved to stand between them.

'Are we sure that Bishop Brodulf found out where this Prince Dagobert was hiding?' Brehon Fíthel demanded, directing his question to Brother Charibert.

'It does no harm to admit it now,' replied Brother Charibert. 'I realised that he had when he warned me to prepare our belongings as we would be leaving this abbey the following day. But he did not tell me where we would be going. I was sure he knew where Prince Dagobert was hiding. I saw he had some texts. I killed him and destroyed the texts.'

The Chief Brehon sat back with a troubled frown. 'The case is simple then, but the punishment is not so simple.'

Abbot Cuán was shaking his head. 'Why so? I know enough of the law to say it stipulates that a killing is basically recompensed by the honour price of the victim, payable to the victim's family. The only matter I can't see is whether Bishop Brodulf was a bishop of high degree in his country and, as a prince, what was his degree? It might be that we are facing the honour price of a king. If he was just a bishop the honour would not be so high.'

Brehon Fíthel took his head. 'It is not just a matter of the honour price. There are other considerations. The bishop was killed while he was a guest in this abbey. Therefore, as abbot, you were extending him hospitality and protection. The matter of *diguin*, the violation of your protection, emerges because the perpetrator is bound to compensate you. That would be the value of your honour price. Thus there are two honour prices to be taken into consideration and the compensations according to the law.'

It was Fidelma who interrupted. 'There is even more to be considered. The status of Brother Charibert. He claimed he was a slave in the house of Wulfoald, the noble in Burgundia, who turns out to be a noble and former steward to King Sigebert, who sent Charibert on his mission to prevent Brodulf assassinating Dagobert.'

Deacon Landric was still on his feet and he turned to them. 'Charibert is a traitor to his king and to his own bishop. Remember he was given his freedom by Wulfoald and went to join the Abbey of Luxovium, where he became inducted as one of the brethren and appointed to serve the bishop. So he stands here as a freeman and one of the brethren of Luxovium. As such he must be punished.'

'There is a more important matter,' Brehon Fíthel said on reflection. 'In this land, Charibert is classed as a *cú glas*.'

Deacon Landric clearly did not understand the term 'grey wolf'.

'*Cú glas* is a legal term,' Brehon Fíthel explained quickly, 'which means one who is a foreigner, an alien born in a country overseas. Thus we must make consideration of that fact, for he seems without rights in this jurisdiction.' There was a pause for some moments and then Brehon Fíthel went on: 'Judging from what has been said, I doubt whether we can class Charibert as a *cheile*, a man with full citizen's rights in this country. I would class him now as a *fuidir* and lower his status accordingly to that of a *daer-fuidir* – a man without any rights.'

'Then what of the fine and compensation?' Abbot Cuán demanded irritably. 'It is obvious that he can't pay them.'

It was Brother Mac Raith who intervened with a solution. 'You know, failing payment, it is the family of the perpetrator who has to pay the fines. If Charibert was accepted into the brethren of Luxovium then that abbey becomes his family.'

Fidelma stood impatiently listening to the legal arguments between the two judges and the steward. In a way she found the academic arguments amusing.

Deacon Landric was still on his feet. 'Does that mean that Charibert is to return to Luxovium and the abbey are to send you the payments for this?' he demanded.

'Not exactly,' Fidelma said. 'There is another way of considering this matter. We have learnt that Charibert was brought up in the family of this noble called Wulfoald. His family had served in that household for several generations. Prior to joining the abbey, Charibert considered himself of the family of Wulfoald. Wulfoald was the close adviser to King Sigebert, the father of Dagobert. Charibert knew Brodulf was a cousin of the current king and was going to assassinate Dagobert and so he killed Brodulf to save Dagobert's life. Would it not then be seen as self-defence? Was it not a killing to prevent the killing of a family member and so no crime is committed? I would contend, under the law, he saw himself as *ceand a cisamh* – or chief protector – of his family.'

'That is ridiculous!' Deacon Landric snapped. 'Charibert was a servant.'

'Ridiculous or not, it is a point in law.' Brehon Fíthel frowned thoughtfully. 'There is such a concept in our law. It does, however, leave the violation of Abbot Cuán's protection of his guest to be considered.'

The abbot was nodding in agreement, satisfied that this aspect was in his favour.

'However,' Brehon Fíthel said heavily, 'to be truly legal we must obtain some clarification of Charibert's allegiance. I presume that he has some idea where this Prince Dagobert is hiding in this country? That is why he killed the bishop. If Charibert was of Dagobert's family, linked through his kin, then he killed in self-defence under the law. But I think Charibert must now call this prince to come forward to confirm that Charibert is a member of his kin.'

Brother Charibert had been sitting silently for a while. Now he rose, shifting his weight slightly, and glanced briefly at Fidelma and then to Brehon Fíthel.

'What is the alternative to refusing to reveal the whereabouts of Prince Dagobert?' he asked softly.

Brehon Fíthel shook his head. 'You retract the claim that you did know his whereabouts as you said earlier?'

'I do not retract it. I will not betray Dagobert, the rightful king of my people.'

'So the alternative will be that a messenger will be sent to King Colgú to discuss with Prefectus Beobba the details of what happened here. There will be a request for fines and payments, to be rendered by the abbey. Until the payments are agreed you will be placed in the custody of Deacon Landric.'

'In other words, you will submit me to torture and death until the whereabouts of Dagobert are revealed? That means his death as well as mine.'

'Torture and death are not our laws. Hopefully, this Dagobert is hiding in this, or some other, abbey. You have only to tell him to come before me and confirm you are protecting him as a member of his kin and the case is dismissed.'

Brother Charibert drew himself up. 'I was born in thralldom to Wulfoald, as were many generations of my family. I served him and have no regrets. I have shown my willingness to serve by the death of one who would kill the future of my people. I now further enact my willingness to protect Prince Dagobert.'

Suddenly the man's body gave a twitch and he uttered a gasp. He staggered a step or two and then collapsed.

It was Luan, the warrior, who reached him as he sank to the floor. Eadulf reached him a moment later, moving aside the injured man's robe. The blood was still pumping and the shaft of a broad-bladed dagger was almost buried up to the hilt under the ribcage and at an angle into the heart. There was no question that death had come upon him instantaneously.

'I was not expecting that,' Fidelma murmured in a resigned tone as Eadulf rejoined her among the rising babble of voices. 'In fact, I was even thinking that I might attempt to argue the laws on *cosnam*, the acts of self-defence that do not require punishment.'

'It could not be helped,' Eadulf replied quietly. 'I have to say, I did not expect such a loyalty to a former master by one who was a slave.'

'You should remember that he was a believer in the Faith, and does not scripture say: "Never let go of loyalty and faithfulness. Tie them around your neck; write them on your heart"? He was certainly loyal to those he considered his kin.'

Eadulf looked dour. 'I presume suicide does not cancel out the previous judgments?'

'Another tricky judgment,' Fidelma sighed. 'The law states that every dead man kills his own liabilities. That is going to be a difficult one to argue when it involves the King of the Franks. To think that I once aspired to the office of Chief Brehon of my brother's kingdom. I am glad my decisions now are not so complicated.'

Eadulf glanced at her in disapproval, unable to evaluate the bitter tone that edged her voice.

The body of Brother Charibert had been removed and Deacon Landric told to confine himself to his chamber until a proper decision could be announced. Yet again, Brehon Fíthel's steward, Urard, was ringing his bell until silence was re-established.

'I remind this court that we have not yet dealt with the death of Brother Garb,' Brethon Fíthel said. 'I assume that we have not done so as it is unrelated to the previous matters, as you have claimed, Fidelma. So are you ready to proceed with this third hearing?'

Once more Fidelma rose and indicated she was prepared.

'This matter is the saddest and perhaps the most horrendous case of all. Yet is the easiest to unravel. So, I will start by asking Eadulf—'

There was an unexpected shout of protest. Everyone looked in astonishment at the source. It was the Prioress Suanach.

'What do you object to?' Brehon Fíthel's brows came together in annoyance.

'I am perturbed that Brother Eadulf is being offered involvement in this matter. He is no longer an onlooker in this hearing and his involvement is not acceptable.'

Brehon Fíthel's eyes widened at her hostility.

'On what grounds? Brother Eadulf is well known for assisting Fidelma of Cashel frequently with her investigations. He has been husband to Fidelma for many years and is father of their son, Alchú. He is known for his services to this kingdom in matters of justice. In his own land he was a *gerefa*, a law giver, before joining the Faith.'

'He is still a foreigner!' the Prioress replied sharply. 'He is just as much a *cú glas,* a grey wolf, as any Burgundian. Marriage to an Eóghanacht, even the sister of the King, does not make him into one of us, far less giving him the ability to act in legal judgment over us.'

Fidelma was about to speak but the Brehon Fíthel motioned her to silence and turned to address the prioress.

'It is through lack of knowledge that you express your opinion, Prioress Suanach. This is, perhaps, due to your long absence from this kingdom. Eadulf is a *fine thacair*, an adopted Eóghanacht. That is, he has been adopted under contract with King Colgú, son of Failbe Flann, with such privileges that may be ascribed. There is only one prohibition – that he cannot stand for any princely role endorsed by the native *derbfine*, nor use a vote as a member of that *derbfine*. All else he can do as a *fine thacair*. Do you now understand why you see him present in this court?'

The prioress clamped her jaw shut and sat down abruptly, almost causing the bench on which she was sitting to shake.

'I should add, I am the one sitting in judgment, Prioress Suanach,' Brehon Fíthel added sourly before he turned to Fidelma and motioned her to continue.

'Very well,' Fidelma almost sighed. 'Since Eadulf has taken the opportunity to hand me the notes I wanted, I no longer need ask him to do so, which was what I was about to do when a point of law arose. However, I do understand the desire on behalf of the prioress to delay this matter for as long as possible.'

The prioress glowered while Brehon Fíthel appeared puzzled, but Fidelma continued.

'While considering the matter of the murder of Brother Garb, I have tried my best to find precedence. As you know, our law is always based on precedence, which gives authority to the texts. The case of murder is clear, and the case of trying to conceal that murder by making it look like suicide is also clear. But the case of the motive is without precedence. Why? Because the motive and the perpetrator of that motive are unique among us, so it will fall to Brehon Fíthel to make a judgment that will itself become the precedent.'

Brehon Fíthel continued to appear bewildered. 'Why would the motive become a precedent?' he asked.

'Because it is a motive that has never been recorded in our legal history before now.'

'Then why and how did Brother Garb die?'

'He was killed because he no longer believed in the Faith.'

It took some time for the uproar in the chapel to fade and allow Abbot Cuán's voice to be heard.

'Do you realise what you are saying, Fidelma? It is Brother Garb of whom we speak. He was one of our leading scholars; so much was he respected and honoured. It was well known that the Venerable Breas had fully intended to appoint him an assistant

professor in the ecclesiastical school here. He had already demonstrated how worthy he was during the now infamous debates with
the late Bishop Brodulf. How can you say that he no longer believed
in the Faith?'

'To save much time, I will simplify the case. Brother Garb was,
indeed, possessed of a great probing mind. Faced with a subject
he did not accept, he probed and analysed it to the utmost degree.
His analytical mind was, perhaps, his undoing. He did not accept
things without close analysis. He told his close friend and fellow
student that he had consulted many records in order to argue with
Bishop Brodulf and, as it turned out, he found himself arguing
with the entire history of the Faith.

'In the words of his friend, he could not believe in a religion
invented mostly by old men sitting discussing and making up rules
in numerous councils in various lands over several centuries. So
he was losing his Faith while his reputation as a scholar was
growing. The final moment coincided with the death of Bishop
Brodulf. Around then, Brother Garb went to his tutor, the one who
had taken such a pride in him as a pupil; the one who thought he
was his faithful disciple, his acolyte. You can imagine that master's
reaction when this most brilliant pupil told him that he no longer
believed.' She paused. 'In fact, you do not have to imagine, for
we heard his views, spoken at the graveside of Brother Garb last
night.'

Prioress Suanach gave a little scream and impulsively reached
forward and grasped the chief professor's hand as everyone turned
to the Venerable Breas. He sat still, not raising his head.

'Your *amra* was powerfully spoken,' Fidelma informed him
softly. 'You had been betrayed by your most admired student; one
whom you had designated to be your assistant and, one day, to
spread the word of the Faith in your name. It was not a betrayal
of the Faith but a personal betrayal. I would hazard that last morning
you offered Garb a drink that had poison in it. It was slow acting

340

and produced a stomach ache, which Garb complained about to the prioress. Unknowing of the cause, she told him to consult Brother Anlón. The physician gave him medication and told him to lie down in the dormitory.

'When the Venerable Breas was told Garb was still sleeping in the dormitory and not yet dead, Breas panicked. Garb might recover and reveal what happened . . . So now Breas brought into use those evil motivations . . . covetousness and resentment.'

'I am not sure where this is leading,' intervened Abbot Cuán, 'but Eadulf's report was that it needed two men to have hoisted Garb's body to the beam in the building where he was found.'

'Exactly so,' confirmed Fidelma.

'The chief professor sits before us. Look to his frail body and the hands that show his rheumatism. He was not capable of this act. Unless you are accusing others associated with him? Perhaps the prioress, who sent him to the disgraced Brother Anlón, who gave him medication and told him to sleep it off in the dormitory. Are you accusing either of them?'

'Prioress Suanach is in love with the Venerable Breas, and has been so since she was a student. Therefore she is protective of him. I am not sure that even now she knows the truth. No, I accuse neither of them. The Venerable Breas now needed someone with youth and strength. Someone who boasted of their strength to me; someone who was jealous of Garb's position and who felt they should have been the leading scholar in his place.'

'It's a lie!' Brother Étaid rose, his voice a curious strangled sound. 'I was Garb's soul friend, his *anam chara*.'

'Only because you were designated the task automatically when you both arrived here as students. Garb's real soul friend, to whom he gave all his conflicting thoughts, was Sister Ingund. By the way, she will be witness to his growing doubts and researches and final decision that he could not accept a Faith made, as he saw it, by the arbitrary votes of old men in councils.'

The Venerable Breas sat, head forward, as if he were not taking part in the proceedings. Fidelma waited for a moment and then continued, addressing Brother Étaid.

'The Venerable Breas sent for you and bribed you with the promise that on Garb's death you would be nominated as the leading scholar in his place. That was so, for Breas admitted you had taken the role. But Garb's death had to be ensured. The rumours about Garb as a suspect for Bishop Brodulf's death were encouraging. Perhaps if a suicide could be faked . . .? So between the time that Sister Ingund saw Garb asleep in the dormitory, probably nearly comatose from the poison, and when we went to find him, you and Breas had removed him. Either way, Étaid, you strangled him, finishing the task Breas had started with his poison. How to disguise this? During the builders' meal break, you and Breas took a rope and ladder and with your strength, Étaid, the both of you arranged to hang the body in the deserted house and make it look like suicide, as we discovered.'

'It is all conjecture!' shouted the prioress defensively. 'You have no facts!'

'Does the Venerable Breas deny it?' Brehon Fíthel questioned.

The chief professor made no reply. He remained sitting, oblivious to his surroundings. The gathering in the chapel was silent, waiting for his answer. There was none.

'No response is an admission of guilt,' pointed out the Chief Brehon.

'I'll respond!' But it was Brother Étaid who shouted. 'I did not strangle Garb. Old Breas did it all. He blackmailed me into helping him. He promised me the position and fame as his acolyte if I did so. I did not . . .'

Fidelma glanced at Eadulf. 'I don't think anyone will object if Eadulf makes a medical comment to help elucidate matters,' she smiled thinly.

'I think that even Brother Anlón will agree that the Venerable

Breas was incapable of asserting the strength needed to strangle someone of Garb's age and physique, even when half comatose with poison,' Eadulf replied. 'It needed someone young and strong to strangle Garb. Anyone can observe Breas' hands. Breas suffers from *ailtidu* – rheumatism. He mentioned it to us on the first occasion we met him.'

Brehon Fíthel turned his gaze to Brother Anlón. 'Do you agree with the contention that he could not have strangled Garb?'

The physician rose and bowed his head. 'I have treated the Venerable Breas for some time, using burdock; its root boiled and used as an ointment. Sometimes willow and fennel help the condition. I would have to agree with Brother Eadulf that, with such a condition, it is not possible to strangle someone.'

Brother Étaid had swung round and was trying to fight his way towards the chapel doors when a blow from Enda rendered him senseless.

Brehon Fíthel quickly ordered that the boy and the Venerable Breas be taken to a secure chamber until a judgment had been reached. Prioress Suanach was hysterical and her removal also had to be ordered.

Brehon Fíthel turned to Fidelma with a grim smile. 'You were wrong, Fidelma,' he observed. 'It was not the crime that involves the precedent but sometimes the methods. An unlawful killing is an unlawful killing and the verdict is laid out under law. The punishments are also the subject of precedence. Abbot Cuán and I must construct the appropriate retribution that has to be met.'

It was the next day when Eadulf and Fidelma were riding back to Cashel, with Enda leading the way. Eadulf seemed buried in thought and finally Fidelma asked him what he was thinking.

'I found it frustrating that the abbot and the keeper of the books would not allow me to look in that secret room and see some of those ancient books that had such an effect on Brother Garb. I recall some of those intriguing titles that Garb told Sister Ingund were there and caused his lack of Faith. Texts like the *Book of Judas*, *Gospel of Thomas*, *Gospel of Mary* . . . think of the information they must contain if Rome tried to destroy them as a danger to their theologies . . .'

'Reading them did not help Brother Garb,' Fidelma returned dryly.

'Do you think Abbot Cúan and Brehon Fíthel gave Breas an appropriate punishment?'

Fidelma turned, disapproving. 'Punishment? You should know by now that our laws do not think in terms of punishment, as such. Law is based on compensation for the victim and rehabilitation for the perpetrator. In this case, the Venerable Breas has been sent to an almost uninhabited island to the south-west with Brother Étaid as his disciple to build a small community of the Faith. There is no escaping from that island because it is barren of trees. A boat will call once in a while to make sure they do not perish until they have learned how to sustain themselves.'

'I found it curious the abbot and Brehon Fíthel agreed to Prioress Suanach's plea to be allowed to go with them.'

'Love is a curious thing, Eadulf.' Fidelma smiled ironically. 'Some will exchange many things for it . . . even their country and culture.'

It was some time before Eadulf realised the hidden extent of the comment.

L'ENVOI

It was early autumn and there was a noticeable chill in the air as Eadulf sat before the log fire in the chambers that he shared with Fidelma in the fortress of her brother, King Colgú of Cashel. He sat in a chair to one side of the fire while before him stood a *clár*, an oak pedestal table, on which was balanced a vellum book that he was reading. It was the universal history by Sinlán moccu Min, the Abbot of Beannchar, written nearly a century before. Eadulf was intrigued for, as he had discovered, it was the first chronicle of events in the Five Kingdoms of Éireann, and Sinlán had incorporated it with a history of other nations.

There was a noise at the door and he looked up as Fidelma entered, clearly excited with some news. He knew she had been down in the town below the fortress to visit her old friend Della. Something unusual must have happened to create such animation in her features.

Before he could ask, she had thrown herself into a chair opposite.

'Do you remember Sister Ingund from that investigation we did into Bishop Brodulf's murder at the Abbey of Imleach three years ago?' she queried without preamble.

Eadulf carefully adjusted the vellum text on the top of the *clár*, on which it had been balanced and glanced at her with a frown as he dredged his memory.

'Wasn't she the little Burgundian student who was in love with Brother Garb, who was murdered? I remember her and felt so sorry for her. She seemed too young and innocent to have encountered such anguish. What makes you recall her now?'

'She has passed through Cashel on her way back to Imleach earlier today. As you know, I was visiting Della and I saw her with some companions at Rumann's tavern where they had stopped for refreshment on their journey. She had just returned from Burgundia and was escorting some new students to Imleach.'

'I am surprised that she even returned to Burgundia after those events years ago. Is she well? Has she overcome her suffering and distress?'

'She has moved on, just as I told her she would,' Fidelma assured him. 'She now escorts those from her abbey in Burgundia who want to come to study further in Imleach.'

Obviously Fidelma was excited and trying to restrain herself from telling him everything in one go.

Eadulf smiled indulgently. 'What news did she impart that has made you so excited?'

'It seemed that Bishop Brodulf was wrong in seeking the exiled Burgundian Prince Dagobert in Imleach.'

'You mean that he was not hiding in that abbey at all?'

'He was not. The story of Bishop Brodulf's search for him, as I explained it at the hearing, was correct. The Burgundian King, Clotaire, had sent Brodulf to find out where Dagobert was hiding and, indeed, to eliminate him. Clotaire is now dead. A war raged among the factions until Dagobert was invited to assume the throne of the Franks. His close supporters had known where he was hiding all along.'

'So he was hiding in another abbey after all?'

'When Dagobert's father, King Sigebert, was assassinated, Bishop Dido of Pictavium sent him into exile to hide here when he was seven years old. He grew up in a Christian community, not in Muman but in Midi, near Tara. He was raised for all these years in the commune that was founded by the Blessed Erc at Sláine na Dela, the Hill of Sláine, where Patricius first lit the Paschal Fires.'

'Surely the High Kings must have known?'

'Perhaps they did. If they did they had managed to keep his whereabouts a secret. And who went to Sláine to bring Dagobert back to Burgundia? None other than Wulfoald, who had been major domo to Sigebert, Dagobert's father.'

'Wulfoald?' Eadulf frowned as the name touched a memory.

'Brother Charibert claimed to have been a slave in the household of Wulfoald, who then sent him to keep a watch on Bishop Brodulf.'

Eadulf grimaced dourly. 'He certainly succeeded in doing that.'

'Wulfoald is again the power and is the major domo of Dagobert's palace. There are a couple of other names who helped Dagobert back to power known to you. Ultan, who is Abbot of Fossail, who also enlisted the help of Wilfrid of Ripon.'

Eadulf grimaced in surprise. 'The same Wilfrid whom you and others argued with at the Council of Streonshalh?'

'The same Wilfrid,' Fidelma agreed.

'Fascinating news,' Eadulf sighed. 'The times are interesting. Plots and murders. Ah well, it seems that Dagobert was not the only foreign prince to seek political refuge in this kingdom. Look at Aldfrith, the son of Oswy of Northumbria. He now lives happily here using the name Flann Fine and writing poetry. Maybe one day the Northumbrians will persuade him to go back there and be their king.'

'If that happens, I hope he declines the offer. Better to live in peace here with his poems.'

'What do you mean?' Eadulf demanded.

'Better live in peace as a poet than inherit great power and be the envy of relatives, and with the constant problem of how to survive the assassins' knives of his siblings or other family claimants.'

'Well, by whatever rule of inheritance, Dagobert is now King of the Franks.'

Fidelma could not help a cynical grimace.

'I cannot help wondering how long it will be before members of his family get together to depose him.'